Nora Roberts is the number one *New York Times* bestseller of more than 200 novels. With over 400 million copies of her books in print, she is indisputably one of the most celebrated and popular writers in the world. She has achieved numerous top five bestsellers in the UK, including number one for *Savour the Moment*, and is a *Sunday Times* hardback bestseller writing as J. D. Robb.

Become a fan on Facebook at
www.facebook.com/norarobertsjdrobb
and be the first to hear all the latest from Piatkus
about Nora Roberts and J. D. Robb.

www.noraroberts.com
www.nora-roberts.co.uk
www.jd-robb.co.uk

By Nora Roberts

Homeport
The Reef
River's End
Carolina Moon
The Villa
Midnight Bayou
Three Fates

Birthright
Northern Lights
Blue Smoke
Montana Sky
Angels Fall
High Noon
Divine Evil

Tribute
Sanctuary
Black Hills
The Search
Chasing Fire
The Witness
Whiskey Beach

The Born In Trilogy:
Born in Fire
Born in Ice
Born in Shame

The Bride Quartet:
Vision in White
Bed of Roses
Savour the Moment
Happy Ever After

The Key Trilogy:
Key of Light
Key of Knowledge
Key of Valour

The Irish Trilogy:
Jewels of the Sun
Tears of the Moon
Heart of the Sea

Three Sisters Island Trilogy:
Dance upon the Air
Heaven and Earth
Face the Fire

The Sign of Seven Trilogy:
Blood Brothers
The Hollow
The Pagan Stone

Chesapeake Bay Quartet:
Sea Swept
Rising Tides
Inner Harbour
Chesapeake Blue

In the Garden Trilogy:
Blue Dahlia
Black Rose
Red Lily

The Circle Trilogy:
Morrigan's Cross
Dance of the Gods
Valley of Silence

The Dream Trilogy:
Daring to Dream
Holding the Dream
Finding the Dream

The Inn Boonsboro Trilogy
The Next Always
The Last Boyfriend
The Perfect Hope

Many of Nora Roberts' other titles are now available in eBook and she is also the author of the In Death series using the pseudonym J.D. Robb. For more information about Nora's work please visit her websites at www.nora-roberts.com or www.nora-roberts.co.uk

NORA ROBERTS

THE REEF

PIATKUS

First published in the US in 1998 by Penguin Putnam Inc.
First published in Great Britain in 1999 by Piatkus
Reprinted 2002 (twice), 2003, 2004, 2005, 2006 (three times), 2007
Reissued by Piatkus in 2009
Reprinted 2009, 2010, 2011, 2012, 2013 (twice), 2014

A CIP catalogue record for this book is available from the British Library.

ISBN 978-0-7499-4092-8

Typeset in Bembo by Phoenix Photosetting, Chatham, Kent
Printed and bound by CPI Group (UK) Ltd, Croydon, CR0 4YY

Papers used by Piatkus are from well-managed forests and other responsible sources.

MIX
Paper from responsible sources
FSC® C104740

Piatkus
An imprint of
Little, Brown Book Group
100 Victoria Embankment
London EC4Y 0DY

An Hachette UK Company
www.hachette.co.uk

www.littlebrown.co.uk

To Ruth Langan and Marianne Willman,
for the past, the present, and the future

Part One

Past

The present contains nothing more than the past, and what is found in the effect was already in the cause.
–Henri Bergson

Prologue

James Lassiter was forty years old, a well-built, ruggedly handsome man in the prime of his life, in the best of health.

In an hour, he'd be dead.

From the deck of the boat, he could see nothing but the clear silky ripple of blue, the luminous greens and deeper browns of the great reef shimmering like islands below the surface of the Coral Sea. Far to the west, the foamy froth and surge of sea surf rose up and crashed against the false shore of coral.

From his stance at the port side, he could watch the shapes and shadows of fish, darting like living arrows through the world he'd been born to share with them.

The coast of Australia was lost in the distance, and there was only the vastness.

The day was perfect, the jewel-clear shimmer of the water, dashed by white facets of light tossed down by the gold flash of sun. The teasing hint of a breeze carried no taste of rain.

Beneath his feet, the deck swayed gently, a cradle on the quiet sea. Wavelets lapped musically against the hull. Below, far below, was treasure waiting to be discovered.

They were mining the wreck of the *Sea Star*, a British merchant ship that had met its doom on the Great Barrier Reef two centuries before. For more than a year, breaking for bad weather, equipment failure and other inconveniences, they had worked, often like dogs, to reap the riches the *Star* had left behind.

There were riches yet, James knew. But his thoughts traveled beyond the *Sea Star*, north of that spectacular and dangerous reef to the balmy waters of the West Indies. To another wreck, to another treasure.

To Angelique's Curse.

He wondered now if it was the richly jeweled amulet that was cursed, or the woman, the witch Angelique, whose power – it was reputed – remained strong in the rubies and diamonds and gold. Legend was that she had worn it, a gift from the husband it was said she murdered, on the day she was burned at the stake.

The idea fascinated him, the woman, the necklace, the legend. The search for it, which he would begin shortly, was taking on a personal twist. James didn't simply want the riches, the glory. He wanted Angelique's Curse, and the legend it carried.

He had been weaned on the hunt, on tales of wrecked ships and the bounty the sea hoarded from them. All of his life, he had dived, and he had dreamed. The dreams had cost him a wife, and given him a son.

James turned from the rail to study the boy. Matthew was nearly sixteen now. He had grown tall, but had yet to fill out. There was potential there, James mused, in the thin frame and ropey muscle. They shared the same dark, unmanageable hair, though the boy refused to have his cut short so that even now as Matthew checked the diving gear, it fell forward to curtain his face.

The face was rawboned, James thought. It had fined down in the last year or two and had lost the childish roundness. An angel face, a waitress had called it once, and had embarrassed the boy into hot cheeks and grimaces.

It had more of the devil in it now, and those blue eyes he'd passed to Matthew were more often hot than cool. The Lassiter temper, the Lassiter luck, James thought with a shake of his head. Tough legacies for a half-grown boy.

One day, he thought, one day soon, he would be able to give his son all the things a father hoped for. The key to it all lay quietly waiting in the tropical seas of the West Indies.

A necklace of rubies and diamonds beyond price, heavy with history, dark with legend, tainted with blood.

Angelique's Curse.

James's mouth twisted into a thin smile. When he had it, the bad luck that had dogged the Lassiters would change. He only had to be patient.

'Hurry up with those tanks, Matthew. The day's wasting.'

Matthew looked up, tossed his hair out of his eyes. The sun was rising behind his father's back, sending light shimmering around him. He looked, Matthew thought, like a king preparing for battle. As always, love and admiration welled up and startled him with its intensity.

'I replaced your pressure gauge. I want to take a look at the old one.'

'You look out for your old man.' James hooked his arm around Matthew's throat for a playful tussle. 'Going to bring you up a fortune today.'

'Let me go down with you. Let me take the morning shift instead of him.'

James suppressed a sigh. Matthew hadn't learned the wisdom of controlling his emotions. Particularly his dislikes. 'You know how the teams work. You and Buck'll dive this afternoon. VanDyke and I take the morning.'

'I don't want you to dive with him.' Matthew shook off his father's friendly arm. 'I heard the two of you arguing last night. He hates you. I could hear it in his voice.'

A mutual feeling, James thought, but winked. 'Partners often disagree. The bottom line here is that VanDyke's putting up most of the money. Let him have his fun, Matthew. For him treasure-hunting's just a hobby for a bored, rich businessman.'

'He can't dive worth shit.' And that, in Matthew's opinion, was the measure of a man.

'He's good enough. Just doesn't have much style at forty feet down.' Tired of the argument, James began to don his wetsuit. 'Buck take a look at the compressor?'

'Yeah, he got the kinks out. Dad–'

'Leave it, Matthew.'

'Just this one day,' Matthew said stubbornly. 'I don't trust that prissy-faced bastard.'

'Your language continues to deteriorate.' Silas VanDyke, elegant and pale despite the hard sun, smiled as he exited the cabin at Matthew's back. It amused him nearly as much as it annoyed him to see the boy sneer. 'Your uncle requires your assistance below, young Matthew.'

'I want to dive with my father today.'

'I'm afraid that would inconvenience me. As you see, I'm already wearing my wetsuit.'

'Matthew.' There was impatient command in James's voice. 'Go see what Buck needs.'

'Yes, sir.' Eyes defiant, he went below decks.

'The boy has a poor attitude and worse manners, Lassiter.'

'The boy hates your guts,' James said cheerfully. 'I'd say he has good instincts.'

'This expedition is coming to an end,' VanDyke shot back. 'And so is my patience and my largesse. Without me, you'll run out of money in a week.'

'Maybe.' James zipped his suit. 'Maybe not.'

'I want the amulet, Lassiter. You know it's down there, and I believe you know where. I want it. I've bought it. I've bought you.'

'You've bought my time, and you've bought my skill. You haven't bought me. Rules of salvage, VanDyke. The man who finds Angelique's Curse owns Angelique's Curse.' And it wouldn't be found, he was sure, on the *Sea Star*. He lifted a hand to VanDyke's chest. 'Now keep out of my face.'

Control, the kind he wielded in board rooms, kept VanDyke from lashing out. He had always won his rounds with patience, with money, and with power. Success in business, he knew, was a simple matter of who maintained control.

'You'll regret trying to double-cross me.' He spoke mildly now, with the faintest hint of a smile curving his lips. 'I promise you.'

'Hell, Silas, I'm enjoying it.' With a quiet chuckle, James stepped inside the cabin. 'You guys reading girlie magazines, or what? Let's get going here.'

Moving quickly, VanDyke dealt with the tanks. It was, very simply, business. When the Lassiters came back on deck, he was hitching on his own gear.

The three of them, VanDyke thought, were pathetically beneath him. Obviously they had forgotten who he was, what he was. He was a VanDyke, a man who had been given or earned or taken whatever he wanted. One who intended to continue to do so, as long as there was profit.

Did they think he cared that they tightened their little triangle and excluded him? It was past time he dismissed them and brought in a fresh team.

Buck, he mused, pudgy, already balding, a foolish foil to his handsome brother. Loyal as a mongrel puppy and just as intelligent.

Matthew, young and eager, brash, defiant. A hateful little worm VanDyke would be pleased to squash.

And James, of course, he mused as the three Lassiters stood together, sharing idle conversation. Tough and more canny than VanDyke had supposed. More than the simple tool he had expected. The man thought he had outwitted Silas VanDyke.

James Lassiter thought he would find and own Angelique's Curse, the amulet of power, of legend. Worn by a witch, coveted by many. And that made him a fool. VanDyke had invested in it, time, money, and effort, and Silas VanDyke never made poor investments.

'There's going to be good hunting today.' James strapped on his tanks. 'I can smell it. Silas?'

'Right with you.'

James secured his weight belt, adjusted his mask and rolled into the water.

'Dad, wait–'

But James just saluted and disappeared under the surface.

The world was silent and stunning. The drenching blue was broken by fingers of sunlight that stabbed through the surface and shimmered clear white. Caves and castles of coral spread out to form secret worlds.

A reef shark, eyes bored and black, gave a twist of its body and slid through the water and away.

More at home here than in the air, James dived deep with VanDyke at his heels. The wreck was already well exposed, trenches dug around it and mined of treasure. Coral claimed the shattered bow and turned the wood into a fantasy of color and shape that seemed studded with amethyst, emerald, ruby.

This was the living treasure, the miracle of art created by seawater and sun.

It was, as always, a pleasure to see it.

When they began to work, James's sense of well-being increased. The Lassiter luck was behind him, he thought dreamily. He would soon be rich, famous. He smiled to himself. After all, he'd stumbled onto the clue, he'd spent days and hours researching and piecing the trail of the amulet together.

He could even feel a little sorry for that asshole VanDyke, since it would be the Lassiters who brought her up, from other waters, on their own expedition.

He caught himself reaching out to stroke a spine of coral as though it were a cat.

He shook his head, but couldn't clear it. The alarm bell sounded in one part of his brain, far off and dim. But he was an experienced diver and recognized the signs. He'd had a brush or two with nitrogen narcosis before. Never at such a shallow depth, he thought dimly. They were well shy of a hundred feet.

Regardless, he tapped his tanks. VanDyke was already watching him, eyes cool and assessing behind his mask. James signaled to surface. When VanDyke pulled him back, signaled toward the wreck, he was only mildly confused. Up, he signaled again, and again VanDyke restrained him.

He didn't panic. James wasn't a man to panic easily. He knew he'd been sabotaged, though his mind was too muddled to calculate how. VanDyke was an amateur in this world, he reminded himself, didn't realize the extent of the danger. So he would have to show him. His eyes narrowed with purpose. He swung out, barely missing a grip on VanDyke's airhose.

The underwater struggle was slow, determined, eerily silent. Fish scattered like colorful silks, then gathered again to watch the drama of predator and prey. James could feel himself slipping, the dizziness, disorientation as the nitrogen pumped into him. He fought it, managed to kick another ten feet toward the surface.

Then wondered why he'd ever wanted to leave. He began to laugh, the bubbles bursting out and speeding high as the rapture claimed him. He embraced VanDyke in a kind of slow whirling dance, to share his delight. It was so beautiful here in the gilded blue light with gems and jewels of a thousand impossible colors waiting, just waiting to be plucked.

He'd been born to dive the depths.

Soon, James Lassiter's merriment would slide toward unconsciousness. And a quiet, comforting death.

VanDyke reached out as James began to flounder. The lack of coordination was only one more symptom. One of the last. VanDyke's sweeping grab pulled the airhose free. James blinked in bemusement as he drowned.

Chapter One

TREASURE. GOLD DOUBLOONS and pieces of eight. With luck, they could be plucked from the seabed as easily as peaches from a tree. Or so, Tate thought as she dived, her father said.

She knew it took a great deal more than luck, as ten years of searching had already proven. It took money and time and exhausting effort. It took skill and months of research and equipment.

But as she swam toward her father through the crystal blue Caribbean, she was more than willing to play the game.

It wasn't a hardship to spend the summer of her twentieth year diving off the coast of St. Kitts, skimming through gloriously warm water among brilliantly hued fish and sculptures of rainbow coral. Each dive was its own anticipation. What might lie beneath that white sand, hidden among the fans and sea grass, buried under the cleverly twisted formations of coral?

It wasn't the treasure, she knew. It was the hunt.

And occasionally, you did get lucky.

She remembered very well the first time she had lifted a silver spoon from its bed of silt. The shock and the thrill of holding that blackened cup in her fingers, wondering who had used it to scoop up broth. A captain perhaps of some rich galleon. Or the captain's lady.

And the time her mother had been cheerfully hacking away at a hunk of conglomerate, the chunk of material formed by centuries of chemical reactions under the sea. The sound of her squeal, then the bray of delighted laughter when Marla Beaumont had unearthed a gold ring.

The occasional luck allowed the Beaumonts to spend several months a year hunting for more. For more luck, and more treasure.

As they swam side by side, Raymond Beaumont tapped his daughter's arm, pointed. Together they watched a sea turtle paddle lazily.

The laugh in her father's eyes said everything. He had worked hard all of his life, and was now reaping the rewards. For Tate, a moment like this was as good as gold.

They swam together, bonded by a love of the sea, the silence, the colors. A school of sergeant majors streaked by, their black and gold stripes gleaming. For no more than the joy of it, Tate did a slow roll and watched the sunlight strike the surface overhead. The freedom of it had a laugh gurgling out in a spray of bubbles that startled a curious grouper.

She dived deeper, following her father's strong kicks. The sand could hold secrets. Any mound could be a plank of worm-eaten wood from a Spanish galleon. That dark patch could blanket a pirate's cache of silver. She reminded herself to pay attention, not to the sea fans or hunks of coral, but to the signs of sunken treasure.

They were here in the balmy waters of the West Indies, searching for every treasure hunter's dream. A virgin wreck reputed to hold a king's treasure. This, their first dive, was to acquaint themselves with the territory they had so meticulously researched through books, maps and charts. They would test the currents, gauge the tides. And maybe – just maybe – get lucky.

Aiming toward a hillock of sand, she began to fan briskly. Her father had taught her this simple method of excavating sand when Tate had delighted him by her boundless interest in his new hobby of scuba diving.

Over the years, he'd taught her many other things. A respect for the sea and what lived there. And what lay there, hidden. Her fondest hope was to one day discover something, for him.

She glanced toward him now, watched the way he examined a low ridge of coral. However much he dreamed of treasure made by man, Raymond Beaumont loved the treasures made by the sea.

Finding nothing in the hillock, Tate moved off in pursuit of a pretty striped shell. Out of the corner of her eyes, she caught the blur of a dark shape coming toward her, swift and silent. Tate's first and frozen thought was shark, and her heart stumbled. She turned, as she had been taught, one hand reaching for her diver's knife, and prepared to defend herself and her father.

The shape became a diver. Sleek and fast as a shark, perhaps, but a man. Her breath whooshed out in a stream of bubbles before she remembered to regulate it. The diver signaled to her, then to the man swimming in his wake.

Tate found herself face mask to face mask with a recklessly grinning face, eyes as blue as the sea around them. Dark hair streamed in the current. She could see he was laughing at her, undoubtedly having guessed her reaction to the unexpected company. He held his hands up, a gesture of peace, until she sheathed her knife. Then he winked and sent a fluid salute toward Ray.

As silent greetings were exchanged, Tate studied the newcomers. Their equipment was good, and included those necessary items of the treasure seeker. The goody bag, the knife, the wrist compass and diver's watch. The first man was young, lean in his black wetsuit. His gesturing hands were wide-palmed, long-fingered, and carried the nicks and scars of a veteran hunter.

The second man was bald, thick in the middle, but as agile as a fish in his undersea movements. Tate could see he was reaching some sort of tacit agreement with her father. She wanted to protest. This was their spot. After all, they'd been there first.

But she could do no more than frown as her father curled his fingers into an 'okay' sign. The four of them spread out to explore.

Tate went back to another mound to fan. Her father's research indicated that four ships of the Spanish fleet had gone down north of Nevis and St. Kitts during the hurricane of July 11, 1733. Two, the *San Cristobal* and the *Vaca*, had been discovered and salvaged years earlier, broken on the reefs near Dieppe Bay. This left, undiscovered and untouched, the *Santa Marguerite* and the *Isabella*.

Documents and manifests boasted that these ships carried much more than cargoes of sugar from the islands. There were jewels and porcelain and more than ten million pesos of gold and silver. In addition, if true to the custom of the day, there would be the hoards secreted by the passengers and seamen.

Both wrecks would be very rich indeed. More than that, discovery would be one of the major finds of the century.

Finding nothing, Tate moved on, bearing north. The competition from the other divers caused her to keep her eyes and her instincts sharp. A school of gem-bright fish speared around her in a perfect vee, a slice of color within color. Delighted, she swam through their bubbles.

Competition or not, she would always enjoy the small things. She explored tirelessly, fanning sand and studying fish with equal enthusiasm.

It looked like a rock at first glance. Still, training had her swimming toward it. She was no more than a yard away when something streaked by her. She saw with faint irritation that scarred, long-fingered hand reach down and close over the rock.

Jerk, she thought, and was about to turn away when she saw him work it free. Not a rock at all, but the crusted handle of a sword that he drew from the scabbard of the sea. Grinning around his mouthpiece, he hefted it.

He had the nerve to salute her with it, cutting a swatch through the water. As he headed up, Tate went after him. They broke the surface in tandem.

She spit out her mouthpiece. 'I saw it first.'

'I don't think so.' Still grinning, he levered up his face mask. 'Anyway, you were slow, and I wasn't. Finders keepers.'

'Rules of salvage,' she said, struggling for calm. 'You were in my space.'

'The way I see it, you were in mine. Better luck next time.'

'Tate, honey.' From the deck of the *Adventure*, Marla Beaumont waved her hands and called out. 'Lunch is ready. Invite your friend and come aboard.'

'Don't mind if I do.' In a few powerful strokes, he was at the stern of the *Adventure*. The sword hit the deck with a clatter, his flippers followed.

Cursing the poor beginning to what had promised to be a wonderful summer, Tate headed in. Ignoring his gallantly offered hand, she hauled herself in just as her father and the other diver broke the surface.

'Nice meeting you.' He dragged a hand through his dripping hair and smiled charmingly at Marla. 'Matthew Lassiter.'

'Marla Beaumont. Welcome aboard.' Tate's mother beamed at Matthew from under the wide brim of her flowered sunhat. She was a striking woman, with porcelain skin and a willowy frame beneath loose and flowing shirt and slacks. She tipped down her dark glasses in greeting.

'I see you've met my daughter, Tate, and my husband, Ray.'

'In a manner of speaking.' Matthew unhooked his weight belt, set it and his mask aside. 'Nice rig here.'

'Oh yes, thank you.' Marla looked proudly around the deck. She wasn't a fan of housework, but there was nothing she liked better than keeping the *Adventure* spit and polished. 'And that's your boat there.' She gestured off the bow. 'The *Sea Devil*.'

Tate snorted at the name. It was certainly apt, she thought, for the man, and the boat. Unlike the *Adventure*, the *Sea Devil* didn't gleam. The old fishing boat badly needed painting. At a distance, it looked like little more than a tub floating on the brilliant platter of the sea.

'Nothing fancy,' Matthew was saying, 'but she runs.' He walked over to offer a hand to the other divers.

'Good eye, boy.' Buck Lassiter slapped Matthew on the back. 'This boy was born with the knack,' he said to Ray in a voice as rough as broken glass, then belatedly held out a hand. 'Buck Lassiter, my nephew, Matthew.'

Ignoring the introductions making their way around the deck, Tate stowed her equipment, then tugged out of her wetsuit. While the others admired the sword, she ducked into the deckhouse and cut through to her cabin.

It wasn't anything unusual, she supposed as she found an oversized T-shirt. Her parents were always making friends with strangers, inviting them onboard, fixing them meals. Her father had simply never developed the wary and suspicious manner of a veteran treasure hunter. Instead her parents shimmered with Southern hospitality.

Normally she found the trait endearing. She only wished they would be a little choosy.

She heard her father offer cheerful congratulations to Matthew on his find, and gritted her teeth.

Damn it, she'd seen it first.

Sulking, Matthew decided as he offered the sword to Ray for examination. A peculiarly female trait. And there was no doubt the little redhead was female. Her copper-toned hair might be cut short as a boy's, but she'd certainly filled out that excuse for a bikini just fine.

Pretty enough, too, he mused. Her face might have been all angles, with cheekbones sharp enough to slice a man's exploring finger, but she had big, delicious green eyes. Eyes, he recalled, that had shot prickly little darts at him in the water, and out.

That only made annoying her more interesting.

Since they were going to be diving in the same pool for a while, he might as well enjoy himself.

He was sitting cross-legged on the forward sundeck when Tate came back out. She gave him a quick glance, having nearly talked herself out of the sulks. His skin was bronzed, and against his chest winked a silver piece of eight hanging from a chain. She wanted to ask him about it, to hear where he'd found it, and how.

But he was smirking at her. Manners, pride and curiosity collided with a wall that kept her unnaturally silent as conversation flowed around her.

Matthew bit into one of Marla's generous ham sandwiches.

'Terrific, Mrs. Beaumont. A lot better than the swill Buck and I are used to.'

'You have some more of this potato salad.' Flattered, she heaped a mound on his paper plate. 'And it's Marla, dear. Tate, you come on and get yourself some lunch.'

'Tate.' Matthew squinted against the sun as he studied her. 'Unusual name.'

'Marla's maiden name.' Ray slipped an arm over his wife's shoulders. He sat in wet bathing trunks, enjoying the warmth and company. His silvered hair danced in the light breeze. 'Tate here's been diving since she was pint-sized. Couldn't ask for a better partner. Marla loves the sea, loves to sail, but she barely swims a stroke.'

With a chuckle, Marla refilled tall glasses of iced tea. 'I like looking at the water. Being in it's something different altogether.' She sat back placidly with her drink. 'Once it gets past my knees, I just panic. I always wonder if I drowned in a former life. So for this one, I'm happy tending the boat.'

'And a fine one she is.' Buck had already assessed the *Adventure*. A tidy thirty-eight footer, teak decking, fancy brightwork. He'd guess she carried two staterooms, a full galley. Without his prescription face mask, he could still make out the massive windows of the pilothouse. He'd liked to have taken his fingers for a walk through the engine and control station.

A look around later was in order, after he had his glasses. Even without them, he calculated that the diamond on Marla's finger was a good five carats, and the gold circle on her right hand was antique.

He smelled money.

'So, Ray . . .' Casually, he tipped back his glass. 'Matthew and me, we've been diving around here for the past few weeks. Haven't seen you.'

'First dive today. We sailed down from North Carolina, started out the day Tate finished her spring semester.'

College girl. Matthew took a hard swallow of cold tea. Jesus. He deliberately turned his gaze away from her legs and concentrated on his lunch. All bets were definitely off, he decided. He was nearly twenty-five and didn't mess with snotty college kids.

'We're going to spend the summer here,' Ray went on. 'Possibly longer. Last winter, we dived off the coast of Mexico a few weeks. Couple of good wrecks there, but mostly played out. We managed to bring up a thing or two though. Some nice pottery, some clay pipes.'

'And those lovely perfume bottles,' Marla put in.

'Been at it awhile, then,' Buck prompted.

'Ten years.' Ray's eyes shone. 'Fifteen since the first time I went down.' He leaned forward, hunter to hunter. 'Friend of mine talked me into scuba lessons. After I'd certified, I went with him to Diamond Shoals. Only took one dive to hook me.'

'Now he spends every free minute diving, planning a dive or talking about the last dive.' Marla let out her lusty laugh. Her eyes, the same rich green as her daughter's, danced. 'So I learned how to handle a boat.'

'Me, I've been hunting more than forty years.' Buck scooped up the last of his potato salad. He hadn't eaten so well in more than a month. 'In the blood. My father was the same. We salvaged off the coast of Florida, before the government got so tight-assed. Me, my father and my brother. The Lassiters.'

'Yes, of course.' Ray slapped a hand on his knee. 'I've read about you. Your father was Big Matt Lassiter. Found the *El Diablo* off Conch Key in 'sixty-four.'

''Sixty-three,' Buck corrected, with a grin. 'Found it, and the fortune she held. The kind of gold a man dreams of, jewels, ingots of silver. I held in my hand a gold chain with a figure of a dragon. A fucking gold dragon,' he said, then stopped, flushed. 'Beg pardon, ma'am.'

'No need.' Fascinated with the image, Marla urged another sandwich on him. 'What was it like?'

'Like nothing you can imagine.' At ease again, Buck chomped into ham. 'There were rubies for its eyes, emeralds in its tail.' Bitterly, he looked down at his hands now and found them empty. 'It was worth five fortunes.'

Caught up in the wonder, Ray stared. 'Yes. I've seen pictures of it. Diablo's Dragon. You brought it up. Extraordinary.'

'The state closed in,' Buck continued. 'Kept us in court for years. Claimed the three-mile limit started at the end of the reef, not at shore. Bastards bled us dry before it was done. In the end they took, and we lost. No better than pirates,' he said and finished off his drink.

'How terrible for you,' Marla murmured. 'To have done all that, discovered all that, only to have it taken.'

'Broke the old man's heart. Never did dive again.' Buck moved his shoulders. 'Well, there are other wrecks. Other treasures.' Buck judged his man, and gambled. 'Like the *Santa Marguerite*, the *Isabella*.'

'Yes, they're here.' Ray met Buck's eye steadily. 'I'm sure of it.'

'Could be.' Matthew picked up the sword, turned it over in his hands. 'Or it could be that both of them were swept out to sea. There's no record of survivors. Only two ships crashed on the reef.'

Ray lifted a finger. 'Ah, but witnesses of the day claim they saw the *Isabella* and the *Santa Marguerite* go down. Survivors from the other ships saw the waves rise and scuttle them.'

Matthew lifted his gaze to Ray's, nodded. 'Maybe.'

'Matthew's a cynic,' Buck commented. 'Keeps me level. I'm going to tell you something, Ray.' He leaned forward, pale blue eyes keen. 'I've been doing research of my own. Five years on and off. Three years ago, the boy and I spent better than six months combing these waters – mostly the two-mile stretch between St. Kitts and Nevis and the peninsula area. We found this, we found that, but we didn't find those two ships. But I know they're here.'

'Well, now.' Ray tugged on his bottom lip, a gesture that Tate knew meant he was considering. 'I think you were looking in the wrong spot, Buck. Not that I want to say I'd know more about it. The ships took off from Nevis, but from what I've been able to piece together, the two lost wrecks made it farther north, just past the tip of St. Kitts before they broke.'

Buck's lips curved. 'I figure the same. It's a big sea, Ray.' He flicked a glance toward Matthew and was rewarded with a careless shrug. 'I've got forty years' experience, and the boy's been diving since he could walk. What I don't have is financial backing.'

As a man who had worked his way up to CEO of a top brokerage firm before his early retirement, Ray knew a deal when it was placed on the table. 'You're looking for a partnership, Buck. We'd have to talk about that. Discuss terms, percentages.' Rising, Ray flashed a smile. 'Why don't we step into my office?'

'Well, then.' Marla smiled as her husband and Buck stepped into the deckhouse. 'I think I'm going to sit in the shade and nap over my book. You children entertain yourselves.' She moved off under a striped awning and settled down with her iced tea and a paperback novel.

'I guess I'll go over and clean up my booty.' Matthew reached for a large plastic bag. 'Mind if I borrow this?'

Without waiting for a response, he loaded his gear into it, then hefted his tanks. 'Want to give me a hand?'

'No.'

He only lifted a brow. 'I figured you might want to see how this cleans up.' He gestured with the sword, waited to see if her curiosity would overpower her irritation. He didn't wait long.

With a mutter, she snatched the plastic bag and took it down the ladder to the swim step and over the side with her.

The *Sea Devil* looked worse close up. Tate judged its sway in the current expertly and hauled herself over the rail. She caught a faint whiff of fish.

Gear was carefully stowed and secured. But the deck needed washing as much as it needed painting. The windows on the tiny wheelhouse where a hammock swung were smudged and smeared with salt and smoke. A couple of overturned buckets, and a second hammock, served as seats.

'It's not the *Queen Mary*.' Matthew stored his tanks. 'But it's not the *Titanic* either. She ain't pretty, but she's seaworthy.'

He took the bag from her and stored his wetsuit in a large plastic garbage can. 'Want a drink?'

Tate took another slow look around. 'Got anything sterilized?'

He flipped open the lid of an ice chest, fished out a Pepsi. Tate caught it on the fly and sat down on a bucket. 'You're living on board.'

'That's right.' He went into the wheelhouse. When she heard him rattling around, she reached over to stroke the sword he'd laid across the other bucket.

Had it graced the belt of some Spanish captain with lace at his cuffs and recklessness in his soul? Had he killed buccaneers with it, or worn it for style? Perhaps he had gripped it in a white-knuckled hand as the wind and the waves had battered his ship.

And no one since then had felt its weight.

She looked up, saw Matthew standing at the wheelhouse door watching her. Furiously embarrassed, Tate snatched her hand back, took a casual drink from her Pepsi.

'We have a sword at home,' she said evenly. 'Sixteenth century.' She didn't add that they had only the hilt, and that it was broken.

'Good for you.' He took the sword, settled with it on the deck. He was already regretting the impulsive invitation. It didn't do much good for him to keep repeating to himself that she was too young. Not with her T-shirt wet and molded against her, and those creamy, just sun-kissed legs looking longer than they had a right to. And that voice – half whiskey, half prim lemonade – didn't belong to a child, but to a woman. Or it should have.

She frowned, watching him patiently working on the corrosion. She hadn't expected those scarred, rough-looking hands to be patient.

'Why do you want partners?'

He didn't look up. 'Didn't say I did.'

'But your uncle–'

'That's Buck.' Matthew lifted a shoulder. 'He handles the business.'

She propped her elbows on her knees, her chin in the heels of her hands. 'What do you handle?'

He glanced up then, and his eyes, restless despite the patience of his hands, clashed with hers. 'The hunt.'

She understood that, exactly, and smiled at him with an eagerness that ignored the sword between them. 'It's wonderful, isn't it? Thinking about what could be there, and that you might be the one to find it. Where did you find the coin?' At his baffled look, she grinned and reached out to touch the disk of silver at his chest. 'The piece of eight.'

'My first real salvage dive,' he told her, wishing she didn't look so appealingly fresh and friendly. 'California. We lived there for a while. What are you doing diving for treasure instead of driving some college boy nuts?'

Tate tossed her head and tried her hand at sophistication. 'Boys are easy,' she drawled, and slid down to sit on the deck across from him. 'I like challenges.'

The quick twist in his gut warned him. 'Careful, little girl,' he murmured.

'I'm twenty,' she said with all the frigid pride of burgeoning womanhood. Or she would be, she amended, by summer's end. 'Why are you out here diving for treasure instead of working for a living?'

Now he grinned. 'Because I'm good. If you'd been better, you'd have this, and I wouldn't.'

Rather than dignify that with a response, she took another sip of Pepsi. 'Why isn't your father along? Has he given up diving?'

'In a manner of speaking. He's dead.'

'Oh. I'm sorry.'

'Nine years ago,' Matthew continued, and kept cleaning the sword. 'We were doing some hunting off of Australia.'

'A diving accident?'

'No. He was too good to have an accident.' He picked up the can she'd set down, took a swallow. 'He was murdered.'

It took Tate a moment. Matthew had spoken so matter-of-factly that the word 'murder' didn't register. 'My God, how–'

'I don't know, for sure.' Nor did he know why he had told her. 'He went down alive; we brought him up dead. Hand me that rag.'

'But–'

'That was the end of it,' he said and reached for the rag himself. 'No use dwelling on the past.'

She had an urge to lay a hand on his scarred one, but judged, correctly, that he'd snap it off at the wrist. 'An odd statement from a treasure hunter.'

'Babe, it's what it brings you now that counts. And this ain't bad.'

Distracted, she looked back down at the hilt. As Matthew rubbed, she began to see the gleam. 'Silver,' she murmured. 'It's silver. A mark of rank. I knew it.'

'It's a nice piece.'

Forgetting everything but the find, she leaned closer, let her finger-tip skim along the gleam. 'I think it's eighteenth-century.'

His eyes smiled. 'Do you?'

'I'm majoring in marine archeology.' She gave her bangs an impatient push. 'It could have belonged to the captain.'

'Or any other officer,' Matthew said dryly. 'But it'll keep me in beer and shrimp for a while.'

Stunned, she jerked back. 'You're going to sell it? You're just going to sell it? For money?'

'I'm not going to sell it for clamshells.'

'But don't you want to know where it came from, who it came from?'

'Not particularly.' He turned the cleaned portion of the hilt toward the sun, watched it glint in the light. 'There's an antique dealer on St. Bart's who'll give me a square deal.'

'That's horrible. That's . . .' She searched for the worst insult she could imagine. 'Ignorant.' In a flash, she was on her feet. 'To just sell it that way. For all you know, it may have belonged to the captain of the *Isabella* or the *Santa*

Marguerite. That would be a historic find. It could belong in a museum.'

Amateurs, Matthew thought in disgust. 'It belongs where I put it.' He rose fluidly. 'I found it.'

Her heart stuttered at the thought of it wasting away in some dusty antique shop, or worse, being bought by some careless tourist who would hang it on the wall of his den.

'I'll give you a hundred dollars for it.'

His grin flashed. 'Red, I could get more than that by melting down the hilt.'

She paled at the thought. 'You wouldn't do that. You couldn't.' When he only cocked his head, she bit her lip. The stereo system she envisioned gracing her college dorm room would have to wait. 'Two hundred then. It's all I have saved.'

'I'll take my chances on St. Bart's.'

Color flooded back into her cheeks. 'You're nothing but an opportunist.'

'You're right. And you're an idealist.' He smiled as she stood in front of him, hands fisted, eyes fired. Over her shoulder, he caught movement on the deck of the *Adventure*. 'And for better or worse, Red, it looks like we're partners.'

'Over my dead body.'

He took her by the shoulders. For one startled minute, she thought he meant to heave her overboard. But he simply turned her until she faced her own boat.

Her heart sank as she watched her father and Buck Lassiter shake hands.

Chapter Two

A BRILLIANT SUNSET poured gold and pink across the sky and melted into the sea. The glory was followed by the finger-snap twilight so usual in the tropics. Over the calm water came the scratchy sound of a portable radio aboard the *Sea Devil* that did little justice to the bouncy reggae beat. The air might have been redolent with the scent of sautéing fish, but Tate's mood was foul.

'I don't see why we need partners.' Tate propped her elbows on the narrow table in the galley and frowned at her mother's back.

'Your father took a real shine to Buck.' Marla sprinkled crushed rosemary into the pan. 'It's good for him to have a man near his own age to pal around with.'

'He has us,' Tate grumbled.

'Of course he has.' Marla smiled over her shoulder. 'But men need men, honey. They've just got to spit and belch now and again.'

Tate snorted at the idea of her impeccably mannered father doing either. 'The point is we don't know anything about them. I mean, they just showed up in our space.' She was still smarting over the sword. 'Dad spent months researching these wrecks. Why should we trust the Lassiters?'

'Because they're Lassiters,' Ray said as he swung into the galley. Bending over, he planted a noisy kiss on the top of Tate's head. 'Our girl's got a suspicious nature, Marla.' He winked at his wife, then because it was his turn for galley duty, began to set the table. 'That's a good thing, to a point. It's not smart to believe everything you see, everything you hear. But sometimes you've got to go with the gut. Mine tells me the Lassiters are just what we need to round out this little adventure.'

'How?' Tate propped her chin on her fist. 'Matthew Lassiter is arrogant and shortsighted and–'

'Young.' Ray finished with a twinkle in his eye. 'Marla, that smells wonderful.' He slipped his arms around her waist and nuzzled the back of her neck. She smelled of suntan lotion and Chanel.

'Then let's sit down and see how it tastes.'

But Tate wasn't willing to let the matter drop. 'Dad, do you know what he plans to do with that sword? He's just going to sell it to some dealer.'

Ray sat and pursed his lips. 'Most salvagers sell their booty, honey. That's how they make a living.'

'Well, that's fine.' Tate took the platter her mother offered automatically and chose her portion. 'But it should be dated and assessed first. He doesn't even care what it is or who it belonged to. To him it's just something to trade for a case of beer.'

'That's a shame.' Marla sighed as Ray poured dinner wine into her glass. 'And I know how you feel, honey. The Tates have always been defenders of history.'

'And the Beaumonts,' her husband put in. 'It's the Southern way. You have a point, Tate.' Ray gestured with his fork. 'And I sympathize. But I also understand Matthew's side of it. The quick turnaround, the quick profit for his efforts. If his grandfather had taken that route, he'd have died a rich man. Instead, he chose to share his discovery and ended up with nothing.'

'There's a middle ground,' Tate insisted.

'Not for some. But I believe Buck and I found it. If we find the *Isabella* or the *Santa Marguerite*, we'll apply for a lease, if we're not outside the limit. Regardless, we'll share what we salvage with the government of St. Kitts and Nevis, a term he agreed to reluctantly.' Ray lifted his glass, eyed the wine. 'He agreed to it because we have something he needs.'

'What do we have?' Tate wanted to know.

'We have a strong enough financial base to continue this operation for some time with or without results. We can afford the time, as we agreed you could defer the upcoming fall semester. And if it becomes an issue, we can afford the equipment needed for an extensive salvage operation.'

'So, they're using us.' Exasperated, Tate pushed her plate aside. 'That's my point, Dad.'

'In a partnership, one-half must have use of the other.'

Far from convinced, Tate rose to pour herself a glass of fresh lemonade. In theory, she wasn't against partnership. From an early age, she'd been taught the value of teamwork. It was this specific team she worried over. 'And what are they bringing into this partnership?'

'In the first place, they're professionals. We're amateurs.' Ray waved a hand as Tate started to protest. 'However much I like to dream otherwise, I've never discovered a wreck, only explored those found and salvaged by others. Oh, we've been lucky a few times.' He picked up Marla's hand, ran a thumb around the gold ring she wore. 'Brought up trinkets others have overlooked. Since my first dive, I've dreamed of finding an undiscovered ship.'

'And you will,' Marla claimed with undiluted faith.

'This could be the one.' Tate dragged a hand through her hair. As much as she loved her parents, their lack of practicality baffled her. 'Dad, all the research you've done, the archives, the manifests, the letters. The way you worked on the records of the storm, the tides, everything. You've put so much work into this.'

'I have,' he agreed. 'And because of that, I'm very interested that a great deal of Buck's research aligns with mine. I can learn so much from him. Do you know he worked for three years in the North Atlantic, in depths of five hundred feet and more? Frigid water, dark water. He's salvaged in mud, in coral, in the feeding area of shark. Imagine it.'

Tate could see he was, the way his eyes unfocused, how his lips curved with dreams. With a sigh, she set a hand on his shoulder. 'Dad, just because he's had more experience–'

'A lifetime more.' Ray reached back, patted her hand. 'That's what he brings to us. Experience, perseverance, the mind of a hunter. And something as basic as manpower. Two teams, Tate, are more efficient than one.' He paused. 'Tate, it's important to me that you understand my decision. If you can't accept it, I'll tell Buck the deals's off.'

And that would cost him, Tate thought, miserably. Pride, because he'd already given his word. Hope, because he was counting on the success of this new team.

'I understand it,' she said, tucking her personal distaste aside. 'And I can accept it. Just one more question.'

'Ask away,' Ray invited.

'How can we be sure that when their team goes down, they won't keep whatever they find to themselves?'

'Because we're splitting the partnership.' He stood to clear the table. 'I'll dive with Buck. You'll dive with Matthew.'

'Isn't that a nice idea?' Marla chuckled to herself at her daughter's horrified expression. 'Who wants a piece of cake?'

Dawn spread over the water in bronze and rose streaks that mirrored the sky. The air was pure as silver and deliciously warm. In the distance, the high bluffs of St. Kitts awoke to the light in misty greens and browns. Farther south, the volcano cone that dominated the little island of Nevis was shrouded in clouds. Sugar-white beaches were deserted.

A trio of pelicans skimmed by, then dived with three quick, nearly soundless plops, shooting the water high in a cascade of individual drops. They rose again, skimmed again, dived again, in comical unity. Wavelets lapped lazily against the hull.

Slowly, beautifully, the light strengthened, and the water was sapphire.

Tate's mood wasn't lifted by the scenery as she suited up. She checked her diver's watch, her wrist compass, the gauges on her tanks. While her father and Buck shared coffee and conversation on the foredeck, she strapped her diver's knife onto her calf.

Beside her, Matthew mirrored the routine.

'I'm not any happier about this than you are,' he muttered. He hefted her tanks, helped her secure them.

'That brightens my mood.'

They attached weight belts, eyeing each other with mutual distrust. 'Just try to keep up, and stay out of my way. We'll be fine.'

'Really.' She spat into her mask, rubbed, rinsed. 'Why don't you stay out of my way?' She plastered a smile on her face as Buck and her father sauntered over.

'Set?' Ray asked her, checking her tank harnesses himself. He glanced at the bright-orange plastic bottle that served as a marker. It bobbed quietly on calm seas. 'Remember your direction.'

'North by northwest – just like Cary Grant.' Tate pecked his cheek, sniffed his aftershave. 'Don't worry.'

He didn't worry, Ray told himself. Of course he didn't. It was just rare that his little girl went down without him. 'Have fun.'

Buck hooked his thumbs in the waistband of his shorts. His legs were stubby trunks knobbed by prominent knees. Covering his bald pate was an oil-smeared Dodgers fielder's cap. His eyes were masked by tinted prescription glasses.

Tate thought he looked like an overweight, poorly dressed gnome. For some reason, she found it appealing. 'I'll keep an eye on your nephew, Buck.'

He grinned at that, his laugh like gravel hitting stone. 'You do that, girl. And good hunting.'

With a nod, Tate executed a smooth back roll from the rail, and headed down. She waited, as a responsible partner, for Matthew's dive. The moment she saw him enter the water, she turned and swam toward the bottom.

Sea fans the color of lilacs waved gracefully in the current. Fish, startled by the intrusion, darted away, a colorful stream of life and motion. If she had been with her father, she might have lingered to enjoy the moment, that always-stunning transition between being a creature of the air, and one of the sea.

She might have taken the time to gather a few pretty shells for her mother, or remained still long enough to coax a fish to glide over and inspect the newcomer.

But with Matthew closing the distance between them, Tate was struck less by the wonder of it than by a keen sense of competition.

Let's see him try to keep up, she decided, and kicking hard, skimmed westward. The water cooled on descent, but remained comfortable. It was a pity, she thought, that they were far from the more interesting reefs and coral gardens, but there was enough to please the senses – the water itself, the sway of fans, a flashing fish.

She kept her eyes peeled for lumps or discolorations in the sand. Damned if she'd miss something and let him surface in triumph again.

She reached for a broken piece of coral, examined it, discarded it. Matthew swam by her, taking the lead. Though Tate reminded herself the change of lead was basic diving procedure, she fretted until she could once more take the point.

They communicated only when strictly necessary. After agreeing to spread out, they kept each other in view. As much, Tate thought, in suspicion as safety.

For an hour, they combed the area where they had found the sword. Tate's first sense of anticipation began to wane when they discovered nothing more. Once she fanned away at sand, her heart thumping as she caught a glint. Her visions of some ancient shoe buckle or plate faded when she uncovered a twentieth-century can of Coke.

Discouraged, she swam farther north. Here, suddenly, a vast undersea garden of brightly patterned shells and coral with darting fish feeding. Lovely branched coral, too fragile to survive the wave action of shallow water, speared and spread in ruby and emerald and mustard yellow. It was home to dozens of creatures that hid in it, fed on it, or indeed fed it.

Pleasure slid through her as she watched a volute with its pumpkin-colored shell creep its laborious way along a rock. A clown fish darted through the purple-tipped tentacles of a sea anemone, immune to their stinging. A trio of regal angelfish glided along, a formation in search of breakfast.

Like a kid in a candy store, Matthew thought, as he watched her. She was holding her position with slow movements, her eyes darting as she tried to take in everything at once.

He'd liked to have dismissed her as foolish, but he appreciated the sea's theater. Both the drama and comedy continued around them – the sunny yellow wrasses busily cleaning the demanding queen trigger-fish, devoted as ladies-in-waiting. There, quick and lethal, the ambushing moray darted from his cave to clamp his jaws over the unwary grouper.

She didn't flinch from her up-close seat of instant death, but studied it. And he had to admit she was a good diver. Strong, skilled, sensible. She didn't like working with him, but she held up her end.

He knew that most amateurs became discouraged if they didn't stumble across some stray coin or artifact within an hour. But she was systematic and apparently tireless. Two other traits he appreciated in a diving partner.

If they were going to be stuck with each other, at least for a couple of months, he might as well make the best of it.

In what he considered a gesture of truce, he swam over, tapped her shoulder. She glanced over, her eyes bland behind her mask. Matthew pointed behind them and watched those eyes brighten with appreciation when she spotted the school of tiny silver-tipped minnows. In a glinting wave, they veered as a mass barely six inches from Tate's outstretched hand, and vanished.

She was still grinning when she saw the barracuda.

It was perhaps a yard off, hovering motionless with its toothy grin and staring eyes. This time she pointed. When

Matthew noted that she was amused rather than afraid, he resumed his search.

Tate glanced back occasionally to be certain their movements didn't attract their audience. But the barracuda remained placidly at a distance. Sometime later when she looked back, he was gone.

She saw the conglomerate just as Matthew's hand closed over it. Disgusted, and certain only her inattention had kept her from finding it first, she swam another few yards to the north.

It irritated her the way he seemed to work in her pocket. If she didn't keep her eye on him, he was practically at her shoulder. In a gesture of dismissal, she kicked away, damned if she'd let him think his misshapen hunk of rock interested her, however promising its pebbly surface.

And that's when she found the coin.

The small spread of darkened sand drew her closer. She fanned more from habit than enthusiasm, imagining she'd probably unearth someone's pocket change or a rusted tin can tossed from a passing boat. But the blackened disk was barely an inch under the silt. She knew the moment she plucked it up that she was holding a legend.

Pieces of eight, she thought, giddy with discovery. A pirate's chant, a buccaneer's booty.

Realizing she was holding her breath, a dangerous mistake, she began to breathe slowly as she rubbed at the discoloration with her thumb. There was the dull sheen of silver at the corner of the irregularly shaped coin.

With a cautious glance over her shoulder to be certain Matthew was occupied, she tucked it into the sleeve of her wetsuit. Smug now, she began to search for more signs.

When a check of her gauge and her watch indicated their time was up, she noted her position, and turned toward her partner. He nodded, jerked a thumb. They began to swim east, ascending slowly.

His goody bag was laden with conglomerate, which he pointed out to her before gesturing to her own empty one. She gave him the equivalent of a shrug and broke the surface just ahead of him.

'Bad luck, Red.'

She suffered his superior smile as they headed in. 'Maybe.' Gripping the ladder of the *Adventure*, she tossed her flippers up to where her father waited. 'Maybe not.'

'How'd it go?' Once his daughter was on deck, Ray relieved her of her weight belt and tanks. Noting her empty bag, he struggled to mask disappointment. 'Nothing worth bringing up, huh?'

'I wouldn't say that,' Matthew commented. He handed Buck his full bag before unzipping his suit. Water dripped from his hair, pooled at his feet. 'Might be something worthwhile once we chip away at it.'

'The boy's got a sixth sense about these things.' Buck set the bag on a bench. His fingers were already itching to start hammering at the conglomerate.

'I'll work on it,' Marla offered. She was wearing her flowered sunhat and a sundress of canary yellow that set off her flame-colored hair. 'I just want to get some videos first. Tate, you and Matthew have a nice cold drink and something to eat. I know these two want to go down and try their luck.'

'Sure.' Tate pushed her wet hair back from her face. 'Oh, and speaking of luck.' She pulled the wrists of her wetsuit. A half dozen coins fell jingling to the deck. 'I had a little myself.'

'Sonofabitch.' Matthew crouched down. He knew by the weight and the shape what she'd found. While the others erupted with excitement, he rubbed a coin between his fingers and looked up coolly into Tate's self-satisfied smile.

He didn't begrudge her the find. But he sure as hell hated that she'd managed to make him look like a fool.

'Where'd you find them?'

'A couple of yards north of where you were harvesting your rocks.' She decided the way annoyance narrowed his eyes almost made up for the sword. 'You were so busy I didn't want to interrupt you.'

'Yeah. I bet.'

'Spanish.' Ray stared down at the coin nestled in his palm. 'Seventeen thirty-three. This could be it. The date's right.'

'Could be from the other ships,' Matthew responded. 'Time, current, storms – they spread things out.'

'They could just as easily be from the *Isabella* or *Santa Marguerite*.' There was a fever in Buck's eyes. 'Ray and me, we'll concentrate on the area where you found these.' He rose from his crouched position, held out a coin to Tate. 'These'll go in the kitty. But I figure you ought to keep one, for yourself. That sit right with you, Matthew?'

'Sure.' He shrugged his shoulders before turning to the ice chest. 'No big deal.'

'It is to me,' Tate murmured as she accepted the coin from Buck. 'It's the first time I've ever found coins. Pieces of eight.' She laughed and leaned forward to give Buck an impulsive kiss. 'What a feeling.'

His ruddy cheeks darkened. Women had always remained a mystery to him and mostly at a distance. 'You hold on to it – that feeling. Sometimes it's a long stretch before you have it again.' He slapped Ray on the back. 'Let's suit up, partner.'

Within thirty minutes, the second team was under way. Marla had spread out a drop cloth and was busily chipping away at the conglomerate. Tate postponed lunch to clean the silver coins.

Nearby, Matthew sat on the deck and polished off his second BLT. 'I tell you, Marla, I might just shanghai you. You sure have a way of putting food together.'

'Anybody can make a sandwich.' Her hammer rang in counterpoint to her molasses-drenched voice. 'You'll have to have dinner with us, Matthew. Then you'll see what cooking's all about.'

He was sure he heard Tate's teeth gnash. 'Love to. I can run over to St. Kitts for you if you need any supplies.'

'That's very sweet.' She'd changed into work shorts and an oversized shirt, and was sweating. Somehow she still managed to look like a Southern belle planning a tea party. 'I could use a little fresh milk to make biscuits.'

'Biscuits? Marla, for homemade biscuits, I'd swim back from the island with the whole cow.'

He was rewarded by her quick, infectious laughter. 'Just a gallon will do me. Oh, not this minute,' she said, waving him back when he started to rise. 'Plenty of time. You enjoy your lunch and the sunshine.'

'Stop trying to charm my mother,' Tate said under her breath.

Matthew scooted closer. 'I like your mother. You've got her hair,' he murmured. 'Her eyes, too.' He picked up another section of sandwich, bit in. 'Too bad you don't take after her otherwise.'

'I also have her delicate bone structure,' Tate said with a clench-toothed smile.

Matthew took his time with his study. 'Yeah, I guess you do.'

Suddenly uncomfortable, she shifted back an inch. 'You're crowding me,' she complained. 'Just like you do on a dive.'

'Here, take a bite.' He held out the sandwich, nearly plowing it into her mouth so that she had little choice but to accept. 'I've decided you're my good-luck charm.'

Rather than choke, she swallowed. 'I beg your pardon?'

'There's a nice Southern flow to the way you say that,' he observed. 'Just a hint of ice under the honey. My good-luck charm,' he repeated. 'Because you were around when I found the sword.'

'You were around when I found it.'

'Whatever. There are a couple of things I don't turn my back on. A man with greed in his eyes, a woman with fire in hers.' He offered Tate more of the sandwich. 'And luck. Good or bad.'

'I'd think it would be smarter to walk away from bad luck.'

'Facing it's better. Usually quicker. Lassiters have had a long run of the bad.' With a shrug, he finished the sandwich himself. 'Seems to me you've brought me some of the good.'

'I'm the one who found the coins.'

'Maybe I'm bringing you some, too.'

'I've got something,' Marla sang out. 'Come and see.'

Matthew rose, and after a moment's hesitation, held out a hand. With matching wariness, Tate took it and let him haul her to her feet.

'Nails,' Marla said, gesturing with one hand as she dabbed a handkerchief over her damp face with the other. 'They look old. And this . . .' She picked up a small disk from amid the rubble. 'Looks like some sort of button. Copper or bronze perhaps.'

With a grunt, Matthew crouched down. There were two iron spikes, a pile of pottery shards, a broken piece of metal that might have been a buckle or pin of some sort. But it was the nails that interested him most.

Marla was right. They were old. He picked one up, turned it in his fingers, imagining it once being hammered into planks that were doomed to storms and seaworms.

'Brass,' Tate announced with delight as she worked off the corrosion with solvent and a rag. 'It is a button. It's got some etching on it, a flower. A little rose. It was probably on a dress of a female passenger.'

The thought made her sad. The woman, unlike the button, hadn't survived.

'Maybe.' Matthew spared the button a glance. 'Odds are we hit a bounce site.'

Tate reached for her own sunglasses to cut the glare. 'What's a bounce site?'

'Just what it sounds like. We probably found the spot where a ship hit while it was being driven in by waves. The wreck's somewhere else.' He lifted his gaze, scanned the sea to the horizon. 'Somewhere else,' he repeated.

But Tate shook her head. 'You're not going to discourage me after this. We haven't come up empty-handed, Matthew. One full dive and we have all this. Coins and nails–'

'Broken pottery and a brass button.' Matthew tossed the nail he held back into the pile. 'Chump change, Red. Even for an amateur.'

She reached out and took hold of the coin that dangled around his neck. 'Where there's some, there's more. My father believes we have a chance at a major find. So do I.'

She was ready to quiver with anger, he noted. Her chin thrust up, sharp as the spikes at their feet, eyes hard and hot.

Christ, why did she have to be a college girl?

He moved his shoulder, and deliberately gave her a light, insulting pat on the cheek. 'Well, it'll keep us entertained.

But it's more often true that where there's some, that's all.' He brushed off his hands and rose. 'I'll clean this up for you, Marla.'

'You're a real upbeat kind of guy, Lassiter.' Tate tugged off her T-shirt. For some reason, the way he'd looked at her, just for an instant, had heated her skin. 'I'm going for a swim.' Moving to the rail, she dove off the side.

'She's her father's daughter,' Marla said with a quiet smile. 'Always sure hard work, perseverance and a good heart will pay off. Life's harder on them than it is for those of us who know those things aren't always enough.' She patted Matthew's arm. 'I'll tidy up here, Matthew. I have my own little system. You go on and get me that milk.'

Chapter Three

TATE FOUND PESSIMISM cowardly. It seemed to her that it was simply an excuse never to face disappointment.

It was even worse when pessimism won out.

After two weeks of dawn-to-dusk double-team diving, they found nothing but a few more scraps of corroded metal. She told herself she wasn't discouraged and hunted on her shift with more care and more enthusiasm than was warranted.

At night, she took to poring over her father's charts, the copies he'd made from his research. The more cavalier Matthew became, the more determined she was to prove him wrong. She wanted the wreck now, passionately. If only to beat him.

She had to admit the weeks weren't a total loss. The weather was beautiful, the diving spectacular. The time she spent on the island when her mother insisted on a break was filled with souvenir shopping, exploring, picnics on the beach. She hunted through cemeteries and old churches, hoping she might find another clue to the secret of the wrecks of 1733.

But most of all, she enjoyed watching her father with Buck. They were an odd pair – one squat and round and cue-ball bald, the other aristocratically lean with a mane of silvering blond hair.

Her father spoke with the slow, sweet drawl of coastal Carolina while Buck's conversation was peppershot with oaths delivered with Yankee quickness. Yet they merged together like old friends reunited.

Often when they surfaced after a dive, they were laughing like boys fresh from some misdemeanor. And one always seemed to have a tale to tell on the other.

It was illuminating for Tate to watch the friendship bloom and grow so rapidly. On land, her father's companions were businessmen, a suit-and-tie brigade of success, moderate wealth and staunch Southern heritage.

Here she watched him bronzing in the sun with Buck, sharing a beer and dreams of fortune.

Marla would snap their picture or pull out her ubiquitous video camera and call them two old salts.

As Tate prepared for her morning dive, she watched them arguing baseball over coffee and croissants.

'What Buck knows about baseball you could swallow in one gulp,' Matthew commented. 'He's been boning up so he can fight with Ray.'

Tate sat down to pull on her flippers. 'I think it's nice.'

'Didn't say it wasn't.'

'You never say anything's nice.'

He sat beside her. 'Okay, it's nice. Hanging with your father's been good for Buck. He's had a rough time the last few years. I haven't seen him enjoy himself so much since . . . for a long time.'

Tate let out a long sigh. It was difficult to work up any annoyance with straight sincerity. 'I know you care about him.'

'Sure I do. He's always been there for me. I'd do anything for Buck.' Matthew pressed a securing hand to his mask. 'Hell, I'm diving with you, aren't I?' With that, he rolled into the water.

Instead of being insulted, she grinned, and rolled in after him.

They followed the marker down. They had been moving the search steadily northward. Each time they tried new territory, Tate felt that quickening surge of anticipation. Each time they went down, she told herself today could be the day.

The water was pleasantly cool on the exposed skin of her hands and face. She enjoyed the way it streamed through her hair on her descent.

The fish had grown used to them. It wasn't unusual for a curious grouper or angelfish to peer into her mask. She'd gotten into the habit of bringing a plastic bag of crackers or bread crumbs with her, and took a few minutes at the start of every dive to feed them, and have them swirl around her.

Invariably the barracuda they'd dubbed 'Smiley' came to call, always keeping his distance, always watching. As a mascot, he wasn't particularly lively, but he was loyal.

She and Matthew developed an easy routine. They worked in sight of each other, rarely crossing the invisible line both recognized as separating their territories. Still, they shared their glimpses of sea life. A hand signal, a tap on the tank to point out a school of fish, a burrowing ray.

He was, Tate decided, easier to tolerate in the silence of the sea than above it. Now and again that silence was broken by the blurred roar of a tourist boat above them. Tate had even heard the eerie echo of music from a blasting portable radio with Tina Turner's raw-throated voice wanting to know what love had to do with it.

Singing in her head, Tate aimed for an odd formation of coral. She startled a grouper, who gave her one baleful glance before gliding off. Amused, she glanced over her shoulder. Matthew was swimming west, but was still in her line of vision. She flipped north toward the pretty soft reds and browns of the formation.

Tate was on top of it before she realized it wasn't coral, but rocks. Bubbles burst from her mouthpiece. If she had been above the water rather than below, she might have babbled.

Ballast rocks. Surely they had to be ballast rocks. From her studies she knew the color meant galleon. Schooners had used the brittle gray egg rock. The ballast of a galleon, she thought with a dreamy sense of unreality. That had been lost, forgotten. And now found.

One of the lost wrecks of 1733 was here. And she had found it.

She let out a shout that did nothing more than spray bubbles that blurred her vision. Remembering herself, she slipped her knife from its sheath and rapped sharply on her tank.

Turning a circle, she saw the shadow of her partner yards away. She thought he was signaling, and impatient, rapped again.

Come here, damn it.

She rapped a third time, putting as much insistence as she could manage into the one-toned signal. With satisfaction, and the beginnings of smugness, she watched him cut through the water toward her.

Be as irritated as you like, hot shot, she thought. And prepared to be humbled.

She could see the moment he recognized the stones, the slight hesitation in rhythm, then the quickening of pace. Unable to help herself, she grinned at him and attempted a watery pirouette.

Behind his face mask his eyes were blue as cobalt, intense, with a recklessness that had her heart thudding hard in response. He circled the pile once, apparently satisfied. When he took her hand, Tate gave his fingers a quick, friendly squeeze. She expected they would surface, announce her discovery, but he tugged her back in the direction from where he'd come.

She pulled back, shaking her head, jerking her thumb up. Matthew pointed west. Tate rolled her eyes, gestured back toward the ballast pile and started to kick toward the surface.

Matthew grabbed her ankle, shocking her with the familiar way his hands worked up her leg as he drew her back down. She considered swinging at him, but he had her arm again and was towing her.

It left her no choice but to go along, and to imagine all the vicious things she would say to him once she could speak.

Then she saw and her mouth fell open in reaction. She readjusted her mouthpiece, remembered to breathe and stared at the cannons.

They were corroded, covered with sea life and half buried in the sand. But they were there, the great guns that had once graced the Spanish fleet, defended it against pirates and enemies of the king. She could have wept for the joy of it.

Instead, she grabbed Matthew in a clumsy hug and spun him around in what passed for a victory dance. Water swirled around them, and a school of silver fish cut around them like blades. Their face masks bumped, and she bubbled out a giggle, still holding on to him as they kicked toward the surface forty feet above.

The moment they broke through, she pushed back her face mask, let her mouthpiece drop. 'Matthew, you saw it. It's really there.'

'Seems to be.'

'We're the first to find it. After more than two hundred and fifty years, we're the first.'

His grin flashed, his legs tangling with hers as they trod water. 'A virgin wreck. And it's all ours, Red.'

'I can't believe it. It's nothing like the other times. Someone else had always been there first, and we just puttered around what they'd overlooked or left behind. But this . . .' She tossed back her head and laughed. 'Oh God. It feels wonderful. Enormous.'

With another laugh, she threw her arms around him, nearly sinking them both, and pressed her lips to his in an innocent kiss of delight.

Her lips were wet and cool and curved. The shock of them against his blanked his mind for a full three heartbeats. He wasn't fully aware that he tugged her lips apart with his teeth, slipped his tongue into her mouth to taste, that he changed the kiss from innocent to hungry.

He felt her breath hitch, and her lips soften. Then heard her low, catchy sigh.

Mistake. The word flashed like neon in his brain. But she was pouring herself into the kiss now, in a surrender as irresistible as it was unexpected.

She tasted salt and sea and man, and wondered if anyone had ever sampled such potent flavors all at once. Sun-showered golden light, diamonds of it dancing on the water; the water cool and soft and seductive. She thought her heart had stopped, but it didn't seem to matter. Nothing mattered in this strange and lovely world but the taste and feel of his mouth.

Then she was cut loose and floundering, the door to that fascinating world slamming shut in her face. She kicked instinctively to keep her head above water and blinked at Matthew with huge, dreamy eyes.

'We're wasting time.' He snapped it at her and cursed himself. When she pressed her lips together as if to recapture the kiss, he bit back a groan and cursed her.

'What?'

'Snap out of it. Somebody your age has been kissed before.'

The hard edge of his voice and the insult beneath it cut away the mists. 'Of course I have. It was just a gesture of congratulations.' That shouldn't have left this hollow sensation in the pit of her stomach.

'Well, save it. We've got to tell the others and put out markers.'

'Fine.' She headed toward the boat with a quick, efficient crawl. 'I don't see what you're so mad about.'

'You wouldn't,' Matthew muttered and started after her.

Determined not to let him spoil the most exciting day of her life, Tate clambered onto the boat.

Marla was sitting under the awning giving herself a manicure. One hand was already tipped with bright-salmon pink. She looked over with a smile. 'You're early, honey. We didn't expect you up for another hour or so.'

'Where are Dad and Buck?'

'In the pilothouse, studying that old map again.' Marla's smile began to crumble at the edges. 'Something's wrong. Matthew.' She scrambled out of her chair, panic darting out of her eyes. Her secret, never-voiced fear of sharks clawed at her throat. 'Is he hurt? What happened?'

'He's fine.' Tate unhooked her weight belt. 'He's right behind me.' She heard his flippers hit the deck, but didn't turn to offer him a hand up. Instead she took a deep breath. 'Nothing's wrong, Mom. Nothing at all. Everything's great. We found it.'

Marla had hurried over to the rail to make certain of Matthew's safety. Her heartbeat began to level again when she saw him whole and unharmed. 'Found what, honey?'

'The wreck.' Tate passed a hand over her face, stunned to see her fingers were trembling. There was a roaring in her ears, a flutter in her chest. 'One of them. We found it.'

'Christ Jesus.' Buck stood at the door to the deckhouse. His normally ruddy face was pale, the eyes behind his lenses stunned. 'Which one?' he said in a strained voice. 'Which one did you find, boy?'

'Can't say.' Matthew shrugged off his tanks. His pulse was scrambling fast, but he knew it had as much to do with the fact he'd nearly devoured Tate as it did with the possibilities of treasure. 'But she's down there, Buck. We found ballast, galleon ballast, and cannon.' He looked beyond Buck to where Ray stood, goggling. 'The other spot was a bounce site, like I figured. But this site has real possibilities.'

'What –' Ray had to clear his throat. 'What was the position, Tate?'

She opened her mouth, closed it again when she realized she'd been too enthralled to mark it. A flush bloomed on her cheeks.

Matthew glanced at her, offered a thin, superior smile before giving Ray the coordinates. 'We'll need to put out marker buoys. You guys want to suit up, I'll show you what we have.' Then he grinned. 'I'd say we're going to put that nice new airlift of yours to use, Ray.'

'Yeah.' Ray looked at Buck. His dazed expression began to clear. 'I'd say you're right.' With a whoop he grabbed Buck. The two men hugged, rocking like drunks.

They needed a plan. It was Tate who, after the noisy celebration that night, offered the voice of reason. A system was required in order to salvage the wreck, and preserve it. Their claim had to be staked legally, and concretely. And the artifacts had to be precisely catalogued.

They needed a good underwater camera to record the sight and the position of artifacts they uncovered, several good notebooks to use for cataloguing. Slates and graphite pencils for sketching underwater.

'Used to be,' Buck began as he helped himself to another beer, 'a man found a wreck, and all it held was his – long as he could hold off pirates and claim jumpers. You had to be cagey, know how to keep your mouth shut, and be willing to fight for what was yours.'

His words slurred a bit as he gestured with his bottle. 'Now there's rules and regulations, and every bloody body wants a piece of what you find with your own work and God-given luck. And there's plenty who're more worried about some planks of worm-eaten timber than about a mother lode of silver.'

'The historical integrity of a wreck's important, Buck.' Ray cruised on his own beer, and the possibilities. 'It's historical value, our responsibility to the past, and the future.'

'Shit.' Buck lighted one of the ten cigarettes he permitted himself a day. 'Time was we blew her to kingdom come if that's what it took to get to the mother lode. Not saying it was smart.' He chuffed out smoke, and his eyes grew dim with memory. 'But it sure as hell was fun.'

'We haven't any right to destroy something to get to something else,' Tate murmured.

Buck glanced over at Tate, grinned. 'Wait, girl, till you get a taste of gold fever. It does something to you. You see that glint come out of the sand. It's shiny and bright, not like silver. Could be a coin, a chain, a medallion, some trinket a long-dead man gave his long-dead woman. There it is, in your hand, true as the day it was made. And all you can think about is more.'

Curious, she tilted her head. 'Is that why you keep going down? If you found all the treasure the *Isabella* and *Santa Marguerite* held – if you found it all and were rich, would you still go down for more?'

'I'll go down till I die. It's all I know. All I need to. Your father was like that,' he added, gesturing to Matthew. 'Whether he struck the mother lode or came back with nothing but a cannonball, he had to go down again. Dying stopped him. That was all that could.' His voice roughened as he looked down at his beer again. 'He wanted the *Isabella*. Spent the last months he lived figuring how and where and when. Now we'll harvest her for him. Angelique's Curse.'

'What?' Ray's brows drew together. 'Angelique's Curse?'

'Killed my brother,' Buck said blearily. 'Damn witch's spell.'

Recognizing the signs, Matthew leaned forward, plucked the nearly empty beer from his uncle's fingers. 'A man killed him, Buck. A flesh-and-blood man. No curse, no spell.' Rising, he hauled Buck to his feet. 'He gets maudlin when he drinks too much,' he explained. 'Next he'll be talking about Blackbeard's ghost.'

'Saw it,' Buck mumbled around a foolish smile. His glasses slid down his nose so that he peered myopically over them. 'Thought I did. Off the coast of Okracoke. Remember that, Matthew?'

'Sure, I remember. We've got a long day ahead of us. Better get back to the boat.'

'Want some help?' Ray rose, was surprised, and a little chagrined to discover he wasn't entirely steady on his feet.

'I can manage. I'll just pour him into the inflatable, row him across. Thanks for dinner, Marla. Never in my life tasted fried chicken to match yours. Be ready at dawn, kid,' he told Tate. 'And for a taste of real work.'

'I'll be ready.' Despite the fact he hadn't asked for help, she went to Buck's other side, draped his arm over her shoulders. 'Come on, Buck, time for bed.'

'You're a sweet kid.' With drunken affection, he gave her a clumsy squeeze. 'Ain't she, Matthew?'

'She's a regular sugar cube. I'm going down the ladder first, Buck. If you fall in, I might let you drown.'

'That'll be the day.' Buck chuckled, shifting his weight onto Tate as Matthew swung over the side. 'That boy'd fight off a school of sharks for me. Lassiters stick together.'

'I know.' Carefully, rocking a bit under his weight, Tate managed to maneuver Buck over the rail. 'Hold on, now.' The absurdity had her giggling as he swayed over the ladder and Matthew cursed from below. 'Hold on, Buck.'

'Don't you worry, girl. There isn't a boat been made I can't board.'

'Goddamn it, you're going to capsize us. Buck, you idiot.' As the dinghy pitched dangerously, Matthew shoved Buck down. Water sloshed in, soaking both of them.

'I'll bail her out, Matthew.' With a good-natured chuckle, Buck began to scoop water out of the bottom with his hands.

'Just sit still.' Matthew took the oars out of the locks, glanced up to see the Beaumonts grinning over the side. 'I should have made him swim for it.'

''Night, Ray.' Buck waved cheerfully as Matthew rowed. 'There'll be gold doubloons tomorrow. Gold and silver and bright, shiny jewels. A new wreck, Matthew,' he mumbled as his chin dropped to his chest. 'Always knew we'd find it. Was the Beaumonts brought us the luck.'

'Yeah.' After securing the oars and the line, Matthew eyed his uncle dubiously. 'Can you make the ladder, Buck?'

'Sure, I can make the ladder. Got the sea legs I was born with, don't I?' Those legs wobbled, as did the small raft as he weaved toward the side of the *Sea Devil.*

Through more luck than design, he gripped a rung and hauled himself up before he could turn the inflatable over. Soaked to the knees, Matthew joined him on deck. Buck was weaving and waving enthusiastically to the Beaumonts.

'Ahoy the *Adventure*. All's well.'

'Let's see if you say that in the morning,' Matthew muttered and half carried Buck to the closet-sized wheelhouse.

'Those are good people, Matthew. First I was thinking we'd just use their equipment, string them along, then take us the lion's share. Be easy for you and me to go down at night, lay off some of the best salvage. Don't think they'd know the difference.'

'Probably not,' Matthew agreed, as he stripped the wet pants off his uncle. 'I gave it some thought myself. Amateurs usually deserve to be fleeced.'

'And we've fleeced a few,' Buck said merrily. 'Just can't do it to old Ray, though. Got a friend there. Haven't had a friend like that since your dad died. There's his pretty wife, pretty daughter. Nope.' He shook his head with some regret. 'Can't pirate from people you like.'

Matthew acknowledged this with a grunt and eyed the hammock strung between the cabin's forward and aft walls. He hoped to God he wouldn't have to heft Buck into it. 'You've got to get into your bunk.'

'Yep. Going to play straight with Ray.' Like a bear climbing into his cave, Buck heaved himself up. The hammock swayed dangerously before he settled. 'Should tell them about Angelique's Curse. Thinking about it, but never told nobody but you.'

'Don't worry about it.'

'Maybe if I don't tell them, they won't be jinxed by it. Don't want to see anything happen to them.'

'They'll be fine.' Matthew unzipped his jeans, peeled them off.

'Remember that picture I showed you? All that gold, the rubies, the diamonds. Doesn't seem like something so beautiful could be evil.'

'Because it can't.' Matthew stripped off his shirt, tossed it after his jeans. He slipped Buck's glasses off his nose, set them aside. 'Get some sleep, Buck.'

'More than two hundred years since they burned that witch and people still die. Like James.'

Matthew's jaw set, and his eyes went cold. 'It wasn't a necklace that killed my father. It was a man. It was Silas VanDyke.'

'VanDyke.' Buck repeated the name in a voice slurred with sleep. 'Never prove it.'

'It's enough to know it.'

'It's the curse. The witch's curse. But we'll beat her, Matthew. You and me'll beat her.' Buck began to snore.

Curse be damned, Matthew thought. He'd find the amulet all right. He'd follow in his father's footsteps until he had it. And when he did, he'd take his revenge on the bastard who had murdered James Lassiter.

In his underwear, he stepped out of the cabin into the balmy, starsplattered night. The moon hung, a silver coin struck in half. He settled under it in his own hammock, far enough away that his uncle's habitual snoring was only a low hum.

There was a necklace, a chain of heavy gold links and a pendant etched with names of doomed lovers and studded with rubies and diamonds. He'd seen the pictures, read the sketchy documentation his father had unearthed.

He knew the legend as well as a man might know fairy tales recited to him as a child at bedtime. A woman burned at the stake, condemned for witchcraft and murder. Her final promise that any who profited from her death would pay in kind.

The doom and despair that had followed the path of the necklace for two centuries. The greed and lust that had caused men to kill for it and women to plot.

He might even believe the legend, but it meant only that the greed and the lust had caused the doom and despair. A priceless jewel needed no curse to drive men to murder.

That he was sure of. That he knew, too well. Angelique's Curse had been the motive behind his father's death.

But it was a man who had planned it, executed it.

Silas VanDyke. Matthew could conjure up his face if he needed to, the voice, the build, even the smell. No matter how many years passed, he forgot nothing.

And he knew, as he had known as a helpless, grief-ravaged teenager, that one day he would find the amulet, and use it against VanDyke.

For revenge.

It was odd, that with such dark and violent thoughts hovering in his mind as he drifted to sleep, he would dream of Tate.

Swimming in impossibly clear waters, free of weight, of equipment, slick and agile as a fish. Deeper and deeper, to where the sun could no longer penetrate. The fans waved and toothy clumps of colors gleamed like jewels and carried bright fish in their pockets.

Still deeper, to where the colors – reds and oranges and yellows – faded to cool, cool blue. Yet there was no pressure, no need to equalize, no fears. Only a bursting sense of freedom that mellowed into complete and utter contentment.

He could stay here forever, in this soundless world, with nothing on his back, neither tanks nor worries.

There. There below him, a child's fairy-tale image of a sunken ship. The masts, the hull, the tattered flags waving in the current. It lay tilted in the bed of sand, impossibly whole and impossibly clear. He could see the cannons, still aimed against ancient enemies. And the wheel waiting for its captain ghost to steer it.

Delighted, he swam toward it, through swirls of fish, past an octopus that curled its tentacles and ballooned away, under the shadow of a gaint ray that danced overhead.

He circled the deck of the Spanish galleon, read the proud lettering that christened her the *Isabella*. The crow's nest creaked above him, like a tree in the wind.

Then he saw her. Like a mermaid, she hovered just out of reach, smiling a siren's smile, gesturing with lovely, graceful hands. Her hair was long, not a flaming cap, but long, silken ropes of fire waving and swirling over her shoulders and naked breasts. Her skin was like a pearl, white and gleaming.

Her eyes were the same, green and amused.

As if a tide had swept him, he was helpless to do anything but go to her.

Her arms went around him, satin chains. Her lips parted for his and were sweet as honey. When he touched her, it was as if he'd waited all his life for that alone. The feel of her skin sliding under his hand, the quiver of muscle as he aroused her. The drum of pulse under flesh.

The taste of her sigh was in his mouth. Then the slick and glorious heat enveloped as he slid inside her, as her legs wrapped around him and her body bowed back to take him deeper.

It was all dreamy movements, endless sensation. They drifted, rolling through the water in a soundless mating that left him weak and stunned and blissfully happy. He felt himself spill into her.

Then she kissed him, softly, deeply and with incredible sweetness. When he saw her face again, she was smiling. He reached for her, but she shook her head and danced away. He gave chase, and they frolicked like children, darting around the sunken ship.

She led him to a chest, laughing as she tossed back the lid and revealed the mountain of gold. Coins spilled as she dipped her hand in. The glint was like sunlight, and scattered with it were jewels of great size. Diamonds as big as his fist, emeralds larger than her eyes, pools of sapphires and rubies. Their color was dazzling against the cool gray of the world around them.

He dragged his hand through the chest, spilled a shower of starshaped diamonds over her hair and made her laugh.

Then he found the amulet, the heavy gold chain, the blood and tears that studded the pendant. He could feel heat from it, as if it lived. Never in his life had he seen anything so beautiful, so compelling.

He held it up, looked at Tate's delighted face through the circle of the chain, then slipped it over her head. She laughed, kissed him, then cupped the pendant in her hand.

Suddenly fire exploded from it, a spear of violent heat and light that slammed him back like a blow. He watched in horror as the fire grew, in size and intensity, covering her in a sheath of flame. All he could see were her eyes, anguished and terrified.

He couldn't reach her. Though he fought and he struggled, the water that had been so calm and peaceful was a whirlwind of movement and sound. A tornado of sand funneled up, blinding him. He heard the lightning crack of the mast splitting, the seaquake roar that burst through the bed of sand and silt to tear through the hull of the ship like cannon fire.

Through it he heard screams – hers, his own.

Then it was gone, the flames, the sea, the wreck, the amulet. Tate. The sky was overhead, with its half disk of moon and splatter of stars. The sea was calm and ink-black, barely whispering against the boat.

He was alone on the deck of the *Sea Devil*, dripping sweat and gasping for breath.

Chapter Four

TATE TOOK TWO dozen pictures of ballast and cannon as she and Matthew explored. He humored her by posing at the mouth of a corroded gun, or manned the camera himself to take shots of her among the rocks and patient fish. Together, they attached a crusted cannonball to a flotation and sent it up to the second team.

Then, after a tug on the line, the work began.

Maneuvering an airlift well requires skill, patience and teamwork. It was a simple tool, hardly more than a pipe, four inches in diameter and about ten feet long with an airhose. Pressurized air ran into the pipe, rising and creating suction that would vacuum water, sand and solid objects. It was as essential to a treasure hunter as a hammer to a carpenter. Used too quickly, or with too much power, it could destroy. Used too carelessly, the pipe would become clogged with conglomerate, shells, coral.

While Matthew ran the airlift, Tate examined and collected its fallout that spewed from the top of the pipe. It was hard and tedious work on both sides. Sand and light debris swirled, obscuring vision in a dirty cloud downcurrent. It took a sharp eye and endless patience to search through the fallout, load the bits and pieces and chunks into buckets to be hauled to the surface.

Matthew continued to make test holes with a steady, almost soothing rhythm. Stingrays basked in the fallout, apparently enjoying the massage of sand and small rock. Tate allowed herself to dream, imagining a slew of glinting gold bursting out of the pipe, like a jackpot in a slot machine.

Fantasies aside, she gathered fused nails, bits of conglomerate and the shards of broken pottery. They were every bit as fascinating to her as gold bullion. Her college studies in the past year had accented her love of history and the fragments of culture buried in the shifting sea.

Her long-term ambitions and goals were very clear. She would study, earn her degree, absorbing all the knowledge she could hold through books, lectures, and most of all, by doing. One day, she would join the ranks of scientists who sailed the oceans, plumbed the depths to discover and analyze the relics of doomed ships.

Her name would make an impact, and her finds from doubloons to iron spikes would matter.

Eventually, there would be a museum carrying the Beaumont name filled with artifacts.

Now and again as she worked, she would catch herself falling behind because she'd paused to wonder over a broken cup. What had it held the last time someone sipped from it?

When she nicked her finger on a sharp edge, she took it philosophically. The thin drip of blood washed away in the swirl.

Matthew signaled her through the cloud. In the hole, perhaps a foot deep, she saw the iron spikes crossed like swords. Caught between their calcified tips was a platter of pewter.

Forty feet of water didn't prevent Tate from expressing her glee. She caught his hand and squeezed it, then blew him a kiss. Efficiently, she unhooked her camera from her belt and documented the find. Records, she knew, were essential to scientific discoveries. She might have spent some time examining it, gloating over it unscientifically, but Matthew was already moving off to dig another hole.

There was more. Each time they transferred the airlift, they would uncover another discovery. A clump of spoons cemented in coral, a bowl that even with a third of it missing caused Tate's heart to slam against her ribs.

Time and fatigue ceased to exist. An audience of thousands watched the progress, small fish scanning the disturbed area for exposed worms. If one got lucky, dozens of others would rush in to search for food in a colorful flood of motion.

At his usual distance, the barracuda remained like a statue, looking on in grinning approval.

Matthew ran the lift like an artist, Tate thought. Probing here, then shifting with a delicacy that seemed to remove sand a grain at a time. He brushed away silt clouds with a wave of the pipe. If the wall of sand was parted by an object, he would back off the pipe, work carefully to prevent damage.

She saw with dazzled eyes a fragile piece of porcelain, a bowl with elegant rosebuds rimming its cup.

He would have left it for the time being, knowing that something that fragile when cemented to coral or some other object could be snapped off at the slightest touch.

But her eyes were so big with wonder, so bright with delight. He wanted to give her the bowl, see her face when she held it. Signaling her back, Matthew began the tedious and time-consuming process of whispering the sand clear. When he was satisfied, he handed her the pipe. Reaching below the bowl to the coral that had claimed it, Matthew worked it free.

It cost him some skin, but when he offered it to her, the nicks and scratches were forgotten. Her eyes glowed, then filled so unexpectedly both of them stared. Disconcerted, Matthew took the pipe back, jerked a thumb to the surface. He cracked the valve on the airlift, released a torrent of bubbles. Together, they swam up in the spray.

She didn't speak, couldn't. Grateful they were hampered by the airlift and her last bucket of conglomerate, she reached the side of the *Adventure*. Her father beamed over the side.

'You've been keeping us busy.' He'd pitched his voice over the roar of the compressor, winced when Buck shut it off. 'We've got dozens of artifacts, Tate.' He hauled up the bucket she held out. 'Spoons, forks, buckets, copper coins, buttons . . .' He trailed off when she held up the bowl. 'My God. Porcelain. Unbroken. Marla.' His voice cracked on the name. 'Marla, come over here and look at this.'

Reverently, Ray took the bowl from Tate. By the time she and Matthew had gotten aboard, Marla was sitting on deck, surrounded by debris, the flowered bowl in her lap, her video camera beside her.

'Pretty piece,' Buck commented. However casual the words, his voice betrayed his excitement.

'Tate liked it.' Matthew glanced toward her. She was standing in her wetsuit, the tears that had threatened forty feet below flowing freely.

'There are so many things,' she managed. 'Dad, you can't imagine. Under the sand. All these years under the sand. Then you find them. Something like this.' After rubbing the heels of her hands over her face, she crouched by her mother, dared to skim a gentle fingertip over the rim of the bowl. 'Not a chip. It survived a hurricane and more than two hundred and fifty years, and it's perfect.'

She rose. Her fingers felt numb as she tugged at the zipper of her wetsuit. 'There was a platter, pewter. It's caught between two iron spikes like a sculpture. You only had to close your eyes to see it heaped with food and set on a table. Nothing I've been studying comes close to doing it, to seeing it.'

'I figure we hit the galley area,' Matthew put in. 'Plenty of wooden utensils, wine jugs, broken dishes.' Grateful, he accepted the cold juice Ray offered him. 'I dug a lot of test holes, about a thirty-foot area. The two of you might want to move a few degrees north of that.'

'Let's get started.' Buck was already suiting up. Casually, Matthew walked over to pour more juice.

'Saw a shark cruising,' he said in an undertone. It was well known among the partners that Marla paled and panicked at the thought of sharks. 'Wasn't interested in us, but it wouldn't hurt to take a couple of bangsticks down.'

Ray glanced toward his wife, who was reverently documenting the latest treasures on video. 'Better safe than sorry,' he agreed. 'Tate,' he called out. 'Want to reload the camera for me?'

Twenty minutes later, the compressor was pumping again. Tate worked at the big drop-leaf table in the deckhouse with her mother, cataloguing every item they'd brought up from the wreck.

'It's the *Santa Marguerite*.' Tate fingered a spoon before setting it in the proper pile. 'We found the ordinance mark on one of the cannons. We found our Spanish galleon, Mom.'

'Your father's dream.'

'And yours?'

'And mine,' Marla agreed with a slow smile. 'Used to be I just went along for the ride. It was such a nice, interesting hobby, I thought. It gave us such adventurous vacations, and was certainly a change from our mundane jobs.'

Tate looked up, a pucker of a frown between her brows. 'I never knew you thought your job was mundane.'

'Oh, being a legal secretary is fine except when you start asking yourself why you didn't have the gumption to be the lawyer.' She moved her shoulders. 'The way I was raised, Tate, honey, a woman didn't move in a man's world except to quietly pick up behind him. Your grandma was a very old-fashioned woman. I was expected to work in an acceptable job until I found a suitable husband.' She laughed and set aside a pewter cup with a missing handle. 'I just got lucky on the husband part. Very lucky.'

This, too, was a new discovery. 'Did you want to be a lawyer?'

'Never occurred to me,' Marla admitted. 'Until I was heading on toward forty. A dangerous time for a woman. I can't say I looked back when your father decided to retire. I did the same, and I thought I was more than content to drift with him, playing at treasure-hunting. Now seeing these things, she picked up a silver coin, 'makes me realize we're doing something important. Valuable in its way. I never thought to make a mark again.'

'Again.'

Marla looked up with a smile. 'I made my mark when I had you. This is wonderful, and it's exciting. But you'll always be treasure enough for your father and me.'

'You've always made me feel like I can do anything. Be anything.'

'You can.' Marla glanced over. 'Matthew, come join us.'

'I don't want to interrupt.' He felt out of his depth, and clumsy, stepping into the family unit.

'Don't be silly.' Marla was already on her feet. 'I bet you'd like some coffee. I've got fresh in the galley. Tate and I are organizing our treasure trove.'

Matthew scanned the scatter of artifacts over the table. 'I think we're going to need more room.'

Marla laughed as she stepped back in with the coffee. 'Oh, I like an optimistic man.'

'Realistic,' Tate corrected and patted the seat on the settee in invitation. 'My diving partner is far from optimistic.'

Not certain if he was amused or insulted, Matthew sat beside her and sampled his coffee. 'I wouldn't say that.'

'I would.' Tate dived into the bowl of pretzels her mother set out. 'Buck's the dreamer. You like the life – sun, sea, sand.' Nibbling, she leaned back. 'No real responsibilities, no real ties. You don't expect to find some crusted chest filled with gold doubloons, but you know how to make do with the occasional trinket. Enough to keep you in shrimp and beer.'

'Tate.' Marla shook her head, muffled a laugh. 'Don't be rude.'

'No, she's hitting it.' Matthew bit into a pretzel. 'Let her finish.'

'You're not afraid of hard work because there's always plenty of time for lying in a hammock, snoozing. There's the excitement of the dive, of the discovery, and always the turnover value rather than the intrinsic value of some small booty.' She handed him a silver spoon. 'You're a realist, Matthew. So when you say we'll need more room, I believe you.'

'Fine.' He realized no matter how he weighed it, he was insulted. He tossed the spoon with a clatter back onto the pile. 'I figure we can use the *Sea Devil* for storage.' When she angled her chin, peered down her nose, he sneered at her. 'Buck and I can bunk here, on deck. We can use the *Adventure* for our work station. We dive from here, we clean the conglomerate and artifacts here, then transport them to the *Sea Devil*.'

'That seems very sensible,' Marla agreed. 'After all, we have two boats, we might as well make full use of both of them.'

'All right. If Dad and Buck agree, so will I. In the meantime, Matthew, why don't you help me bring in another load from on deck?'

'Fine. Thanks for the coffee, Marla.'

'Oh, you're welcome, sweetie.'

'I'm going to have to run to St. Kitts later,' Tate began as they started out. 'To have the film developed. Want to come with me?'

'Maybe.'

She caught the edge to his voice and smothered a smile. 'Matthew.' To stop his progress, she touched a hand to his arm. 'Do you know why I think we work so well together down there?'

'No.' He turned. Her skin was still an impossible alabaster even after weeks at sea. He could smell the cream she used to protect it, and the perfume that was salt and sea air that clung to her hair. 'But you're going to tell me.'

'I think it's because you're realistic, and I'm idealistic. You're reckless, I'm cautious. Contradicting traits inside ourselves and against each other. Somehow we make a balance.'

'You really like to analyze things, don't you, Red?'

'I guess I do.' Hoping he was unaware of how much courage it took, she shifted closer. 'I've been analyzing why you were so angry after you kissed me.'

'I wasn't angry,' he corrected evenly. 'And you kissed me.'

'I started it.' Determined to finish it, she kept her eyes on his. 'You changed it, then you got mad because it surprised you. What you felt surprised you. It surprised me, too.' Lifting her hands, she spread them on his chest. 'I wonder if we'd be surprised now.'

He wanted, more than anything he could remember, he wanted to swoop down and plunder that fresh and eager mouth. The hunger to taste it came in swift, sharp waves, and made his hands rough as they snagged her wrists.

'You're moving into dark water, Tate.'

'Not alone.' She wasn't afraid any longer, she realized. Why, she wasn't even nervous. 'I know what I'm doing.'

'No, you don't.' He shoved her back, arm's-length, hardly realizing his hands were still cuffed around her wrists. 'You figure there aren't any consequences, but there are. If you don't watch your step, you'll pay them.'

A shiver worked up her spine, deliciously. 'I'm not afraid to be with you. I want to be with you.'

The muscles in his stomach twisted. 'Easy to say, with your mother in the galley. Then again, maybe you're more clever than you look.' Furious, he tossed her hands down and strode away.

The implication brought a bright bloom to her cheeks. She had been teasing him, she realized. Taunting him. To see if she could, needing to know if he felt even half of this draw toward her that she felt toward him. Ashamed, contrite, she hurried after him.

'Matthew, I'm sorry. Really I–'

But he was over the side with a splash and swimming toward the *Sea Devil*. Tate let out a huff of breath. Damn it, the least he could do was listen when she apologized. She dived in after him.

When she dragged herself onto the deck, he was popping the top on a beer.

'Go home, little girl, before I toss you overboard.'

'I said I was sorry.' She dragged wet hair out of her eyes. 'That was unfair and stupid, and I apologize.'

'Fine.' The quick swim and cold beer weren't doing much to scratch the itch. Hoping to ignore her, he swung into his hammock. 'Go home.'

'I don't want you to be mad.' Determined to make amends, she marched to the hammock. 'I was only trying to . . . I was just testing.'

He set the open beer on the deck. 'Testing,' he repeated, then lunged before she could draw in the breath to gasp. He hauled her onto the hammock atop him. It swung wildly as she clawed at the sides to keep from upending. Her eyes popped wide with shock when his hands clamped intimately over her bottom.

'Matthew!'

He gave her a quick, not altogether loving tap, then shoved her off. She landed in a heap on the butt he'd just explored.

'I'd say we're even now,' he stated, and reached for his beer.

Her first impulse was to spring to attack. Only the absolute certainty that the result would be either humiliating or disastrous prevented her. Mixed with that was the lowering thought that she'd deserved just what she'd gotten.

'All right.' With calm and dignity, she rose. 'We're even.'

He'd expected her to lash at him. At the very least to blubber. The fact that she stood beside him, cool, composed, touched off a glint of admiration in his eyes. 'You're okay, Red.'

'Friends again?' she asked and offered a hand.

'Partners, anyway.'

Crisis avoided, she thought. At least temporarily. 'So, do you want to take a break? Maybe do some snorkeling?'

'Maybe. Couple of masks and snorkels in the wheelhouse.'

'I'll get them.' But she came back with a sketchbook. 'What's this?'

'A silk tie. What does it look like?'

Overlooking the sarcasm, she sat on the edge of the hammock. 'Did you do this sketch of the *Santa Marguerite?*'

'Yeah.'

'It's pretty good.'

'I'm a regular Picasso.'

'I said "pretty good." It would have been great to see her like this. Are these figures measurements?'

He sighed again, thinking of amateurs. 'If you want to try to figure out how much area the wreck covers, you've got to do some calculations. We hit the galley today.' He swung his legs over until he was sitting beside her. 'Officers' cabins, passengers' cabins.' He laid a fingertip on the sketch at varying points. 'Cargo hold. Best way is to imagine a gull's-eye view.' To demonstrate, he flipped a page and began to sketch out a rough grid. 'This is the sea floor. Here's where we found the ballast.'

'So the cannon is over here.'

'Right.' In quick deft moves, he penciled them in. 'Now we dug test holes from here to here. We want to move more midship for the mother lode.'

Her shoulder bumped his as she studied the sketch. 'But we want to excavate the whole thing, right?'

He glanced up briefly, then continued to draw. 'That could take months, years.'

'Well, yes, but the ship itself is as important as what it holds. We have to excavate and preserve all of it.'

From his viewpoint, the ship itself was wood and worthless. But he could humor her. 'We'll be in hurricane season before too much longer. We could be lucky, but we concentrate on finding the mother lode. Then you can afford to take as much time as you want on the rest.'

For himself, he'd take his share and split. With gold jingling in his pocket, he could afford the time to build that boat, to finish his father's research on the *Isabella*.

To find Angelique's Curse and VanDyke.

'I guess that makes sense.' She glanced up, startled by the hard, distant gleam in his eye. 'What are you thinking about?' It was foolish, of course, but she thought it looked like murder.

He shook himself back. Here and now, he thought, was what mattered most. 'Nothing. Sure it makes sense,' he continued. 'Before long, word's going to get out that we've found a new wreck. We'll have company.'

'Reporters?'

He snorted. 'They're the least of it. Poachers.'

'But we have a legal claim,' Tate began, and broke off when he laughed at her.

'Legal don't mean jack, Red, especially when you've got the Lassiter luck to deal with. We'll have to start sleeping as well as working in shifts,' he went on. 'If we start to bring up gold, Red, hunters will smell it from Australia to the Red Sea. Believe me.'

'I do.' And because she did, she hopped down to fetch the snorkeling equipment. 'Let's check on Dad and Buck. Then I want to get that film developed.'

By the time Tate was ready to go ashore, she had a list of errands in addition to the film. 'I should have known Mom would give me a grocery list.'

Matthew hopped into the *Adventure's* little tender with her, cranked the engine. 'No big deal.'

Tate merely adjusted her sunglasses. 'You didn't see the list. Look!' She gestured west where a school of dolphin leapt before the lowering sun. 'I swam with one once. We were in the Coral Sea and a school of them followed the boat. I was twelve.' She smiled and watched them flash toward the horizon. 'It was incredible. They have such kind eyes.'

Tate rose as Matthew cut speed. She timed the distance to the pier, braced her legs and secured the line.

Once the boat was secure, they started across the strip of beach.

'Matthew, if we hit the mother lode, and you were rich, what would you do?'

'Spend it. Enjoy it.'

'On what? How?'

'Stuff.' He moved his shoulders, but he knew by now generalities wouldn't satisfy her. 'A boat. I'm going to build my own as soon as I have the time and means. Maybe I'd buy a place on an island like this.'

They moved by guests of the nearby hotel as they baked lazily in the lowering sun. Staff with flowered shirts and white shorts strolled across the sand with trays of tropical drinks.

'I've never been rich,' he said half to himself. 'It couldn't be too hard to get used to it, to live like this. Fancy hotels, fancy clothes, being able to pay to do nothing.'

'But you'd still dive?'

'Sure.'

'So would I.' Unconsciously she took his hand as they walked through the hotel's fragrant gardens. 'The Red Sea, the Great Barrier Reef, the North Atlantic, the Sea of Japan. There're so many places to see. Once I finish college, I'm going to see them all.'

'Marine archeology, right?'

'That's right.'

He skimmed a glance over her. Her bright cap of hair was tousled by the salt and wind. She wore baggy cotton slacks, a skimpy T-shirt and square, black-framed sunglasses.

'You don't look much like a scientist.'

'Science takes brains and imagination, not looks or fashion sense.'

'Good thing about the fashion sense.'

Unoffended, she shrugged. In spite of her mother's occasional despair, Tate never gave clothes or style a thought. 'What's the difference, as long as you've got a good wetsuit? I don't need a wardrobe to excavate and that's what I'm going to spend my life doing. Imagine getting paid to go on treasure hunts, to examine and study artifacts.' She shook her head at the wonder of it. 'There's so much to learn.'

'I never thought a whole lot of school myself.' Of course, they had moved around so much, he'd never had a choice. 'I'm more a fan of on-the-job training.'

'I'm certainly getting that.'

They took a cab into town where Tate could drop off her film. To her pleasure, Matthew didn't seem to mind when she wanted to poke around the shops, dallying over trinkets. She sighed for a while over a small gold locket with a single pearl dripping from its base. Clothes were for keeping out the weather, but baubles were a nice, harmless weakness.

'I didn't think you went in for stuff like that,' he commented, leaning on the counter beside her. 'You don't really wear any bangles.'

'I had this little ruby ring Mom and Dad gave me for Christmas when I was sixteen. I lost it on a dive. It really broke my heart, so I stopped wearing jewelry in the water.' She tore her eyes away from the delicate locket and tugged on his silver piece. 'Maybe I'll take that coin Buck gave me and wear it as a charm.'

'Works for me. You want to get a drink or something?'

She touched her tongue to her top lip. 'Ice cream.'

'Ice cream.' He thought it over. 'Let's go.'

Sharing cones, they strolled along the sidewalk, explored narrow streets. He charmed her by plucking a creamy white hibiscus from a bush, tucking it carelessly behind her ear. While they shopped for Marla's essentials, he had her gurgling with laughter over the story of Buck and Blackbeard's ghost.

'We were off Ocracoke, on Buck's birthday. His fiftieth. The idea of half a century behind him had Buck so depressed he'd finished off half a bottle of whiskey. I helped him work on the other half.'

'I bet.' Tate chose a bunch of ripening bananas and added it to her basket.

'He was going on about all these might have's – you know what I mean. We might have found that wreck if we'd looked another month. If we'd gotten there first, we might have hit the mother lode. If the weather had held, we might have struck it rich. Between the whiskey and the boredom, I passed out on deck. That melon's not ripe. This one.'

He switched fruit, chose the grapes himself. 'Anyway, the next thing I know, the engines are roaring and the boat's lurching off southeast at a good twelve knots. Buck's at the wheel, screaming about pirates. Scared the shit out of me. I jumped up, tripped, knocked my head on the rail so hard I saw stars. Nearly went overboard when he swung to starboard. He's yelling for me and I'm cursing him, fighting to stay upright as he circles the boat. His eyes are about six inches out from his face and white. You know he can't see more than three feet in front of him without his glasses. But he's pointing out to sea and shouting all this pirate cant. "Avast, ahoy, shiver me timbers." '

Tate's laughter turned heads. 'He did not say "shiver me timbers." '

'Hell, he didn't. He nearly capsized us doing a jig and singing "yo, ho, ho." 'The memory of it had a grin tugging at his mouth. 'I almost had to knock him out to get the wheel away from him. "The ghost, Matthew. Blackbeard's ghost. Don't you see it?" I told him he wasn't going to be seeing anything either after I poked his eyes out. He tells me it's there, right there, ten degrees off the forward bow. There's not a damn thing there but a little mist. But to Buck, it was Blackbeard's severed head, smoke curling from the beard. He claimed it was a sign, and if we dived there the next day, we'd find Blackbeard's treasure, the one everyone else figured was buried on land.'

Tate paid for the groceries, Matthew hefted the bags. 'And you went down the next morning,' she said, 'because he asked you to.'

'That and because if I hadn't, I'd never have heard the end of it. We didn't find a damn thing, but he sure got over turning fifty.'

It was nearly dusk when they got back to the beach. Matthew stowed the bags and turned to see Tate had rolled up her pants legs so she could stand in the surf.

Light gilded her hair, her skin. Suddenly he was painfully reminded of his dream and how she had looked aglow in the water. How she had tasted.

'It's so beautiful here,' she murmured. 'It's like nothing else exists. How can there be anything wrong with the world when there are spots like this? When there are days like this?'

She was sure he was unaware that this had been the most romantic day of her life. Such simple things like a flower for her hair, a hand to hold as she walked along the beach.

'Maybe we shouldn't leave here, ever.' With a laugh in her voice, she turned. 'Maybe we should just stay and . . .'

She trailed off, her throat closing at the look in his eyes. They were so dark, so intense, so suddenly focused on her. Only her.

She didn't think, didn't hesitate, but walked to him. Her hands slid up his chest, linked behind his head. His eyes stayed on hers, a dozen frantic pulse beats, then he dragged her against him and flashed fire in her blood.

Yes, she'd been kissed before. But she knew the difference between boy and man. It was a man who held her, drew from her. It was a man she wanted. Eager and quick, she pressed against him, racing her lips over his face in frenzied kisses until they found his again on a sob of pleasure.

She was so slim, so willing, so avid to accept any demand. She flowed like water under each pass of his hands, and her mouth clung greedily to his. Each hum and whimper of desire that sounded in her throat cut through him, a blade of fire that ruptured new needs.

'Tate.' His voice was rough, nearly desperate. 'We can't do this.'

'We can. We are.' God, she couldn't breathe. 'Kiss me again. Hurry.'

His mouth crushed down on hers. The taste of her seemed to explode inside him. Everything about it was painful, nearly agonizing, as heat would be after cold.

'This is crazy,' he murmured against her mouth. 'I'm out of my mind.'

'Me, too. Oh, I want you, Matthew. I want you.'

And that struck him hard. He jerked back, gripped unsteady hands on her shoulders. 'Listen, Tate . . . What the hell are you smiling at?'

'You want me, too.' She lifted a hand, laid it gently against his cheek and almost unmanned him. 'For a while I thought you didn't. And it hurt because I want you so much. I didn't even like you at first, and wanted you anyway.'

'Jesus.' To gain control of himself, he let his brow rest on hers. 'I thought you said you were the careful one.'

'Not about you.' Full of love and trust, she nuzzled into him. Heart to heart. 'Never about you. When you kissed me the first time, I knew you were what I'd been waiting for.'

He had no compass, no direction, but he knew it was essential to reverse course. 'Tate, we have to take this slow. You're not ready for what I'm thinking of. Believe me.'

'You want to make love with me.' Her chin came up. Her eyes, all at once, were a woman's, and just as mysterious. 'I'm not a child, Matthew.'

'Then I'm not ready. And I'm not willing to do something that would hurt your parents. They've been straight with me and Buck.'

Pride, she thought. Pride, loyalty and integrity. Was it any wonder she loved him? Her lips curved. 'All right. We'll take it slow. But it's between us, Matthew. What we decide, and what we want.' She leaned forward, touched her lips to his. 'I can wait.'

Chapter Five

STORMS SWEPT IN and made diving impossible for the next two days. When the first wave of impatience passed, Tate settled down on the boatdeck of the *Adventure* to clean and catalogue the pieces of the *Santa Marguerite* her father and Buck had brought up on the last dive.

Rain drummed on the tarp stretched overhead. The islands had vanished in the mist, leaving only restless seas and angry skies. Their world had whittled down to water, and each other.

In the deckhouse, a marathon poker game was in progress. Voices, a laugh, a curse, drifted out to her over the monotonous patter of rain. Tate cleaned the corrosion from a crudely made silver cross, and knew she'd never been happier in her life.

With a mug of coffee in each hand, Matthew ducked under the tarp. 'Want some help?'

'Sure.' Just looking at him had her heart cartwheeling into her throat. 'Is the poker game breaking up?'

'No, but my luck is.' He sat beside her, offered a mug. 'Buck just blew down my full house with a straight flush.'

'I can never keep straight what beats what. I'm better at gin.' She held up the cross. 'Maybe the ship's cook wore this, Matthew. It would have banged against his chest when he beat batter for biscuits.'

'Yeah.' He fingered the silver. It was an ugly piece, more likely fashioned by a blacksmith than a jeweler. Neither did it have weight. Matthew dismissed it as little value. 'What else you got here?'

'These rigging hasps. See, they've still got traces of rope in them. Imagine.' She handled the black metal reverently. 'How they would have fought to save the ship. The wind would have been screaming, the sails in tatters.'

She looked beyond into the mist and saw what had been. 'Men clinging to lines and masts as the ship heeled. Passengers terrified. Mothers holding their children while the ship pitched and heeled. And we're finding what's left of them.'

She set the fitting down and lifted a clay pipe with both hands. 'A seaman kept this tucked in his pocket, stood on deck after his watch to light it and enjoy a quiet smoke. And this tankard would have been filled with ale.'

'Too bad it's missing the handle.' He plucked it up, turned it over. He didn't want to admit her vision had moved him. 'Devaluates it.'

'You can't just think about the money.'

He grinned. 'Sure I can, Red. You take the drama, I'll take the dough.'

'But–' He cut off her objection with a quick, sneaky kiss.

'You look so cute when you're indignant.'

'Really?' She was young enough, and in love enough, to be flattered. Picking up her coffee, she sipped, watching him over the rim. 'I don't believe you're nearly as mercenary as you pretend.'

'Believe it. History's fine if you can make something from it. Otherwise, it's just dead guys.' He glanced up, barely noticing her frown. 'Rain's slowing down. We'll dive tomorrow.'

'Restless?'

'Some. The trouble is hanging out here, having your mother put a plate under my nose every time I blink. I could get used to it.' He lifted a hand, ran it over her hair. 'It's a different world. You're a different world.'

'Not so different, Matthew,' she murmured and turned her lips to his. 'Maybe just different enough.'

His fingers tensed, relaxed slowly. She hadn't seen enough of the world, his world, he thought, to know the difference. If he were a good man, a kind one, he knew he wouldn't be touching her now, tempting them both toward a step that could only be a mistake.

'Tate–' He was riding the wire between pushing her away or bringing her closer, when Buck stuck his head under the tarp.

'Hey, Matthew, you–' Buck's jaw dropped open as they broke apart. His unshaven cheeks bloomed with color. 'Ah, 'scuze me. Ah, Matthew . . .' While Buck searched for what to say, Tate calmly picked up her pen and catalogued the clay pipe.

'Hi, Buck.' Tate sent him a bright, easy smile while the two men eyed each other uncertainly. 'I heard you were having a run of luck at the poker table.'

'Yeah. Yeah, I, ah . . .' He jammed his hands into his pockets, shifted his feet. 'Rain's slacking off,' he announced. 'Me and Matthew, we'll load this stuff up, store it on the *Sea Devil*.'

'I'm just finishing cataloguing.' Meticulously, Tate capped the pen. 'I'll give you a hand.'

'No, no, we'll do her.' Buck dragged his hand out of his pocket long enough to shove his glasses back up his nose. 'Me and Matthew, we've got to do some tinkering with the engine over there anyhow. Your mama said something about you being on kitchen duty tonight.'

'She's right,' Tate said with a sigh. 'I guess I'll get started.' She unfolded her legs and rose before tucking her notebook under her arm. 'I'll see you at dinner.'

The men said little as they wrapped and loaded the booty. Matthew's suggestion that they might need to rent a room or a garage for storage was met by a grunt and a shrug. Buck waited until they were putting toward the *Sea Devil* before he exploded.

'Have you lost your mind, boy?'

Matthew jogged the wheel slightly. 'I don't need you crawling up my back, Buck.'

'If I got to crawl up your back to get to your brain, then that's what I'll do.' He rose smoothly when Matthew cut the engine. 'Haven't you got more sense than to mess around with that young thing?'

'I haven't been messing around with her,' Matthew said between his teeth. He secured the bow line. 'Not like you mean.'

'Thank God for that.' Agilely, Buck shouldered the first tarp, hooked his foot on the ladder. 'You got no business playing games with Tate, boy. She ain't a loose one.'

'I know what she is.' Matthew hauled the second tarp. 'And I know what she isn't.'

'Then you remember it.' Buck carried his tarp into the wheelhouse, unrolled it carefully on the counter. 'The Beaumonts are good, decent people, Matthew.'

'And I'm not.'

Surprised at the bitterness in the tone, Buck looked up as Matthew set down his tarp. 'Never said you weren't good or decent, boy. But we ain't like them. Never have been. Maybe you figure it's okay to dally around with her before we move on, but a girl like that expects things.'

He took out a cigarette, lighted it, peering at his nephew through the smoke. 'You going to tell me you're thinking about giving them to her.'

Matthew pulled out a beer, swallowed long to wash some of the anger out of his throat. 'No, I'm not going to tell you that. But I'm not going to hurt her, either.'

Wouldn't mean to, Buck thought. 'Change your course, boy. There's plenty of females out there if you've got an itch.' He saw the fury flash into Matthew's eyes and met it equably. 'I'm telling you 'cause I'm the one who's got to. A man hooks up with the wrong woman, it can ruin both of them.'

Struggling for calm, Matthew set the half-drained bottle of beer aside. 'Like my mother and father.'

'That's true enough,' Buck said, but his voice had gentled. 'They set sparks off each other, sure. Got themselves tangled before either of them thought it through. Left them both pretty scraped up.'

'I don't think she did a hell of a lot of bleeding,' Matthew shot back. 'She left him, didn't she? And me. Never came back. Never looked back as far as I can tell.'

'She couldn't take the life. Ask me, most women can't. No use blaming them for it.'

But Matthew could. 'I'm not my father. Tate's not my mother. That's the bottom line.'

'I'll give you the bottom line.' Eyes heavy with concern, Buck crushed out his cigarette. 'That girl over there's having herself some fun and excitement for a few months. You're a good-looking man, so it's natural you'd be part of that fun and excitement. But when it's over, she'll go back to college, get herself a fancy job, a fancy husband. That leaves you high and dry. If you forget that, and take advantage of the stars in her eyes, both of you'll be the worse for it.'

'It wouldn't occur to you that I might be good enough for her.'

'You're good enough for anybody,' Buck corrected. 'Better'n most. But being right for somebody's different.'

'So speaks the voice of experience.'

'Maybe I don't know a goddamn thing about women. But I know you.' Hoping to calm the waters, he laid a hand on Matthew's rigid shoulder. 'We got a chance at the big time here, Matthew. Men like us look all our lives, only a few of us find it. We found it. All we have to do is take it. You can make something out of yourself with your share. Once you do, there'll be plenty of time for women.'

'Sure.' Matthew picked up his beer, tipped it back. 'No sweat.'

'There you go.' Relieved, Buck gave his shoulder a slap. 'Let's take a look at the engine.'

'I'll be right there.'

Alone, Matthew stared at the bottle in his hand until he'd willed back the clawing urge to smash it into jagged pieces. There was nothing Buck had told him that he hadn't already told himself. And less kindly.

He was a third-generation treasure hunter with a legacy of bad luck that had dogged him like a bloodhound all of his life. He'd lived by his wits, and the occasional flip side of that luck. He had no ties but to Buck, no property other than what he could strap on his back.

He was a drifter, nothing more, nothing less. The prospect of fortune forty feet beneath his feet would make the drifting more comfortable, but it wouldn't change it.

Buck was right. Matthew Lassiter of no fixed address and less than four hundred dollars tucked into a cigar box had no right picturing himself with Tate Beaumont.

Tate had other ideas. It was frustrating to discover over the next few days that the only time she found herself alone with Matthew was underwater. There communication and physical contact were hampered.

She would change that, she promised herself as she searched the fallout from the airlift. And she would change it today. After all, it was her twentieth birthday.

Carefully, she picked among the nails, the spikes, the shells, eyes peeled for the valuables that scattered. Ship fittings, a sextant, a small, hinged brass box, a silver coin embedded in a hunk of coral. A wooden crucifix, an octant and a lovely china cup sliced delicately in two.

All this she gathered, ignoring the pings of debris against her back, the occasional nick on her hand.

A glint of gold shot by her. Tate's heart careened in her chest as she scanned the cloud for the telltale flash of it. The small, quick gleam had her darting forward, dipping toward the sand and sending the burrowing rays rising in a swirling cloud.

Her mind was screaming treasure, doubloons, jewels of great price and age. But when her hand closed around the piece of gold, her eyes began to swim.

It wasn't a coin, or jewelry long buried beneath the waves. Not a priceless artifact, but priceless nonetheless. She lifted the gold locket with the single pearl dripping from its point.

When Tate turned back, she saw that Matthew was pointing the airlift pipe away and watching her. He sketched letters in the water with his finger. H. B. D. Happy birthday. With a gurgle of laughter, she swam toward him. Undaunted by tanks and hoses, she took his hand, pressed it to her cheek.

He let it lie there a moment, then waved her away. His signal an obvious 'Stop loafing.'

Once more the airlift sucked at sand. Ignoring the fallout, Tate carefully secured the necklace by looping it around her wrist. She went back to work with love soaring in her heart.

Matthew concentrated on the offshore end of the ballast mound. Patiently, he cut into the sand, creating an ever-widening circle with sloping sides. He was a foot down, then two, while Tate worked busily to pick through the fallout. A school of triggerfish darted by. Matthew glanced up and saw through the murky cloud that the barracuda was grinning at him.

On impulse, he shifted his position. He wouldn't have considered himself superstitious. As a man of the sea he followed signs and lived by lore. The toothy fish hovered in nearly the same spot day after day. It wouldn't hurt to use the mascot as a marker.

Curious, Tate looked over as Matthew hauled the airlift several feet north where he was already forming a new hole. Tate let her attention drift and watched a kaleidoscope of fish whirl through the clouded water hunting for the seaworms displaced by the cut of the pipe.

Something clinked against her tank. Efficiently, she turned back to resume her chores. The first glint of gold barely registered. She stared through the roiling water at the bed of sand. The flashes of brightness were scattered around her like flowers that had just bloomed. Stupefied, she reached down and plucked up a doubloon. The long-dead Spanish king stared back at her.

The coin dropped from her numbed fingers. In a sudden fever, she began to harvest them, pushing them into her wetsuit, jamming them into her lobster bag and ignoring the solid objects that drifted down in the thick column of fallout. The conglomerate rained, but she was oblivious to it, facedown, scanning the seafloor like a miner panning for gold.

Five coins, then ten. Twenty and more. Her breath rushed out in a shriek of laughter. She couldn't seem to get enough air. When she looked up, she saw Matthew grinning at her, his eyes dark and wild. Behind her mask, her face was bone white.

They'd hit the mother lode.

He gestured to her. As if in a dream, she swam over and her trembling hand reached for his. Sand trickled down into the test hole, but she saw the sparkle of crystal from a perfectly preserved goblet, the sheen of coins and medallions. And everywhere the calcified shapes of artifacts. And there the blackened streak of sand that every hunter knew meant a river of silver.

Behind them the ballast pile loomed. And beneath, the shining prize of the galleon *Santa Marguerite* and all her treasure.

There was a roaring in Tate's ears as she reached down and closed her hand over a thick gold chain. Slowly she drew it up. From it dangled a heavy cross crusted by sea life. And by emeralds.

Her vision blurred as she held it out to Matthew. With sudden formality she carefully lifted the chain over his head. The simple generosity of the gesture touched him. He wished he could have held her, told her. All he could do was point a finger up. He cracked the valve on the airlift and followed her to the surface.

She couldn't speak. Even now it took all of her effort just to draw air in and out of her lungs. She was trembling like a leaf when she hoisted herself aboard. Strong arms lifted her.

'Honey, you okay?' Buck's face, lined with worry, loomed over her, 'Ray, Ray, come on out here. Something wrong with Tate.'

'Nothing wrong,' she managed and sucked in air.

'Just lie still.' Fretting like a mother hen, he eased off her face mask and nearly shuddered with relief when he heard Matthew clattering over the side. 'What happened down there?' he demanded without turning around.

'Not much.' Matthew let his weight belt fall.

'Not much, my ass. Girl's white as a sheet. Ray, get us some brandy here.'

But Ray and Marla were already rushing out. Voices buzzed in Tate's head. Hands were poking and probing for injury. She got her breath back on a giggle, then couldn't stop.

'I'm all right.' She had to press both hands over her mouth to hold back a fresh stream of hysterical laughter. 'I'm fine. We're both fine, aren't we, Matthew?'

'Fine and dandy,' he agreed. 'We just had a little excitement.'

'Come on, honey, let's get you out of that suit.' With some impatience, Marla shot a glance at Matthew. 'Just what kind of excitement? Tate's shaking.'

'I can explain.' Tate snorted behind her hands. 'I gotta get up. Would you let me up?' Tears began to stream from her eyes as she fought to control the laughter. Brushing away restraining hands, she got unsteadily to her feet. Trembling with breathless giggles, she upended her goody bag, tugged open her suit.

Coins rained gold onto the deck.

'Fuck me,' Buck croaked and sat down heavily.

'We found the mother lode.' Tate threw back her head and screamed at the sun. 'We found the mother lode.'

She threw her arms around her father, whirled him into a dance, only to break off and swing her mother. She planted a big smacking kiss on Buck's bald head as he continued to sit and stare at the coins at his feet.

With their voices babbling around her, Tate turned a circle and launched herself into Matthew's arms. By the time he'd managed to regain his balance, her mouth was clinging to his.

His hands went to her shoulders. He knew he should push her away, keep the kiss a product of the moment's excitement. But a current of helplessness swamped him, and his hands slid to her back, crossed, embraced.

So it was she who drew away, her eyes still glowing, her face flushed now and eager. 'I thought I was going to faint. When I looked down and saw the coins, all the blood drained out of my head. The only other time I've ever felt like that is when you kissed me.'

'We're not a bad team.' He ran a hand over her hair.

'We're a great team.' She clamped a hand over his and dragged him to where Buck and Ray were already suiting up. 'You should have seen it, Dad. Matthew moved the airlift like it was a divining rod.'

Happily recounting every minute of the discovery, she helped Buck and her father with their tanks. Only Matthew noticed that Marla remained silent, and the warmth in her eyes had been cooled by concern.

'I'm going down to take pictures,' Tate announced, hooking on fresh tanks. 'We have to document everything. Before we're done, we'll have the cover of *National Geographic*.'

'Don't go pulling them in yet.' Buck sat on the side, rinsed his mask. 'We gotta keep this quiet.' He looked around as if expecting a dozen boats to come speeding in on the claim. 'Finds like this are one in a million, and there're plenty who'd do whatever it took to get a piece.'

Tate only grinned. 'Eat your heart out, Jacques Cousteau,' she said, and rolled into the water.

'Get some champagne chilling,' Ray called to his wife. 'We'll have a double celebration tonight. Tate's earned herself a hell of a birthday party.' He flashed a smile at Buck. 'Ready, partner?'

'Ready and willing, hoss.' After lowering the airlift, they disappeared beneath the surface.

Matthew fueled the compressor, murmuring a thanks when Marla brought him a tall frosted glass of lemonade.

'An exciting day,' she commented.

'Yeah. You don't get many like this.'

'No. Twenty years ago today I thought this is the happiest I can ever be.' She sat on a deck chair, tilted her sunhat to shade her eyes. 'But over the years I've had a lot of happy moments. Tate's been a joy to her father and me right from the first. She's bright, eager, generous.'

'And you want me to keep my distance,' Matthew concluded.

'I'm not sure.' Marla sighed, tapped her finger against her own glass. 'I'm not blind, Matthew. I've seen the signs between the two of you. It's natural enough. You're healthy attractive people, working and living in close quarters.'

He took off the cross, ran a thumb over the glint of grass-green stones. Like Tate's eyes, he thought, and set the chain aside. 'Nothing's happened.'

'I appreciate your telling me that. But you see, if I haven't given Tate the foundation to know how to make her own decisions, then I've failed as a parent. I don't believe I have.' She smiled a little. 'That doesn't stop me from worrying. She has so much ahead of her. I can't help wanting her to have all of it, and at the right time. I suppose what I'm asking you to do is be careful with her. If she's in love with you–'

'We haven't talked about that,' Matthew said quickly.

Under other circumstances, Marla might have smiled at the panic in his voice. 'If she's in love with you,' Marla repeated, 'it will block everything else. Tate thinks with her heart. Oh, she thinks she's practical, sensible. And she is. Until her emotions are stirred. So be careful with her.'

Now she did smile, and rose. 'I'm going to fix you some lunch.' Laying a hand on his arm, she lifted to her toes and kissed his cheek. 'Sit in the sun, honey, and enjoy your moment of triumph.'

Chapter Six

IN A MATTER of days, the seabed was riddled with holes. The *Santa Marguerite* gave up her stores generously. Between the airlift, and the simple tools of coal shovel and bare hands the team mined both the spectacular and the ordinary. A wooden worm-eaten bowl, a dazzling gold chain, pipe bowls and spoons, a sumptuous cross crusted with pearls. All were lifted from the sandy vault where they had rested for centuries, and hauled into the light in buckets.

Now and again a pleasure boat would cruise by and hail the *Adventure*. If Tate was onboard, she would lean on the rail and chat. There was no disguising the murky cloud from the airlift that stained the surface. Word of the underwater excavation was spreading. They were careful to downplay their progress. But each day, they worked harder and faster as the prospect of rival treasure hunters arriving increased.

'A legal claim don't mean squat to some of these pirates,' Buck told her. He zipped his thick torso into his wetsuit. 'You gotta be alert, and you gotta be tough.' He winked at her as he passed her his glasses. 'And cagey. We'll dig out that mother lode, Tate, and we'll play her out.'

'I know we will.' She handed him his face mask. 'We've already found more than I ever imagined.'

'You start imagining bigger.' He grinned, spat into his mask. 'It's good having a couple of young ones like you and Matthew along. Figure you could work twenty hours out of twenty-four if you had to. You're a good diver, girl. And a good hunter.'

'Thanks, Buck.'

'Don't know many females who can handle it.'

Her brow shot up as he rinsed out his mask. 'Really?'

'Now don't go shooting that equal stuff at me. Just stating a fact. Plenty of girls like to dive all right, but when it comes to pulling their weight on a dig, they ain't got what it takes. You do.'

She thought it through, then smiled at him. 'I'll take that as a compliment.'

'Should. Best damn team I ever worked with.' He settled into position, slapped a hand on Ray's shoulder. 'Since I hunted with my old man and my brother. 'Course once we get it all up, I'm going to have to kill hoss here.' Buck grinned as he lowered his mask into place. 'Figure on beating him to death with his own flippers.'

'I'm on to you, Buck.' Ray slipped over the side. 'I've already decided to smother you with a boat cushion. The treasure's mine.' He let out a wild, evil laugh. 'Mine, do you hear? All mine.' Rolling his eyes madly, Ray plugged in his mouthpiece and did a surface dive.

'I'm after you, hoss. Going to run him through with a coal shovel,' Buck promised and splashed into the water.

'They're crazy,' Tate decided. 'Like a couple of bad little boys playing hooky.' She turned to grin at Matthew. 'I've never seen Dad have so much fun.'

'Buck's not this loose unless he's got a quart of whiskey in him.'

'It's not just the treasure.' She held out a hand so that he would join her at the rail.

'No, I guess it's not.' Looking out over the water, Matthew linked his fingers with hers. 'But it helps.'

She leaned her head on his shoulder and chuckled. 'It doesn't hurt. But they'd have clicked without it. So would we.' She turned her head so that her lips could graze his jaw. 'We'd have found each other, Matthew. We were supposed to.'

'Like we were supposed to find the *Marguerite.*'

'No.' She turned into his arms. 'Like this.'

Her lips were warm and soft. Irresistible. He could feel himself sinking into them, slowly, weightlessly, until he was steeped in the seduction that was Tate. She seemed to surround him, tastes and scents and flavors so unique he would have recognized them, recognized her, if he'd been deaf, dumb and blind.

There had never been another woman who could twist his system into such shivering, slippery knots with one quiet kiss. He wanted her so desperately it terrified him.

And when she drew away, her eyes dreamy, her lips curved, he knew she had no notion of his need, his desperation or his terror.

'What's wrong?' Tate lifted a hand to his cheek. 'You look so serious.'

'No. Nothing.' Pull yourself together, Lassiter. She's not ready for what's running through your mind. With an effort, he smiled. 'I was just thinking it's too bad.'

'What is?'

'That after Buck takes care of Ray, I'll have to get rid of you.'

'Oh.' Willing to play, she tilted her head. 'And just how do you propose to do that?'

'I figured I'd just strangle you.' He circled her throat with his hand. 'Then toss you overboard. We're going to keep Marla, though. Chain her to the stove. A man's gotta eat.'

'Very practical of you. Of course, that only works if I don't get you first.' She wiggled her brows, then dug her fingers into his ribs.

Helpless laughter buckled his knees. He made a weak grab, but she was darting away. By the time he'd gotten his breath back, she was around the starboard side of the deckhouse.

'Want to play rough?' He charged the port side to cut her off. He'd nearly made the bow when he saw her, and the bucket. Before he could dodge, she'd heaved the load of cool seawater.

While he choked and dripped, she held her sides. But when he'd blinked the stinging water out of his eyes, she saw their intent. With a shriek, she went into full retreat.

Her only mistake was in dropping the bucket.

Marla came out of the deckhouse, where she'd been cleaning cob coins, and ran headlong into Tate.

'Goodness. Is there a war?'

'Mom.' Giddy with laughter, Tate ducked behind her mother just as Matthew rounded the cabin, armed with a freshly loaded bucket.

He skidded to a halt. 'You'd better stand aside, Marla. This could get messy.'

Choking with laughter, Tate wrapped her arms around her mother's waist, using her ruthlessly as a shield. 'She's not going anywhere.'

'Now, children.' Marla patted Tate's hand. 'Behave.'

'She started it,' Matthew claimed. He couldn't wipe the grin off his face. It had been years since he had felt this free, this foolish. 'Come on, coward. Stand clear and take your medicine.'

'No way.' Smug, Tate sneered at him. 'You lose, Lassiter. You wouldn't use that with my mother between us.'

He narrowed his eyes, frowned down at the bucket. When he looked back up, Tate was fluttering her lashes at him. 'Sorry, Marla,' he said, and drenched them both.

Female shrieks rang in his ears as he raced to the side for more ammunition.

It was a messy battle, ripe with ambush and retaliation. Since Marla threw herself into the war with an enthusiasm Matthew hadn't anticipated, he found himself outgunned and outmaneuvered.

He did the manly thing. He dived overboard.

'Good aim, Mom,' Tate managed before she collapsed weakly against the rail.

'Well.' Marla fluffed a hand over her tangled hair. 'I did what had to be done.' She'd lost her hat somewhere during combat, and her crisp blouse and shorts were limp and running with water. Still, she was all gracious Southern hospitality as she peered over to where Matthew was warily treading water. 'You give up, Yankee?'

'Yes, ma'am. I know when I'm licked.'

'Then haul yourself aboard, honey. I was about to fix up some nice beer-battered shrimp when I was interrupted.'

He swam toward the ladder, but shot Tate a cautious look. 'Truce?'

'Truce,' she agreed and held out a hand. When their hands locked, she slitted her eyes. 'Don't even think about it, Lassiter.'

He had. The idea of toppling her into the water had its merits. But it wasn't nearly as much fun since she was on to him. Revenge could wait. He dropped lightly on deck, slicked his hair out of his eyes.

'That cooled us off, anyway.'

'I never thought you'd blast Mom.'

He grinned, settled on a boat cushion. 'Sometimes the innocent have to suffer. She's terrific, you know. You're lucky.'

'Yeah.' Tate settled beside him, stretched out her legs. She couldn't remember ever being more content. 'You've never mentioned your own mother.'

'I don't remember her much. She took off when I was a kid.'

'Took off?'

'Lost interest,' he said with a shrug. 'We were based in Florida then, and my father and Buck were doing some boat building and repair on the side. Things were pretty lean. I remember them fighting a lot. One day she sent me over to the neighbors. Said she had errands to run and didn't want me underfoot. She never came back.'

'That's terrible. I'm so sorry.'

'We got by.' And after so many years, the hurt had healed over with only the occasional unexpected throb. 'After my father died, I found divorce papers and a letter from a lawyer dated a couple of years after she'd left. She didn't want custody or visitation rights. She just wanted her freedom. She got it.'

'You haven't seen her?' It was incomprehensible to Tate that a mother, any mother, could walk so carelessly away from a child she had carried and held and watched grow. 'Never once since then?'

'Nope. She had her life, we had ours. We moved around a lot. Up the coast, California, the islands. We did okay. Better than okay, now and then. We got work doing straight salvage up in Maine, and my father hooked up with VanDyke.'

'Who's that?'

'Silas VanDyke. The man who murdered him.'

'But–' She sat up, her face pale and tense. 'If you know who . . .'

'I know,' Matthew said quietly. 'They were partners for about a year. Well, maybe not partners so much as my father worked for him. VanDyke picked up diving as a hobby, and got interested in treasure-hunting along the way, I guess. He's one of these business tycoons who figures he can buy anything he wants. That's the way he looked at treasure. Something to buy. He was looking for a necklace. An amulet. He thought he'd traced it to a ship that went down on the Great Barrier Reef. He wasn't much of a diver, but he had money, pots of money.'

'So, he hired your father?' Tate prompted.

'The Lassiters still had a rep back then. He was the best and VanDyke wanted the best. My father trained him, taught him everything, and got caught up in the legend. Angelique's Curse.'

'What does that mean?' she demanded. 'Buck was talking about that.'

'It's the necklace.' Matthew rose to go to the ice chest, fished out two cans of Pepsi. 'Supposedly it belonged to a witch who was executed in the fifteen hundreds somewhere in France. Gold, rubies, diamonds. Priceless. But it's the power it's said to hold that caught VanDyke's interest. He even claimed he had some sort of family connection way back to the witch.'

He sat again, passed her a chilled can. 'Bullshit, of course, but men kill for less.'

'What kind of power?'

'Magic,' he said with a sneer. 'There's a spell on it. Whoever has it, and can control it, will have untold riches and power – whatever their heart desires. If it controls them, they lose whatever's most precious to them. Like I said,' he added, swallowing deep. 'Bullshit. But VanDyke's big on control.'

'It's fascinating.' And she made up her mind to do some research on the legend at the first opportunity. 'I've never heard the story before.'

'There's not a lot of documentation. Bits and pieces. The necklace bounced around, wreaking havoc supposedly and gaining a rep.'

'Like the Hope Diamond?'

'Yeah, if you go for that stuff.' He eyed her. 'You would.'

'It's interesting,' she said with some dignity. 'Did VanDyke find it?'

'No. He thought my father had. Got the idea in his head that my father was holding back on him. He was right.' Matthew took a long, cold drink. 'Buck told me that my father had found some papers that made him think the necklace had been sold to this rich Spanish merchant or aristocrat or something. He spent a lot of time researching, really got into it. He decided it was on the *Isabella*, but kept it between him and Buck.'

'Because he didn't trust VanDyke.'

'He should have trusted him less.' The memory glinted like a sword in Matthew's eyes. 'I heard them going at it the night before that last dive. VanDyke accused him of hiding the necklace. He still figured it was on the wreck they were digging. My father just laughed at him. Told him he was crazy. The next day, he was dead.'

'You never told me how he died.'

'He drowned. They said it was bad tanks, that the equipment hadn't been properly rigged. That was a fucking lie. I was in charge of the equipment. There was nothing wrong with it when I checked it that morning. VanDyke sabotaged it. And when my father was eighty feet down, he was taking in too much nitrogen.'

'Nitrogen narcosis. Rapture of the deep,' Tate murmured.

'Yeah. VanDyke claimed he tried to get him up when he realized something was wrong, but my father fought him off. There was a struggle, he said. VanDyke's story is he started up for help, but my father kept pulling him back. I went down right away once the bastard came up with the story, but he was already dead.'

'It could have been an accident, Matthew. A terrible accident.'

'It wasn't an accident. And it wasn't Angelique's Curse the way Buck likes to think. It was murder. I saw that bastard's face when I brought my father up.' His tensed fingers crushed the can in his hand. 'He was smiling.'

'Oh, Matthew.' To comfort, she cuddled against him. 'How horrible for you.'

'One day I'll find the *Isabella*, and I'll find the necklace. VanDyke will come looking for me. I'll be waiting.'

She shivered. 'Don't. Don't think about it.'

'I don't very often.' Wanting to change the mood, he draped an arm over her shoulders. 'Like I said, the past is past. And it's too nice a day to think about it. Maybe we should take some time off later in the week. Rent some skis or try some parasailing.'

'Parasailing.' She looked up at the sky, relieved that his voice was casual again. 'Have you ever done it?'

'Sure. The next best thing to being under the water is being over it.'

'I'm game if you are. But if we're going to talk the rest of this crew into a day off, we'd better get to work. Get your hammer, Lassiter. It's back to the chain gang.'

They'd barely begun to work on conglomerate, when they heard a shout over the port side. Tate brushed off her hands and strolled over.

'Matthew,' she said in a thin voice. 'Come here. Mom.' She cleared her throat. 'Mom! Come out. Bring the camera. Oh, God. Hurry.'

'For heaven's sake, Tate, I'm frying shrimp.' Exasperated, Marla came on deck with the video camera swinging from her arm. 'I don't have time to take movies.'

Tate, with her hand vised on Matthew's, turned and grinned idiotically. 'I think you'll want to take one of this.'

Marla scooted to Tate's other side, and the three of them looked over the rail.

Both Buck and Ray bobbed in the water, faces beaming maniacally. Each gripped the side of a bucket that shimmered and dripped with gold doubloons.

'Jesus Christ,' Matthew breathed. 'Is that thing full?'

'To the brim,' Ray called out. 'And we've filled two more below.'

'You ain't seen nothing like it, boy. We're rich as kings.' Water trickled down Buck's face, from his eyes. 'There are thousands of them, thousands, just lying there. You gonna haul this up, or you want us to pitch them to you one at a time?'

Ray howled with laughter, and the two men batted each other on the head. Coins spilled out of the bucket, like loose fish.

'Wait, wait, I have to get you in frame.' Marla fumbled, cursed, laughed. 'Oh hell, I can't find the record button.'

'I'll do it.' Tate snatched the camera, bobbled it. 'Hold it steady, guys, and smile.'

'They're going to drown each other.' Matthew gripped the rope and drew the bucket up. 'Christ, it's heavy. Give me a hand here.'

Marla grunted, nearly upended over the rail, but hauled the rope with him while Tate gleefully recorded the scene. 'I'm going to go down with the underwater camera.' Awed, she plunged her hand into the coins when Matthew set the bucket on deck. 'God, who'd have imagined it? I'm up to my elbow in doubloons.'

'Told you to imagine big, girl,' Buck shouted. 'Marla, you get out your fanciest dress 'cause we're going dancing tonight.'

'That's my wife, pal.'

'Not after I kill you, hoss. Going to get another bucket.'

'Not if I get there first.'

Tate sprang up and raced for her wetsuit. 'I'm going down with the underwater camera. I want to get this on film, give them a hand.'

'I'll be right with you. Marla.' Matthew snapped his fingers in front of Marla's glazed eyes. 'Marla, I think your shrimp's burning.'

'Oh. Oh, my lord.' Still clutching a handful of doubloons, she dashed to the galley.

'Do you know what this means?' Tate demanded as she fought her way into her wetsuit.

'That we're stinking rich.' Matthew snatched her off her feet and whirled her around.

'Think of the equipment we can buy. Sonar, magnetometers, a bigger boat.' She gave him a sloppy kiss before wriggling away. 'Two bigger boats. I'll get a computer for listing artifacts.'

'Maybe we should get a submersible while we're at it.'

'Good. Put that down. One submersible with robotics so we can mine the abyss on our next expedition.'

He hooked on his weight belt. 'What about fancy clothes, cars, jewelry?'

'Not a priority, but I'll keep it in mind. Mom! We're going down to give Dad and Buck a hand.'

'See if you can catch me some more shrimp.' Marla poked her head out, held out a platter filled with blackened blobs. 'These aren't fit to eat.'

'Marla, I'm going to buy you a trawler of shrimp, another of beer.' On impulse, Matthew caught her face in his hands and kissed her full on the mouth. 'I love you.'

'Might try telling me that,' Tate mumbled under her breath, then jumped off the side. She went in feet first, then tucked neatly and began to swim. Following the line, she kicked through the murky cloud, and into the clear.

There Ray and Buck hovered at the bottom, a second bucket of gold beside them as they plucked through the pay dirt. She snapped a picture as Buck handed her father a blackened brick that was an ingot of silver.

Fish swam around them, a living carousel, as they mined the sand. Medallions, more coins, oblong bricks of discolored silver. Ray found a dagger, its handle and blade crusted with sea life. Feigning a dueling stance, he jabbed it playfully at Buck, who hefted an ingot and mimed a defense.

Beside Tate, Matthew shook his head, circled his finger around his ear.

Yes, she thought, they were crazy. And wasn't it great?

She swam clear to take her pictures from different angles. She wanted a good composition of the little pyramid of ingots, another of the odd sculpture of coins and medals fused together beside the glinting bucket.

National Geographic, she thought gleefully, here I come. The Beaumont Museum just found its cornerstone.

She accepted the dagger her father offered. With her diver's knife she scraped delicately at the handle. Her eyes rounded at the glint of a ruby. Like a buccaneer she tucked it into her weight belt.

Through signals, Buck indicated that he and Matthew would haul up the next load. Ray pantomimed opening a bottle of champagne, drinking. This met with unanimous agreement. Giving the 'okay' sign, Buck and Matthew kicked toward the surface with a bucket between them.

Tate gestured for her father to stand with one flipper poised on the pile of ingots and snapped pictures as he happily hammed it up for her. She was bubbling with laughter when she let the camera drop by its strap.

And then she noticed the stillness.

It was odd, she thought absently. All the fish were gone. Even Smiley seemed to have whisked himself away. Nothing stirred in the water, and the silence was suddenly and eerily heavy.

She glanced up through the murk and saw the shadow of Matthew and Buck as they carried their rich burden to the surface.

And then she saw the nightmare.

It came so fast, so quiet, that her mind rejected it. First there was nothing but the figures of the men swimming through the cloudy water, the sun fighting through it in thin misty streams. Then the shadow bulleted out of nowhere.

Someone screamed. Later her father would tell her the sound had come from her, and had alerted him. But by that time she was already clawing her way up.

The shark was longer than a man, perhaps ten feet. In her horror, she could see that its jaw was already open for the kill. She saw the moment they understood the danger and screamed again because she knew it was too late.

The men broke apart, as if propelled. Gold poured down through the water like dazzling rain. With terror digging talons into her throat, Tate watched the shark take Buck in his vicious mouth, shake him like a dog shakes a rat. The force of the attack ripped off his mask and mouthpiece as the shark tore him through the blood-smeared water. Somehow her knife was in her hand.

The shark dived, still thrashing as Matthew plunged his blade into its flesh, aiming for and missing the brain. The desperate jab left a gash, but the fish, frenzied on blood, held on to its prey and rammed his attacker.

Lips peeled back from his teeth, Matthew stabbed and hacked. Buck was dead. He knew Buck was dead. And his only thought was to kill. The shark's black, glasslike eye fixed on him, rolled back white. Buck's body drifted free in the swirling blood as the fish sought fresh prey and mindless revenge.

Matthew braced himself, prepared to kill or die. And Tate burst through the hideous murk like a warrior angel, an ancient dagger in one hand, a diver's knife in the other.

He thought his fear had reached his limit. But it doubled then, almost paralyzed him, as the shark turned toward the movement and charged her. Blind with terror, he kicked forward through the curtain of blood, rammed hard against the wounded shark to impede its progress. With a strength born of hot panic, Matthew plunged his knife into its back to the hilt.

And prayed as he had never known he could.

Grimly, he held on while the shark rolled and thrashed. He saw that while his blade had found its mark, so had hers. She'd ripped open its belly.

Matthew let the carcass go and saw that Ray was struggling toward them with his knife freed in one hand while he hauled Buck's limp body. Knowing what the bloody water could bring, Matthew dragged Tate toward the surface.

'Get in the boat,' he ordered. But her face was chalk white, her eyes beginning to roll back. He slapped her once, twice, until she focused. 'Get in the fucking boat. Haul anchor. Do it.'

She nodded, breath sobbing, and struck out in awkward strokes as he dived again. Her hands kept slipping on the ladder, and she'd forgotten to pull off her flippers. She couldn't find the air to call out. Her mother had turned on the radio, and Madonna was slyly claiming to be just like a virgin.

Her tanks clattered on deck, and the noise had Marla strolling over from the starboard side. In an instant, she was crouched beside Tate.

'Mama. Shark.' Tate rolled over to her hands and knees and choked up water. 'Buck. Oh God.'

'You're all right?' Marla's voice was high and thin. 'Oh, baby, are you all right?'

'It's Buck. Hospital. He needs a hospital. Pull up the anchor. Hurry.'

'Ray, Tate. Your father?'

'He's all right. Hurry. Radio the island.'

As Marla raced off, Tate pushed herself up; she dragged off her belt, turning her eyes away from the blood on her hands. She stood, swayed, bit her lip hard to keep from passing out. As she ran to the side, she dragged off her tanks.

'He's alive.' Ray grabbed for the ladder. Between them, he and Matthew supported Buck's body. 'Help us get him onboard.' His eyes, full of horror and pain, met hers. 'Hold on to yourself, baby.'

As they lifted Buck's unconscious form into the boat, she saw why he had warned her. The shark had taken his leg below the knee.

Bile rose to her throat. Grimly, she swallowed it, gritting her teeth until the nausea and dizziness passed. She heard her mother gasp, but when she turned, her movements slow and sluggish, Marla was moving forward briskly.

'We need blankets, Tate. And towels. Plenty of towels. Hurry. And the first-aid kit. Ray, I radioed ahead. They're expecting us at Frigate Bay. You'd better take the wheel.' She pulled off her blouse beneath which she wore a pretty white lace bra. Without a wince she used the crisp cotton to staunch the blood at the stub of Buck's leg.

'Good girl,' she murmured when Tate ran back with armloads of towels. 'Matthew, pack these around the wound. Hold them firmly against it. Matthew.' Her voice was dead calm and with enough steel to have his head jerking up. 'He needs lots of pressure on that leg, understand me. We're not having him bleed to death.'

'He's not dead,' Matthew said dully as she took his hands and pressed them to the towels she'd packed against the wound. There was already a sickening pool of blood welling on the deck.

'No, he's not dead. And he's not going to be. We'll need a tourniquet.' Her eyes stung as she noticed Buck was still wearing his left flipper, but her hands were quick and efficient. They never trembled as she fixed the tourniquet above the gory stump of his right leg.

'We need to keep him warm,' she said calmly. 'We'll have him to the hospital in a few minutes. In just a few minutes.'

Tate covered Buck with a blanket, then knelt on the bloody deck to take his hand. Then she reached for Matthew's and linked the three of them.

She held on as the boat flew through the water toward land.

Chapter Seven

MATTHEW SAT ON the floor in the hospital corridor and tried to keep his mind blank. If he let down his guard, for even an instant, he was back in the bloody swirl of water, staring into the doll's eyes of the shark, seeing those wicked rows of teeth slice into Buck.

He knew he would see it hundreds, thousands of times in his sleep – the blinding scream of bubbles, the thrashing of man and fish, the blade of his own knife plunging and hacking.

Each time the scene rolled through his brain, what had taken only minutes stretched hideously into hours, each movement slowed into horrible clarity. He could see it all, from the first bump when Buck had shoved him out of the shark's attack path and through to the rush and noise of the Emergency Room.

Slowly, he lifted his hand, flexed it. He remembered how Buck's fingers had tightened on it, gripped hard on that race to the island. He'd known then that Buck was alive. And that was somehow worse, because he couldn't convince himself that Buck would stay that way.

It seemed that the sea delighted in taking the people he cared for most.

Angelique's Curse, he thought on a wave of guilt and grief. Maybe Buck had been right. The fucking necklace was down there, just lying in wait for a victim. The search for it had taken two people he'd loved.

It wasn't going to get another.

He opened his hand, rubbed it hard over his face like a man waking from a long sleep. He thought he must be going a little crazy, thinking this way. A man had killed his father, and a shark had killed Buck. It was a pitiful defense against his own failure to save them that had him blaming an amulet he'd never even seen.

However bloody that ancient necklace and the lore surrounding it might be, Matthew knew he couldn't point the guilt at anyone or anything but himself. If he'd been quicker, Buck would still be whole. If he'd been smarter, his father would still be alive.

As he was alive. As he was whole. He would have to carry that weight for the rest of his life.

For a moment, he rested his brow on his knees, fought to clear his head again. He knew the Beaumonts were just down the hall in the waiting room. They'd offered him comfort, support, unity. And he'd had to escape. Their quiet compassion had all but destroyed him.

He already knew that if Buck had even a slim chance of survival, it wasn't due to him, but to Marla's quick, calm and unflinching handling of a crisis. It was she who had taken control, even down to remembering to grab clothes from the boat.

He hadn't even been able to fill out the hospital forms, but had only stared at them until she'd taken the clipboard from him, gently asked the questions and filled in the blanks herself.

It was frightening to discover that he was, essentially, useless.

'Matthew.' Tate crouched in front of him, took his hands and wrapped them around a cup of coffee. 'Come in and sit down.'

He shook his head. Because the coffee was in his hands he lifted it and sipped. He could see that her face was still pale and glossy with shock, her eyes red. But the hand she rested on his updrawn knee was steady.

In one terrifying mental blip, he saw her hurtling through the water toward the jaws of the shark.

'Go away, Tate.'

Instead, she sat beside him, draped an arm around his shoulders. 'He's going to make it, Matthew. I know it.'

'What, are you a fortune teller now, on top of everything else?'

His voice was cold and sharp. Though it wounded, she leaned her head on his shoulder. 'It's important to believe it. It helps to believe it.'

She was wrong. It hurt to believe it. Because it did, he jerked away from her, got to his feet. 'I'm going for a walk.'

'I'll go with you.'

'I don't want you.' He whirled on her, letting all the fear, the guilt, the grief explode into fury. 'I don't want you anywhere near me.'

Her stomach quaked, her eyes stung, but she held her ground. 'I'm not leaving you alone, Matthew. You'd better get used to it.'

'I don't want you,' he repeated, and stunned her by putting a hand just under her throat and pushing her against the wall. 'I don't need you. Now, why don't you go get your nice, pretty family and take off?'

'Because Buck matters to us.' Though she managed to swallow the tears, they roughened her voice. 'So do you.'

'You don't even know us.' Something was screaming inside him to get out. To keep it hidden even from himself, he pushed her. His face, inches from hers, was hard, cold, merciless. 'You're just out for a lark, taking a few months in the sun to play at treasure-hunting. You got lucky. You don't know what it's like to go month after month, year after year and have nothing to show for it. To die and have nothing.'

Her breath was hitching now no matter how she fought to control it. 'He's not going to die.'

'He's already dead.' The fury died from his eyes like a light switched off and left them blank and flat. 'He was dead the minute he pushed me out of the way. The goddamn idiot pushed me out of the way.'

There it was, the worst of it, out, ringing on the sterilized hospital air. He turned from it, covered his face, but couldn't escape it.

'He pushed me out of the way, got in front of me. What the hell was he thinking of? What were you thinking of?' Matthew demanded, spinning back to her with all the helpless anger rolling back into him like a riptide. 'Coming at us that way. Don't you know anything? When a shark's got blood it'll attack anything. You should have headed for the boat. With that much blood in the water, we were lucky it didn't draw a dozen sharks in to feed. What the hell were you thinking of?'

'You.' She said it quietly and stayed where she was, backed against the wall. 'I guess both Buck and I were thinking about you. I couldn't have handled it if anything had happened to you, Matthew. I couldn't have lived with it. I love you.'

Undone, he stared at her. There had been no one, in his whole life, who had said those three words to him. 'Then you're stupid,' he managed, and pulled unsteady fingers through his hair.

'Maybe.' Her lips were trembling. Even when she pressed them hard together, they vibrated with the power of her roiling emotions. 'I guess you were pretty stupid, too. You didn't leave Buck. You thought he was dead and you could have gotten away while the shark had him. You didn't. Why didn't you head for the boat, Matthew?'

He only shook his head. When she stepped forward to put her arms around him, he buried his face in her hair. 'Tate.'

'It's all right,' she murmured, running soothing strokes up his rigid back. 'It's going to be all right. Just hold on to me.'

'I'm bad luck.'

'That's foolish. You're just tired now, and worried. Come in and sit down. We'll all wait together.'

She stayed beside him. The hours passed in that dream state so common to hospitals. People came and went. There was the soft flap of crepesoled shoes on tile as nurses passed the doorway, the smell of overbrewed coffee, the sharp tang of antiseptic that never quite masked the underlying odor of sickness. Occasionally there was the faint swish as the elevator doors opened and closed.

Then softly, gently, rain began to patter on the windows.

Tate dozed with her head pillowed on Matthew's shoulder. She was awake and aware the instant his body tensed. Instinctively, she reached for his hand as she looked toward the doctor.

He came in quietly, a surprisingly young man with lines of fatigue around his eyes and mouth. His skin, the color of polished ebony, looked like folded black silk.

'Mr. Lassiter.' Despite the obvious weariness, his voice was as musical as the evening rain.

'Yes.' Braced for condolences, Matthew pushed himself to his feet.

'I am Doctor Farrge. Your uncle has come through the surgery. Please sit.'

'What do you mean, come through?'

'He has survived the operation.' Farrge sat on the edge of the coffee table, waited for Matthew to settle. 'His condition is critical. You know he lost a great deal of blood. More than three liters. If he had lost even a fraction more, if it had taken you even ten minutes longer to get him here, there would have been no chance. However, his heart is very strong. We're optimistic.'

Hope was too painful. Matthew simply nodded. 'Are you telling me he's going to live?'

'Every hour his chances improve.'

'And those chances are?'

Farrge took a moment to measure his man. With some, kindness didn't comfort. 'He has perhaps a forty percent chance of surviving the night. If he does, I would upgrade that. Further treatment will be necessary, of course, when he is stabilized and stronger. When this time comes I can recommend to you several specialists who have good reputations in treating patients with amputated limbs.'

'Is he conscious?' Marla asked quietly.

'No. He will be in recovery for some time, then in our Critical Care Unit. I would not expect him to be alert for several hours. I would suggest that you leave a number where you can be reached at the nurses' station. We'll contact you if there is any change.'

'I'm staying,' Matthew said simply. 'I want to see him.'

'Once he is in CCU, you'll be able to see him. But only for a short period.'

'We'll get a hotel.' Ray rose, laid a hand on Matthew's shoulder. 'We'll take shifts here.'

'I'm not leaving.'

'Matthew.' Ray squeezed gently. 'We need to work as a team.' He glanced at his daughter, read what was in her eyes. 'Marla and I will find us some rooms, make the arrangements. We'll come back and relieve you and Tate in a few hours.'

There were so many tubes snaking out from the still figure in the bed. Machines beeped and hummed. Outside the thin curtain Matthew could hear the quiet murmurings of the nurses, their brisk steps as they went about the business of tending lives.

But in this room, narrow and dim, he was alone with Buck. He forced himself to look down at the sheet, at the odd way it lay. He would have to get used to it, he thought. They would both have to get used to it.

If Buck lived.

He barely looked alive now, his face slack, his body so strangely tidy in the bed. Buck was a tosser, Matthew remembered, a man who tugged and kicked at sheets, one who snored violently enough to scrape the paint from the walls.

But he was as still and silent now as a man in a coffin.

Matthew took the broad, scarred hand in his, a gesture he knew would have embarrassed both of them had Buck been conscious. He held it, studying the face he'd thought he knew as well as his own.

Had he ever noticed how thick Buck's eyebrows were, or how the gray peppered them? And when had the lines around his eyes begun to crisscross that way? Wasn't it strange that his forehead, which rose into that egg-shaped skull, was so smooth? Like a girl's.

Jesus, Matthew thought, and squeezed his eyes tight. His leg was gone.

Fighting off panic, Matthew leaned down. He was nearly comforted by the sound of Buck's breathing.

'That was a damn stupid thing to do. You made a mistake getting in front of me that way. Maybe you figured on wrestling with that shark, but I guess you're not as quick as you used to be. Now you probably figure I owe you. Well, you've got to live to collect.'

He tightened his grip. 'You hear that, Buck? You've got to live to collect. Think about that. You kick off on me, you lose, and me and the Beaumonts will just split your share of the *Marguerite* on top of it. Your first big strike, Buck, and if you don't pull out of this, you won't get to spend the first coin.'

A nurse parted the curtain, a gentle reminder that the time was up.

'It'd be a real shame if you didn't get to enjoy some of that fame and fortune you've always wanted, Buck. You keep that in mind. They're tossing me out of here, but I'll be back.'

In the corridor, Tate paced, as much from nerves as the need to keep herself awake. The moment she saw Matthew come through the doors, she hurried over.

'Did he wake up at all?'

'No.'

Taking his hand, Tate struggled with her own fears. 'The doctor said he wouldn't. I suppose we were all hoping otherwise. Mom and Dad are going to take a shift now.' When he started to shake his head, she squeezed his fingers impatiently. 'Matthew, listen to me. We're all a part of this. And I think he's going to need all of us, so we may as well start now. You and I are going to the hotel. We're going to get a meal, and we're going to sleep for a few hours.'

As she spoke, she drew him down the corridor. After sending her parents a bolstering smile, she steered Matthew toward the elevators.

'We're all going to lean on each other, Matthew. That's the way it works.'

'There has to be something I can do.'

'You're doing it,' she said gently. 'We'll be back soon. You just need to rest a little. So do I.'

He looked at her then. Her skin was so pale it seemed he could pass his hand through it. Smudges of exhaustion bruised her eyes. He hadn't been thinking of her, he realized. Nor had he considered that she might have needed to lean on him.

'You need sleep.'

'I could use a couple of hours.' Keeping her hand on his, she stepped into the elevator car, pushed the button for the lobby. 'Then we'll come back. You can sit with Buck again until he wakes up.'

'Yeah.' Matthew stared blankly at the descending numbers. 'Until he wakes up.'

Outside, the wind kicked at the rain, swept through palm fronds. The cab bumped along the narrow, deserted streets, its tires sluicing at puddles. It was like driving through someone else's dream – the dark, the huddle of unfamiliar buildings shifting in the glare of headlights, the monotonous squeak of the wipers across the windshield.

Matthew fished Caribbean bills from his wallet as Tate climbed out. In seconds, the rain plastered her hair to her head.

'Dad gave me the room keys,' she began. 'It's not the Ritz.' She tried another smile as they entered the tiny lobby crowded with wicker chairs and leafy plants. 'But it's close to the hospital. We're on the second floor.'

They took the steps with Tate jingling the keys nervously in her hand. 'This is your room. Dad said we were right next door.' She looked down at the keys, studied the number. 'Matthew, can I come in with you? I don't want to be by myself.' She shifted her gaze to his. 'I know it's stupid, but–'

'It's okay. Come on.' He took the key from her, unlocked the door.

There was a bed with a spread of brightly colored orange and red flowers, a small dresser. The lamp's shade was askew. Marla had brought him a kit from the boat, and had left it neatly at the foot of the bed. Matthew switched on the lamp. Its glow was yellowed by the crooked shade. Rain beat against the window in angry fists.

'It's not much,' Tate murmured. Compelled, she reached out to straighten the lampshade, as if the little homemaker's gesture would make the room less sad.

'Not what you're used to, I guess.' Matthew strode into the adjoining bath and came out with a thin towel the size of a place mat. 'Dry your hair.'

'Thanks. I know you need to sleep. I should probably leave you alone.'

He sat on the side of the bed, concentrated on removing his shoes. 'You can sleep in here if you want. You don't have to worry about anything.'

'I wouldn't be worried.'

'You should.' On a sigh, he rose and, taking the towel, rubbed it briskly over her hair himself. 'But you don't have to. Take off your shoes, and stretch out.'

'You'll lie down with me?'

He glanced over as she sat and fumbled tiredly with the laces of her sneakers. He knew he could have her – one touch, one word. He could lose himself and all of this misery in her. She would be soft, and willing, and sweet.

And he would hate himself.

Saying nothing, he turned down the spread. He stretched out on the sheet, held out a hand to her. Without hesitation, she lay down beside him, curled her body to his, pillowed her head on his shoulder.

There was one keen slice of need low in his gut. It mellowed to a dull ache as she settled her palm on his chest. He turned his face into her rain-scented hair and found a baffling mix of comfort and pain.

Safe, lulled by trust, she let her eyes close. 'It's going to be all right. I know it's going to be all right. I love you, Matthew.'

She slipped into sleep as easily as a child. Matthew listened to the rain and waited for dawn.

The shark shot through the water, a sleek gray bullet armed with ready teeth and a lust for blood. The water was red and roiling, choking her as she struggled to escape. She was screaming, gasping for air she couldn't find. Those jaws opened, hideously wide. Then closed over her with a pain too excruciating to name.

She came awake with a scream locked in her throat. Curling into a ball, she fought her way out of the nightmare. She was in Matthew's room, she reminded herself. She was safe. He was safe.

And she was alone.

Lifting her head, she saw the murky sunlight just easing in the window. Panic came first that he had somehow gotten word that Buck had died, and had gone back to the hospital without her. Then she realized what she thought was rain was the shower.

The storm was over, and Matthew was here.

She let out a long breath, pushed at her disheveled hair. She could be grateful he hadn't been with her when she'd had the nightmare. He was already carrying so much weight, she thought. She wouldn't add to it. She would be brave and strong, and give him whatever support he needed.

When the bathroom door opened, Tate had a smile ready. Despite her worries, her heart did a quick tumble at the sight of him, damp from his shower, bare chested, his jeans carelessly unfastened.

'You're awake.' Matthew hooked his thumbs into his front pockets and tried not to think about how she looked sitting with her arms wrapped around her knees in the middle of the bed. 'I thought you might sleep awhile longer.'

'No, I'm fine.' Suddenly awkward, she moistened her lips. 'The rain stopped.'

'I noticed.' Just as he noticed how big and soft and aware her eyes had become. 'I'm going to head back to the hospital.'

'We're going back to the hospital,' she corrected. 'I'll go shower and change.' She was already climbing off the bed, picking up her key. 'Mom said there was a coffee shop next door. I'll meet you there in ten minutes.'

'Tate.' He hesitated when she stopped at the door, turned back. What could he say? How could he say it? 'Nothing. Ten minutes.'

They were back at the hospital in thirty. Both Ray and Marla rose from the bench outside of CCU, where they had taken up the watch.

They looked, Matthew thought, rumpled. It had always impressed him that no matter what the circumstances, the Beaumonts were so neatly groomed. Now, their clothes were wrinkled and limp. Ray's face was shadowed by a night's growth of beard. In all the weeks they'd worked together, he'd never seen Ray unshaven. For reasons

Matthew couldn't pinpoint, he focused on that one small fact. Ray hadn't shaved.

'They won't tell us much,' Ray began. 'Only that he had a restful night.'

'They let us go in for a few minutes every hour.' Marla took Matthew's hand, gave it a squeeze. 'Did you get some rest, honey?'

'Yeah.' Matthew cleared his throat. She hadn't brushed her hair, he thought foolishly. Ray hadn't shaved, and Marla hadn't brushed her hair. 'I want to tell both of you how much I appreciate–'

'Don't insult us.' Marla deliberately laced a scold into her voice. 'Matthew Lassiter, you use that polite tone with that polite phrase on strangers when you feel obligated. Not with friends who love you.'

He'd never known anyone else who could shame and touch him at the same time. 'What I meant was I'm glad you're here.'

'I think his color's better.' Ray put an arm around his wife, gave her a quick, warm hug. 'Don't you, Marla?'

'Yes, I do. And the nurse said Doctor Farrge would be looking in on him shortly.'

'Matthew and I will take over now. I want the two of you to go get some breakfast, and a little more sleep.'

Ray studied his daughter's face, judged her fit, and nodded. 'We'll do just that. You call the hotel if there's any change. Otherwise, we'll be back by noon.'

When they were alone, Tate took Matthew's hand. 'Let's go see him.'

Maybe his color was better, Matthew thought a few moments later when he stood over his uncle's bed. Buck's face was still drawn, but that horrible gray wash had faded.

'His chances go up every hour,' Tate reminded him, and slipped her hand over Buck's. 'He made it through surgery, Matthew, and he made it through the night.'

The dim glow of hope was more painful than despair. 'He's tough. See that scar there.' With a fingertip, Matthew traced a jagged pucker along Buck's right forearm. 'Barracuda. Yucatán. I was running the airlift, and Buck and the fish ran into each other in the fallout cloud. Went and got himself stitched up. Was back in the water within an hour. He's got a beaut on his hip where–'

'Matthew.' Tate's voice was shaky. 'Matthew, he squeezed my hand.'

'What?'

'He squeezed my hand. Look. Look at his fingers.'

They flexed on Tate's, a slow curl. Matthew's skin went cold, then hot as he looked at his uncle's face. Buck's eyelids fluttered.

'I think he's coming around.'

A tear leaked out of the corner of Tate's eye as she gave Buck's hand an answering squeeze. 'Talk to him, Matthew.'

'Buck.' With his heart skidding in his chest, Matthew leaned closer. 'Goddamn it, Buck, I know you hear me. I'm not going to waste my time talking to myself.'

Buck's eyelids fluttered again. 'Shit.'

'Shit.' Tate began to weep quietly. 'Did you hear that, Matthew? He said "shit." '

'He would.' Matthew grabbed Buck's hand as his throat burned. 'Come on, you candy ass. Wake up.'

'I'm 'wake. Jesus.' Buck opened his eyes, saw blurs. Shapes swam and shivered. He had the sensation of floating, found it not altogether unpleasant. His vision cleared enough for him to make out Matthew's face. 'What the hell. Thought I was dead.'

'That makes two of us.'

'He didn't get you, did he?' Buck's voice slurred as he struggled to get the words around his tongue. 'That bastard didn't get you?'

'No.' Guilt crashed down on Matthew like cold, honed steel. 'No, he didn't get me. It was a tiger, about a ten-footer,' he said, understanding that Buck would want to know. 'We killed him, Tate and me. He's fish bait now.'

'Good.' Buck closed his eyes again. 'Fucking hate sharks.'

'I'll go tell the nurse,' Tate said quietly.

'Fucking hate them,' Buck repeated. 'Ugly bastards. Probably a rogue, but make sure we got bats and bangsticks.'

He opened his eyes again. Gradually the machines and the tubes came into focus. His brow puckered. 'Not the boat.'

Matthew's heart began to thud in his throat. 'No. You're in the hospital.'

'Hate hospitals. Goddamn doctors. Boy, you know I hate hospitals.'

'I know.' Matthew concentrated on soothing the panic he saw in Buck's eyes. He'd worry about his own reaction later. 'Had to bring you in, Buck. The fish hurt you.'

'A couple of stitches . . .'

Matthew could see the instant Buck began to remember. 'Take it easy, Buck. You've got to take it easy.'

'Got hold of me.' The sensations rushed back, one tumbled over another like nasty children in a street brawl. Fear, pain, horror and a skittering dread that triumphed over the rest.

He remembered the agony, the helplessness of being shaken and torn, choking on his own blood, blinded by it. That last clear memory of staring into those black, hate-filled eyes as they rolled up white with cold pleasure.

'Son of a bitch got hold of me.' Buck's voice jerked as he fought against Matthew to sit up. 'How bad? How bad he get me, boy?'

'Calm down. You've got to calm down.' Struggling to keep his hands gentle, Matthew pinned Buck to the bed. It was pitifully easy. 'If you act like this, they'll knock you out again.'

'Tell me.' Panic darting in his eyes, Buck took a fistful of Matthew's shirt. The grip was so weak, Matthew could have shaken it off with a shrug. But he didn't have the heart. 'You tell me what that bastard did to me.'

Of all the things that had been between them, there had never been lies. Matthew covered Buck's hands with his, looked him square in the eyes.

'He took your leg, Buck. The fucker took your leg.'

Chapter Eight

'You're not going to blame yourself.'

Tate stopped her restless pacing to sit beside Matthew on the bench outside CCU. It had been a full day since Buck had regained consciousness. The better the outlook for his recovery, the deeper Matthew sank into depression.

'I don't see anyone else around here to blame.'

'Things sometimes happen that aren't anyone's fault. Matthew . . .' Patience, she warned herself. The snap of her temper wouldn't help him. 'What happened was horrible, tragic. You couldn't stop it. You can't change it now. All you can do, all we can do, is see him through it.'

'He lost his goddamn leg, Tate. And every time he looks at me, we both know it should have been me.'

'Well, it wasn't you.' The thought that it could have been haunted her relentlessly. 'And thinking it should have been is stupid.' Weary of reasoning, drained from the struggle to stay strong and supportive, she dragged a hand through her hair. 'He's afraid now, and he's angry and depressed. But he isn't blaming you.'

'Isn't he?' Matthew looked up. Grief now warred with bitterness in his eyes.

'No, he's not. Because he isn't as shallow and self-important as you.' She sprang up from the bench. 'I'm going in to see him. You can sit here and wallow in self-pity by yourself.'

Head high, she sailed across the corridor and through the doors to Critical Care. The moment she was out of Matthew's sight, she stopped, took time to compose herself. After fixing on a sunny smile, she nudged Buck's curtain aside.

His eyes opened when she came in. Behind his thick lenses, his eyes were dull.

'Hey.' As if he'd greeted her with a wink and a wave, she marched over to kiss his cheek. 'I hear they're moving you down to a regular room in a day or two. One with a TV and better-looking nurses.'

'Said they might.' He winced as pain in his phantom leg plagued him. 'Thought you and the boy'd gone back to the boat.'

'No, Matthew's right outside. Do you want him?'

Buck shook his head. He began to pleat the sheet between his fingers. 'Ray was in before.'

'Yes, I know.'

'Said there was some specialist in Chicago I'm supposed to go to once they let me out of here.'

'Yeah. He's supposed to be brilliant.'

'Not smart enough to put my leg back on.'

'They'll give you an even better one.' She knew her voice was over-bright, but couldn't control it. 'Did you ever see that show, Buck? The one with the bionic man. I loved it when I was a kid. You'll be "Bionic Buck." '

The corner of his mouth twitched briefly. 'Yeah, sure, that's me. Bionic Buck, king of the cripples.'

'I'm not going to stay if you talk that way.'

He shrugged a shoulder. He was too tired to argue. Almost too tired to feel sorry for himself. 'Better if you didn't. You should get back to the boat. Got to get that booty up before somebody else does.'

'You shouldn't worry about that. We've got our claim.'

'You don't know nothing,' he snapped at her. 'That's the trouble with amateurs. Word's out by now. It's out all right, after this especially. Shark attacks are always news, especially in tourist waters. They'll be coming.' His fingers began to drum a quick tattoo on the mattress. 'You locked up what we got already, didn't you? Someplace nice and tight?'

'I–' She hadn't given the treasure a thought in two days. Doubted anyone had. 'Sure.' She had to swallow on the lie. 'Sure, Buck, don't worry.'

'Got to go down, get the rest up quick. Did I tell Ray?' His eyes fluttered and he forced them open again. 'Did I tell him? Fucking medication makes my head foggy. Got to get it up. All that gold. Like blood to sharks.' He laughed as his head lolled back on the pillow. 'Like blood to sharks. Ain't that a kick in the ass? Got the treasure. Only cost me my goddamn leg. Get it up, lock it away, girl. You do that.'

'Okay, Buck.' Gently, she stroked his brow. 'I'm going to take care of it. Rest now.'

'Don't go down alone.'

'No, of course not,' she murmured and slipped his glasses off.

'Angelique's Curse. She don't want anyone to win. Be careful.'

'I will. Just rest.'

When she was sure he was asleep, she went out quietly. Matthew was no longer on the bench, nor in the corridor.

A check of her watch told her that her parents would be there in less than an hour.

She hesitated, then walked decisively to the elevators. She'd take care of things herself.

She felt at home the moment she stepped aboard the *Adventure*. Someone, her mother she imagined, had washed down the decks. There was no trace of blood, and the equipment was once again tidily stowed away.

Rather than try to remember what they had left aboard before Buck's accident, she ducked into the deckhouse for her notebook.

The moment she did, she knew something was wrong.

Everything was tidy. The cushions were plumped, the table gleaming. The galley beyond the living area was spotless. But there was no notebook on the table. There were no artifacts carefully set there, or on the counter for cleaning and cataloguing.

After the first shiver of alarm had passed, she told herself her parents had probably done just what she had come to do. They had gathered up the booty and taken it to the hotel. Or out to the *Sea Devil*.

The boat was more logical, she decided. They would keep it all together. Wouldn't they?

She looked back to shore, wondering if she should go and find them. But here, alone, Buck's urgency began to claw at her. She would go out to the *Sea Devil* and check for herself. It was a short trip, one she could easily handle alone.

Calmer now that she had a goal, she went to the bridge, weighed anchor. An hour, she thought. No more for a quick round-trip. Then she could reassure Buck that everything was taken care of.

As she cruised out to open sea, her tension dissolved. Life always seemed so simple with a deck under her feet.

Overhead, gulls swooped and scolded, and the sea, the sheer blue stretch of it, beckoned. With the wind on her face and the wheel under her hands, she wondered if she would have found this fascinating world if she'd had different parents. Would the lure have been there if she had been raised conventionally, without tales of the sea and treasures as her bedtime stories?

Just then, with the sea shimmering around her, she was sure she would. Destiny, she thought, was a patient master. It waited.

She had found hers, earlier than some, she supposed. Already she could see her life with Matthew unfolding before her. Together they would sail the world, unlocking secrets from the sea's vault. Partners, she mused, in every way.

In time, he would come to learn that the value of what they did went beyond the flash of gold. They would build a museum, and bring the thrill and the pulse of history to hundreds of people.

One day they would have children, make a family, and she would write a book about their adventures. He'd come to understand that there was nothing they couldn't do, nothing they couldn't be, with each other.

Like destiny, Tate would be patient.

She was smiling over her daydreams when she caught sight of the *Sea Devil*. The smile faded into puzzlement. Anchored off its port was a gleaming white yacht.

It was a stunner, a hundred feet of luxury and shine. She could see people on deck. A uniformed man carrying a tray of glasses, a woman sunbathing lazily, and apparently naked, a seaman polishing the brightwork on the foredeck. Glass that ribboned the deckhouse and bridge tossed back the sun.

Under different circumstances, she would have admired it, the lovely, somehow feminine lines, the celebration ripple of the brightly striped umbrellas and awnings, but the telltale murk on the surface of the water had already caught her eye.

Someone was below, running an airlift.

Almost shaking with fury, Tate cut her speed, maneuvered the *Adventure* to starboard of the *Sea Devil.* With quick efficiency, she moored her boat.

Now she could smell it, the unmistakable rotten-egg scent that was perfume to treasure hunters. The gases released from a wreck. Without hesitation, she darted from the bridge. Taking time only to pry off her sneakers, she dived over the side and swam to the *Sea Devil.*

Shaking her wet hair out of her eyes, she hauled herself on deck. The tarps she and Matthew had used to cover the booty from the *Santa Marguerite* were in place. But it took only one swift glance to see that much of what they had recovered was missing.

It was the same in the cabin. The emerald cross, the bucket that had been filled with silver coins, the fragile porcelain, the pewter she and her mother had carefully cleaned. Gone. Teeth gritted, she looked back toward the yacht.

Armed with temper and a sense of righteousness, she dived back in the water. She was snarling by the time she climbed the ladder onto the glossy mahogany deck of the yacht.

A blonde, wearing sunglasses, a headset and a thong bottom lounged in a padded chaise.

Tate marched to her, rapped her sharply on the shoulder. 'Who's in charge here?'

'*Qu'est-ce que c'est*?' After a huge yawn, the blonde tipped down the oversized glasses and studied Tate over them with bored blue eyes. '*Qui le diable es-tu*?'

'Who in hell are you?' Tate shot back in angry, fluent French. 'And what do you think you're doing with my wreck?'

The blonde moved a creamy shoulder and slipped off her headphones. 'American,' she decided in poor and irritated English. 'You Americans are so tedious. *Allez*. Go away. You're dripping on me.'

'I'm going to do more than drip on you in a minute, Fifi.'

'Yvette.' With an amused cat smile, she took a long brown cigarette from the pack at her elbow and struck the flame on a slim, gold lighter. 'Ah, what a noise.' She stretched, the movement as feline as her smile. 'All the day and half the night.'

Tate set her teeth. The noise Yvette complained about was the compressor busily running the airlift. 'We have a claim on the *Santa Marguerite*, and you have no right to work her.'

'Marguerite? *C'est qui, cette* Marguerite?' She blew out a fragrant stream of smoke. 'I am the only woman here.' Lifting a brow, she scanned Tate from head to toe. 'The only,' she repeated. Her gaze drifted beyond Tate, and warmed. '*Mon cher*, we have company.'

'So I see.'

Tate turned and saw a slim man in crisp buff-colored shirt and slacks, a tie of muted pastel stripes knotted handsomely at his neck. He wore a panama at a rakish angle over pewter-colored hair. Gold winked against his tanned skin at his wrist and neck. His face, as smooth as a boy's, glowed with health and good cheer. It was strikingly handsome with its long, narrow nose, neatly arched silver brows and thin, curved mouth. His eyes, a translucent blue, were bright with interest.

Tate's first impression was of money and manners. He smiled and offered a hand so charmingly that she nearly accepted before she remembered why she was there.

'Is this your boat?'

'Yes, indeed. Welcome aboard the *Triumphant*. It isn't often we have visits from water nymphs. André,' he called out, his voice cultured and vaguely European. 'Bring a towel for the lady. She's quite wet.'

'I don't want a damn towel. I want you to get your divers up here. That's my wreck.'

'Really? How odd. Won't you sit down, Miss . . .'

'No, I won't sit down, you thieving pirate.'

He blinked, and his smile never wavered. 'It seems you've mistaken me for someone else. I'm sure we can clear up this little misunderstanding in a civilized manner. Ah.' He took the towel from a uniformed steward. 'We need champagne, André. Three glasses.'

'It's going to get real uncivilized,' Tate warned. 'If you don't cut off that compressor.'

'It does make conversation difficult.' He nodded to his steward, then sat. 'Please, do sit down.'

The longer he talked in that calm, lovely voice, smiled that easy, charming smile, the more she felt like a clumsy fool. As a sop to her dignity, she sat stiffly on a deck chair. She would, she determined, be cool, logical and as mannered as he.

'You've taken property off my boats,' Tate began.

He lifted a brow, turning his head so that he could study the *Sea Devil*. 'That unfortunate thing is yours?'

'It belongs to my partners,' Tate muttered. Beside the *Triumphant*, the *Sea Devil* resembled a secondhand garbage scow. 'A number of items are missing from the *Sea Devil* and the *Adventure*. And–'

'My dear girl.' He folded his hands, smiled benignly. A square-cut diamond the size of a Scrabble tile winked on his pinkie. 'Do I look as though I need to steal?'

She said nothing as the steward uncorked a bottle of champagne with a rich, echoing pop. Her voice was as honeyed as the breeze. 'Not everyone steals because they need to. Some people simply enjoy it.'

Now his eyes rounded with delight. 'Astute, as well as attractive. Impressive attributes for one so young.'

Yvette mumbled something uncomplimentary in French, but he only chuckled and patted her hand. '*Ma belle*, do cover yourself. You're embarrassing our guest.'

While Yvette pouted and fastened a scrap of electric blue over her magnificent breasts, he offered Tate a flute of champagne. She had her hand around the stem before she realized she'd been maneuvered.

'Listen–'

'I'd be happy to,' he agreed. He sighed as the compressor fell silent. 'Ah, that is better. Now, you were saying you're missing some property?'

'You're well aware of it. Artifacts from the *Santa Marguerite*. We've been excavating for weeks. We have a legitimate claim.'

He studied her face with obvious interest. It was always a pleasure for him to observe someone so animated and bold, particularly when he had already won. He pitied those who didn't appreciate the true challenge of the business deal, and the true triumph of winning. 'There may be some confusion about that. The claim.' He pursed his lips, then sampled his champagne. 'We are in free water here. The government often disputes such things, which is why I contacted them several months ago to apprise them of my plans to dig here.' He drank again. 'It's unfortunate you weren't informed. Of course, when I arrived I did notice that someone had been poking about. But then, there was no one here.'

Several months ago, my ass, Tate thought, but forced herself to speak calmly. 'We had an accident. One of our team is in the hospital.'

'Oh, how unfortunate. Treasure-hunting can be a dangerous business. It's been a hobby of mine for some years now. I've been quite lucky all in all.'

'The *Sea Devil* was left here,' Tate continued. 'Our markers were here. The rules of salvage–'

'I'm willing to overlook the impropriety.'

Her mouth fell open. '*You're* willing?' The hell with calm. 'You jump our claim, you steal artifacts and records from our boats–'

'I don't know anything about this property you're missing,' he interrupted. His voice firmed, as it would with a difficult underling. 'I suggest you contact the authorities on St. Kitts or Nevis about that.'

'You can be sure I will.'

'Sensible.' He plucked the champagne from its silver bucket, poured more into his glass, into Yvette's. 'Don't you care for Taittinger's?'

Tate set the flute down with a snap. 'You're not going to get away with this. We found the *Marguerite*, we worked her. One of our team nearly died. You're not going to sail in and take what's ours.'

'Ownership in such matters is a foggy area.' He paused a moment to study the wine in his glass. And ownership, of course, was what life was all about. 'You can of course dispute it, but I'm afraid you'll be disappointed with the outcome. I have a reputation for winning.' He beamed at her and stroked a fingertip down Yvette's gleaming arm. 'Now,' he said and rose. 'Perhaps you'd like a tour. I'm very proud of the *Triumphant*. She has some very unique features.'

'I don't give a damn if you've done the head in solid gold.' Her own control surprised her as she rose and stared him down. 'Fancy boats and a European flair don't negate piracy.'

'Sir.' The steward cleared his throat politely. 'You're wanted forward.'

'I'll be along in a moment, André.'

'Yes, Mr. VanDyke.'

'VanDyke,' Tate repeated, and her stomach trembled. 'Silas VanDyke.'

'My reputation precedes me.' He seemed only more pleased that she knew of him. 'How remiss of me not to have introduced myself, Miss . . .'

'Beaumont. It's Tate Beaumont. I know who you are, Mr. VanDyke, and I know what you've done.'

'That's flattering.' He lifted his glass, toasting her before finishing off the frothy wine. 'But then, I've done many things.'

'Matthew told me about you. Matthew Lassiter.'

'Oh, yes, Matthew. I'm sure he has spoken, none too kindly, of me. And since he has, you're probably aware that there is one particular item that interests me.'

'Angelique's Curse.' Her palms might have been damp, but Tate lifted her chin. 'Since you've already killed for it, stealing shouldn't be an obstacle.'

'Ah, young Matthew's been filling your head with nonsense,' he said pleasantly. 'It's understandable that the boy had to blame someone for his father's accident, particularly when his own negligence might have caused it.'

'Matthew isn't negligent,' she snapped back.

'He was young, and hardly to blame. I might have offered to help them financially at the time, but I'm afraid he was unreachable.' He moved his shoulders gently. 'And as I said, Miss Beaumont, treasure-hunting is a dangerous business. Accidents happen. I can make one thing very clear for all of us, however. If the amulet is on the *Marguerite*, it's mine. As is anything else she holds.' The light in his eyes was brighter now, chillingly gracious. 'And I always take, and treasure, what's mine. Isn't that true, *ma belle*?'

Yvette ran a hand down one gleaming thigh. 'Always true.'

'You don't have it yet, do you?' Tate walked to the rail. 'And we'll see who holds the rights to the *Santa Marguerite*.'

'I'm sure we will.' VanDyke turned the empty flute in his hands. 'Oh, and Miss Beaumont, be sure to give the Lassiters my regards, and my regrets.'

Tate heard him chuckling as she dived into the water.

'Silas.' Yvette lighted another cigarette and snuggled down in her chaise. 'What was that annoying American babbling about?'

'Did you find her annoying?' With a pleased smile, Silas watched Tate swim strongly back to the *Adventure*. 'I didn't. I found her fascinating – young, foolishly bold and rather sweetly naive. In my circles, I rarely come across such qualities.'

'So.' Yvette blew out smoke, sulked. 'You think she's attractive with her skinny body and hair like a boy.'

Because his mood was mellow, VanDyke sat on the edge of the chaise and prepared to placate. 'Hardly more than a child. It's women who interest me.' He touched his lips to Yvette's pouty ones. 'You who fascinate me,' he murmured, reaching behind to tug loose the knot of her brief top. 'That's why you're here, *ma chère amie*.'

And would be, he thought as he cupped one of her perfect breasts in his hand. Until she began to bore him.

Leaving Yvette's feathers smoothed, VanDyke rose. With a smile, he watched Tate pilot the *Adventure* toward St. Kitts.

There was something to be said for youth, he thought. It was something even his money, and his business skills couldn't buy. He had a feeling it would take a long, long time for someone as fresh as Tate Beaumont to grow tedious.

He strolled forward, a hum on his lips. There, his divers had spread the latest haul over a tarp. His heart began to sing. What was there, corroded, calcified or gleaming, was his. Success. Profit for investment. It was only more thrilling that it had belonged to the Lassiters.

No one spoke as VanDyke knelt and began to pick through the booty with his jeweled and manicured fingers. It was so satisfying for him to know that he had brought up treasure while the brother of James Lassiter had been fighting for his life.

It only enhanced the legend, didn't it? he mused as he lifted a cob coin, turned it in his hand. Angelique's Curse would strike them down, strike all down who searched for it. But him.

Because he'd been willing to wait, to bide his time, to use his resources. Time and again, his business sense had told him to forget it, to cut his losses, which had been considerable to date. Yet the amulet remained, always in the back of his mind.

If he didn't find it, own it, he would have failed. Failure was simply unacceptable. Even in a hobby. He could justify the time and the money. He had more than enough of both. And he hadn't forgotten that James Lassiter had laughed at him, had tried to outwit him on a deal.

If Angelique's Curse haunted him, there was a reason for it. It belonged to him.

He glanced up. His divers waited. The crew looked on in silence, ready to obey any order. Such things, VanDyke thought with contentment, money could buy.

'Continue the excavation.' He rose, brushed fussily at the knees of his sharply creased slacks. 'I want armed guards, five on deck, five at the wreck. Deal discreetly, but firmly, with any interference.' Satisfied, he flicked a glance out to sea. 'Don't harm the girl should she return. She interests me. Piper.' With a crook of his finger, he gestured to his marine archeologist.

VanDyke moved briskly through the forward doors and into his office, with Piper on his heels like a loyal hound.

Like the rest of the yacht, VanDyke's floating office was stylish and efficient. The walls were paneled in glossy rosewood, the floor gleamed with its polish of hot wax. The desk, securely anchored, was a nineteenth-century antique that had once graced the home of a British lord.

Rather than typical seafaring decor, he preferred the feel of a manor house, complete with a Gainsborough and heavy brocade drapes. Due to the tropical weather, the small marble fireplace housed a thriving bromeliad rather than crackling logs. The chairs were buttery leather in tones of burgundy and hunter green. Antiques and priceless artifacts were displayed with taste that just edged toward opulence.

With a practical nod to the twentieth century, the office was fully outfitted with the finest electronic equipment.

Never one to shrug away work, VanDyke had crowded his desk with charts and logs and copies of the documents and manifests that guided him on his search for treasure. Hobby or business, knowledge was control.

VanDyke sat behind his desk, waited a few beats. Piper wouldn't sit until he was told. That small and vital twist of power pleased. Prepared to be benign, VanDyke gestured to a chair.

'You've finished transferring the notebooks I gave you onto disk?'

'Yes, sir.' Piper's thick-lensed glasses magnified the dog-like devotion in his brown eyes. He had a brilliant mind that VanDyke respected. And an addiction to cocaine and gambling VanDyke detested and used.

'You found no mention of the amulet?'

'No, sir.' Piper folded his always-nervous hands, pulled them apart. 'Whoever was in charge of the cataloguing did a first-class job, though. Everything, down to the last iron spike, is listed, dated. The photographs are excellent, and the notes and sketches detailing the work are clear and concise.'

They hadn't found the amulet, he mused. He had known it, of course, in his heart, in his gut. But he preferred tangible details.

'That's something. Keep whatever might be of use and destroy the rest.' Considering, VanDyke tugged at his earlobe. 'I'll want a full accounting of today's haul by ten tomorrow morning. I realize that will keep you busy most of the night.' He unlocked a drawer, took out a small vial of white powder. Necessity overcame disgust as he saw the desperate gratitude on Piper's face. 'Use this sensibly, Piper, and privately.'

'Yes, Mr. VanDyke.' The vial disappeared into Piper's baggy pocket. 'You'll have everything by morning.'

'I know I can count on you, Piper. That's all for now.'

Alone, VanDyke leaned back. His eyes scanned the papers on his desk as he sighed. It was possible that the Lassiters had simply lucked onto a virgin wreck, and it had nothing to do with the amulet. Years of indulging in his hobby, and the search, had given him a true appreciation for luck.

If that was the case, he would simply take what they'd found and add to his own fortune.

But if the amulet was on the *Santa Marguerite*, it would soon be his. He would excavate every inch of her and the surrounding sea until he was sure.

James had found something, he mused, tapping his steepled fingers to his lips. Something he had refused to share. And oh, how that grated still. After all this time, the search around Australia and New Zealand had gone cold. There was a piece of documentation missing. VanDyke was sure of it.

James had known something, but had he had the time or the inclination to share that something with his fool of a brother, or the son he left behind?

Perhaps not. Perhaps he had died clutching the secret to himself. He detested not being sure, detested knowing he might have miscalculated. The fury of that, the slim chance that he had mistaken his man had VanDyke balling his pampered hands into fists.

His eyes darkened with temper, his handsome mouth thinned and trembled while he fought back the tantrum as a man might fight a wild beast snapping at his throat. He recognized the signs – the thundering heartbeat, the pounding of blood in his head, behind his eyes, the roaring in his ears.

The violent moods were coming on him more often, as they had when he'd been a boy and had been denied some wish.

But that had been before he'd learned to use his strength of will, before he'd groomed his power to manipulate and win. The vicious, furious waves of black rage rolled over him, taunted him to drum his heels, to scream, to break something. Anything. Oh, how he despised being thwarted, how he loathed losing the upper hand.

Still, he would not give in to weak and useless emotions, he ordered himself. He would, under all circumstances, stay in control, stay cool and clearheaded. Losing the grip on emotions made a man vulnerable, caused him to make foolish mistakes. It was vital to remember it.

And to remember how his mother had lost that battle, and had lived her last years drooling on her silk blouses in a locked room.

His body shivered once with the final effort to battle back rage. He took a long, steadying breath, straightened his tie, massaged his tensed hands.

It was possible, he thought with utter calm now, that he had been a bit impatient with James Lassiter. It wasn't a mistake he would make with the others. Years of search had only strengthened him, added wisdom and knowledge. Made him more aware of the value of the prize, the power of its possession.

It waited for him just as he waited for it, he reminded himself, and saw that his hands were again perfectly steady. Neither he nor Angelique's Curse would tolerate any interlopers. But, interlopers could be used before they were discarded.

Time would tell, VanDyke thought and closed his eyes. There was no sea, no ocean, no pond where the Lassiters could sail without him being aware.

One day, they would lead him to Angelique's Curse and the one fortune that continued to allude him.

Chapter Nine

OUT OF BREATH and pale with fury, Tate rushed into the hospital. She spotted her parents and Matthew in a huddle at the end of the corridor and barely prevented herself from calling out. She headed for them at a jog that had her mother turning and staring.

'Tate, for goodness sake, you look as though you've been swimming in your clothes.'

'I have. We have trouble. There was a boat. They're excavating. There was nothing I could do to stop them.'

'Slow down,' Ray ordered and put both hands on her shoulders. 'Where have you been?'

'I went out to the site. There's a boat there, a hell of a boat, luxury yacht, fully loaded. First-class excavation equipment. They're working the *Marguerite*. Saw the airlift cloud.' She paused half a second to catch her breath. 'We have to get out there. They've been aboard the *Adventure* and the *Sea Devil*. My catalogues are gone, and a lot of the artifacts are missing. I know he took them. He'll deny it, but I know.'

'Who?'

Tate shifted her gaze from her father and looked at Matthew. 'VanDyke. It's Silas VanDyke.'

Before she could speak again, Matthew gripped her arm, whirled her to face him. 'How do you know?'

'His steward called him by name.' The fear she'd experienced onboard the *Triumphant* was nothing compared to seeing murder leap into the eyes of the man she loved. 'He knew you. He knew what happened to Buck. He said – Matthew.' Alarm trembled in her voice as he strode down the hall. 'Wait.' She managed to catch him, brace herself in front of him. 'What are you going to do?'

'What I should have done a long time ago.' His eyes were cold and flat and frightening. 'I'm going to kill him.'

'Get a hold of yourself.' Though Ray's voice was calm, he had Matthew's arm in a surprisingly strong grip. Tate recognized the tone and breathed a small sigh of relief. Little or nothing got past her father in this mood. Not even murderous rage. 'We have to be careful, and we have to be sensible,' he continued. 'There's a lot at stake.'

'That bastard isn't going to walk away this time.'

'We'll go out. Marla, you and Tate wait here. Matthew and I will straighten this out.'

'I'm not waiting here.'

'Neither of us is waiting here.' Marla ranged herself with her daughter. 'This is a team operation, Ray. If one goes, we all go.'

'I don't have time for family debates.' Matthew shook himself free. 'I'm going now. You can hang here and see if you can control your women.'

'You ignorant–'

'Tate.' Marla took a deep breath to control her own temper. 'Let's consider the circumstances.' She aimed a look at Matthew that could have melted steel. When she spoke again, the southern honey in her voice was frozen over ice. 'You're right about one thing, Matthew, we're wasting time.' With this, she sailed to the elevator, jabbed the down button.

'Idiot,' was all Tate said.

When they were aboard the *Adventure*, Tate joined her mother at the rail. Ray and Matthew were at the bridge, piloting the boat and, she imagined, discussing strategy. The insult of it burned in her blood.

More frightened than she wanted to admit, Marla turned to her daughter. 'What was your impression of this man? This VanDyke?'

'He's slick.' It was the first word to come to Tate's mind. 'With a nasty layer under the shine. Smart, too. He knew there was nothing I could do, and he enjoyed that.'

'Did he frighten you?'

'He offered me champagne and a tour of the boat. Genial host to welcomed guest. He was reasonable, entirely too reasonable.' Tate flexed her hand on the rail. 'Yes, he frightened me. I could see him as a Roman emperor, nibbling on sugared grapes while the lions tore the Christians to shreds. He'd enjoy the show.'

Marla suppressed a shudder. Her daughter was whole and safe and here, she reminded herself. But she kept a hand over Tate's as reassurance. 'Do you believe he killed Matthew's father?'

'Matthew believes it. There.' She lifted a hand to point. 'There's the boat.'

On the bridge, Matthew studied the *Triumphant*. It was new, he noted, more luxurious than the rig they had used in Australia. As far as he could see, the decks were deserted.

'I'm going over, Ray.'

'Let's take this one step at a time.'

'VanDyke's already taken too many steps.'

'We'll hail them first.' Ray maneuvered the boat between the *Triumphant* and the *Sea Devil*, cut the engines.

'Get the women in the cabins, keep them there.' Matthew picked up a diving knife.

'And what are you going to do?' Ray demanded. 'Clamp that between your teeth and swing over on a rope? Use your head.' Hoping the scathing tone worked, he left the bridge. On deck, he glanced at his wife and daughter before going to the rail.

'Ahoy the *Triumphant*,' he called out.

'There was a woman,' Tate supplied. The hair on her arms and neck began to tingle as Matthew joined them. 'Crew-seamen and stewards. Divers.'

Now, the *Triumphant* looked like a ghost ship, silent but for the flap of awnings and lap of the water on its hull.

'I'm going over,' Matthew said again. As he readied to dive into the water, VanDyke strolled out on deck.

'Good afternoon.' His beautiful voice carried over the water. 'Gorgeous day for a sail, isn't it?'

'Silas VanDyke?'

Like a pose, VanDyke leaned on the rail, ankles crossed, arms folded.

'Yes, indeed. And what can I do for you?'

'I'm Raymond Beaumont.'

'Ah, of course.' In a gallant gesture, he tipped the brim of his panama. 'I've met your charming daughter. Lovely to see you again, Tate. And you must be Mrs. Beaumont.' He bowed slightly in Marla's direction. 'I see where Tate gets her fresh and intriguing beauty. And it's young Matthew Lassiter, isn't it? How interesting to meet you here.'

'I knew you were a murderer, VanDyke,' Matthew called out. 'But I didn't know you'd sink to piracy.'

'You haven't changed.' VanDyke's teeth flashed. 'I'm glad. It would be a shame to have all those rough edges polished away. I'd invite you all onboard, but we're rather busy at the moment. Perhaps we can arrange a little dinner party for later in the week.'

Before Matthew could speak, Ray clamped a hand on his arm, fingers vising. 'We have first claim on the *Santa Marguerite*. We discovered her, and we've been working her for several weeks. The necessary paperwork was filed with the government of St. Kitts.'

'I'm afraid we disagree.' Gracefully, Silas took a slim silver case from his pocket, chose a cigarette. 'You're welcome to check with the authorities if you find it necessary. Of course, we are beyond the legal limit. And when I arrived, there was no one here. Just that unfortunate, and empty, boat.'

'My partner was seriously injured a few days ago. We had to postpone the excavation.'

'Ah.' VanDyke lighted his cigarette, took a contemplative drag. 'I heard about poor Buck's accident. How difficult for him, for you all. My sympathies. However, the fact remains that I'm here, and you're not.'

'You took property from our boats,' Tate shouted out.

'That's a ridiculous accusation, and one you'll have a great deal of difficulty proving. Of course, you're welcome to try.' He paused to study and admire a pair of pelicans in their dance from sky to sea and back again. 'Treasure-hunting is a frustrating business, isn't it?' he said conversationally. 'And often heartbreaking. Do give my best regards to your uncle, Matthew. I hope this bad luck that runs in your family ends with you.'

'Fuck this.' Even as Matthew vaulted to the rail, Tate sprang to stop him. He'd barely shaken her off when Ray shoved him back.

'Top deck,' he murmured. 'Forward and aft.'

Two men had stepped into view, each with rifles shouldered and aimed.

'I believe in guarding my possessions,' VanDyke explained. 'A man in my position learns that security isn't merely a luxury, but a vital business tool. Raymond, I'm sure you're a sensible man, sensible enough to keep young Matthew from getting himself hurt over a few trinkets.' Well satisfied with the situation, he took another drag on his cigarette as the pelicans plopped gleefully into the water between them. 'And I would be devastated if a stray bullet happened to strike you, or either of those precious jewels beside you.' His smile spread. 'Matthew would be the first to tell you that accidents, tragic accidents, happen.'

Matthew's fingers were bone white on the rail. Everything inside him screamed to take his chances, to dive in. 'Get them inside.'

'If he shoots you, what happens to Buck?'

Matthew shook his head, riding on the rush of blood to his head. 'I only need ten seconds. Ten goddamn seconds.' And a knife across VanDyke's throat.

'What happens to Buck?' Ray insisted.

'You're not going to ask me to walk away from this.'

'No, I'm telling you.' Fear and fury helped Ray muscle Matthew back from the rail. 'This isn't worth your life. And it sure as hell isn't worth the lives of my wife and daughter. Take the wheel, Matthew. We're heading back to St. Kitts.'

Even the thought of retreat made him ill. If he'd been alone . . . But he wasn't. Saying nothing, he turned on his heels and headed for the bridge.

'Very wise, Raymond,' VanDyke commented with a glint of admiration in his voice. 'Very wise. The boy is a tad reckless, I'm afraid, not as mature and sensible as men like us. It was a pleasure to meet you all. Mrs. Beaumont, Tate.' He tipped the brim of his hat again. 'Good sailing.'

'Oh, Ray.' As the boat circled around, Marla crossed to her husband on jellied knees. 'They would have killed us.'

Feeling unmanned, helpless, Ray stroked her hair and watched the dashing figure of VanDyke grow smaller with distance. 'We'll go to the authorities,' he said quietly.

Tate left them, rushed to the bridge. There Matthew gripped the wheel, the course set.

'There was nothing we could do,' she began. Something about his stance warned her against touching him in any way. When he said nothing, she stepped closer, but kept her hands locked together. 'He would have had them shoot you, Matthew. He wanted to. We'll report him as soon as we dock.'

'And what the fuck do you think that will do?' There was something mixed with the bitterness in his voice. Something she didn't recognize as shame. 'Money talks.'

'We went through all the proper channels,' she insisted. 'The records–'

He cut her off with one flaming look. 'Don't be stupid. There won't be any records. There won't be anything he doesn't want there to be. He'll take the wreck. He'll strip her, take it all. And I let him. I stood there, just the way I did nine years ago, and I did nothing.'

'There was nothing you could do.' Ignoring her own instincts, she laid a hand on his back. 'Matthew . . .'

'Leave me alone.'

'But, Matthew–'

'Leave me the hell alone.'

Hurt and helpless, she did what he asked.

That evening, she sat alone in her room. She imagined this was what was meant by being shell-shocked. The day had been a series of hard slaps, ending with her father's shaken announcement that there was no record of their claim. None of the paperwork they had so meticulously filed existed, and the clerk Ray had worked with personally denied ever having seen him before.

There was no longer any doubt that Silas VanDyke had won. Again.

Everything they had done, all the work, the suffering Buck had endured was for nothing. For the first time in her life, she was faced with the fact that being right, and doing right, didn't always matter.

She thought of all the beautiful things she had held in her hands. The emerald cross, the porcelain, the bits and pieces of history she had lifted out of its blanket of sand and brought into the light.

She would never touch them again, or study them, see them winking behind glass at a museum. There would be no discreet card heralding them as pieces of the Beaumont-Lassiter collection. She would not see her father's name in *National Geographic*, or pore over photographs she'd taken herself on those glossy pages.

They'd lost.

And it shamed her to realize how much she had wanted those flashes of glory. She'd imagined herself going back to college, impressing her professors, sailing through to her degree on a wave of triumph.

Or simply sailing off with Matthew, riding on the current of their victory on the way to the next.

Now there was nothing but bitter failure.

Too restless to stay in her room, she headed out. She would walk on the beach, she decided. Try to clear her head and plan the future.

It was there she found him, standing with his face to the sea. He'd chosen the spot where they had once come onto the island. Where she had looked, seen him look, and had known she loved him.

Her heart squeezed with sorrow for him, then settled. For she was sure now what to do.

She walked to his side and stood, letting the breeze ruffle her hair. 'I'm so sorry, Matthew.'

'It's nothing new. Bad luck's my usual kind.'

'This had to do with cheating and stealing. Not with luck.'

'It always has to do with luck. If I'd had better, I'd have gotten to VanDyke alone.'

'And done what? Rammed his boat, boarded it, fought off his armed crew single-handedly?'

It didn't matter now how foolish she made it sound. 'I'd have done something.'

'Gotten yourself shot,' she agreed. 'A lot of good that would have done any of us. Buck needs you, Matthew. I need you.'

He hunched his shoulders. A poor defense, he thought. Being needed didn't suit him. 'I'll see to Buck.'

'We'll see to him. There are other wrecks, Matthew. Waiting. When he's better, we'll find them.' Needing to let hope surge, she took his hands. 'He can even dive again if he wants to. I talked to Doctor Farrge. They're doing amazing things with prostheses. We can take him to Chicago next week. The specialist there will have him up and around in no time.'

'Right.' As soon as he figured out how to pay for a trip to Chicago, a specialist, therapy.

'When he gets the go-ahead, we'll go someplace warm where he can recuperate. That'll give us time to research another wreck. The *Isabella*, if it's still what he wants. What you want.'

'You can't spend time researching wrecks in college.'

'I'm not going back to college.'

'What the hell are you talking about?'

'I'm not going back.' Delighted with her decision, she threw her arms around his neck. 'I don't know why I thought I needed to. I can learn everything I have to learn by doing. What difference does a degree make?'

'That's stupid talk, Tate.' He reached up to pry her arms loose, but she pressed against him.

'No, it's not. It's absolutely logical. I'll stay with you and Buck in Chicago until we decide where to go next. Then we'll go.' She touched her lips to his. 'Anywhere. As long as we're together. Can't you see it, Matthew, sailing wherever we want, whenever we want, on the *Sea Devil*.'

'Yeah.' The fact that he could, all too well, made his limbs weak.

'Mom and Dad will join us when we find another wreck. And we will find one, better than the *Marguerite*. VanDyke won't beat us, Matthew, unless we let him.'

'He already has.'

'No.' With her eyes closed, she laid her cheek against his. 'Because we're here, we're together. And we have everything ahead of us. He wants the amulet, but he doesn't have it. And I know, I just know he never will. Whether we find it or not, Matthew, we have more than he ever can.'

'You're dreaming.'

'What if I am?' She drew back and was smiling again. 'Isn't that what hunting for treasure's all about? Now we can dream together. I don't care if we never find another wreck. Let VanDyke take it all, every last doubloon. You're what I want.'

She meant it. The certainty of that made him giddy with need, terrified with guilt. He had only to snap his fingers and she would go with him wherever he asked. She would leave everything she had, or could have, behind.

And before long she would hate him nearly as much as he hated himself.

'Seems to me you're not giving a lot of thought to what I want.' His voice was cool as he tipped up her chin and gave her a careless kiss.

'I don't know what you mean.'

'Listen, Red, things went to hell here. I put in a lot of work and had to watch it slip right through my fingers. That sucks, but it's not even the worst of it. I'm already saddled with a cripple. What makes you think I want to take you on as well?'

The cut was so quick, so sharp, she barely felt it. 'You don't mean that. You're still upset.'

'Upset doesn't cover it. If you and your by-the-book family hadn't gotten in the way, I wouldn't be standing here empty-handed. Ray just had to go through channels. How the hell do you think VanDyke got on to us?'

Color leeched from her cheeks. 'You can't blame him.'

'Hell I can't.' He tucked his hands into his pockets. 'Me and Buck, we ran a different kind of operation. But you had the dough. Now we've got nothing. All I have left after months of work is a gimpy uncle.'

'That's a horrible thing to say.'

'Plain fact,' he corrected and ignored the coating of disgust in his throat. 'I'll get him set up somewhere. I owe him that. But you and me, Red, that's a different can of worms. Passing the time for a few weeks, a little entertainment on the side to break the monotony is one thing.

And it's been fun. But you hanging around my neck now that the deal's in the toilet – that cramps my style.'

She felt as if someone had hollowed her out in one vicious scoop. He was looking at her with a faint grin on his mouth, cool amusement in his eyes. 'You're in love with me,' she insisted.

'You're dreaming again. Hey, you want to weave a little romantic fantasy with me in the starring role, fine. But don't expect to sail off into the sunset.'

It had to be worse, he decided. He had to be worse. Words alone wouldn't shake her loose, wouldn't save her from him. Even as his own actions revolted him, he cupped his hands over her hips, drew her intimately close.

'I didn't mind playing the game, honey. Hell, I enjoyed every minute of it. As lousy as things turned out, why don't we try to cheer each other up. End things with a real bang.'

He clamped his mouth over hers, hard. He wanted nothing soft or sweet in the kiss. It was greedy, demanding and just a little mean. Even as she started to struggle, he slipped a hand under her blouse, closed it over her breast.

'Don't.' This was wrong, she thought frantically. It wasn't supposed to be like this. It couldn't be like this. 'You're hurting me.'

'Come on, baby.' Christ, her skin was like satin. He wanted to stroke it, savor it, seduce it. Instead he bruised it, knowing whatever marks he left there would fade much sooner than the ones he was leaving on himself. 'You know we both want it.'

'No.' Sobbing, she shoved and clawed herself free. In defense, she hugged her arms tight. 'Don't touch me.'

'Just a tease after all.' He forced himself to meet her haunted eyes. 'All talk, no action, Tate?'

She could barely see him for the tears spilling out of her eyes. 'You don't care about me at all.'

'Sure I do.' He heaved a sigh. 'What's it going to take to get you in the sack? You want poetry? I can dig some up. Too shy to do it on the beach? Fine. I've got a room your old man's paying for.'

'None of us meant anything to you.'

'Hey. I pulled my weight.'

'I loved you. We all cared.'

Already past tense, he thought. It wasn't so hard to kill love. 'Big fucking deal. Partnership's dissolved. You and your parents go back to your nice, tidy lives. I go on with mine. Now, do you want to go bounce on the mattress a while, or do I go find somebody else?'

Part of her mind wondered that she could still stand, still speak, when he had torn out her heart. 'I never want to see you again. I want you to stay away from me and my parents. I don't want them to have to know what a bastard you are.'

'No problem. Run on home, kid. I got places to go.'

She told herself she wouldn't, that she would walk, head high. But after a few steps, she did just that. She fled, with her tattered heart bleeding.

When she was gone, Matthew sat down in the sand, laid his aching head on his knees. He figured he'd just completed the first heroic act of his life, by saving hers.

And he decided as the ache pulsed through him, that he wasn't cut out to be a hero.

Chapter Ten

'I CAN'T IMAGINE where Matthew could be.' Marla spoke in undertones, fretting as she paced the hospital corridor. 'It's not like him to miss his visit to Buck. And especially today, when they're transferring Buck to a regular room.'

Tate shrugged. Even that hurt, she discovered. She'd spent a sleepless night mourning a broken heart, giving it every tear inside her. Still, in the end, she had salvaged her pride and now braced against it.

'He probably found a more interesting way to spend his day.'

'Well, it's not like him.' Marla glanced over when Ray stepped out of Buck's room.

'He's settling in.' The bolstering smile did little to erase the concern in Ray's eyes. 'He's a little tired, doesn't really feel up to visitors. Matthew come in yet?'

'No.' Marla looked down the hall as if she could will the elevator doors to open up, and Matthew to stroll out. 'Ray, did you tell him about Silas VanDyke, the treasure?'

'I didn't have the heart.' Wearily Ray sat down. The last ten minutes with Buck had sapped him. 'I think it's just beginning to sink in about his leg. He's angry and bitter. Nothing I said seemed to help. How could I tell him everything we'd worked for is gone?'

'It can wait.' Knowing there was little else they could do, Marla sat down beside him. 'Don't start blaming yourself, Ray.'

'I keep going over that moment in my mind,' he murmured. 'One instant we were flying. We were kings. Midases turning everything we touched into gold. Then there was horror and fear. Could I have done something, Marla, moved faster? I don't know. It all happened in a heartbeat. Angelique's Curse.' Ray lifted his hands, let them fall. 'That's what Buck keeps saying.'

'It was an accident,' Marla insisted, though a shiver raced through her. 'It has nothing to do with curses or legends. You know that, Ray.'

'I know Buck's lost his leg, and the dream that was just at our fingertips turned into a nightmare. There's nothing we can do about it. That's the worst of it. There's nothing we can do.'

'You need rest.' Briskly, Marla rose, took his hands. 'We all do. We're going back to the hotel and putting all of this aside for a few hours. In the morning, we'll do whatever needs to be done.'

'Maybe you're right.'

'You two go ahead.' Tate tucked her hands in her pockets. The idea of sitting in her room for the rest of the afternoon was far from appealing. 'I think I'll go for a walk, maybe sit on the beach awhile.'

'That's a good idea.' Marla slipped an arm around Tate's shoulders as they walked to the elevators. 'Get yourself some sun. We'll all feel better for a little break.'

'Sure.' Tate managed a smile as they stepped into the elevator. But she knew nothing was going to make her feel better for a long, long time.

As the Beaumonts went their separate ways, Matthew sat down in Dr. Farrge's office. Already that day he'd put into play several of the decisions he'd made during the night. Decisions, he felt, that were necessary for everyone.

'I need you to contact that doctor you told me about, the one in Chicago,' Matthew began. 'I have to know if he'll take care of Buck.'

'I can do that for you, Mr. Lassiter.'

'I'd appreciate it. And I need an accounting of what I owe here plus what it's going to cost to transfer him.'

'Your uncle is without medical insurance?'

'That's right.' Matthew braced his shoulders against the fresh weight. It was always humiliating to owe more than you could pay. He doubted a professional treasure hunter was a prime candidate for a loan. 'I'll give you what I've got. I'll have more tomorrow.' From the sale of the *Sea Devil* and most of the equipment. 'I'll need some sort of payment schedule for the rest. I've made some calls myself. I've got a line on a couple of jobs. I'm good for it.'

Farrge sat back, rubbed a finger along the side of his nose. 'I'm sure we can make arrangements. In your country there are programs–'

'Buck's not going on welfare,' Matthew interrupted, a bite of fury in his voice. 'Not as long as I can work. Just figure up the bottom line. I'll deal with it.'

'As you wish. Mr. Lassiter, it's fortunate that your uncle is a strong man. I have no doubt that he will recover physically. He could, in fact, dive again. If he chooses. But his emotional and mental recovery will be slower even than the physical. He'll need your support. You will need help to–'

'I'll deal with it,' Matthew repeated and rose. At the moment, he didn't think he could stand hearing about psychiatrists and social workers. 'The way I figure it, you saved his life. I owe you for that. Now I've got to take it from here.'

'It's a great deal to shoulder alone, Mr. Lassiter.'

'That's the breaks, isn't it?' Matthew said with cool dispassion. 'For better or worse, mostly worse, I'm all he's got.'

That was his personal bottom line, Matthew thought as he headed down to Buck's floor. He was the only family Buck had left. And Lassiters, whatever their failings, paid their debts.

Oh, maybe they skipped out on a bar bill now and again when times were lean. And he'd been known to fleece a tourist or two by inflating the price and history of a clay pipe or broken jug. If some idiot paid through the nose for some chipped wine jar just because a stranger claimed it was from Jean Lafitte's personal stash, they deserved what they got.

But there were matters of honor that couldn't be shaken. Whatever it took, Buck was his responsibility.

The treasure was gone, he thought, giving himself a moment in the corridor before going in to Buck. The *Sea Devil* was history. All he had left were clothes, his wetsuit, flippers, mask, and his tanks.

He'd hustled the sales. Hustling was something that came easily, he thought with a thin smile. The money in his pocket would get them to Chicago.

After that . . . Well, after that, they'd see.

He pushed open Buck's door, relieved to find his uncle alone.

'Wondered if you'd show.' Buck scowled and fought back the bitter tears that stung his eyes. 'Least you could do is be around when they go poking and prodding and wheeling me all over hell and back in this place.'

'Nice room.' Matthew glanced toward the curtain that separated Buck from the patient in the next bed.

'It's crap. I'm not staying here.'

'Not for long. We're taking a trip to Chicago.'

'What the hell is there in Chicago for me?'

'A doctor who's going to fix you up with a new leg.'

'New leg my ass.' The leg was gone, and only the nagging pain was left to remind him he'd once stood like a man. 'Piece of plastic with hinges.'

'We could always strap a peg on you instead.' Matthew pulled a folding chair to the bedside and sat. He couldn't remember the last time he'd really slept. If he could get through the next couple of hours, he promised himself he'd zero out for another eight. 'I thought the Beaumonts might be around.'

'Ray was in.' Buck frowned, tugged on his sheet. 'Sent him away. Don't need his damn long face in here. Where's that damn nurse?' Buck fumbled for his call button. 'Always around when you don't want 'em. Sticking needles in you. I want my pills,' he barked the minute the nurse stepped in. 'I'm in pain here.'

'After your meal, Mr. Lassiter,' she said patiently. 'Your dinner will be here in a few moments.'

'I don't want any of that goddamn slop.'

The more she tried to placate him, the louder he shouted, until she stalked off with blood in her eye.

'Nice way to make friends, Buck,' Matthew commented. 'You know, if I were you, I'd be a little more careful with a woman who could come back at me with a six-inch needle.'

'You're not me, are you? You got two legs.'

'Yeah.' Guilt ate a ragged hole in his gut. 'I got two legs.'

'Lot of good the treasure's gonna do me now,' Buck muttered. 'Finally got all the money a man could ever want, and it can't make me whole again. What am I gonna do? Buy some big fucking boat and spin around it in a wheelchair? Angelique's Curse is what it is. Goddamn witch gives with one hand and takes the best away with the other.'

'We didn't find the amulet.'

'It's down there. It's down there all right.' Buck's eyes began to glimmer with bitterness and hate. 'It didn't even have the goodness to kill me. Better if it had. Nothing but a cripple. A rich cripple.'

'You can be a cripple if you want,' Matthew said wearily. 'That part's up to you. But you're not going to be rich. VanDyke's taken care of that.'

'What the hell are you talking about?' The color fury had pumped into Buck's cheeks drained away like water. 'What about VanDyke?'

Do it now, Matthew ordered himself. All at once. 'He jumped our claim. And he's taken it all.'

'It's our wreck. Me and Ray, we even registered it.'

'Funny thing about that. The only paperwork anybody can find is VanDyke's. All he had to do was bribe a couple of clerks.'

To lose it all now was unthinkable. Without his share of the treasure he'd not only be a cripple, he'd be a helpless one. 'You gotta stop him.'

'How?' Matthew shot up, pressed his hands against Buck's shoulders to keep him in bed. 'He's got a full crew, armed. They're working around the clock. I'll guarantee he's already transported what he's brought up, and what he took off the *Sea Devil* and the *Adventure*.'

'You're just gonna let him get away with it?' Fueled by desperation, Buck gripped Matthew by the shirtfront.

'You're just gonna turn around and walk away from what's ours? It cost me my leg.'

'I know what it cost you. And yeah, I'm walking away. I'm not going to die for a wreck.'

'Never thought you'd turn coward.' Buck released him, turned his head away. 'If I wasn't laid up here . . .'

If you weren't laid up here, Matthew thought, I wouldn't have to walk away. 'It looks like you'd better work at getting up and out of here so you can handle it your way. Meantime, I'm in charge and we're going to Chicago.'

'How the hell are we going to get there? We've got nothing.' Unconsciously, he reached down to where his leg should have been. 'Less than nothing.'

'The *Sea Devil*, the equipment and some odds and ends brought in a few thousand.'

Glassily pale, Buck turned back. 'You sold the boat? What right did you have to sell the boat? The *Sea Devil* belonged to me, boy.'

'It was half mine,' Matthew said with a shrug. 'When I sold my share, yours went with it. I'm doing what I have to do.'

'Running away,' Buck said and turned his head again. 'Selling out.'

'That's right. Now I'm going to go book us a flight to Chicago.'

'I ain't going to Chicago.'

'You're going to go where I tell you. That's the way it is.'

'Well, I'm telling you to go to hell.'

'As long as we go by way of Chicago,' Matthew said and walked out.

The bottom line, Matthew learned, was a great deal steeper than he had imagined. Swallowing his pride left his throat raw. He soothed it with a cold beer while he waited for Ray in the hotel lounge.

His life, he decided, was about as bad as it could get. Funny, a few months before, he'd had basically nothing. A boat that had seen better days, a little cash in a tin box, no urgent plans, no urgent problems. Looking back, he supposed he'd been happy enough.

Then, suddenly, he'd had so much. A woman who loved him, the prospect of fame and fortune. Success, the kind he'd never really believed in, had been briefly his. Revenge, which he'd dreamed of for nine years, had been almost within his grasp.

Now he'd lost it all, the woman, the prospects, even the bits of nothing he'd once considered more than enough. It was so much harder to lose once you'd won.

'Matthew.'

He looked up at the clap on his shoulder. Ray slid onto the stool beside him. 'Thanks for coming down.'

'Glad to. I'll have a beer,' he told the bartender. 'Another for you, Matthew?'

'Yeah, why not?' It was only the beginning of what Matthew planned for one long night of stinking drunkenness.

'We've been missing each other the last few days,' Ray began, then tapped his bottle against Matthew's fresh one. 'Kept figuring we'd run into you at the hospital. Though we haven't been there as much as we'd like. Buck's not feeling up for company much.'

'No.' Matthew tipped the bottle back, let the chilled beer run down his throat. 'He won't even talk to me.'

'I'm sorry, Matthew. He's wrong taking it out on you this way. There was nothing you could have done.'

'I don't know which he's taking harder. The leg or the *Marguerite*.' Matthew moved a shoulder. 'I guess it doesn't matter.'

'He'll dive again,' Ray stated and stroked a fingertip down the condensation on the bottle. 'Doctor Farrge told me his physical recovery is ahead of schedule.'

'That's one of the things I needed to talk to you about.' There was no way to put it off any longer, Matthew reminded himself. He would have preferred getting roaring drunk first, but that little pleasure would have to wait. 'I've got the go-ahead to take him to Chicago. Tomorrow.'

'Tomorrow?' Torn between pleasure and alarm, Ray set his beer down with a clack. 'That's so quick. I had no idea arrangements were already made.'

'Farrge says there's no reason to delay it. He's strong enough to make the trip, and the sooner he gets hooked up with this specialist, the better.'

'That's great, Matthew. Really. You'll keep in touch, won't you? Let us know about his progress. Marla and I will take a trip up ourselves as soon as you think he's up to it.'

'You're . . . you're the best friend he ever had,' Matthew said carefully. 'It would mean a lot if you come to see him when you can manage it. I know he's hard to deal with right now, but–'

'Don't worry about that.' Ray spoke quietly. 'A man lucky enough to make that kind of a friend, he doesn't toss it away because times are rough. We'll come, Matthew. Tate's decided to start college in September after all. But I'm sure she'd like to go up with us on her first break.'

'She's going back to college in September,' Matthew murmured.

'Yes, Marla and I are pleased she's decided not to defer after all. She's so down about this whole business right now that I can't think of anything better for her than getting back into routine. I know she's not sleeping well. Tate's so young to have to face all we've had to face these last few days. Concentrating on her studies is the best thing for her.'

'Yeah. You're right.'

'I don't want to pry, Matthew. But I get the feeling you and Tate have had some sort of disagreement.'

'No big deal.' Matthew signaled for another beer. 'She'll land on her feet.'

'I don't doubt it. Tate's a strong-willed and sensible girl.' Ray frowned down at the circles of damp his bottle left on the bar. Rings within rings, he thought. 'Matthew, I'm not blind. I realize the two of you were becoming involved.'

'We had a few laughs,' Matthew interrupted. 'Nothing serious.' He looked at Ray, and answered the unspoken question. 'Nothing serious,' he repeated.

Relieved, Ray nodded. 'I'd hoped I could trust both of you to be responsible. I know she's not a child anymore, but a father still worries.'

'And you wouldn't want her to hook up with someone like me.'

Ray glanced over, met the cool derision in Matthew's eyes with some surprise. 'No, Matthew. I'd be sorry, at this point in her life, to see her hooked up seriously with anyone. With the right motivation, Tate would throw everything she'd hoped to accomplish to the winds. I'm grateful she's not doing that.'

'Fine. Terrific.'

Ray let out a long breath. Something he hadn't even considered had just jumped out and slapped him in the face. 'If she knew you were in love with her, she wouldn't be going back to North Carolina.'

'I don't know what you're talking about. I told you we had a few laughs.' But the compassion in Ray's eyes had him turning away, dropping his face in his hands. 'Shit. What was I supposed to do? Tell her to pack it up and come with me?'

'You could have,' Ray said quietly.

'I've got nothing for her but bad times and worse luck. Once I get Buck to Chicago, I'm taking a job on a salvage boat off Nova Scotia. Lousy conditions, but decent pay.'

'Matthew–'

But he shook his head. 'The thing is, Ray, it's not going to be enough, money-wise. Especially at first. I can pretty well square things here. Back in the States with the fancy doctor and the fancy treatment, it's going to be another story. Farrge worked it so they'd cut us a break. Buck's kind of an experiment,' he added with a sneer. 'And they're talking about social security and Medicaid or Medicare or some such shit. Even with that . . .' He swallowed more beer along with his pride. 'I need money, Ray. There's nobody else I can ask for it, and I gotta say it doesn't go down real good to have to ask you.'

'Buck's my partner, Matthew. And my friend.'

'Was your partner,' Matthew corrected. 'Anyway, I need ten thousand.'

'All right.'

The mild tone slashed like a blade across the throat of his pride. 'Don't agree so fast. Goddamn it.'

'Would it really help if I made you beg for it? If I outlined terms and conditions?'

'I don't know.' Matthew gripped the bottle, fighting furiously the need to hurl it, hear it shatter. Like that pride. 'It's going to take me some time to pay it back. I'm going to pay it back,' he said between his teeth before Ray could speak. 'I need enough to set Buck up for the operation, for the therapy and the prosthesis. And he's going to need a place to live after. But I've got work, and when that job peters out, I'll get another one.'

'I know you're good for the money, Matthew, just as you know I don't care about being paid back.'

'I care.'

'Yes, I understand that. I'll write you a check on the condition that you keep me apprised of Buck's progress.'

'I'll take the check. On the condition that you keep this between the two of us. Just the two of us, Ray. All of it.'

'In other words you don't want Buck to know. And you don't want Tate to know.'

'That's right.'

'You're hoeing a hard row for yourself, Matthew.'

'Maybe, but that's the way I want it.'

'All right, then.' If it was all he could do, he would do it as he was asked. 'I'll leave the check at the front desk for you.'

'Thanks, Ray.' Matthew offered a hand. 'For everything. Mostly it was a hell of a summer.'

'Mostly it was. There'll be other summers, Matthew. Other wrecks. The time might come when we'll dive for one together again. The *Isabella*'s still down there.'

'With Angelique's Curse.' Matthew shook his head. 'No thanks. She costs too much, Ray. The way I'm feeling right now, I'd just as soon leave her for the fish.'

'Time will tell. Take care of yourself, Matthew.'

'Yeah. Tell . . . tell Marla I'll miss her cooking.'

'She'll miss you. We all will. And Tate? Anything you want me to tell her?'

There was too much to tell her. And nothing to tell her. Matthew only shook his head.

Alone at the bar, Matthew shoved his beer aside. 'Whiskey,' he told the bartender. 'And bring the bottle.'

It was his last night on the island. He couldn't think of one good reason to spend it sober.

Part Two

Present

The now, the here, through which all future plunges to the past.
–James Joyce

Chapter Eleven

THERE WERE TWENTY-SEVEN crew members aboard the *Nomad*. Tate was delighted to be one of them. It had taken her five years of intense year-round work and study to earn her master's degree in the field of marine archeology. Friends and family had often worried, told her to slow down. But that degree had been the one goal she felt she could control.

She had it. And in the three years since, had put it to use. Now through her association with the Poseidon Institute and her assignment with SeaSearch aboard the *Nomad*, she was taking the next step to earning her doctorate, and her reputation.

Best of all, she was doing what she loved.

This expedition was for science as well as profit. To Tate's mind that was the proper and only logical rank of priority.

The crew quarters were a bit on the spare side, but the labs and equipment were state of the art. The old cargo vessel had been meticulously refitted for deep-sea exploration and excavation. Perhaps it was slow and unhandsome as ships went, she mused, but she'd learned long ago that an attractive outer layer meant nothing compared to what was within.

One summer of naive dreams had taught her that, and more.

The *Nomad* had a great deal within. She was manned by the top scientists and technicians in the field of ocean research.

And she was one of them.

The day was as fine as anyone could ask for. The waters of the Pacific gleamed like a blue jewel. And beneath it, fathoms deep where the light never reached and man could never venture, lay the side-wheeler *Justine*, and her treasure trove.

In her deck chair, Tate settled her laptop on her knees to complete a letter to her parents.

We'll find her. The equipment on this ship is as sophisticated as any I've seen. Dart and Bowers can't wait to put their robot to use. We've dubbed it 'Chauncy.' I'm not sure why. But we're putting a lot of faith in the little guy. Until we find the Justine *and begin to excavate, my duties are light. Everybody pitches in, but there's a lot of free time just now. And the food, Mom, is incredible. We're expecting an airdrop today. I've managed to charm a few recipes from the cook though you'll have to cut them down from the bulk necessary to feed almost thirty people.*

After nearly a month at sea, there have been squabbles. Family-like, we snipe and fight and make up. There are even a couple of romances. I think I told you about Lorraine Ross, the chemist who shares a cabin with me. The assistant cook, George, has a major crush on her. It's kind of sweet. Other flirtations are more to pass the time, I think, and will fade away once the real work begins.

So far the weather's been with us. I wonder how it is back home. I imagine the azaleas will bloom within a few weeks, and the magnolias. I miss seeing them, and I miss seeing you. I know you'll be leaving for your trip to Jamaica soon, so I hope this letter reaches you before you ship out. Maybe we can mesh schedules in the fall. If things go well, my dissertation will be complete. It would be fun to do a little diving back home.

Meanwhile I should get back. Hayden's bound to be poring over the charts again, and I'm sure he could use a little help. We don't have a mail drop until the end of the week, so this won't go out until then. Write back, okay? Letters are like gold out here. I love you.

Tate

She hadn't mentioned the tedium, Tate thought as she took the laptop back to the cabin she shared with Lorraine. Or the personal loneliness that could strike without warning when you were surrounded by mile after mile of water. She knew a great many of the crew were beginning to lose hope. The time, the money, the energy that was tied up in this expedition were extensive. If they failed, they would lose their backers, their share of the trove, and perhaps most important, their chance to make history.

Once inside the narrow cabin, Tate automatically scooped up the shirts and shorts and socks scattered over the floor. Lorraine might have been a brilliant scientist, but outside of the lab she was as disorganized as a teenager. Tate piled the clothes on Lorraine's unmade bunk, her nose twitching at the musky perfume that haunted the air.

Lorraine, Tate concluded, was determined to drive poor George insane.

It still amazed and amused her that she and Lorraine had managed to become friends. Certainly no two women were more different. Where Tate was neat and precise, Lorraine was careless and messy. Tate was driven, Lorraine was unapologetically lazy. Over the years since college, Tate had experienced one serious relationship that had ended amicably while Lorraine had gone through two nasty divorces and innumerable volatile affairs.

Her roommate was a tiny, fairylike woman with a curvy body and a halo of golden hair. She wouldn't so much as turn on a Bunsen burner unless she was wearing full makeup and the proper accessories.

Tate was long, lean and had only recently let her straight red hair grow to her shoulders. She rarely bothered with cosmetics and was forced to agree with Lorraine's statement that she was fashion-impaired.

She didn't think to glance in the full-length mirror Lorraine had hung on the door of the head before she left the cabin.

Turning left, she proceeded to the metal stairs that would take her to the next deck. The clattering and wheezing above made her smile.

'Hey, Dart.'

'Hey.' Dart came to a red-faced halt at the base of the stairs. Unlike his name, he was anything but slim and sharp. Pudgy, with all his edges softly rounded, he resembled an overweight St. Bernard. His thin, sandy-brown hair flopped into his guileless brown eyes. When he smiled, he added another chin to the two he habitually carried. 'How's it going?'

'Slow. I was going up to see if Hayden wanted some help.'

'I think he's up there, buried in his books.' Dart flipped his hair back again. 'Bowers just relieved me at Ground Zero, but I'm going back in a couple minutes.'

Tate's interest peaked. 'Something interesting on screen?'

'Not the *Justine*. But Litz is up there having multi-orgasms.' Dart referred to the marine biologist with a shrug. 'Lots of interesting critters when you get down below a couple thousand feet. Bunch of crabs really got him off.'

'That's his job,' Tate pointed out, though she sympathized. No one was fond of the cold, demanding Frank Litz.

'Doesn't make him less of a creep. See you.'

'Yeah.' Tate made her way forward to Dr. Hayden Deel's workroom. Two computers were humming. A long table bolted to the floor was covered with open books, notes, copies of logs and manifests, charts held down with more books.

Hunkered over them and peering through black horn-rims, Hayden ran fresh calculations. Tate knew he was a brilliant scientist. She had read his papers, applauded his lectures, studied his documentaries. It was a bonus, she thought, that he was simply a nice man.

She knew he was roughly forty. His dark-brown hair was sprinkled with gray and tended to curl. Behind the lenses, his eyes were the color of honey, and usually distracted. There were character-building lines that fanned from his eyes and scored his brow. He was tall, broad-shouldered and just a little clumsy. As usual, his shirt was wrinkled.

Tate thought he looked a bit like Clark Kent approaching middle age.

'Hayden?'

He grunted. As that was more than she'd expected, Tate took a seat directly across from him, folded her arms on the table and waited until he'd finished muttering to himself.

'Hayden?' she said again.

'Huh? What?' Blinking like an owl, he looked up. His face became quietly charming when he smiled. 'Hi. Didn't hear you come in. I'm recalculating the drift. I think we're off, Tate.'

'Oh, by much?'

'It doesn't take much out here. I decided to start from the beginning.' As if preparing for one of his well-attended lectures, he tapped papers together, folded his hands over them.

'The side-wheeler *Justine* left San Francisco on the morning of June eighth, 1857, en route to Ecuador. She held one hundred and ninety-eight passengers, sixty-one crew. In addition to the passengers' personal belongings, she carried twenty million dollars in gold. Bars and coins.'

'It was a rich time in California,' Tate murmured. She'd read the manifests. Even for a woman who had spent most of her life studying and diving for treasure, it had boggled her.

'She took this route,' Hayden continued, tapping keys on the computer so that the graphics mirrored the doomed ship's journey south through the Pacific. 'She went into port at Guadalajara, discharging some passengers, taking on others. She pulled out on June nineteenth, with two hundred and two passengers.'

He pushed through copies of old newspaper clippings. ' "She was a bright ship," ' he quoted, ' "and the mood was celebrational. The weather was calm and hot, the sky clear as glass." '

'Too calm,' Tate said, well able to imagine the mood, the hope. Elegantly dressed men and women parading the decks. Children laughing, perhaps watching the sea for a glimpse of a leaping dolphin or sounding whale.

'One of the survivors noted the brilliant, almost impossibly beautiful sunset on the night of June twenty-first,' Hayden continued. 'The air was still and very heavy. Hot. Most put it down to their nearness to the equator.'

'But the captain would have known then.'

'Would have, or should have.' Hayden moved his shoulders. 'Neither he nor the log survived. But by midnight on the evening of that beautiful sunset, the winds came – and the waves. Their route and speed put them here.' He took the computer-generated *Justine* south and west. 'We have to assume he would have headed for land, Costa Rica by most accounts, hoping he could ride it out. But with fifty-foot swells battering his ship, there wasn't much of a chance.'

'All that night and all the next day, they fought the storm,' Tate added. 'Terrified passengers, crying children. You'd hardly be able to tell day from night, or hear your own prayers. If you were brave, or frightened enough to look, all you would see would be wall after wall of water.'

'By the night of the twenty-second, the *Justine* was breaking apart,' Hayden continued. 'There was no hope of saving her, or of reaching land in her. They put the women, the children, and the injured in the lifeboats.'

'Husbands kissing their wives goodbye,' Tate said softly. 'Fathers holding their children for the last time. And all of them knowing it would take a miracle for any of them to survive.'

'Only fifteen did.' Hayden scratched his cheek. 'One lifeboat outwitted the hurricane. If they hadn't, we wouldn't even have these small clues as to where to find her.' He glanced up, noticed with alarm that Tate's eyes were wet. 'It was a long time ago, Tate.'

'I know.' Embarrassed, she blinked back the tears. 'It's just so easy to see it, to imagine what they went through, what they felt.'

'For you it is.' He reached over and gave her hand an awkward pat. 'That's what makes you such a fine scientist. We all know how to calculate facts and theories. Too many of us lack imagination.'

He wished he had a handkerchief to offer her. Or better yet, the nerve to brush away the single tear that had escaped to trail down her cheek. Instead, Hayden cleared his throat and went back to his calculations.

'I'm going to suggest we move ten degrees south, southwest.'

'Oh, why?'

Delighted she'd asked, he began to show her.

Tate rose, moved behind him to view his screens and his hastily scribbled notes over his shoulder. Occasionally, she laid her hand on it or leaned closer to get a better look or ask a question.

Each time she did, Hayden's heart would stutter. He called himself a fool, even a middle-aged fool, but it didn't stop the hitch.

He could smell her – soap and skin. Each time she laughed in that low, carelessly sexy way, his mind would cloud. He loved everything about her, her mind, her heart, and when he let himself fantasize, her wonderfully willowy body. Her voice was like honey poured over brown sugar.

'Did you hear that?'

How could he hear anything but her voice when he was all but swimming in it. 'What?'

'That.' She pointed overhead, toward the sound of engines. Planes, she realized, and grinned. 'It must be the food drop. Come on, Hayden. Let's go up top, get some sun and watch them.'

'Well, I haven't quite finished my–'

'Come on.' Laughing, she grabbed his hand and pulled him to his feet. 'You're like a mole in here. Just a few minutes on deck.'

He went with her, of course, feeling very much like a mole chasing a butterfly. She had the loveliest legs. He knew he shouldn't stare at them, but they were the most incredible shade of alabaster. And there was that enchanting little freckle just above the back of her right knee.

He'd like to press his mouth just there. The thought of doing it, of perhaps being invited to do it, made his head swim.

He cursed himself for being an idiot, reminding himself he was thirteen years her senior. He had a responsibility to her and to the expedition.

She was onboard the *Nomad* due to his agreement with the recommendation that had come straight from Trident through its Poseidon arm. He'd been delighted to agree. After all, she'd been his best and brightest student.

Wasn't it wonderful the way the sun gilded the flame of her hair?

'Here comes another one!' Tate shouted and cheered along with the other crew who had gathered as the next package splashed off the stern.

'We'll eat like kings tonight.' Lorraine, her lush little body stuffed into a snug halter and shorts, leaned over the rail. Below, crew were manning a dinghy. 'Don't leave anything behind, boys. I put in a request for some Fume Blanc, Tate.' She winked, then turned to flutter her gilded lashes at Hayden. 'Doc, where have you two been hiding out?'

'Hayden's running new figures.' Tate leaned over the rail to shout encouragement as the dinghy putted out to retrieve the supplies. 'I hope they remembered the chocolate.'

'You only eat sweets because you're repressed.'

'You're just jealous because M&M's go straight to your thighs.'

Lorraine pursed her lips. 'My thighs are terrific.' She ran a fingertip along one, slanted Hayden a sly look. 'Aren't they, doc?'

'Leave Hayden alone,' Tate began, then squealed when she was grabbed from behind.

'Break time.' Bowers, tough and sinewy, scooped her up. While others applauded, he dashed to one of the ropes they'd rigged. 'We're going swimming, babycakes.'

'I'll kill you, Bowers.' She knew their robotics and computer expert loved nothing better than to play. Still laughing, she struggled weakly. 'This time I mean it.'

'She's nuts about me.' With one muscled arm, he snagged the rope. 'Better hold on, honey child.'

She looked down as his eyes rolled in his glossy ebony face. He bared his teeth, made her giggle helplessly. 'How come you always pick on me?'

''Cause we look so fine together. Grab hold. Me Tarzan, you Jane.'

Tate gripped the rope, sucked in her breath. With Bowers's wild Tarzan yell ringing in her ears, she pushed off with him into space. She screamed, because it felt good. The wide, wide sea tilted beneath her, and as the rope arched, she let go. The air whisked over her, the water rushed up. She heard Bowers cackling like a loon an instant before she hit.

It was bracingly cool. She let it bathe her before kicking her way to the surface.

'Only an 8.4 from the Japanese judge, Beaumont, but they're picky devils.' Bowers winked at her, then shaded his eyes. 'Oh Christ almighty, here comes Dart. Everybody out of the pool.'

From the rail, Hayden watched Tate and his associates play like children freshly released to recess. It made him feel old, and more than a little stodgy.

'Come on, doc.' Lorraine gave him her quick, flirtatious smile. 'Why don't we take a dip?'

'I'm a lousy swimmer.'

'So, wear a flotation, or better yet, use Dart as a raft.'

That made him smile. At the moment, Dart was bobbing around in the Pacific like a bloated cork. 'I think I'll just watch.'

Keeping her smile in place, Lorraine shrugged her bare shoulders. 'Suit yourself.'

More than three thousand miles away from where Tate frolicked in the crystal Pacific, Matthew shivered in the frigid waters of the North Atlantic.

The fact that he headed the salvage team was a small point of pride. He'd worked his way up in Fricke Salvage over the years, taking on all and any assignments that paid. Now he was in charge of the underwater dig and hauled in ten percent of the net profits.

And he hated every minute of it.

There wasn't a nastier cut to the pride of a hunter than crewing a big, ugly boat on straight metal salvage. There was no gold, no treasure to be discovered on the

Reliant. The World War II vessel was crusted with the icy mud of the North Atlantic, its value solely in its metal.

Often when his fingers felt like icicles and the exposed skin around his mouth was blue with cold, Matthew dreamed about the days when he'd dived for pleasure as well as profit.

In warm, mirrorlike water in the company of jeweled fish. He remembered what it had felt like to see that flash of gold, or a blackened disk of silver.

But treasure-hunting was a gamble, and he was a man with debts to pay. Doctors, lawyers, rehab centers. Jesus, the more he worked, the more he owed. Ten years before, if anyone had suggested his life would turn out to be a cycle of work and bills to be paid, he would have laughed in their faces.

Instead, he'd discovered that life was laughing in his.

Through the murk, he signaled to his team. It was time to start the slow rise to the surface. The damned ugly *Reliant* lay on its side, already half hacked away by the crew. Matthew poured salt on his own wounds by studying it as he stopped at the first rest point.

To think he'd once dreamed of galleons and man o' wars. Privateers bursting at the seams with bullion. Worse, he'd had one only to lose it. And everything else.

Now he was little better than a junkyard dog, harvesting and guarding scraps. Here, the sea was a cave, dark, hostile, almost colorless, cold as fish blood. A man never felt quite human here – not free and weightless as a diver felt in the live waters, but distant and alien where there was little to see that wasn't eating or being eaten.

A careless movement sent an icy spurt of water down the neck of his suit, reminding him that like it or not, human he was.

He kicked to the next point, knowing better than to hurry. However cold the water, however tedious the dive, biology and physics were kings here. Once, five years before, he'd watched a careless diver collapse on deck and die painfully from the bends because he'd hurried the rest stops. It wasn't an experience Matthew intended to have.

Once he'd boarded, Matthew reached for the hot coffee a galley mate offered. When his teeth stopped chattering, he gave his orders to the next team. And he damn well intended to tell Fricke that the men were getting a bonus on this trip.

It pleased him that Fricke, the miserly bastard, was just enough afraid of him to dip a little deeper into his tight pockets.

'Mail came in.' The mate, a scrawny French Canadian who went only by LaRue, shouldered Matthew's tanks. 'Put yours in your cabin.' He grinned, showing a gleaming gold front tooth. 'One letter, many bills. Me, I get six letters from six sweethearts. I feel so bad, maybe I give one to you. Marcella, she not so pretty, but she fuck you blind, deaf and dumb, eh?'

Matthew peeled off the hood of his wetsuit. The chill Atlantic air breathed frigidly on his ears. 'I'll pick my own women.'

'Then why don't you? You need you a good bounce or two, Matthew. LaRue, he can spot these things.'

Matthew brooded out toward the cold, gray sea. 'Women are a little scarce out here.'

'You come with me to Quebec, Matthew. I show you where to get a good drink and a good lay.'

'Get your mind off sex, LaRue. At this rate, we're going to be out here another month.'

'If my mind's all I can get on sex, then it's going to stay there,' LaRue called out as Matthew stalked away.

Chuckling to himself, he took out his precious tobacco pouch to roll one of his favored fat, foul-smelling cigarettes. The boy needed guidance, the wisdom of an older man, and a good fuck.

What Matthew wanted were warm clothes and another shot of coffee. He found the first in his cabin. After he'd tugged on a sweater and jeans, he poked through the envelopes braced under a rock on the small table that served as his desk.

Bills, of course. Medical, the rent on Buck's apartment in Florida, the lawyer Matthew had hired to square things when Buck had wrecked a bar in Fort Lauderdale, the last statement from the last rehabilitation center he'd hauled Buck into in hopes of drying out his uncle.

They wouldn't break him, he mused. But they sure as hell weren't going to leave him a lot to play with. The single letter gave him some pleasure.

Ray and Marla, he thought as he sat down with the rest of his coffee to enjoy it. They never failed. Once a month, rain or shine, wherever he happened to be, they'd get a letter to him.

Not once in eight years had they let him down.

As usual it was a chatty letter of several pages. Marla's looping, feminine handwriting was offset by Ray's quick scrawl in notes and messages in the margins. Nearly five years earlier, they'd moved to the Outer Banks of North Carolina and built a cottage on the sound side of Hatteras Island. Marla would pepper the letters with descriptions of Ray's puttering around the house, her luck, good or bad, with her garden. Woven through were details of their adventures at sea. Their trips to Greece, Mexico, the Red Sea, their impulsive dives along the coast of the Carolinas.

And of course, they wrote of Tate.

Matthew knew she was nearing thirty, working on her Ph.D., joining varying expeditions. Yet he still saw her as she'd been that long-ago summer. Young and fresh and full of promise. Over the years when he thought of her, it was with a vaguely pleasant nostalgic tug. In his mind, she and those days they'd spent together had taken on a burnished golden hue. Almost too perfect for reality.

He'd long ago stopped dreaming of her.

There were debts to be paid, and plans, still in the dim future, to be settled.

Matthew savored each word on each page. The expected invitation for him to visit touched a chord, making him both wistful and bitter. Three years before, he'd browbeaten Buck into making the trip. The four-day visit had been anything but a success.

Still, he could remember how quietly at home he felt, looking at the serene waters of the sound through the fan of pines and bay trees, smelling Marla's cooking, listening to Ray talk of the next wreck and the next shot at gold. Until Buck had managed to hitch a ride over to Ocracoke on the ferry and get himself stinking drunk.

There wasn't any point in going back, Matthew thought. Humiliating himself, putting the Beaumonts in that miserable position. The letters were enough.

When he shuffled the last page to the front, Ray's crablike handwriting shot Tate, and that summer in the West Indies, into sharp and painful focus.

Matthew, I've got some concerns I haven't shared with Marla. I will, but I wanted to get your thoughts first. You know Tate is in the Pacific, working for SeaSearch. She's thrilled with the assignment. We all were. But a few days ago, I was researching some stocks for an old client. I had an impulse to invest in SeaSearch myself, a kind of personal tribute to Tate's success. I discovered that the company is an arm of Trident, which in turn is a part of The VanDyke Corporation. Our VanDyke. Obviously this concerns me. I don't know if Tate is aware. I strongly doubt it. There's probably no need for me to worry. I can't imagine Silas VanDyke would take a personal interest in one of his marine archeologists. It's doubtful he even remembers her, or would care. And yet, I'm uncomfortable knowing she's so far away and even remotely associated with him. I haven't decided if I should contact Tate and let her know what I've learned, or leave well enough alone. I'd very much like your thoughts on this.

Matthew, I'd like them in person, if you can find a way to come to Hatteras. There's something more I want very much to discuss with you. I made an incredible find only a few weeks ago – something I've been searching for, for nearly eight years. I want to show it to you. When I do, I hope you'll share my excitement. Matthew, I'm going back for the Isabella. *I need you and Buck with me. Please, come to Hatteras and take a look at what I've put together before you reject the idea.*

She's ours, Matthew. She's always been ours. It's time for us to claim her.

Fondly,

Ray

Jesus. Matthew skipped back to the beginning of the page and read it a second time. Ray Beaumont didn't believe in dropping his bombshells lightly. In a couple of quick paragraphs he had set off charges that exploded from Tate to VanDyke to the *Isabella*.

Go back? Suddenly, fiercely angry, Matthew slapped the letter down on the table. Damned if he'd go back and dredge up his most complete and horrendous failure. He was making his life, wasn't he? Such as it was. He didn't need old ghosts tempting him back toward that glint of gold.

He wasn't a hunter anymore, he thought as he lunged out of the chair to pace the small cabin. He neither wanted nor needed to be. Some men could live on dreams. He had once – and didn't intend to do so again.

It was money he needed, he fumed, money and time. When both were in his pocket, he would finish what was begun half a lifetime ago over his father's body. He would find VanDyke, and he would kill him.

And as for Tate, she wasn't his problem. He'd done her a good turn once, Matthew remembered, and scowled down at the letter on the table. The best turn of her life. If she'd screwed it up by getting hooked into one of VanDyke's schemes, it was on her head. She was a grown woman now, wasn't she? With a potload of education and fancy degrees. Goddamn it, she owed him every bit of it, and no one had the right to make him feel responsible for her now.

But he could see her, as she'd been then, awed by a simple silver coin, glowing in his arms, courageously attacking a shark with a diver's knife.

He swore again, viciously. Then again, quietly. Leaving the letter and the mug where they were, he headed out to the radio room. He needed to make some calls.

Tate entered the room the crew had dubbed 'Ground Zero.' It was crammed with computers, keyboards, monitors. The sonar dial glowed green as the needle swept. Remotes for the cameras that took stereophotos were easily at hand.

At the moment, however, the area was more of a rec room for adolescents than a scientific lab.

Dart was in a corner with Bowers, relieving tedium by trouncing the computer at a game of Mortal Combat.

It was late, nearly midnight, and she'd have been better off in her cabin, getting a good night's sleep or working on her dissertation. But she was restless, and Lorraine had been edgy. The cabin had seemed too small for both of them.

Taking a handful of Dart's candy, she settled down to watch the monitor that showed the sweep of the seafloor.

It was so dark, she mused. Cold. Tiny luminescent fish hunted food. They moved slowly, surrounded by points of phosphorescence that resembled stars. The soft, even sediments of the sea plane were featureless. Yet there was life. She saw a seaworm, hardly more than a primitive stomach, glide by the camera's range. The huge eyes of a cystosoma made her smile.

It was, in its own way, a kind of fairy land, she thought. Hardly the wasteland a number of oceanographers had once thought. And certainly not the dumping ground certain industries chose to regard it as. It was colorless, true, but those magically transparent, pulsing fish and animals turned it into an eerie wonder.

Tate was comforted by it, the continuity, the antiquity. The monitor lulled her like an old late-night movie until she was nearly dozing in the chair.

Then she was blinking, her subconscious struggling to transmit to her eyes what she was viewing.

Coral crabs. They would colonize any handy structure. And they were busily doing so. It was wood, she realized, leaning forward. It was the hull of a ship, encrusted with life of the deep sea.

'Bowers.'

'Just a minute, Tate, I gotta finish ragging on this boy.'

'Bowers, now!'

'What's the hurry?' Forehead furrowed, he swiveled back to her. 'Nobody's going anywhere. Holy hell.' Staring at the monitor, he slipped his chair forward, hitting the necessary controls to stop the camera's sweep.

But for the beep of the equipment, the room was silent as the three of them stared at the screen.

'It could be her.' Tate's voice was thin with excitement.

'Could be,' Bowers replied and got to work. 'Handle the digitals, Dart. Tate, signal the bridge for full stop.'

They didn't speak again for several moments. While the tapes ran, Bowers zoomed in closer and sent the camera on a slow sweep.

The wreck was teaming with life. Tate imagined that Litz and the other biologists on board would soon be singing hosannahs. With her lips pressed together, she held her breath. Then let it out on an explosive puff.

'Oh Christ, look! Do you see it?'

Dart's answer was a nervous giggle. 'It's the wheel. Look at that honey lying there, just waiting for us to come along and find her. She's a side-wheeler, Bowers. It's the goddamn beautiful *Justine*.'

Bowers halted the camera. 'Children,' he said and got shakily to his feet. 'At a moment like this, I believe I should say something profound.' He laid a hand on his heart. 'We've done did it.'

With one wild hoot, he grabbed Tate and did a fast boogie. Laughter and excitement had tears rushing to her eyes.

'Let's wake up the ship,' she decided and dashed off.

She raced to her own cabin first to rouse a cranky Lorraine. 'Get down to Ground Zero, now.'

'What? Are we sinking? Go away, Tate. I'm busy being seduced by Harrison Ford.'

'He'll wait. Get down there.' To ensure obedience, Tate ripped the sheet off Lorraine's curled, naked body. 'But for God's sake put a robe on first.'

Leaving Lorraine swearing at her, she dashed down the corridor to Hayden's cabin. 'Hayden?' Struggling with giggles, she pounded on his door. 'Come on, Hayden, red alert, all hands on deck, get the lead out.'

'What is it?' His eyes owlishly wide without his glasses, his hair sticking straight up and a blanket held modestly around his waist, he blinked at Tate. 'Is somebody hurt?'

'No, everybody's wonderful.' In that moment, she was sure he was quite simply the sweetest man she had ever met. Following impulse, she threw her arms around him, nearly knocking him down, and kissed him. 'Oh, Hayden, I can't wait to–'

The first shock of his mouth closing hungrily over hers had her going still. She knew desire when she tasted it on a man's lips, knew need when she felt it trembling in a man's arms.

For both of them, she relaxed, lifting a hand gently to his cheek until the kiss played out.

'Hayden–'

'I'm sorry.' Appalled, he stepped stiffly back. 'You caught me off guard, Tate. I shouldn't have done that.'

'It's all right.' She smiled, laid both hands on his shoulders. 'Really it's all right, Hayden. I'd say we caught each other off guard, and it was nice.'

'As associates,' he began, terrified he might stammer. 'As your superior, I had no right to make an advance.'

She suppressed a sigh. 'Hayden, it was only a kiss. And I kissed you first. I don't think you're going to fire me over it.'

'No, of course not. I only meant–'

'You meant you wanted to kiss me, you did, and it was nice.' Patiently, she took his hand. 'Let's not go crazy over it. Especially since we've got a lot more to go crazy over. You want to know why I beat on your door, dragged you out of bed and threw myself at you?'

'Well, I . . .' He pushed at glasses he wasn't wearing and poked himself in the nose. 'Yes.'

'Hayden, we found the *Justine*. Now hold onto yourself,' she warned, 'because I'm going to kiss you again.'

Chapter Twelve

THE DROID DID the work. And that was the problem. A week into the excavation of the *Justine*, Tate found herself struggling with a vague sense of dissatisfaction.

It was everything they'd hoped for. The wreck was rich. There were gold coins, gold bars – some of them a full sixty pounds. Artifacts were transferred to the surface in abundance. The droid worked busily, digging, lifting, shifting booty with Bowers and Dart working the controls at Ground Zero.

Now and again Tate took a break from her own work to watch the monitor and observe how the machine would haul a heavy load in its mechanical arms, or snag a sea sponge delicately with its pincers for the biologists to study.

The expedition was a complete success.

Tate was suffering through a profound sense of envy for an ugly metal robot.

At her station in a forward cabin, she photographed, examined and catalogued the bits and pieces of mid-nineteenth-century life. A cameo brooch, bits of crockery, spoons, a pewter inkwell, a child's worm-eaten wooden top. And, of course, the coins. Both silver and gold were stacked on her worktable. They glittered, thanks to Lorraine's work in the lab, as though they were freshly minted.

Tate picked up a five-dollar gold piece, a beautiful little disk dated 1857, the year the *Justine* sank. How many hands had it passed through? she wondered. Perhaps only a few. It might have been tucked into a lady's purse or a gentleman's pocket. Maybe it had paid for a bottle of wine or a Cuban cigar. A new hat. Or maybe it had never been used, only held in anticipation of some small treat it could buy at the end of the journey.

Now it was in her hand, part of so many lost treasures.

'Pretty, isn't it?' Lorraine came in. She carried a tray of artifacts newly decalcified and cleaned in her lab.

'Yeah.' Tate replaced the coin, logged it in her computer. 'There's enough work here for a year.'

'You sound real happy about it.' Curious, Lorraine tilted her head. 'Scientists are supposed to be pleased when they have themselves steady field work.'

'I am pleased.' Tate meticulously logged the brooch, set it aside in a tray. 'Why wouldn't I be? I'm involved in one of the most exciting finds of my career, part of a team of top scientists. I have the very best equipment, better-than-average working and living conditions.' She picked up the child's toy. 'I'd be crazy not to be pleased.'

'So why don't you tell me why you're crazy?'

Lips pursed, Tate gave the toy a quick spin. 'You've never dived. It's hard to explain to someone who's never gone down, never seen it.'

Lorraine sat down, tipped her feet up on the edge of the table. A tattoo of a unicorn rode colorfully over the inside of her ankle. 'I've got some time. Why don't you try?'

'This isn't hunting for treasure,' she began, her voice sharp with annoyance fully self-directed. 'It's computers and machines and robotics, and it's marvelous in its way. We'd never have found the *Justine* or been able to study her without the equipment, obviously.'

A fresh wave of restlessness had her pushing back from her work-table, pacing to the porthole that was her miserly view of the sea. 'It couldn't be excavated or studied without it. The pressure and temperature at that depth make diving impossible. It's basic biology, basic physics. I know it. But damn it, Lorraine, I want to go down. I want to touch it. I want to fan away the sand and find some piece of yesterday. Bowers's droid's having all the fun.'

'Yeah, he's always bragging about it.'

'I know it sounds stupid.' Because it did, Tate was able to smile as she turned back. 'But diving a wreck, being there, is an incredible high. And this is all so sterile. I didn't know I'd feel this way, but every time I come in here to work, I remember what it was like. My first dive, my first wreck, working the airlift, hauling up conglomerate. All the fish, the coral, the mud and sand. The work, Lorraine, the physical strain of it. You feel like you're part of it.' She spread her arms, let them fall. 'This seems so removed, so cold and intrusive somehow.'

'So scientific?' Lorraine put in.

'Science without participation, for me, anyway. I remember when I found my first coin, a silver piece of eight. We had a virgin wreck in the West Indies.' She sighed, sat again. 'I was twenty. It was a very eventful summer for me. We found a Spanish galleon, and lost it. I fell in love and had my heart broken. I've never been that involved with anything or anyone again. I haven't wanted to be.'

'Because of the ship or the man?'

'Both. In a few weeks, I experienced absolute joy and absolute grief. A difficult ride at twenty. I went back to college that fall with my goals very well defined. I would get my degree and be the very best in my field. I would do exactly what I'm doing now and keep a logical, professional distance. And here I am, eight years later, wondering if I've made some terrible mistake.'

Lorraine cocked a brow. 'You don't like your work?'

'I love my work. I'm just having a hard time letting machines do the best part of it for me. Keeping me at that logical, professional distance.'

'It doesn't sound like a crisis to me, Tate. It just sounds like you need to strap on your tanks and have a little fun.' She studied the nails she'd recently manicured. 'If that's the way you define fun. When's the last time you took a vacation?'

'Oh, let's see . . .' Tate leaned back, closed her eyes. 'That would have been about eight years ago, unless we count a couple of quick weekends and Christmases at home.'

'We don't,' Lorraine said definitely. 'Doctor Lorraine's prescription is very simple. What you've got here is a case of the blues. Take a month off when we're done here, go someplace with lots of palm trees and spend lots of time with fish.'

Lorraine developed a sudden avid interest in her manicure and peered at the coral-pink enamel. 'If you wanted company, Hayden would jump at the chance to go with you.'

'Hayden?'

'To use a technical term, the man's nuts about you.'

'Hayden?'

'Yes, Hayden.' Lorraine jerked back so that her feet slapped on the floor. 'Christ, Tate, pay attention. He's been mooning over you for weeks.'

'Hay–' Tate began before she caught herself. 'We're friends, Lorraine, associates.' Then she remembered the way he'd kissed her the night they'd found the *Justine*. 'Well, hell.'

'He's a terrific man.'

'Of course he is.' Baffled, Tate dragged a hand through her hair. 'I just never thought about him that way.'

'He's thinking about you that way.'

'It's not a good idea,' Tate murmured. 'It's not a good idea to get involved with someone you're working with. I know.'

'Your choice,' Lorraine said carelessly. 'I just thought it was time somebody gave the guy a break and let you know. I'm also supposed to let you know that some reps from SeaSearch and Poseidon are coming to examine and transport some of the loot. And they're bringing a film crew.'

'A film crew.' Automatically, Tate filed the problem of Hayden in the back of her mind. 'I thought we were doing our own video records.'

'They'll use ours as well. We're going to be a cable documentary, so don't forget your mascara and lipstick.'

'When are they due?'

'They're on their way.'

Hardly realizing it, Tate picked up the wooden top, cupped it possessively in her hands. 'They're not moving anything I haven't finished studying and cataloguing.'

'You be sure to tell them that, champ.' Lorraine headed for the door. 'But remember, we're just the hired help.'

The hired help, Tate thought and set the top carefully aside. Maybe that was the crux of it. Somehow she'd gone from being an independent woman looking for adventure to a competent drone who worked for a faceless corporation.

It made her work possible, she reminded herself. Scientists were always beggars. And yet . . .

There were a lot of 'and yets' in her life, she realized. She was going to have to take some time and decide which ones mattered.

Matthew decided he had lost his mind. He'd quit his job. A job he'd hated, but one that had paid the bills and left enough to spare to keep a couple of small dreams from dying. Without the job, the boat he'd been building bit by bit over the years would never be completed, his uncle would be forced to live on subsidies and he would be lucky to be able to afford a decent meal in six months' time.

Not only had he quit his job, but he'd been maneuvered into taking LaRue along with him. The man had simply packed up and shipped out with him with no encouragement at all. As Matthew saw it, he was now stuck with two dependents, two men who spent most of their time arguing with each other and pointing out his flaws.

So here he sat, outside a trailer in southern Florida wondering when he had gone mad.

It was the letter from the Beaumonts that had started it. The mention of Tate, of VanDyke, and of course, the *Isabella*. It had brought back too many memories, too many failures and too much hope. Before he'd let himself think through the consequences, he'd been packing his gear.

Now that his bridges were burning at his back, Matthew had plenty of time to think. What the hell was he going to do with Buck? The man's drinking was out of hand again.

Big surprise, Matthew thought. Every year, he came back to Florida and spent his month on shore struggling to get his uncle dry. And every year he went back to sea, hampered with guilt, regrets and the grief that he would never be able to make a difference.

Even now, he could hear Buck's voice lifted in drunken bitterness. Despite the rain that was falling in steady, sodden sheets, Matthew remained outside under the rusted, leaking awning.

'What is this slop?' Buck demanded, clattering into the tiny kitchen.

LaRue didn't bother to glance up from the book he was reading. 'It is bouillabaisse. A family recipe.'

'Slop,' Buck said again. 'French slop.' Unshaven, wearing the clothes he'd slept in, Buck slammed open a cabinet door in search of a bottle. 'I don't want it smelling up my house.'

In answer, LaRue turned a page.

'Where the fuck's my whiskey?' Buck stabbed his hand into the cupboard, knocking over and scattering the meager supplies. 'I had a bottle in here, goddamn it.'

'Me, I prefer a good Beaujolais,' LaRue commented. 'At room temperature.' He heard the screen door open and marked his place in his Faulkner novel. The evening show was about to begin.

'You been stealing my whiskey, you fucking Canuk?'

As LaRue's tooth gleamed in a snarl, Matthew stepped in. 'There isn't any whiskey. I got rid of it.'

Hampered more by his morning's drinking than by his prosthesis, Buck turned on him. 'You got no right to take my bottle.'

Who was this man, Matthew thought, this stranger? If Buck was somewhere in that bloated, unshaven face, in those red-rimmed, bleary eyes, he could no longer see him. 'Right or not,' he said calmly, 'I got rid of it. Try the coffee.'

In response, Buck grabbed the pot from the stove and hurled it against the wall.

'So don't try the coffee.' Because he was tempted to ball them into fists, Matthew tucked his hands into his pockets. 'You want to drink, you're going to have to do it somewhere else. I'm not going to watch you kill yourself.'

'What I do's my business,' Buck muttered, crunching over broken glass and slopped coffee.

'Not while I'm around.'

'You're never around, are you?' Buck nearly skidded on the wet tile, righted himself. His face went pink with humiliation. Every step he took was a reminder. 'You blow in here when you please, and blow out the same way. You got no business, boy, telling me what to do in my own house.'

'It's my house,' Matthew said softly. 'You're just dying in it.'

He could have dodged the blow. He took Buck's fist on his jaw philosophically. In some perverse part of his brain, he was pleased to note that his uncle could still pack a punch.

While Buck stared at him, Matthew wiped the blood from his mouth with the back of his hand. 'I'm going out,' he said and left.

'Go away, walk away.' Buck shambled to the door to shout after him over the drumming rain. 'Walking away's what you're best at. Why don't you keep walking? Nobody here needs you. Nobody needs you.'

LaRue waited until Buck lumbered back toward the bedroom, then rose to turn down the heat on his stew. He took his jacket, and Matthew's, and slipped out of the trailer.

They had only been in Florida three days, but LaRue knew just where Matthew would go. Adjusting the brim of his cap so that the rain sluiced off in front of his face, he made his way down to the marina.

It was nearly deserted, and the lock was off the door of the concrete garage that Matthew rented by the month. He found Matthew inside, sitting in the bow of a nearly finished boat.

It was a double hull, almost as wide as it was long. LaRue's first glimpse of it after they'd arrived had impressed him. It was a pretty thing, not dainty by any means, but sturdy and tough. The way LaRue preferred his boats, and his women.

Matthew had designed the deck section to lie across the top of the hulls so that it would stay clear in rough seas. Each bow had an inward curve that would create a cushioning effect and lead to not only a smoother ride, but a faster one. There was plenty of storage area and seating. But the genius of the design in LaRue's opinion was the sixty square feet of open deck forward.

Treasure room, LaRue thought.

All it lacked were the finishing touches. The paint and brightwork, the bridge equipment, navigational devices. And, LaRue thought, a suitable name.

He climbed up, impressed again by the sharp, cutting look of the bows. It would take the water, he mused. It would fly.

'So, when you finish this thing, eh?'

'I've got the time now, don't I?' Matthew envisioned the rails. Brass and teak. 'All I need's the money.'

'Me, I got plenty of money.' Thoughtfully, LaRue took out a leather pouch and began the slow and, to him, pleasurable process of rolling a cigarette. 'What do I spend it on but women? And they don't cost so much as most men think. So maybe I give you the money to finish it, and you give me part of the boat.'

Matthew let out a sour laugh. 'What part do you want?'

LaRue leaned into the backrest, carefully sealing the cigarette paper around the tobacco. 'A boat a man builds is a good place to come when he wants to brood. Tell me this, Matthew, why did you let him hit you?'

'Why not?'

'Seems to me he'd be better if you hit him.'

'Right. That would be great. It would do a lot of good for me to knock down a–'

'Cripple?' LaRue finished mildly. 'No, you never let him forget he's not what he was.'

Furious, surprised into hurt, Matthew lunged to his feet. 'Where the hell do you come off saying that? What the hell do you know about it? I've done everything I can for him.'

'You've done.' LaRue struck a match, let it flare on the edge of the neatly rolled cigarette. 'You pay for the roof over his head, the food in his belly, the whiskey he kills himself with. All it costs him is his pride.'

'What the hell am I supposed to do, toss him out into the street?'

LaRue shrugged. 'You don't ask him to be a man, so he's not a man.'

'Butt out.'

'I think you like your guilt, Matthew. It keeps you from doing what you want, and maybe failing at it.' He only grinned when Matthew hauled him up by the shirtfront. 'See, me, you treat like a man.' He cocked up his chin, not entirely sure it wouldn't be broken in the next ten seconds. 'You can hit me. I'll hit you back. When we're finished, we'll make a deal for the boat.'

'What the hell are you doing here?' In disgust, Matthew shoved him back. 'I don't need company, I don't need another partner.'

'You do, yes. And I like you, Matthew.' LaRue sat again, neatly tapping the ash from his cigarette into his palm. 'And I figure this. You're going to go back for that ship you once told me about. Maybe you'll go after this VanDyke you hate so much. Maybe you'll even go back for the woman you want. I'm going, because I don't mind being rich. I like to see a good fight, and me, I have a soft spot for romance.'

'You're an asshole, LaRue. Christ knows why I ever told you about that shit.' He lifted his hands and rubbed them over his face. 'I must have been drunk.'

'No, you never let yourself get drunk. You were talking to yourself, *mon ami*. I was just there.'

'Maybe I'll go back for the wreck. And maybe, if I get lucky, I'll cross paths with VanDyke again. But there's no woman anymore.'

'There's always a woman. If not one, another.' LaRue shrugged his bony shoulders. 'Me, I don't understand why men lose their minds over a woman. One leaves, another comes along. But an enemy, that's worth working for. And money, well, it's easier to be rich than poor. So we finish your boat, eh, and go looking for fortune and revenge.'

Wary, Matthew eyed LaRue. 'The equipment I want isn't cheap.'

'Nothing worthwhile is cheap.'

'We may never find the wreck. Even if we do, mining her is going to be hard, dangerous work.'

'Danger is what makes life interesting. You've forgotten that, Matthew.'

'Maybe,' he murmured. He began to feel something stir again. It was the blood he'd let settle and cool over the years. He held out a hand. 'We finish the boat.'

*

It was three days later when Buck made his way into the garage. He'd gotten a bottle somewhere, Matthew deduced. The sour stench of whiskey surrounded him.

'Where the hell you think you're going to take this tub?'

Matthew continued to lovingly sand the teak for the rail. 'Hatteras to start. I'm hooking up with the Beaumonts.'

'Shit, amateurs.' A little rocky on his feet, Buck walked to the stern. 'What the hell did you build a catamaran for?'

'Because I wanted to.'

'Single hull's always been good enough for me. Good enough for your father, too.'

'It's not your boat. It's not his boat. It's mine.'

That stung. 'What kind of color is this you're painting her. Damn sissy blue.'

'Caribbean blue,' Matthew corrected. 'I like it.'

'Probably sink the first time you hit weather.' Buck sniffed and stopped himself from caressing one of the hulls. 'I guess all you and Ray are good for now is pleasure sailing.'

Experimentally, Matthew ran the pad of his thumb over the teak. It was satin smooth. 'We're going after the *Isabella*.'

Silence sparked like naked wires crossed. Matthew hefted the sanded rail over his shoulder and turned. Buck had a hand on the boat now, braced as he swayed like a man already at sea.

'The hell you are.'

'Ray's decided to go. He found something he wants to show me. As soon as I can get things done here, I'm heading up. Regardless of what Ray's come up with, I'm going after her. It's long past time I did.'

'Are you out of your mind, boy? Do you know what she cost us? Cost me?'

Matthew set the rail aside for varnishing. 'I've got a pretty good idea.'

'You had a treasure, didn't you? You let her go. You let that bastard VanDyke dance off with it. You lost it for me when I was half dead. Now you think you're going back and leaving me here to rot?'

'I'm going. What you do is your business.'

Panicked, Buck slammed the heel of his hand into Matthew's chest. 'Who's going to see to what I need here? You go off like this, the money'll be gone in a month. You owe me, boy. I saved your worthless life. I lost my leg for you. I lost everything for you.'

The guilt still came, waves of it a strong man could drown in. But this time, Matthew shook his head. He wasn't going under again. 'I'm finished owing you, Buck. Eight years I've worked my ass off so you could drink yourself into a coma and make me pay for every breath I took. I'm done. I'm going after something I'd convinced myself I couldn't have. And I'm going to get her.'

'They'll kill you. The *Isabella* and Angelique's Curse. And if they don't, VanDyke will. Then where will I be?'

'Just where you are now. Standing on two legs. One of them I paid for.'

He didn't take the punch this time. Instead he caught Buck's fist in his hand an inch before it struck his face. Without thinking he shoved back so that Buck stumbled into the stern of the boat.

'Try that again, and I'll take you down, old man or not.' Matthew planted his feet, prepared to face-off if Buck lunged again. 'In ten days, I'm leaving for Hatteras with LaRue. You can pull yourself together, or you can go fuck yourself. It's your choice. Now get the hell out. I've got work to do.'

With a shaking hand, Buck wiped his mouth. His phantom leg began to throb, a nasty, grinning ghost that never quite gave up the haunting. Sick at heart, he hurried off to find a bottle.

Alone, Matthew hefted another section of rail and went to work like a man possessed.

Chapter Thirteen

As far as Silas VanDyke was concerned, Manzanillo was the only place to spend the first breaths of spring. His cliff house on the western Mexican coast afforded him the most spectacular view of the restless Pacific. There was nothing more relaxing than standing by his wall of windows and watching the waves crash and spew.

Power never failed to fascinate him.

As an Aquarian, he considered water his element. He loved the sight of it, the smell of it, the sound of it. Though he traveled extensively for both business and pleasure, he could never be away from his element for long.

All of his homes had been bought or built near some body of water. His villa in Capri, his plantation in Fiji, his bungalow on Martinique. Even his brownstone in New York afforded him a view of the Hudson. But he had a particular fondness for his hideaway in Mexico.

Not that this particular trip was one of leisure. VanDyke's work ethic was as disciplined as the rest of him. Rewards were earned – and he had earned his. He believed in labor, the exercise of the body as well as the mind. It was true that he had inherited a great deal of his wealth, but he had not whiled away his time or whittled away his resources. No, he had built on them doggedly and shrewdly until he had easily tripled the legacy passed to him.

He considered himself discreet and dignified. No publicity-seeking Trump, VanDyke pursued his personal and business affairs quietly and with a subtle flare that kept his name out of the press and tabloid news.

Unless he put it there. Publicity, of the proper type, could shade a business deal and tip the scales when necessary.

He had never married, though he admired women greatly. Marriage was a contract, and the negating of that contract was too often messy, too often public. Heirs were often a result of that contract, and heirs could be used against a man.

Instead, he chose his companions with care, treated them with the same respect and courtesy as he would treat any employee. And when a woman ceased to entertain him, she was generously dispatched.

Few complained.

The little Italian socialite he had recently grown weary of had been a bit of a problem. The icy diamonds he'd offered as a parting gift hadn't cooled her hot temper. She'd actually threatened him. With some regret, he'd arranged for her to be taught a lesson. But he'd given strict orders that there were to be no visible scars.

After all, she'd had a lovely face and body that had given him a great deal of pleasure.

It seemed to him that violence, well-skilled violence, was a tool no successful man could afford to ignore. In the last few years, he had used it often, and he thought, quite well.

The oddest thing was that it gave him so much more pleasure than he had expected. A kind of cheap, emotional profit, he decided. Privately, he could admit that by paying for it, he often soothed those black tempers that raged over him.

So many men he knew, men who, like him, controlled great wealth and managed responsibilities, lost their edge by accepting certain failures, making too many concessions. Or they simply burned themselves out by fighting to stay on top. Frustrations, he thought, unreleased, festered. A wise man took his relief and always, always, counted the profit.

Now he had business to attend to, business to entertain him. At the moment, his priority was the *Nomad*, its crew, and its brilliant find.

As he'd ordered, the reports were on his desk. He'd handpicked the team for his expedition, from the scientists to the technicians and down to the galley staff. It pleased him to know that once again, his instincts had been on target. They hadn't failed him. When the expedition was complete, VanDyke would see to it that each and every member of the *Nomad* team received a bonus.

He admired scientists tremendously, their logic and discipline, their vision. He was more than satisfied with Frank Litz, both as a biologist and as a spy. The man kept him up to date on the personal dynamics and intimacies of the *Nomad's* crew.

Yes, he thought Litz a happy find, particularly after the disappointment of Piper. The young archeologist had had potential, VanDyke mused. But that one little flaw had made him sloppy.

Addictions led to a lack of order. Why, he himself had given up smoking years before simply to make a point. Inner strength equaled power over personal environment. A pity Piper had lacked inner strength. In the end, VanDyke had harbored no regrets in offering him the uncut cocaine that had killed him.

In truth, it had been rather thrilling. The ultimate termination of an employee.

Settling back, he studied the reports from Litz and his team of marine biologists on the ecosystem, the plants and animals that had colonized the wreck of the *Justine*. Sponges, gold coral, worms. Nothing was beneath VanDyke's interest.

What was there could be harvested and used.

With the same respect and interest, he studied the reports of the geologists, the chemist, those of the representatives he had sent to observe the operation and its results.

Like a child with a treat, he saved the archeologist's report for last. It was meticulously organized, thorough and clear as new glass. No detail was omitted, down to the last shard of crockery. Each artifact was described, dated and photographed, each item catalogued according to the date and time it was discovered. There was a cross-reference with the chemist's report as to how the article was treated, tested, cleaned.

A father's pride swept through VanDyke as he read the carefully typed pages. He was glowingly pleased with Tate Beaumont, considered her a protégée.

She would make a fine replacement for the unfortunate Piper.

Perhaps it had been impulse that had urged him to have her education monitored over the years. But the impulse had more than paid off. The way she had faced him onboard the *Triumphant* with fury and intelligence firing her eyes. Oh, he admired that. Courage was a valuable asset, when tempered with a well-ordered mind.

Tate Beaumont possessed both.

Professionally, she had more than exceeded his early expectations of her. She'd graduated third in her class, publishing her first paper in her sophomore year. Her postgraduate work had simply been brilliant. She would earn her doctorate years before the majority of her contemporaries.

He was thrilled with her.

So thrilled he had opened several doors for her along the way. Doors that even with her skills and tenacity might have been difficult for her to unlatch. Her opportunity to research in a two-man sub off Turkey in depths of six hundred feet had come through him. Though like an indulgent uncle, he had taken no credit. Yet.

Her personal life earned his admiration as well. Initially, he'd been disappointed that she hadn't remained attached to Matthew Lassiter. A continued connection would have been one more method of keeping tabs on Matthew. Yet he'd been pleased that she'd shown the obvious good taste to shrug off a man so clearly beneath her.

She'd concentrated on her studies, her goals, as he would have expected from his own daughter, had he a daughter. Twice she had explored relationships. The first no more than the rebellion of youth, in VanDyke's opinion. The young man she'd attached herself to in the initial weeks after her return to college had been little more than an experiment, he was sure. But she'd soon shaken herself loose from the muscle-bound empty-headed jock.

A woman like Tate required intellect, style, breeding.

Indeed, after graduation she had been drawn into a liaison with a fellow postgraduate student who shared many of her interests. That had lasted just under ten months, and had caused VanDyke some concern. But that, too, had ended when he'd arranged to have the man offered a position at his oceanographic institute in Greenland.

To fully realize her potential, he felt Tate needed to limit her distractions, as he had over the years. Marriage and family would only tilt her priorities.

He was delighted that she was now working for him. He intended to keep her on the fringes for the present. In time, if she continued to prove worthy, he would draw her into the core.

A women of her intelligence and ambitions would recognize the debt she owed him, and would understand the value of what he could continue to offer.

One day they would meet again, work side by side.

He was a patient man and could wait for her. As he waited for Angelique's Curse. His instincts told him that when the time was finally right, one would lead him to the other.

Then he would have everything.

VanDyke glanced over as his fax began to hum. Rising, he poured himself a large tumbler of freshly squeezed orange juice. If he hadn't had such a full schedule that day, he would have added just a dollop of champagne. Such small luxuries could wait.

He lifted a brow as he picked up the fax. It was his latest report on the Lassiters. So, he mused, Matthew had jumped ship and gone back to his uncle. Perhaps he would stick the drunken fool in another rehab center. It continued to surprise him that Matthew didn't simply leave the old man to wallow in his own vomit and disappear.

Family loyalty, he thought, shaking his head. It was something VanDyke knew existed, but had never experienced. If his own father hadn't conveniently died at fifty, VanDyke would have implemented his plans for a takeover. Fortunately, he had no siblings to rival with, and his mother had faded quietly away in an exclusive mental hospital when he'd been barely thirteen.

He had only himself, VanDyke thought, sipping the chilled juice. And his fortune. It was well worth using a small part of it to keep an eye on Matthew Lassiter.

Family loyalty, he thought again with a small smile. If it ran true, Matthew's father had found a way to pass his secret to his son. Sooner or later, Matthew would be compelled to hunt for Angelique's Curse. And VanDyke, patient as a spider, would be waiting.

Rough weather hit the *Nomad* and halted excavation for forty-eight hours. High seas had half the crew down for the count despite seasick pills and patches. Tate and her cast-iron constitution rode out the storm with a Thermos of coffee at her worktable.

She'd left the cabin to a moaning, green-faced Lorraine.

The rock and roll of the boat didn't stop her from cataloguing the newest additions to the trove.

'I thought I'd find you here.'

She looked up, let her fingers pause on her keyboard and smiled at Hayden. 'I thought you were lying down.' She tilted her head. 'You're a little pale yet, but you've lost that interesting green tinge.' Her smile widened wickedly. 'Want a cookie?'

'Feeling smug?' Warily, he kept his eyes averted from the plate of cookies on the table. 'I hear Bowers is having a great time finding new ways to describe pork to Dart.'

'Hmm. Bowers and I, and a few of the others, enjoyed quite a hardy breakfast this morning.' She laughed. 'Rest easy, Hayden, I won't describe it to you. Have a seat?'

'It's embarrassing for the team leader to lose his dignity this way.' Grateful, he lowered himself into a folding chair. 'Too much time in the classroom, not enough in the field, I guess.'

'You're doing okay.' Happy to have company, she turned away from the monitor. 'The entire film crew's down. I hate to be pleased with anyone's misfortune, but it's a relief not to have them hovering for a couple days.'

'A documentary will pump up interest in this kind of expedition,' he pointed out. 'We can use the exposure, and the grants.'

'I know. It isn't often you have the benefit of a privately funded expedition, or one that pays off so successfully. Look at this, Hayden.' She lifted a gold watch, complete with chain and fob. 'Beautiful, isn't it? The detail of etching on the cover. You can practically smell the roses.'

Lovingly, she rubbed a thumb over the delicately etched spring of buds before carefully opening the clasp.

' "To David, my beloved husband, who makes time stop for me. Elizabeth. 2/4/49." '

Her heart sighed over it. 'There was a David and Elizabeth MacGowan on the manifest,' she told Hayden in a voice that had thickened. 'And their three children. She and her eldest daughter survived. She lost a son, another daughter, and her beloved David. Time stopped for them, and never started again.'

She closed the watch gently. 'He'd have been wearing this when the ship went down,' she murmured. 'He'd have kept it with him. He might have even opened it, read the inscription one last time after he said goodbye to her and their children. They never saw each other again. For a hundred and fifty years, this token of how much she loved him has been waiting for someone to find it. And remember them.'

'It's humbling,' Hayden said after a moment, 'when the student outstrips the teacher. You have more than I ever did,' he added when Tate glanced up in surprise. 'I would see a watch, the style, the manufacturer. I would note the inscription down, pleased to have a date to corroborate my calculation of its era. I might give David and Elizabeth a passing thought, certainly I would have looked for them in the manifest. But I wouldn't see them. I wouldn't feel them.'

'It isn't scientific.'

'Archeology is meant to study culture. Too often we forget that people make culture. The best of us don't. The best of us make it matter.' He laid a hand over hers. 'The way you do.'

'I don't know what to do when it makes me sad.' She turned her hand over so that their fingers linked. 'If I could, I'd take this and I'd find their great-great-grandchildren so I could say – look, this is part of David and Elizabeth. This is who they were.' Feeling foolish, she set the watch aside. 'But it doesn't belong to me. It doesn't even belong to them now. It belongs to SeaSearch.'

'Without SeaSearch, it would never have been found.'

'I understand that. I do.' Needing to clarify her own feelings, she leaned closer. 'What we're doing here is important, Hayden. The way we're doing it is innovative and efficient. Over and above the fortune we're bringing up, there's knowledge, discovery, theory. We're making the *Justine*, and the people who died with her, real and vital again.'

'But?'

'That's where I stumble. Where will David's watch go, Hayden? And the dozens and dozens of other personal treasures people carried with them? We have no control over it, because no matter how important our work, we're employees. We're dots, Hayden, in some huge conglomerate. SeaSearch to Poseidon, Poseidon to Trident, and on.'

His lips curved. 'Most of us spend our working lives as dots, Tate.'

'Are you content with that?'

'I suppose I am. I'm able to do the work I love, teach, lecture, publish. Without those conglomerates, with their slices of social conscience, or eye for a tax write-off, I'd never be able to take time for this kind of hands-on field work and still eat on a semi-regular basis.'

It was true, of course. It made perfect sense. And yet . . . 'But is it enough, Hayden? Should it be enough? How much are we missing by being up here? Not risking anything, or experiencing the hunt. Not having some claim or control over what we do, and what we discover. Aren't we in danger of losing the passion that pulled us into this in the first place?'

'You aren't.' His heart began to accept what his head had told him all along. She would never be for him. She was an exotic flower to his simple, plodding drone. 'You'll never lose it, because it's what defines you.'

In a symbolic farewell to a foolish dream, he lifted her hand and pressed his lips to her knuckles.

'Hayden . . .'

He could read the concern, the regret and, painfully, the sympathy in her eyes. 'Don't worry. Just a token of admiration from colleague to colleague. I have a suspicion we're not going to be working together much longer.'

'I haven't decided,' she said quickly.

'I think you have.'

'I have responsibilities here. And I owe you, Hayden, for recommending me for this position.'

'Your name was already on the list,' he corrected. 'I merely agreed with the choice.'

'But I thought–' Her brow creased.

'You've earned a reputation, Tate.'

'I appreciate that, Hayden, but … Already on the list, you said. Whose list?'

'Trident's. The brass there was impressed with your record. Actually, I got the feeling there was some definite pressure to put you on, from one of the moneymen. Not that I wasn't happy to go along with the recommendation.'

'I see.' For reasons she couldn't name, her throat felt dry. 'Who would that be, the moneyman?'

'Like you said, I'm just a dot.' He shrugged his shoulders as he rose. 'Anyway, should you decide to resign before the expedition is finished, I'd be sorry to lose you, but it's your choice.'

'You're getting ahead of me.' It made her nervous to realize she'd been singled out somehow, but she smiled at Hayden. 'But thanks.'

When he left her, she rubbed her hands over her mouth. Where had this spooky feeling come from? she wondered. Why hadn't she known about a list, or that her name had been on it?

Turning to her monitor, she clattered keys, eyes narrowed on the screen. Trident, Hayden had said. So she would bypass Poseidon and SeaSearch for the moment. To find where the power was at any level, you looked for the money.

'Hey, friends and neighbors.' Bowers strolled in, gnawing on a chicken leg. 'Lunch is up, in more ways than one.' He wiggled his brows at Tate and waited for her to chuckle.

'Give me a hand here, Bowers.'

'Sure, sweet thing. My hand is your hand.'

'Just work your magic on the computer. I want to find out who the big backers are in Trident.'

'Going to write thank-you notes?' Setting his lunch aside, he wiped his hands on his shirtfront and started in.

'Hmm ... a lot of layers here,' he murmured after a moment. 'Good thing I'm the best. You're hooked up to the main here, so the data we need's in there somewhere. Always is. You want board of directors, or what?'

'No,' she said slowly. 'Forget that. Ownership of the *Nomad*, Bowers, under the corporation. Who owns the ship?'

'Ownership shouldn't be tough to find. Not with your friendly technology. SeaSearch owns it, baby. Hold on ... donated. God, I love philanthropists. Some cat named VanDyke.'

Tate stared at the screen. 'Silas VanDyke.'

'He's a big wheel and a big deal. You musta heard of him. Finances a lot of expeditions. We ought to give the man a big, sloppy kiss.' His grin faded when he looked down at Tate's face. 'What's up?'

'I am.' She gritted her teeth against the fury. 'That son of a bitch put me on here. That ... Well, I'm taking myself off.'

'Off?' Baffled, Bowers stared at her. 'Off what?'

'He thought he could use me.' Almost blind with temper, she stared at the artifacts carefully arranged on her worktable. David and Elizabeth's watch. 'For this. The hell with him.'

Matthew hung up the phone, picked up his coffee. Another bridge burned, he thought. Or maybe, just maybe, the first couple of planks set in place on a new one.

He was sailing for Hatteras in the morning.

If nothing else, he mused, it would be a good test of the *Mermaid*'s seaworthiness.

The boat was finished, painted, polished and named. He and LaRue had taken her out several times over the last few days on short runs. She sailed like a dream.

Matthew sat back now, pleasantly tired. Maybe he'd finally done something that would last.

Even the name had personal significance for him. He'd had the dream again, the one of Tate in the deep, dark sea. He didn't need Freud to explain it to him. He'd been in contact with Ray often over the last few weeks. Tate's name had come up, as had the *Isabella*, and memories of that summer.

Naturally, it had made him think, and look back, so the dream had come.

Tate might have been no more than a wistful memory, but the dream had been so immediate that he'd felt compelled to christen the boat for it. Or in a roundabout way, he supposed, for her.

He wondered if he would see her, doubted it. And letting himself slide into relaxation, told himself it didn't matter one way or the other.

The screen door whined open, slammed. LaRue came in with bags of takeout burgers and fries. 'You made your phone call?' he asked.

'Yeah. I told Ray we'd start out in the morning.' Lifting his arms over his head, Matthew linked his fingers and stretched. 'Weather looks good. Shouldn't take us more than three or four days at an easy clip. That'll give us a chance to shake her down.'

'I look forward to the meeting of him and his wife.' LaRue dug up paper plates. 'He didn't tell you more about what he found?'

'He wants me to see it in person.' Suddenly ravenous,

Matthew helped himself to a burger. 'He's set on heading out for the West Indies by the middle of April. I told him that suited us.'

LaRue's gaze met Matthew's, and held. 'The sooner the better.'

'You're crazy going back there.' Face haggard, Buck stepped in from the bedroom. 'The place is cursed. The *Isabella*'s cursed. Took your father, didn't it?' His gait slow, measured, he came forward. 'Nearly took me. Should have.'

Matthew doused his fries with enough salt to make LaRue wince. 'VanDyke took my father,' he said calmly. 'A shark took your leg.'

'Angelique's Curse caused it.'

'Maybe it did.' Matthew chewed thoughtfully. 'If it did, I figure I've got a claim on it.'

'That thing's bad luck to the Lassiters.'

'It's time I changed my luck.'

Unsteady, Buck braced a hand on the tiny linoleum-topped table. 'Maybe you figure I only care what happens to you 'cause of what'll happen to me. That ain't the way it is. Your father expected I'd look after you. I did the best I could long as I could.'

'I haven't needed looking after for a long time.'

'Maybe not. And maybe I've been fucking up when it comes to you, when it comes to me the past few years. You're all I've got, Matthew. Truth is, you're all I ever gave most of a damn about.'

Buck's voice broke, causing Matthew to close his eyes and will away the worst edge of guilt. 'I'm not spending the rest of my life paying for something I couldn't stop, or watching you finish the job the shark started.'

'I'm asking you to stay. I figure we could start a business. Take tourists out, fishermen, that kind of thing.' Buck swallowed hard. 'I'd pull my weight this time around.'

'I can't do it.' Appetite gone, Matthew pushed his food aside and stood. 'I'm going after the *Isabella*. Whether I find her or not, I'm picking up my life again. There are plenty of wrecks out there, and I'm damned if I'm going to spend the rest of my life salvaging metal or chauffeuring tourists instead of hunting gold.'

'There's nothing I can do to stop you.' Buck looked down at his trembling hands. 'I didn't figure there was.' He took a deep breath, straightened his shoulders. 'I'm going with you.'

'Look, Buck–'

'I haven't had one fucking drink in ten days.' Buck fisted his hands, forced them to relax again. 'I'm dry. Maybe I'm a little rocky yet, but I'm dry.'

For the first time, Matthew looked at him. There were shadows under the eyes, but the eyes were clear. 'You've gone ten days before, Buck.'

'Yeah. But not on my own. I got a stake in this, too, Matthew. Scares the hell out of me, the thought of going back. But if you go, I go. Lassiters stick together,' he managed before his voice cracked again. 'You want me to beg you not to leave me behind?'

'No. Christ.' He rubbed a hand over his face. There were a dozen logical, viable reasons to refuse. And only one to agree. Buck was family. 'I can't baby-sit you, or worry about you sneaking a bottle. You have to work, earn your space on the boat.'

'I know what I gotta do.'

'LaRue' – Matthew turned to the man quietly eating his takeout dinner – 'you've got a stake in this. Where do you stand?'

Politely, LaRue swallowed, dabbed his mouth with a paper napkin. 'Me, I figure two more hands don't get in the way, long as they're steady.' He shrugged his shoulder. 'If they shake, you can take him for ballast.'

Humiliated, Buck set his jaw. 'I'll pull my weight. James wanted the *Isabella*. I'll help you get her for him.'

'All right.' Matthew nodded. 'Pack your gear. We leave at first light.'

Chapter Fourteen

THE LITTLE PLANE bounced on the runway and woke Tate out of a half doze. For the past thirty-eight hours she had been almost constantly on the move, juggling herself from boats to planes to cabs. She'd crossed a hefty slice of the Pacific, an entire continent, and all the varying time zones.

Her eyes told her it was day, but her body didn't have a clue.

At the moment, she felt as though she were made out of thin, fragile glass that would easily shatter at a loud noise or a careless bump.

But she was home. Or as close to home as the tiny airport in Frisco on Hatteras Island. All that was left was one quick car ride, and then, she vowed, she would avoid anything that moved for at least twenty-four hours.

Shifting carefully, she reached down for her carry-on. The tuna can with propellers she'd caught in Norfolk was empty but for her and the pilot. Once he'd taxied to a halt, he turned and gave her a thumbs-up sign which she returned with a vague gesture and an even vaguer smile.

She knew she had a great deal to think over, but her mind simply wouldn't function. Since she'd discovered the connection with VanDyke, she'd been in a tearing hurry to get home. Fate had played a hand. She'd been stuffing her gear into bags when she'd received a call from her father, asking her to come as soon as she was able to break away from the expedition.

Well, she'd broken away, she thought. In record time.

Since then, she'd done nothing but work and travel, catching snatches of sleep in between. She hoped VanDyke had already been informed she was thousands of miles from her post. She hoped he knew she'd thumbed her nose at him.

With her briefcase in one hand, the carry-on slung over her shoulder, she negotiated the narrow steps to the tarmac. Her knees wobbled, and she was grateful for the shaded glasses that cut the glare of the brilliant sun.

She saw them almost immediately, waving cheerfully while she waited for the pilot to unload her suitcase from cargo.

How little they changed, she mused. Maybe there was a touch more gray threading through her father's hair, but they were both so straight and slim and handsome. Both of them were grinning like fools, holding hands while they waved manically.

Half of Tate's travel fatigue drained just looking at them.

But what in the hell have you gotten yourselves into? she wondered. Secrets that couldn't be shared over the phone. Plots and plans and adventures. That damned amulet, that damned wreck. The damned Lassiters.

It had been Ray's enthusiasm about the possibility of hooking up with the Lassiters again that had weighed the scales in favor of Tate's trip directly to Hatteras instead of to her own apartment in Charleston. She only hoped he'd listened to her and held off contacting Matthew. It was incomprehensible to her that any of them would want a repeat of that horrendous summer.

Well, she was here now, she told herself as she gripped the strap and rolled her suitcase behind her. And she would talk some sense into her wonderful, but naive, parents.

'Oh, honey. Honey, it's so good to see you.' Marla's arms came around her, gripped tight. 'It's been so long. Nearly a year this time.'

'I know. I've missed you.' On a laugh, she let her carry-on drop so that she could pull her father into the embrace. 'I've missed both of you. Oh, and you look terrific.' Tearing up, she pulled back to take a long, close-up look. 'Really terrific. Mom, you've changed your hair. It's almost as short as mine used to be.'

'Do you like it?' Womanlike, Marla patted her sassily cropped do.

'It's great. Totally now.' And so youthfully flattering, Tate wondered how this pretty, smooth-faced woman could be her mother.

'I'm doing so much gardening now. It always seemed to be in the way. Honey, you're so thin. You've been working too hard.' Brow creased, she turned to her husband. 'Ray, I told you she's been working too hard.'

'You told me,' he agreed and rolled his eyes. 'Over and over. How was the trip, baby?'

'Endless.' She wriggled her shoulders to loosen them as they walked through the small terminal to where Ray had parked his jeep. Stifling a yawn, she shook her head. 'The bottom line is, I'm here.'

'We're glad you are.' Ray stowed the luggage in the back of the jeep. 'We wanted you in on this trip, Tate, but

I feel guilty knowing you resigned from your expedition. I know it was important to you.'

'Not as important as I thought.' She climbed into the back of the jeep, let her head fall back. She didn't want to bring up VanDyke, and his connection. Not yet at least. 'I'm glad I was part of it. I really admire the people I was working with, and I'd be thrilled to work with any of them again. And the whole process was fascinating. But it was impersonal. By the time any of the artifacts got to me, they'd been through so many other hands, it was almost like taking something out of a display case to examine.' Wearily, she concluded: 'You understand?'

'Yes.' Because Marla had warned him, Ray repressed his need to rattle away about his own plans. Give her a little time, Marla had insisted. Take it slow.

'You're home now,' Marla said. 'The first thing you're going to do is have a good, hot meal and a nap.'

'No argument. Once my head clears, I want to hear all about this idea of yours to go after the *Isabella*.'

'When you've read through my research,' Ray said cheerfully as he turned toward the village of Buxton, 'you'll see why I'm so eager to get moving.' He opened his mouth to continue, noticed his wife's warning glance and subsided. 'After you've rested a bit, we'll get it all together.'

'At least tell me what you found that started the ball rolling,' she began as he turned through a break in the pines and drove up the sandy lane. 'Oh, the azaleas are blooming.'

She was caught, leaning out the window to draw in the scent of pine and bay and blooms mixed with the aroma of water. It looked, as Tate remembered, like a fairy tale.

Marla had cleverly interspersed flowering shrubs among the trees, naturalized with spring and summer bulbs so that splashes and flows of color seemed gloriously wild and unplanned.

Near the two-story cedar house with its wide-screened porch, flower beds were only slightly more formal, with low-growing rock cress, sunny primroses and flowering sage giving way to nodding columbine and larkspur. Annuals and perennials thrived, while others waited for their season.

'You've created a rock garden,' Tate observed, craning her head when the jeep turned into a widened slot facing the sound.

'My new project. We've so much shade here I have to be very choosy. And you should see my herb bed around back by the kitchen.'

'Everything looks fabulous.' Tate stepped out of the jeep and looked at the house. 'And it's so quiet,' she said softly. 'Just the water, the birds, the breeze through the pines. I don't know how you ever leave it.'

'Whenever we come back from one of our little jaunts, we love it that much more.' Ray hefted her bags. 'It'll be a great place to retire.' He winked at his wife. 'When we're ready to grow up.'

'That'll be the day.' More delighted than she'd imagined to be there, Tate started along the walking stones set into the gentle slope. 'I suppose I'll be ready for knitting or bingo long before either of–' She halted at the back door. The colorful hammock she'd bought her father during a trip to Tahiti was stretched in its usual patch of sun. But it was occupied. 'You have company?'

'No, not company. Old friends.' Marla opened the screen door. 'They arrived just before dusk last night. We're loaded with weary travelers, aren't we, Ray?'

'Got a full house.'

Tate could see little more than a mop of dark hair that flopped over mirrored glasses, a hint of a tanned, muscular body. It was enough to have her stomach clench into several painful knots.

'What old friends?' she asked in a carefully neutral tone.

'Buck and Matthew Lassiter.' Marla was already in the kitchen, checking the clam chowder she'd had heating for lunch. 'And their shipmate LaRue. An interesting character, isn't he, Ray?'

'You bet.' Ray kept a bright smile on his face. He hadn't gotten around to mentioning to Marla their daughter's objection to the renewal of the old partnership. 'You'll get a kick out of him, Tate. I'm just going to put your things in your room.' And escape.

'Where's Buck?' Tate asked her mother. Though she'd gone into the kitchen, she kept her eye on the hammock through the window.

'Oh, he's around somewhere.' She sampled the chowder, nodded. 'He looks so much better than he did the last time we saw him.'

'Drinking?'

'No. Not a drop since he's been here. Sit down, honey. Let me fix you a bowl.'

'Not just yet.' Tate set her shoulders. 'I think I'll go out and renew acquaintance.'

'That's nice. You tell Matthew his lunch is ready.'

'Right.' She intended to tell him a great deal more than that.

The sand and springy grass muffled her footsteps. Though she was certain she could have marched up with a brass band and he wouldn't have stirred. The sunlight slanted over him. Beautifully, she thought, infuriated.

He was beautiful. No amount of resentment and disdain could deny it. His hair was mussed and obviously hadn't seen a barber's care for some time. In sleep his face was relaxed, that gorgeous mouth soft. It was a bit bonier than it had been eight years ago, she supposed, deepening the hollows of his cheeks. And that only added to the instant, sexual punch. His body was trim, muscled, and looked hard as granite with its covering of ripped jeans and faded T-shirt.

She let herself take a good long look, scrupulously monitoring her own reaction as she would monitor any lab experiment. An initial jump of the pulse, maybe, she judged. But that was only natural when a woman came across a stunning animal.

She was grateful to report that after that one visceral jolt, she felt nothing but annoyance, resentment and good, old-fashioned anger at finding him napping on her turf.

'Lassiter, you bastard.'

He didn't stir; his chest continued to rise and fall rhythmically. With a grim smile, she planted her feet, took a good hold on the edge of the hammock. Putting her back into it, she heaved.

Matthew came awake halfway through the roll. He had a quick glimpse of the ground rushing up, threw his hands out instinctively to catch himself. He grunted when he hit, swore when a prickly needle of a thistle jabbed his thumb. Groggy and disoriented, he shook his head. Tossing his hair back, he shifted until he was sitting on the ground.

The first thing he saw were small, narrow feet encased in practical and well-worn walking boots. Then there were the legs. A lot of them. Long, feminine and wonderfully shaped in snug black leggings. Under different circumstances, he could have passed a great deal of time happily studying them.

Shifting his gaze a bit higher, he encountered a black shirt, mannish with its tail sweeping hips that were definitely not a man's. Lovely breasts, high, adding a nice curve to the shirt.

Then the face.

The juices the body had stirred went directly to simmer.

She'd changed, unfairly, he thought. Gorgeously. Mouth-wateringly. While she'd been fresh, lovely and sweet at twenty, the woman she'd become was heart-stopping.

Her skin was ivory, almost transparently pure with just a blush of rose. Her unpainted mouth was full, luscious, and set in a badtempered pout that had his own mouth going bone-dry. She'd let her hair grow, and it was swept back now in a no-nonsense ponytail that left that face unframed. Behind her shaded lenses, her eyes were hot with anger.

Realizing he was on the edge of gawking, Matthew unfolded himself. In defense, he tilted his head and offered a quick, careless smile.

'Hey, Red. Long time.'

'What the hell are you doing here, getting my parents tangled up in some ridiculous scheme?'

In a negligent move, he leaned on a tree. His knees were water. 'Nice to see you, too,' he said dryly. 'And you've got it backwards. Ray's got the scheme. I'm going along for the ride.'

'Taking him for a ride more likely.' Disgust fountained up. It wasn't possible to swallow all of it. 'The partnership was dissolved eight years ago, and it's going to stay that way. I want you to go back to whatever hole you climbed out of.'

'You running things around here now, Red?'

'I'll do whatever I have to, to protect my parents from you.'

'I never did anything to Ray or Marla.' He lifted a brow. 'Or to you, for that matter. Though in that area I had plenty of opportunity.'

Her cheeks heated. She hated him for it, hated those damned glasses that hid his eyes and tossed her own reflection back at her. 'I'm not a young girl with stars in her eyes now, Lassiter. I know exactly what you are. An opportunist with no sense of loyalty or responsibility. We don't need you.'

'Ray thinks differently.'

'He's soft-hearted.' She angled her chin. 'I'm not. Maybe you've conned him into putting his money into some wild plan, but I'm here to put a stop to it. You're not going to use him.'

'Is that how you see it? I'm using him?'

'You're a born user.' She said it mildly, pleased with her control. 'And when things get rough, you walk. Like you walked on Buck, leaving him in some hole-in-the-wall trailer park in Florida while you sailed off. I was there.' All but shimmering with resentment, she stepped closer. 'Almost a year ago, I went to see him. I saw that sty you dropped him in. He was all alone, sick. There was barely any food. He said he couldn't remember the last time you'd been there, that you were off diving somewhere.'

'That's true enough.' He'd have sawed off his tongue with his own pride before he would have told her differently.

'He needed you, but you were too self-involved to give a damn. You left him to drink himself half to death. If my parents knew how callous, how cold you really are, they'd pitch you out on your ass.'

'But you know.'

'Yes, I know. I knew eight years ago when you were considerate enough to show me. That's the only thing I owe you, Matthew, and I'll pay you back by letting you have the chance to bow out of this business gracefully.'

'No deal.' He folded his arms. 'I'm going after the *Isabella,* Tate, one way or the other. I've got my own debts to pay.'

'You won't use my parents to pay them.' She turned on her heel and strode off.

Alone, Matthew gave himself a minute to let the storm of emotions settle. Slowly he sat on the hammock, braced his feet to keep it from rocking.

He hadn't expected her to greet him with open arms and a sunny smile. But he hadn't expected such complete and utter loathing. Dealing with it would be difficult, but necessary.

Yet that wasn't the worst of it. Not by a long shot. He'd been so sure he was over her. She'd barely been more than a passing thought in his life for years. It was a jolt, an embarrassing, devastating jolt to realize that rather than being over her, he was desperately, foolishly in love with her.

Still.

Before Marla could repeat her offer of lunch, Tate had sailed through the kitchen, into the homey, cluttered living room, down the steps to the foyer and out the front door.

She needed to breathe.

At least she'd held on to her temper, she told herself as she stormed over the sandy soil toward the sound. She hadn't decked him the way she'd wanted to. And she'd made her position crystal clear. She would see to it that Matthew Lassiter was packed and gone by nightfall.

Tate took another gulp of air as she stepped on the narrow dock. Moored there was the *New Adventure*, the forty-two-foot cruiser her parents had christened only two years before. She was a beauty, and though Tate had only managed one brief run on her, she knew the boat to be quick and agile.

She might have gone onboard, just to spend a few minutes alone with her anger, if there hadn't been another boat on the other side of the pier.

She was frowning at it, its unusual lines and double-hull construction, when Buck came on deck.

'Ahoy there, pretty girl.'

'Ahoy yourself.' Grinning, she hurried onto the pier. 'Permission to come aboard, sir.'

'Permission granted.' He laughed, holding out a hand as she leapt gracefully down.

She could see instantly that he'd lost some of the weight the bloat of drink and bad food had ballooned on him. His color was ruddy again, his eyes clear. When she hugged him, there was no stale scent of whiskey and sweat.

'It's good to see you,' she told him. 'You look renewed.'

'I'm getting by.' He shifted uncomfortably. 'You know what they say, a day at a time.'

'I'm proud of you.' She pressed her cheek to his, but sensing his embarrassment, pulled back. 'Well, tell me about this.' She spread her arms wide to encompass the boat. 'How long have you had her?'

'Matthew finished her only a few days before we sailed up.'

Her smile faded; her arms dropped back to her sides. 'Matthew?'

'He built her,' Buck said with pride ringing in every syllable. 'Designed her, worked on her off and on for years.'

'Matthew designed and built this boat, himself?'

'Just about single-handed. I'll show you around.' As he led her around the deck from bow to stern, he ran a commentary on the design, the stability, the speed. Every few minutes, his hand would run along a rail or fitting with affection.

'I gave him grief over her,' Buck admitted. 'But the boy proved me wrong. We ran into a squall off of Georgia, and she took it like a lady.'

'Umm-hmm.'

'She carries two-hundred-gallon freshwater capacity,' he went on, bragging like a doting papa. 'And storage, the way he set her out, she's got as much as you find on a sixty-footer. Got twin motors, a hundred and forty-five shaft horsepower.'

'Sounds like he's in a hurry,' she muttered. When she stepped into the pilothouse, her eyes widened. 'God, Buck, the equipment.'

Stunned, she walked through, examining. Top-of-the-line sonar, depth finders, magnetometer. The cockpit held excellent and pricey navigational equipment, a radio-telephone, radio direction finder, a Nav Tex for offshore weather data and, to her complete amazement, an LCD-screen video plotter.

'The boy wanted the best.'

'Yes, but–' She wanted to ask how he'd paid for it, but was afraid the answer might be her parents. Instead she took a deep breath and promised to find the answer herself, later. 'It's quite a setup.'

The pilothouse boasted full visibility, access from starboard and port. There was a wide flat chart table, empty now, and glossy cabinets with brass fittings for storage. Even a settee berth with thick navy padding over wood had been built into a corner.

A far cry, she mused, from the *Sea Devil.*

'Come take a look at the cabins. Hell, guess I should call 'em staterooms. Got two of them, with heads. Sleep snug as a bug down there. And the galley's one even your ma would be proud of.'

'Sure, I'd love to see. Buck,' she began as they exited to stern. 'How long has Matthew been planning on going back to look for the *Isabella*?'

'Can't say. Probably since we left the *Marguerite*. Ask me, it's been preying on his mind all along. All he lacked was the time and the means.'

'The means,' Tate repeated. 'Did he come into some money then?'

'LaRue bought in.'

'LaRue? Who–'

'Did I hear my name?'

Tate saw a figure at the base of the companionway. As she stepped down she made out a thin, nattily dressed man somewhere between forty and fifty. Gold winked out of his grin as he offered a hand to help her down.

'Ah, mademoiselle, my head spins.' He swept her hand up to his lips.

'Don't pay this scrawny Canuk any mind, Tate. He thinks he's a ladies' man.'

'A man who reveres and appreciates women,' LaRue corrected. 'I'm enchanted to meet you at last, and to have such beauty grace our humble home.'

At a glance, the neat, shipshape deckhouse looked anything but humble. Wood gleamed on the dining bar where colorfully padded stools stood waiting. Someone had hung framed charts, yellowed with age, on the walls. She was astonished to see a vase of fresh daffodils on a table.

'Guess it's a big step up from the *Sea Devil*,' Buck commented.

'From *Sea Devil* to *Mermaid*.' LaRue grinned. 'Can I offer you tea, mademoiselle?'

'No.' She was still blinking in shock. 'Thanks. I have to get back. There are a number of things I have to talk over with my parents.'

'Ah, yes. Your father, he was thrilled that you would be going with us. Me, I'm delighted to know two such lovely ladies will be adding charm to the journey.'

'Tate's not just a lady,' Buck said. 'She's a hell of a diver, a natural born treasure hunter, and she's a scientist.'

'A woman of many talents,' LaRue murmured. 'I'm humbled.'

Baffled, she stared at him. 'You shipped with Matthew?'

'Indeed. It has been my trial to try to induce some culture into his life.'

Buck snorted. 'Shit with an accent's still shit. Begging your pardon, Tate.'

'I've got to get back,' she said again, dazed. 'Nice to have met you, Mr. LaRue.'

'LaRue only.' He kissed her hand again. '*A bientôt*.'

Buck shouldered LaRue aside. 'I'll walk back with you a ways.'

'Thanks.' Tate waited until they were back on the pier and headed for shore. 'Buck, you said Matthew's been working on that boat on and off for years?'

'Yeah, whenever he had a little extra time or money. Musta done a dozen drawings and designs 'fore he settled on this one.'

'I see.' That kind of ambition, and tenacity, was more than she would have given him credit for. Unless...

'All right.' She put a friendly hand on his arm. 'I hope you won't take this the wrong way, but I'm not sure any of this is a good idea.'

'You mean us partnering up with Ray and Marla and going back?'

'Yes. Finding the *Marguerite* was practically a miracle. The odds of it happening twice are very dim. I know it took a long time for all of us to get over the disappointment before. I hate to see you, and my parents, go through all of it again.'

Buck paused to shove his glasses back into place. 'I can't say I'm happy about it myself.' Automatically, he reached down to rub the artificial leg. 'Bad memories, bad luck. Matthew's set, though. And I owe him.'

'That's not true. He owes you. He owes you his life.'

'Maybe he did.' Buck grimaced. 'Fact is, I made him pay for it. I didn't save his father. Don't know if I could have, but I didn't. Never went after VanDyke. Don't know what good it woulda done, but I didn't. Then when my time came to pay, I didn't take it like a man should.'

'Don't talk like that.' She hooked a protective arm through his. 'You're doing wonderfully.'

'Now. For a couple of weeks. Don't really make up for all the years between. I let the boy shoulder it all, the work and the blame.'

'He left you alone,' Tate said furiously. 'He should have stayed by you. Supported you.'

'Done nothing but support me. Worked at a job he hated so I could have what I needed. I took it, used it and tossed it in his face every chance I got. I'm ashamed of that.'

'I don't know what you're talking about. The last time I came to see you–'

'I lied to you.' He stared down at his feet, knowing he had to risk her affection for his own self-respect. 'I made it seem like he pushed me off, didn't come around, didn't do nothing for me. Maybe he didn't come around much, but it's hard to blame him. But he sent me money, took care of things best he could. Paid to have me in detox I don't know how many times.'

'But I thought–'

'I wanted you to think. Wanted him to think it, too, 'cause it was easier for me if everybody was miserable. He did the best he could.'

Far from convinced, she shook her head. 'He should have stayed with you.'

'He did what he had to do,' Buck insisted, and Tate bowed to unshakable family loyalty.

'Regardless, this new brainstorm strikes me as being impulsive and dangerous. I'm going to do my best to talk my parents out of it. I hope you understand.'

'Can't blame you for thinking twice about hooking up with the Lassiters again. You do what you have to do, Tate, but I'll tell you, your daddy's got the wind in his sails.'

'I'll just have to change his course.'

Chapter Fifteen

BUT THERE WERE times when the wind ran strong and true and defeated even the most determined sailor.

Tate tolerated Matthew's presence at dinner. She made conversation with Buck and LaRue at the big chestnut table. She listened to their stories, laughed at their jokes.

Her heart simply wasn't hard enough to spoil the celebratory mood, or dim the light of delight in her father's eyes with cold, hard facts and logic.

Because she was sharp enough to notice her mother's occasional looks of concern in her direction, Tate managed to be marginally polite to Matthew. Though she did her best to limit contact to the obligatory 'pass the salt.'

When the meal was over, she maneuvered the situation in her favor by insisting on clearing up the dishes alone with her father.

'Bet you haven't had a meal like that in a month of Sundays,' he commented, humming under his breath as he stacked dishes.

'In a year of Sundays. I'm sorry I had to pass on the pecan pie.'

'You'll have some later. That LaRue's something, isn't he? Exchanging recipes with your mother one minute and arguing foreign policy the next with a side trip into baseball and eighteenth-century art.'

'He's a regular Renaissance man,' she murmured. But she was holding out on judgment of him. Any friend of Matthew's, she thought, required careful scrutiny. Even if he was interesting, well read and charming. Particularly if he was. 'I haven't figured out what he's doing with Matthew.'

'Oh, I think they suit each other well enough.' Ray filled the sink with soapy water for the pots as Tate loaded the dishwasher. 'Matthew's always had a lot going for him, he's just never had much chance to put it all to use.'

'I'd say he's a man who knows how to make the most of an opportunity. Which is something I want to discuss with you.'

'The *Isabella*.' Sleeves pushed up, Ray began to attack pans in the sink. 'We're going to get to that, honey. Soon as everyone's had a chance to settle in for the evening. I held off saying anything more to the rest until you got here.'

'Dad, I know how you felt when we found that virgin wreck eight years ago. I know how I felt, so I understand that you may think it's a good idea to go back. But I'm not sure you're considering all the details, the pitfalls.'

'I've thought of them a great deal over the years, and little else for the last nine months. We had our share of luck, good and bad, the last time. But we've got a hell of a lot more going for us this time around.'

'Dad.' Tate slipped another plate into the dishwasher, straightened. 'If I have the right information, Buck hasn't dived since his accident, and LaRue worked on ship as a cook. He's never had on tanks in his life.'

'That's all true. Maybe Buck won't go under, but we can always use another hand on deck. As for LaRue, he's willing to learn, and I have a feeling he's a quick study.'

'There are six of us,' Tate went on, trying futilely to chip away at the optimism. 'Only three of whom can dive. I haven't done any serious diving myself in nearly two years.'

'Like riding a bike,' Ray said easily and set a pan aside to drain. 'We need people to read and run the equipment in any case. Now we've got a professional marine archeologist on hand, not one in training.' He sent her a beaming smile. 'Maybe you'll do your thesis on this expedition.'

'I'm not concerned about my thesis right now,' she said, straining for patience. 'I'm concerned about you. You and Mom have spent the last several years playing at hunting, Dad. Exploring established wrecks, pleasure diving, shell collecting. That's nothing compared to the full out physical labor needed for something like you have in mind.'

'I'm in shape,' he told her, vaguely insulted. 'I work out three times a week, dive regularly.'

Wrong tactic, she thought. 'Okay. What about the expense? It could take months of your time, plus the cost of supplies, equipment. This isn't a vacation you're talking about, or a hobby. Who's backing this venture?'

'Your mother and I are very stable financially.'

'Well.' Fighting temper, she snatched up a dishrag to swipe the counters. 'That answers my last question. You're putting your money on the line, which means you're carrying the Lassiters.'

'It's not a matter of carrying them, honey.' Genuinely puzzled, he pulled his hands out of the water and wiped them dry. 'It's a partnership, just like before. Any imbalance will be taken out of the profits once we salvage the wreck.'

'What if there isn't any wreck?' she exploded. 'I don't care if you toss your last penny away on a dream. I want you to enjoy everything you've worked for. But how can I stand by while you let that self-serving, opportunistic bastard take you for a ride?'

'Tate.' Alarmed at the way her voice carried, he patted her on the shoulder. 'I didn't know you were upset. I thought when you said you were coming back, you were committing to the idea.'

'I came back to try to stop you from making a mistake.'

'I'm not making one.' His face closed up in the way she knew it could when he was hurt. 'And there is a wreck. Matthew's father knew it, I know it. The *Isabella* is there, and Angelique's Curse is with her.'

'Not the amulet again.'

'Yes, the amulet again. That's what James Lassiter was looking for, what Silas VanDyke wants, and what we're going to have.'

'Why is it so important? This wreck, this necklace?'

'Because we lost something that summer, Tate,' he said quietly. 'More than the fortune that thief stole from us. More even than Buck's leg. We lost the joy in what we'd done, what we could do. We lost the magic of what could be. It's time we got it back.'

She let out a sigh. How could she fight dreams? Didn't she have her own, still? The museum she'd planned for, hoped for, most of her life. And someday she'd see it realized. Who was she to try to block her father's one abiding wish?

'All right. We can go back, just the three of us.'

'The Lassiters are part of it now, just as they were then. And if anyone has a right to find that wreck, and that amulet, it's Matthew.'

'Why?'

'Because it cost him a father.'

She didn't want to think of that. She didn't want to be able to visualize the young boy who had grieved helplessly over his dead father's body.

'The amulet doesn't mean any more to him than a means to an end, something to be sold to the highest bidder.'

'That's for him to decide.'

'That makes him,' she corrected, 'little better than VanDyke.'

'He hurt you that summer. Matthew.' Gently, Ray took her face in his hands. 'I knew there was something between you, but I didn't realize it had cut so deep.'

'This has nothing to do with that,' she insisted. 'It has to do with who and what he is.'

'Eight years is a long time, honey. Maybe you should step back and take another look. In the meantime, there are things I need to show you, all of you. Let's get everybody into my den.'

With reluctance, Tate joined the group in the warmly paneled room where her father did his research and wrote his articles for diving magazines. Deliberately, she moved to the opposite end of the room from Matthew and settled on the arm of her mother's chair.

With the windows open to the scents and music of the sound, it was just cool enough to indulge in a quiet fire. Ray walked behind his desk, cleared his throat like a nervous lecturer about to begin his speech.

'I know you all are curious about what prompted me to begin this venture. All of us know what happened eight years ago, what we found and what we lost. Every time I'd dive after that, I'd think about it.'

'Brood about it,' Marla corrected with a smile.

Ray smiled back at her. 'I couldn't let it go. I thought I had for a time, but then something would remind me, and set me off again. One day I had the flu, and Marla wouldn't let me out of bed. I passed the time with some television and happened across a documentary on salvaging. It was a wreck off Cape Horn, a rich one. And who was backing it, who was pulling in the glory, but Silas VanDyke.'

'Bastard,' Buck muttered. 'Probably pirated that one, too.'

'Might have, but the point is, he'd decided to film the proceedings. He wasn't on-camera much himself, but he did talk a little about some of the diving he'd done, other wrecks he'd discovered. The sonofabitch talked about the *Santa Marguerite*. He never bothered to mention it had already been found, excavated. The way he told it, he did it all, then being the generous soul he is, donated fifty percent of the proceeds to the government of St. Kitts.'

'In bribes and kickbacks,' Matthew decided.

'It got my blood up. I started researching again right then and there. I figured he'd gotten one wreck, but he wasn't going to get the other. I spent the better part of two years digging up every snatch of information I could find on the *Isabella*. No reference to that ship, that crew, that storm was too small or insignificant. That's how I found it. Or, how I found two very vital pieces to the puzzle. A map, and a reference to Angelique's Curse.'

Carefully, he lifted a book out of the top drawer. Its cover was tattered and held together by tape. Its pages were dry and yellowed.

'It's falling apart,' Ray said unnecessarily. 'I found it in a used-book store. *A Sailor's Life*. It was written in 1846, by the great-grandson of a survivor of the *Isabella*.'

'But there were no survivors,' Tate put in. 'That's one of the reasons the wreck's been so hard to find.'

'No recorded survivors.' Ray stroked the book as though it were a well-loved child. 'According to this, stories and legends the author transcribed from his grandfather's tales, José Baltazar washed ashore on the island of Nevis. He was a seaman on the *Isabella*, and he watched her go down as he clung half conscious to a plank probably from the wrecked *Santa Marguerite*. Matthew, I think your father had traced this same clue.'

'If that's true, what was he doing in Australia?'

'He was following Angelique's Curse.' Ray paused for effect. 'But he was a generation too soon. A British aristocrat, Sir Arthur Minnefield, had acquired the amulet from a French merchant.'

'Minnefield.' Buck narrowed his eyes in concentration. 'I remember seeing that name in James's notes. The night before he died he told me he'd been looking in the wrong place. He said how VanDyke had it wrong, how that damned necklace had gotten around. That's how he said it, "that damned necklace," and he was excited. When we were finished on the reef, he said how we were going to shake loose of VanDyke, turn the tables on him before he turned them on us. Said how we had to be careful of VanDyke and not move too fast. He had a lot more studying and figuring to do before we went after her.'

'My theory is he found another reference to the amulet, or to Baltazar.' Ray set the book carefully on his desk. 'You see, the amulet didn't go down on the reef, the ship did, Minnefield did, but Angelique's Curse survived. Details are sketchy for the next thirty years. Maybe it washed up on the beach or someone found it while exploring the reefs. I can't find any mention of it between 1706 and 1733. But Baltazar saw it around the neck of a young Spanish woman aboard the *Isabella*. He described it. He heard the legend, and he recounted it.'

Far from convinced, Tate folded her hands. 'If there's a reference to the amulet that places it on the *Isabella*, why hasn't VanDyke found it, and gone after the *Isabella* himself?'

'He was dead sure it was in Australia,' Buck told her. 'He was fired up about it, obsessed. He got it into his head James knew something more, dogged him about it.'

'And killed him for it,' Matthew said flatly. 'VanDyke's had teams working that wreck and that area for years.'

'But if my father found a reference that indicated the necklace was elsewhere,' Tate continued with stubborn logic, 'and your father found a reference, it's only reasonable that a man with VanDyke's resources, and his greed, would have found it as well.'

'Maybe the amulet didn't want him to find it.' LaRue spoke passively as he patiently rolled a cigarette.

'It's an inanimate object,' Tate retorted.

'So is the Hope Diamond,' LaRue said. 'The philosopher's stone, the Ark of the Covenant. Yet the legends surrounding them are vital.'

'The operative word is "legend." '

'All those degrees made you cynical,' Matthew commented. 'Too bad.'

'I think the point is,' Marla cut in, recognizing the warrior light in her daughter's eyes, 'that Ray has found something, not whether or not this amulet holds some sort of power.'

'Well put.' Ray rubbed the side of his nose. 'Where was I? Baltazar was captivated by the amulet, even after word began to pass about the curse, and the crew became uneasy. He believed the ship was wrecked because of the curse, and that he survived to tell the tale. He told it well,' Ray added. 'I've copied several pages of his reminiscences of the storm. You'll see when you read them that it was a hellish battle against the elements, a hopeless one. Of these two ships, the *Marguerite* succumbed first. As the *Isabella* broke up, passengers and crew were swept into the sea. He claims to have seen the Spanish lady, the amulet like a jeweled anchor around her neck, go down. Of course, that tidbit might have been for artistic effect.'

Ray passed out copied pages. 'In any case, he survived. The wind and the waves carried him away from land, from St. Kitts, or St. Christopher's as it was known then. He'd given up all hope, lost his sense of time when he saw the outline of Nevis. He didn't believe he could make it to shore as he was too weak to swim. But eventually he drifted in. A young native boy found him. He was delirious and near death for weeks. When he recovered, he had no desire to serve the Armada. Instead he let the world believe him dead. He remained on the island, married and passed down his stories of his adventures at sea.'

Ray took another paper from his pile. 'And, he drew maps. A map,' Ray continued, 'from an eyewitness who places the *Isabella* several degrees south-southeast from the wreck of the *Marguerite*. She's there. Waiting.'

Matthew rose to take the map. It was crude, and sparse, but he recognized the points of reference – the whale's tail of the peninsula of St. Kitts, the rising cone of Mount Nevis.

An old, almost forgotten need surged in him. The need to hunt. When he looked up, the grin he flashed was the one from his youth. Bold, reckless and irresistible.

'When do we leave?'

Tate couldn't sleep. There was too much racing inside her head, swimming in her blood. She understood, and struggled to accept, that the momentum was out of her hands. There would be no stopping her father from taking on this quest. None of the logic nor the personal doubts she used would sway him from partnering with the Lassiters.

At least the timing worked. She'd just tossed an enormous career advancement aside for principle. That gave her some satisfaction. And it also gave her the opportunity to help launch the expedition for the *Isabella*.

At least if she was there, right on hand, she could keep her eye on everyone. Matthew in particular.

So she was thinking of him when she stepped outside to face the moon and the wind that washed through the top of the pines.

She had loved him once. Over the years, she'd told herself it had been merely a crush, a young woman's infatuation with wild good looks and an adventurer's heart.

But that was a coward's lie.

She had loved him, Tate admitted, and tugged her jacket tighter against the night's moist breeze. Or had loved the man she'd thought he was, and could be. Nothing and no one had embraced her heart so completely before him. Just as nothing and no one had ever broken it so totally, and so callously.

She tugged a leaf from a fragrant bay laurel, spun it under her nose as she walked toward the water. It was a night for reflections, she supposed. The moon, nearly full, rode a sky crowded with hot stars. The air was full of perfume and promise.

Once she would have been seduced by that alone. Before her romantic side had been sliced away. She considered herself fortunate that she could now appreciate the night for what it was, and not spin dreams around it.

In a way, she knew she had Matthew to thank for opening her eyes. Rudely, painfully, but he'd opened them. She understood now that princes and pirates were for young, foolish girls to dream of. She had more solid goals than that.

If she had to put those goals aside for a time, she would. Everything she was, everything she'd accomplished, she owed to her parents' support and belief in her. There was nothing she wouldn't do to protect them. Even if it meant working shoulder-to-shoulder with Matthew Lassiter.

She stopped near the water, downcurrent from where the boats were docked. Her parents had built up the bank here with duck weed and wild grasses to fight erosion. Always the water stole from the land. Always the land adjusted.

It was a good lesson, she supposed. Things had been stolen from her. She'd adjusted.

'It's a nice spot, isn't it?'

Tate's shoulders tightened at the sound of his voice. She wondered how she hadn't sensed him. But for a man who spent his life at sea, he moved quietly on land.

'I thought you'd gone to bed.'

'We're bunked down in the boat.' He knew she didn't want him beside her, so perversely he stepped forward until their shoulders nearly brushed. 'Buck still snores like a freighter. Doesn't bother LaRue. But then, he sleeps like a corpse.'

'Try earplugs.'

'I'll just string a hammock out on deck. Like old times.'

'These are new times.' She took a bracing breath before she turned to him. As she'd expected, perhaps feared, he looked magnificent in the moonlight. Bold, exciting, even dangerous. How lucky she was that such traits no longer appealed to her. 'And we'd better lay out the ground rules.'

'You were always more into rules than me.' To suit himself he sat on a bale of duck grass, patted the space beside him in invitation. 'You go first.'

She ignored the invitation, and the half-empty bottle of beer he offered. 'This is a business arrangement. As I understand it, my parents are fronting the bulk of the expenses. I intend to keep an accurate account of your share.'

Her voice still carried those lovely liquid vowels of the south, he mused, the consonants blurring like soft shadows. 'Fine. Bookkeeping's your department.'

'You will pay them back, Lassiter. Every penny.'

He took a swallow of beer. 'I pay my debts.'

'I'll see to it you pay this one.' She paused a moment before moving from one practical matter to another. The moon mirrored prettily on the calm water, but she paid no heed to it. 'I understand you're teaching LaRue to dive.'

'I've been working with him.' Matthew moved his shoulders. 'He's catching on.'

'Will Buck dive?'

Even in the shadows, she saw his eyes glint. 'That's up to him. I'm not pushing him.'

'I wouldn't want you to.' She softened enough to move closer. 'He matters to me. I – I'm glad he's looking so well.'

'You're glad he's off the bottle.'

'Yes.'

'He's been off it before. Lasted a whole month once.'

'Matthew.' Before she'd realized it, she laid a hand on his shoulder. 'He's trying.'

'Aren't we all?' Abruptly, he grabbed her hand, tugged her down beside him. 'I'm tired of looking up at you. Besides, I can see you better down here, in the moonlight. You always had a face for moonlight.'

'Personal rule,' she said briskly. 'You keep your hands off me.'

'No problem. I don't need the frostbite. You've sure chilled down over the years, Red.'

'I've simply developed a more discerning taste.'

'College men.' His smile was a sneer. 'Always figured you'd go for the academic type.' Deliberately, he looked down at her hands, then back into her eyes. 'No rings. How come?'

'Let's keep our private lives private.'

'That's not going to be easy, seeing as we're going to be working in close quarters for some time.'

'We'll manage. And as to working arrangements, when we dive, one member of your team goes down with a member of ours. I don't trust you.'

'And you hid it so well,' he muttered. 'That's fine,' he continued. 'That suits me. I like diving with you, Tate. You're good luck.' He leaned back on his elbows, looked up at the stars. 'It's been a while since I dived in warm water. The North Atlantic's a bitch. You learn to hate her.'

'Then why did you dive there?'

He slanted her a look. 'Doesn't that come under the heading of private?'

She looked away, cursing herself. 'Yes, though it was professional curiosity that made me ask.'

So, he'd oblige her. 'There's money to be made salvaging metal wrecks. In case you haven't heard, World War II played hell with ships.'

'I thought the metal you were interested in was gold.'

'Whatever pays, sweetheart. I've got a feeling this trip's going to pay off big.' Because it pleased him almost as much as it hurt, he continued to study her profile. 'You're not convinced.'

'No, I'm not. But I am convinced this is something my father needs to do. The *Isabella* and the *Santa Marguerite* have fascinated him for years.'

'And Angelique's Curse.'

'Yes, from the moment he heard of it.'

'But you don't believe in curses anymore. Or magic. I guess you educated it out of your system.'

She couldn't have said why it stung to hear him say what was only the truth. 'I believe the amulet exists, and knowing my father, that it was aboard the *Isabella*. Finding it will be another matter altogether. And its value will come from its age and its stones and the weight of its gold, not from some superstition.'

'There's no more mermaid left in you, Tate.' He said it quietly, and stopped himself before his hand lifted to stroke her hair. 'You used to remind me of something fanciful that was as much at home in the sea as in the air. With all sorts of secrets in your eyes, and endless possibilities shimmering around you.'

Her skin shivered, not from the nippy little breeze, but from heat. In defense, her voice was flat and cool. 'I doubt very much if you had any sort of romantic flights of fancy where I was concerned. We're both aware of what you thought of me.'

'I thought you were beautiful. And even more out of reach than you are right now.'

Hating the fact that such careless lies could make her pulse jump, she rose quickly. 'It won't work, Lassiter. I'm not along on this trip to amuse you. We're business partners. Fifty-fifty since my father wants it that way.'

'Isn't that interesting?' he murmured. He set the bottle down and rose slowly until they were toe to toe. Until he could smell her hair. Until his fingers throbbed with the memory of how her skin felt under them. 'I still get to you, don't I?'

'Your ego's still in the same place.' She schooled her features to mild disdain. 'Just below the button of your jeans. Tell you what, Lassiter, if things get a little tedious and I'm desperate enough to try anything to break the monotony, I'll let you know. But until that unlikely event, try not to embarrass yourself.'

'I'm not embarrassed.' He grinned at her. 'Just curious.' Hoping to loosen some of the knots in his gut, he sat again. 'Any more rules, Red?'

She needed a minute before she could trust her voice. Somehow her heart had lodged in her throat. 'If, by some miracle, we find the *Isabella*, I will, as marine archeologist, catalogue and assess and preserve all the artifacts. Everything gets logged, down to the last nail.'

'Fine. Might as well put those degrees to use.'

She bristled at his obvious lack of respect for her field. 'That's just what I intend to do. Twenty percent of whatever we find will go to the government of St. Kitts and Nevis. And though it's only fair that it be put to a vote, I'll set aside what artifacts I find appropriate to donate.'

'Twenty percent's hefty, Red.'

'Try a little fame along with your fortune, Lassiter. If things work out as we hope, I'm going to negotiate with the government to establish a museum. The Beaumont-Lassiter Museum. If the wreck's as rich as reputed, you can spare ten percent of your share and still not have to work another day in your life. It'll keep you in shrimp and beer.'

Again he flashed a grin. 'Still stewing over that sword. You surprise me.'

'As long as we keep our cards on the table, there won't be any surprises. Those are my terms.'

'I can live with them.'

She nodded. 'There's one more. If we do find Angelique's Curse, it goes to the museum.'

He picked up his beer, drained it. 'No. You've had your terms, Tate. I've only got one of my own. The amulet's mine.'

'Yours?' She would have laughed if her teeth hadn't been clenched together. 'You don't have any stronger claim on it than the rest of us. Its potential value is tremendous.'

'Then you can assess it, catalogue it and deduct it from the rest of my take. But it's mine.'

'For what?'

'To pay off a debt.' He rose, and the look in his eyes had her backing up a step before she could stop herself. 'I'm going to wrap it around VanDyke's neck, and strangle him with it.'

'That's foolish.' Her voice shook. 'Crazy.'

'That's a fact. You live with that one, Tate, because that's how it's going to be. You've got your rules.' He cupped her chin in his hand and made her tremble. Not from the touch, not this time, but from the hotblooded murder boiling in his eyes. 'I've got mine.'

'You can't expect any of us to stand by while you plan to kill someone.'

'I don't expect anything.' He'd stopped expecting long ago. 'It just wouldn't be smart to get in my way. Now you'd better get some sleep. We've got a lot of work ahead of us.'

He was lost in the shadows of the trees almost immediately. To ward off the chill, Tate wrapped her arms tight around her body.

He'd meant it. She couldn't pretend otherwise. But she could tell herself that he'd lose this thirst for revenge in the hunt.

The odds were they'd never find the *Isabella*. And if they did, the odds were even higher against finding the amulet.

For the first time, she prepared to go on an expedition hoping for failure.

Chapter Sixteen

IT WAS BLISSFULLY easy to fall back into the old routine. Tate found herself pushing the purpose of the voyage to the back of her mind and simply enjoying the ride.

They left Hatteras Island behind on a bright spring morning with the seas at a light chop. The wind was just brisk enough for a jacket and she'd pulled her hair through the hole in the back of a Durham Bulls baseball cap. At her father's insistence, she had first shift at the wheel. And took the Atlantic.

They sailed toward Ocracoke with its pirate ghosts, waving at passengers on a passing ferry as seagulls swooped and called in their wake. Then land became a shadow to the west, and there was only sea.

'How's it feel, Skipper?' Ray slipped in behind her, hugging an arm over her shoulders.

'It feels good.' Tate lifted her face to the wind that rushed through the partially open windows of the bridge. 'I guess I've been a passenger too long.'

'Sometimes your mother and I will hop aboard and sail to nowhere for a day or two. I've enjoyed that.' Eyes on the horizon, he sighed deeply. 'But it sure feels good to be sailing to somewhere. I've been wanting this for a long time.'

'I guess I thought you'd put the *Isabella*, and all of it, pretty much behind you. I didn't realize how much you still wanted her.'

'I didn't either, really.' Out of habit, he checked the course. She, the boat and his daughter, was right on the mark. 'After we lost the *Marguerite*, and you went off to college, I just drifted awhile. It seemed like the right thing to do. I felt so helpless about Buck. He and Matthew off in Chicago, and Buck just wouldn't let me connect.'

'I know that hurt you,' she murmured. 'You'd gotten so close that summer.'

'He lost a leg. I lost a friend. All of us lost a fortune. Neither Buck nor I handled it very well.'

'You did the best you could,' Tate corrected. She had lost her heart, she thought, and she, too, had done the best she could.

'I never knew what to say, or what to do. Sometimes I'd pop one of the videos your mother had taken during those months – watch and remember. It got easier to just drop a letter in the mail now and again. Matthew never let on how bad it was. We might never have found out if we hadn't taken a trip to Florida and gone by the trailer.'

He shook his head, remembering what a shock it had been to see his friend drunk, stumbling around a filthy trailer, surrounded by trash, covered in shame.

'The boy should have told us what a bind he was in.'

'Matthew?' She glanced back in surprise. 'It sounds to me as if Buck was the one in trouble. Matthew should have stayed and taken care of him.'

'If he'd stayed, he couldn't have taken care of Buck. He had to work, Tate. Hell, money doesn't just float in on the tide. It must have taken him years to pay off the medical bills. Fact is, I doubt he's managed it yet.'

'There are programs for people in Buck's situation. Subsidies, assistance.'

'Not for people like Matthew. He'd ask for a loan, but never a handout.'

Disturbed by the idea, she frowned. 'That's stupid pride.'

'Pride, anyway,' Ray agreed. 'It was after I saw Buck again that the *Isabella* started preying on my mind. I couldn't shake it. All those what ifs. So I went back over my old research, started new.'

He looked far out, toward something she couldn't see. Or had forgotten to look for. 'I guess I started thinking if I could find some new clue, it would be a way to pay Buck back for what he'd lost as my partner.'

'Dad, that was no one's fault.'

'Not a matter of blame, honey. A matter of what's right. It's come full circle, Tate. Something tells me it was supposed to.' Shaking off the mood, he smiled down at her. 'I know, it's not logical.'

'You don't have to be logical.' She rose on her toes to kiss him. 'I'll take care of that part.'

'And your mother'll keep things shipshape.' Over the memories, the old excitement began to brew. 'We make a good team, Tate.'

'Always did.'

'*Mermaid* off the port bow,' he murmured.

So it was, Tate saw. She had to admit, it was a stunner of a boat. Those twin hulls cut through the water like diamonds through glass. Though the sun tossed light from the windows of the pilothouse, she could make out Matthew at the helm.

He pulled alongside until there was barely ten feet between them. She saw him turn his head in her direction, and sensed his challenging grin.

'Looks like he wants a race,' Ray said.

'Oh, does he?' Planting her feet a bit farther apart, she gripped the throttle. 'Well, we'll just give him one.'

'That's my girl.' With a hoot, he raced from the bridge, calling for Marla.

'Okay, Lassiter,' Tate muttered to herself. 'You're on.'

She punched the throttle, turning the wheel to give him her wake. The thrill of the competition had her laughing out loud as she felt the power hum under her hands. The *New Adventure* wasn't any Sunday cruiser, and with the Atlantic spread before her, Tate let it have its head.

At twelve knots, it was purring.

It didn't surprise her to see the *Mermaid* coming alongside. She wanted a run. When their bows were even, she shot forward again, sprinting to fifteen knots.

Again he crept steadily even with her, and again, Tate pumped her speed until his bow trailed her stern. In lieu of thumbing her nose, Tate rocked the wheel so that her boat danced. She was chuckling to herself, feeling smug until the *Mermaid* shot by like a bullet.

By the time she'd closed her mouth, he was fifty feet ahead. She bore down, took her engines to full. Her mother's wild, appreciative laughter swam up from the bow. Infectious, it had Tate giggling as she gained ground. But try as she might, she couldn't match the *Mermaid*.

'That's some boat,' she said to herself. 'Hell of a boat.'

And though she knew she should be insulted when Matthew maneuvered a wide circle and came up alongside again, she wasn't.

Damn him, he made her smile.

★

On the evening of their third day, they moored at Freeport, just ahead of a storm that swept in thundering rain and choppy seas. A group dinner was planned aboard the *Mermaid* with LaRue's shrimp jambalaya as the centerpiece.

By the time second helpings were being dispensed, LaRue and Marla were deep into cooking theories while Buck and Ray fell back into their old habit of arguing baseball. Since neither topic fell into Tate's area of expertise, she found herself uncomfortably paired with Matthew.

Because silence seemed cowardly, Tate turned to ingrained Southern manners. 'I'd forgotten you were interested in boat-building,' she began. 'Buck said you designed the *Mermaid* yourself.'

'Yeah. I toyed with a few designs over the years. This one worked for me.' He scooped up more stew. 'I guess I always figured I'd go back.'

'Did you? Why?'

His eyes shot up to hers, held. 'Because I never finished what I started. You must have thought about it now and again.'

'Not really.' Manners aside, lies were safer. 'I've been busy with other things.'

'Looks like college suited you.' She'd taken to wearing her hair in one fat braid that trailed down her back, he noted. That, too, suited her. 'I hear we'll be calling you "Doctor" Beaumont before long.'

'I have some work to do yet.'

'You earned a pretty good rep on that Smithsonian thing a couple years ago.' Her surprised look made him shrug. 'Ray and Marla passed things along.' There wasn't any point in mentioning that he'd gotten a copy of the magazine and read the five-page article twice. 'They were jazzed about the idea of you identifying artifacts from some ancient Greek ship.'

'I was hardly in charge. I was part of a team. Hayden Deel headed the archeological end. He was a professor of mine,' she added. 'He's brilliant. I was with him on the *Nomad*, my last assignment.'

'I heard about that, too.' It grated that she'd been a part of a VanDyke operation. 'A sidewheeler.'

'That's right. The depths were too great for diving. We used computers and robotics.' Comfortable with shop talk, she rested her chin on her fist. 'We have incredible film of plant and animal colonization.'

'Sounds like a barrel of fun.'

'It was a scientific expedition,' she said coolly. 'Fun wasn't a prerequisite. The equipment that was devised to search for and excavate the *Justine* was stunningly successful. We had a team of top scientists and technicians. And,' she added with a bite, 'beyond the scientific value and knowledge, we mined gold. That, I'm sure, you'd understand. A fortune in gold coins and bars.'

'So, VanDyke gets richer.'

He knew, she realized, and felt her face go cold, stiff. 'That's beside the point. The scientific and historic benefit outweighs–'

'Bullshit. Nothing VanDyke does is beside the point.' It infuriated him that she should have changed so much to believe it. 'Don't you care who writes your paycheck?'

'SeaSearch–'

'VanDyke owns Trident, which owns Poseidon, which owns SeaSearch.' Sneering, he lifted his glass of red wine, toasted. 'I'm sure VanDyke's happy with your work.'

For a moment, she could only stare. It felt as though a fist had plunged into her stomach. That he would think so little of her, of her character, and of her heart, hurt more than she had believed it could. She could see herself standing dripping and defiant, facing VanDyke on his own yacht. And she remembered the fury, the fear, and the terrible sense of loss.

Saying nothing, she pushed away from the table and walked out into the rain. On a muttered oath, Matthew shoved his bowl aside and went after her.

'Is this how you handle things now when somebody puts a mirror up to your face, Red? Walk away?'

She stood at the starboard rail, gripping it tight while the rain poured over her. To the north, lightning cracked the sky.

'I didn't know.'

'Right.'

'I didn't know,' she repeated. 'Not when I signed on. If I had, I wouldn't … I would never have been a part of anything connected with VanDyke. I wanted to work with Hayden again, to be a part of something big and important. So I never looked beyond the opportunity.' She was ashamed now, as she hadn't been when the anger and resentment had been so huge. 'I should have.'

'Why? You had a chance, you took it. That's the way things work.' He hooked his thumbs in his pockets to keep himself from touching her. 'You made your choices, and so what? Bottom line is VanDyke's not your fight anyway.'

'The hell he isn't.' Fresh fury had her whirling around. Rain streamed from her hair and face. Thunder grumbled in the distance. 'He isn't your personal demon, Matthew, whatever you think. He took from all of us.'

'So you took something back from him. You earned a little fame and fortune on the *Nomad*. Like you said, you don't care who paid for it.'

'Goddamn you, Lassiter, I said I didn't know. The minute I found out, the minute I realized he'd arranged to have me on the ship, I packed up and left.'

'You packed up and left because you were afraid I'd take advantage of your parents. Don't pull this crap, Tate. I know he called you, told you what was going down. You were on Hatteras in record time.'

'That's right, and one of the reasons I could be was because I'd already tendered my resignation and arranged for transport. The hell with you,' she said wearily. 'I don't have to prove anything to you. I don't have to justify anything to you.'

But she realized she had to justify it to herself. Impatient, she pushed dripping hair back from her face. 'I thought I'd gotten the assignment because Hayden had recommended me.'

A little kernel of jealousy glowed green just under his heart. 'You and this Hayden got a thing going?'

'He's a colleague,' she said between her teeth. 'A friend. He told me that my name was on the approved list before it got to him.'

'So?'

'Follow the logic, Lassiter. I did. Why would someone have done that? I wanted to know why, and who, and I found out. VanDyke chose me. He didn't strike me as a man who forgets. How many Tate Beaumonts with a master's in marine archeology do you figure are out there?'

Because it was starting to make sense, he began to feel like a fool. 'At a guess, I'd say one.'

'Right.' She turned back to the rail. 'He had to know who I was,' she said quietly. 'And he wanted me on the *Nomad*. Whether you believe me or not, I was leaving the expedition before my father contacted me.'

He let out a long breath, rubbed his hands over his wet face. 'I believe you. Maybe I was out of line, but I was steamed over the idea that you'd work for him just to build your rep.' The quick, cold look she shot over her shoulder had him feeling like a worm. 'I said I was out of line. I should have known better.'

'Yes, you should have known better.' Now she sighed. Why should he have trusted me? she asked herself. They didn't really know each other anymore. 'It doesn't matter. I'm glad we cleared the air about it, anyway, I've been stewing over it. I don't like knowing he'd used me. I like knowing less he's been looking over my shoulder all these years.'

It was a possibility that hadn't occurred to him. As it took root, the violent emotion that bloomed from it dimmed jealousy. He gripped her arms, lifting her to her toes. 'Did he ever contact you, try anything?'

'No.' To keep her balance, Tate splayed her hands on Matthew's chest. Rain beat down on them in fat, warm drops. 'I haven't seen him since the day he threatened to have us shot. But obviously, he's kept track of me. My first postgraduate expedition was for Poseidon, in the Red Sea. For Poseidon,' she repeated. 'And now I have to wonder how many projects I've been involved with he's had a hand in. How many doors he opened for me, and why.'

'Why's easy. He saw you had potential, and he could use it.' He recognized the look on her face and gave her a quick shake. 'He wouldn't have opened a door if he hadn't been sure you could have done it for yourself. He doesn't do favors, Red. You got where you are because you're smart and went after what you wanted.'

'Maybe. But that doesn't change the fact that he's been there, behind the scenes.'

'No, it doesn't.' His grip had gentled. He hadn't forgotten he was holding her. It crossed his mind that she was upset enough that she might not freeze if he drew her to him. Instead, he ran his hands from her shoulders to her wrists. And let her go. 'There's something else to consider.'

'What?' Distracted, she fought off a shiver. That small, careless gesture had been so familiar.

'If he knew you were aboard the *Nomad*, he knows you left. By now, he knows you've teamed up with me again, and where we're going.'

She was cold now, icily so. 'What are we going to do about it?'

'We're going to beat him.'

'How?' She turned away again, clamped her hands on the wet rail. 'He has the resources, the contacts, the means.' And he would, she realized as her insides quaked, use her to get to Matthew. 'Our best hope is to throw him off track. If I left, went back to the *Nomad*, or someplace, anyplace else, he might follow my trail. I could even leak something about your talking my parents into a wild-goose chase toward Anguilla, or Martinique.' She spun back. 'I could lead him away.'

'No. We stick together.'

'It only makes sense, Matthew. If he respects me professionally, wouldn't he believe that if I had no interest in this hunt, there wasn't anything to it? He'd be more likely to leave you alone.'

'We stick together,' he repeated. 'And we beat him together. Face it, Tate, we need each other.' He took her arm and pulled her with him.

'Where are you going?'

'We're going to the bridge. There's something I want to show you.'

'We need to tell the others about this. I should have told them before.' She clattered up the short flight of stairs. 'Everyone has a right to input, to the decision.'

'The decision's made.'

'You're not in charge here, Lassiter.'

He kicked the door shut behind him, grabbed a jacket off a hook. 'If you think anyone's going to vote that you go off on your own, you're not as smart as you look. Put this on.' He tossed the jacket at her. 'You're shivering.'

'I'm angry,' she corrected, but jammed her arms into the windbreaker. 'I'm not going to let VanDyke use me to hurt you.'

He stopped in the process of pouring the brandy he'd taken from a cupboard. 'I wouldn't think that would bother you.'

She angled her chin. 'I don't mind seeing you hurt, but I'd prefer doing it myself, not as someone's tool.'

His lips curved. He brought her a stubby glass with two fingers of brandy. 'You know, Red, you always did look terrific wet, especially when you were indignant on top of it. The way you are now.' He clinked his glass to hers. 'I know you'd like to slice me up and use me for chum. Just like I know you'll wait until the job's done.'

'I wouldn't use you for chum, Lassiter.' With a smile, she sipped the brandy. 'I have too much respect for fish.'

He laughed, and threw her off balance by giving her wet braid a quick, friendly tug. 'You know what you have, Tate, besides a good brain, a fierce sense of loyalty and a stubborn chin?'

She moved her shoulders and walked over to stand at the wheel and watch the rain.

'Integrity,' he murmured. 'It flatters you.'

Closing her eyes, she fought off a wave of emotion. He still had a way of sneaking past any defense and seducing the heart of her. 'It sounds as though you're flattering me, Matthew.' Steadying, she turned to face him again. 'Why?'

'Just calling it as I see it, Tate. And wondering if, with all those other fine virtues, you've managed to hang on to that shining sense of curiosity and empathy that made you special.'

'I was never special to you.'

'Yes, you were.' He shrugged again to cover the painful truth. 'If you hadn't been, you wouldn't have left St. Kitts a virgin.'

Color rose in her cheeks like flags of war. 'Why, you arrogant, conceited bastard.'

'Facts are facts,' he countered, pleased that he'd distracted her from her worry over VanDyke. Setting his brandy aside, he crouched to open a storage compartment under a padded bench. 'Stay put,' he said mildly when she headed for the door. 'You'll want to see this. And believe me …' Still crouched, he glanced over his shoulder at her. 'I'm not interested in seducing you. At least not right now.'

Tate's fingers tightened on the glass she'd neglected to set down. It was a pity, she thought, that there were only a few drops left in it. Not enough to make an impression if she poured them over his head.

'Lassiter, you've got as much chance of seducing me as a rabid skunk does of becoming my favored pet. And there's nothing you could have that I want to see.'

'A few pages of Angelique Maunoir's diary.'

It stopped her in her tracks, her hand on the door. 'Angelique Maunoir. Angelique's Curse.'

'VanDyke has the original diary. He tracked it down almost twenty years ago and had it translated.' Matthew took a small metal box from the compartment and straightened. 'I heard him tell my father he traced the descendants of Angelique's maid. Most of them were in Brittany. That's where the legend started. It was VanDyke's father who told him about it. Import-export, shipping, lots of tales and legends get passed around in those types of industries. And they had a personal interest as they were supposed to be some distant relations to Angelique's father-in-law. That's why VanDyke considers the amulet his.'

Though he realized she was staring at the box, Matthew sat, set it in his lap. 'VanDyke liked the idea of being descended from a count, even one, or maybe especially one, with an unsavory reputation. The way VanDyke told it, the count got the amulet back. He had to kill the maid to do it, but she was only a maid. He still had it when he died, quite miserably, I imagine, of syphilis a year later.'

Tate moistened her lips. She didn't want to be fascinated. 'If you knew all this, why didn't you tell us before?'

'Some I knew, some I didn't. My father talked to Buck, and Buck kept most of it to himself. He kept most of my father's papers to himself, too. I didn't come across them until a couple of years ago when he was in rehab and I was shoveling out the trailer. The whole business spooked him.'

Matthew watched her as he tapped a finger on the box. 'See, the problem was VanDyke told my father too much. Arrogance made him careless. I imagine he thought he was close to finding the amulet, and he wanted to gloat. He told my father how he'd traced the amulet through the count's family. Several of whom died young and violently. Those who lived suffered poverty. The amulet was sold, began its journey and developed its reputation.'

'How did your father copy pages of the diary?'

'According to his journal, he was worried about VanDyke. He suspected a double-cross, or worse, and decided to do some research on his own. He had a chance when winter set in and they had to take a break from diving. He used the time to work on his own. That's when he must have come across the *Isabella*. His notes were cryptic after that. Maybe he was worried VanDyke would find them.'

The old frustration came back, rough around his heart. 'It's mostly speculation, Tate. I was a kid, there was a lot he didn't tell me. Shit, he didn't tell me anything. Putting it together is like trying to put him together. And I'm not even sure I knew who he was.'

'Matthew.' Her voice was gentle now, Drawn, she went to sit beside him, lay a hand over his. 'You were only a boy. You can't blame yourself for not having a clear picture.'

He stared at their hands, hers narrow and white, his beneath it big, scarred and rough. That, he supposed, illustrated the difference between them as well as anything could.

'I didn't know what he was planning. I guess I knew something was going on. I know I didn't want him to go down with VanDyke that day. I'd heard them going at each other the night before. I asked him not to dive, or at least to let me go with him. He just laughed it off.'

He shook off the memory. 'But that doesn't answer your question. The best I can piece together is that my father got into VanDyke's cabin and searched it. He found the diary and copied down the relevant pages. It couldn't have been long before he did, because that's part of what they were arguing about. The diary, the amulet.'

'Why are you telling me this, Matthew? Why go back over something so painful that can't be changed?'

'Because I know you won't stay because I tell you to.'

She withdrew her hand. 'So it's a play on my sympathies.'

'It's background. Scientists need background, facts and theories, right? I know you don't believe we'll find the

Isabella.' His gaze held hers, measuring. 'You're not convinced we'll ever find the amulet, or, if we do, that it's anything but an interesting and valuable piece of antique jewelry.'

'All right, that's true. Nothing you've told me convinces me otherwise. I understand why you need to believe, but it doesn't change the facts.'

'But we're not hunting facts, Tate.' He opened the box and handed her papers covered with cramped, hurried writing. 'I don't think you've forgotten that. If you have, maybe this will remind you.'

October 9, 1553

In the morning they will kill me. I have only one night left on earth, and spend it alone. They have taken even my dear Colette from me. Though she went weeping, it is for the best. Not even her prayers, as pure and selfless as they are, can aid me now, and she would have suffered needlessly in this cell, waiting for dawn. Companionship. I have already learned to live without it. With Etienne's death six long weeks ago, I lost not only my dearest companion, my love, my joy, but also my protector.

They say I poisoned him, plying him with one of my witch brews. What fools they are. I would have given my life for his. Indeed, I am doing so. His illness was deep within, and beyond my powers to cure. So quickly it came on him, so violently, the fever, the pain. No potion, no prayer I devised could halt his death. And I as his wife am condemned. I, who once treated the ills and suffering of the village, am reviled as a murderess. And a witch. Those whose fevers I cooled, whose pains I eased have turned against me, shouting for my death like beasts howling at the moon.

It is the count who leads them. Etienne's father who hates and desires me. Does he watch from his castle window as they build the pyre that will be my deathbed? I'm sure he does with his greedy eyes glinting and his thin, wicked fingers twisted in prayer. Though I will burn tomorrow, he will burn for eternity. A small but useful revenge.

If I had succumbed to him, if I had betrayed my love even after his death and gone to the bed of Etienne's father, perhaps I would live. So he promised me. I have faced the tortures of this damnable Christian court with more joy than that.

I hear my jailers laughing. They are drunk with the excitement of tomorrow. But they do not laugh when they come into my cell. Their eyes are wide and frightened as they fork their fingers in the sign against witchcraft. Such fools to believe that such a small, pitiful gesture could stop true power.

They have cut my hair. Etienne often called it his angel fire and ran his fingers through its length. It was my vanity, and even that is stripped from me. My flesh is wasting on my bones from sickness, scarred from their relentless tortures. For this one night, they will leave me in peace. That is their mistake.

However weak my body now, my heart grows stronger. I will be with Etienne soon. And that is comfort. I no longer weep at the thought of leaving a world that has become cruel, that uses God's name to torture and condemn and murder. I will face the flames, and I swear on Etienne's soul that I will not cry out for mercy from the merciless or call out to the God they use to destroy me.

Colette has smuggled the amulet to me. They will find it and steal it, of course. But for tonight

I wear it around my neck, the heavy gold chain, its bright tear-shaped ruby framed in more gold and etched with Etienne's name and mine, studded with more rubies and diamonds. Blood and tears. I close my hand around it and feel Etienne close to me, see his face.

And with it, I curse the fates that killed us, that will kill the child only I and Colette know stirs within me. A child who will never know life, with its pleasures and its pains.

For Etienne and our child I gather what strength I have, I call on whatever forces listen, loose whatever power I hold. May those who condemn me suffer as we have suffered. May those who would take from me all that I value never know joy. I curse whoever wrests this amulet from me, this last earthly link between myself and my love. I pray to all the forces of heaven and hell that he who takes this, Etienne's last gift to me, will know strife and pain and tragedy. He who seeks to profit will only lose what is most precious, most dear. My legacy to my murderers and those who follow them is generations of grief.

Tomorrow they burn me as a witch. I pray they are right, and my powers, like my love, are enduring.

Angelique Maunoir

Tate couldn't speak for a moment. She handed Matthew back the papers and rose to go to the window. The rain had slowed, nearly stopped without her being aware.

'She was so alone,' Tate murmured. 'How cruel for her to be in that cell knowing she would die so horribly in the morning. Still grieving for the man she loved, not being able to feel joy for the child she carried. No wonder she prayed for retribution.'

'But did she get it?'

With a shake of her head, Tate turned to see he had risen as well and was standing with her. Her eyes were wet. The words written so long ago tore at her heart. But when Matthew lifted a hand and laid it on her damp cheek, she jerked back.

'Don't.' She watched his eyes go flat before she stepped away. 'I stopped believing in magic, black or white, a long time ago. The necklace was obviously vitally important to Angelique, a link to the man she'd loved. A curse is a different matter altogether.'

'Funny, I'd have thought someone who spends her time handling and researching old things would have more imagination. Haven't you ever picked up something that has been buried for centuries and felt the punch of it? The power.'

She had. Indeed she had. 'My point is,' she continued, evading, 'that I'm convinced. We stick together, beat him together. We do whatever it takes to keep the amulet out of VanDyke's hands.'

Matthew acknowledged this with a nod that was much more casual than his jerking pulse. 'That's the answer I wanted. I'd offer to shake on it, but you don't like me to touch you.'

'No, I don't.' She started to step around him, but he shifted to block her. Her eyes went cold. 'Really, Matthew, let's not be any more ridiculous than necessary.'

'When we start diving, you're going to have to tolerate me touching you when it's necessary.'

'I can work with you. Just don't crowd me.'

'That's what you used to say.' He moved back, gestured. 'There's plenty of room.'

She took advantage of it and crossed to the door. She shrugged out of the borrowed windbreaker, replaced it on its hook. 'I appreciate your showing me the papers, Matthew, and giving me more of the background.'

'We're partners.'

She glanced back. Odd how alone he looked standing there with the wheel at his back and the sea behind him. 'So it seems. Good night.'

Chapter Seventeen

SILAS VANDYKE WAS extremely disappointed. The reports he'd just read had completely ruined his morning. He tried to recapture some of the charm of the day by having lunch on his patio overlooking the sea.

It was certainly a spectacular spot, the crash of waves thundering, Chopin soaring from the speakers hidden cannily among the lush spread of his tropical gardens. He sipped champagne and picked at a succulent fruit salad, knowing his companion of the moment would be back from her shopping expedition shortly.

Naturally, she'd be willing to distract him with an afternoon of sex. But he simply wasn't in the mood.

He was calm, he assured himself. Still in charge. He was simply disappointed.

Tate Beaumont had betrayed him. He took it quite personally. After all, he'd watched her blossom as any of his well-tended blooms. Like a kindly uncle, he'd given her career little boosts along the way. Always anonymously, of course. He hadn't been looking for gratitude.

Just loyalty.

Her work on the *Nomad* would have catapulted her to the very top of her field. With her looks, her enthusiasm, her youth, she would have outstripped such quietly respected scientists as Hayden Deel. Then, when she was at her peak, he would have stepped out of the shadows and offered her the world.

She would have headed his expeditions. His labs, his funding, his finest equipment would have been at her disposal. She would have joined him in his quest for Angelique's Curse. Since that day eight years before, when she had stood on the deck of the *Triumphant*, he had known intuitively that she was his link to it. Over the years, he'd come to realize that the fates had put her in his path as a sign, a symbol. And he had kept her there, patiently waiting for the moment to come.

With her, he would have succeeded. He was sure of it.

But she had betrayed him. Left her post.

Betrayed him.

His teeth clenched and sweat popped out hot on his skin. Fury hazed his vision, overtook him so that he hurled the crystal over the sea wall, heaved the table so that china and silver and luscious fruit smashed and splattered onto the patio.

Payment, there would be payment. Desertion was a highly punishable offense. A killing offense. His nails dug red welts into his palms. She would have to pay for that, and more, for the bad taste of aligning herself once more with his enemies.

They thought they'd outwitted him, VanDyke raged as he stalked the patio, yanked a creamy hibiscus from the bush beside him. Their mistake, of course. Tate's mistake.

She owed him loyalty, and he would have it. He demanded it. A feral grin on his lips, he ripped the delicate blossom. Then he ripped off more, still more, until the bush and his beautiful suit were in tatters.

Panting, his head swimming with the volcanic fury inside him, he yanked himself back, back. As his vision cleared, he saw the shattered remains of his elegant lunch, the ruin of his possessions. His head ached abominably, and his hands were raw.

He couldn't quite remember causing the destruction, only the black cloud that had smothered him.

For how long? he wondered in jittering panic. For how long had he been lost?

He looked desperately at his watch, winking gold on his wrist, but he couldn't remember when the mood had taken him away.

It didn't matter, he soothed himself. The servants would say nothing, would think nothing but what he ordered them to think. In any case, he hadn't caused this nasty destruction of food and china.

It was they who had caused the destruction, he reminded himself. The Lassiters. The Beaumonts. He'd simply reacted, perhaps a bit rashly, to his keen disappointment. But he'd cleared his mind again. As he always did. As he always would.

Now that he was calm, he would think, and he would plan. He'd give them time, he decided. He'd give them room. Then, he'd destroy them. This time, he would destroy them utterly for causing him to lose his dignity.

He would have control, VanDyke told himself, breathing slow and deep. His father had not been able to control his mother. His mother had been unable to control herself.

But he had learned strength and will.

It was slipping now, and he feared that the way a child fears the monsters in the closet. There were monsters, he remembered, and had to force himself to stop his eyes from darting in search of them. The monsters in the dark, the monsters in the doubt. In failure.

He was losing the control over self that he had fought so hard to develop.

Angelique's Curse. He knew now, was sure now, that the amulet was the answer. With it, he would be strong, fearless, powerful. He believed the witch had put her soul into it. Oh yes, he believed that now, and wondered why he had ever doubted it, ever considered it simply a valuable, much-desired trinket.

It was his destiny, of course. He laughed a little, taking a linen handkerchief from his pocket with a trembling hand to wipe his face. His destiny, and perhaps his salvation. Without it, he would taste failure, and more. He might find himself trapped in that black, numbing world of slathering rage without a key.

The amulet was the key. Gently now, he plucked another blossom, stroked it delicately to prove he could.

Angelique had put her soul into metal and stone. She had haunted him for years, taunted him, teased him by letting him get just so close and no further.

Well, he would beat her, as his long-dead ancestor had beaten her. He would win because he was a man who knew how to win.

And as for Tate … He crushed the flower in his hand, letting his neatly manicured nails rip through the dewy petals.

She'd made her choice.

The West Indies. Tropical islands lush with flowers and palms, towering with cliffs. White sand glittering in the sun and kissed by gilded blue water. Fragrant breezes swaying majestic palms. It was everyone's image of paradise.

As Tate stepped on deck just after sunrise, she was no exception. The cone of Nevis's sleeping volcano was shrouded in mists. The gardens and cabanas of the resort that had been built since her last visit seemed to sleep as well. Nothing stirred but the gulls.

She decided she would go ashore later that morning on the supply run. But for now, she would enjoy a quiet, solitary swim.

She slipped into the water, letting it flow over her shoulders as she tipped her head back. It was just cool enough to refresh. Treading water lazily, she turned a slow circle. Her sigh of delight turned into a gasp as something grabbed her leg and pulled her under.

She sputtered furiously to the surface. Behind his mask, Matthew's eyes glinted.

'Sorry, hard to resist. I was just doing some free diving and saw these legs poke through the water. You've got great legs, Red. All the way up.'

'It's a very big sea, Matthew,' she said primly. 'Go play somewhere else.'

'Why don't you go get a mask and come down with me?'

'Not interested.'

'I've got a bag of crackers in the pocket of my trunks.' He reached over to pluck a strand of wet hair from her face. 'Don't you want to feed the fish?'

She did, but only if she'd thought of it first. 'No.' Giving him her shoulder, she swam deliberately away.

He did a neat surface dive, swam under her and came up in her face again. 'You used to be fun.'

'You used to be marginally less annoying.'

He matched his pace to hers. 'Of course, you'd be out of practice diving, spending all your time with computers and robots. That's probably why even a little snorkeling worries you.'

'I'm not worried. I dive as well as I ever did. Better.'

'We'll have to do some swim-overs while we're looking for the *Isabella*. I say you need the practice.'

'I do not need to practice snorkeling.'

'Prove it,' he challenged and kicked away from her.

She lectured herself, cursed him, but she ended up hauling herself back aboard the boat for snorkel gear. The man was an idiot, of course, she told herself, as she dropped into the water again. But he knew what buttons to push. Her only satisfaction would be to show him just how good she was.

Adjusting her mouthpiece, she skimmed onto the surface. She'd forgotten, until the moment her gaze swept through water to fish and sand, how long it had been since she'd dived – free or scuba – for pleasure only.

She paddled along dreamily, the challenge forgotten. Until Matthew streaked past beneath her, rolling until they were nearly mask-to-mask. He was grinning, then water fountained out of his pipe above the surface. He cocked his head, gestured down. Without waiting, he jackknifed and left her behind.

It was all the motivation she needed. She filled her lungs with air and kicked after him.

This was a world that always lived in her heart. Waving patches of sea grass, clear water, the plains and hillocks of sand. And when Matthew released the broken crackers from the bag he carried, teams of greedy fish.

They swarmed around her, bodies bright as they nipped and gobbled the feast. One or two were curious enough to stare into her face mask before darting off to join the competition for food. Her lungs were aching before she kicked up, blew her pipe clear and drew in more air.

Nearly an hour passed before she kicked to the surface. Tate pulled up her mask and lay contentedly on her back to float.

'Maybe you haven't lost your touch,' Matthew commented.

'I haven't spent all my time in a lab.'

Because her eyes were closed, he indulged himself and let his fingers comb through the hair that flowed red and silky on the water. 'You didn't come in when we docked at San Juan.'

'I was busy with other things.' But she'd seen him, swimming powerfully through the water, and working with LaRue on diving lessons.

'Your thesis.'

'That's right.' A faint tug on her hair had her brushing a hand back. Her fingers collided with his.

'Sorry. What's your thesis on?'

Cautious, she let herself drift a few inches away from where he trod water. 'You wouldn't be interested.'

He said nothing for a moment, surprised by the hot surge of resentment. 'You're probably right.'

Something in his tone had her opening her eyes again.

'I barely got through high-school term papers. What would I know about doctorates and theses?'

'I didn't mean it that way.' Ashamed of herself, she reached out for his arm before he could go under again. 'I didn't. I only meant I didn't think you'd care about some long-winded technical paper when you've already done everything I could write about. And the truth is, I want the damned thing over.'

'I thought you liked that stuff.'

'I do. I–' Annoyed with herself, she floated again, closed her eyes again. 'I don't know what I mean. My thesis is on the inherent versus the monetary value of artifacts. It's not terribly original, but I thought I might focus on one piece, tracing it from its beginnings through to its discovery and analysis. Or I might scrap the whole thing and go back to my first idea of how technological advancements have improved and depersonalized the science of marine archeology. Or… '

She opened one eye. 'You can see why I'm not thrilled you tried to pin me down.'

'So, you haven't made up your mind yet. What's the hurry?'

'I thought there was one.' How could she explain that she felt as though she'd been on a treadmill for years. One of her own choosing, certainly. But that she'd suddenly, and impulsively, leapt off. She didn't have her feet under her yet, and wasn't sure how to get back on when the time came.

'You always got that line, right there, when you tried to out-think yourself.' He skimmed a fingertip between her brows.

She batted his hand aside. 'Go away, Lassiter. I'm having a good time stewing over a professional crisis.'

'Looks to me like you have to be taught how to relax all over again.' He planted a hand firmly on her face and pushed.

She went under, but she was quick enough to snag him on the way down. She got her chin above water, and would have been more successful pulling in air if she hadn't been giggling. When he closed a hand over her ankle, she kicked out with her other foot and had the satisfaction of meeting flesh before he dragged her down again.

Rather than struggle, she went limp. The instant his grip loosened, she gave him a solid butt, then struck out for the boat. She wasn't certain if he was quicker than he'd once been, or if she was slower, but she didn't make it four strokes.

By the time she clawed her way to the surface again, she was weak and out of breath.

'You're drowning me.'

'I'm saving you,' he corrected. Indeed he was holding her up. Their legs were tangled so he used one arm to keep them buoyant while the other stayed wrapped around her.

'Maybe I am out of shape.' She fought to get her breath back and used one hand to swipe hair out of her eyes.

'Not from where I'm swimming.'

It took a moment for the laughter to fade from her face, a moment before she realized she was clinging to him, that his body was hard, nearly naked and pressed close to hers. It took a moment to read the desire in his eyes and for the raw echo of it to sound through her.

'Let me go, Matthew.'

He could feel her trembling now, and she'd gone pale. But he knew it wasn't from fear. She'd often looked and felt just like this before. When she'd wanted him.

'Your heart's pounding, Tate. I can practically hear it.'

'I said–'

He leaned forward, caught her bottom lip lightly between his teeth and watched her eyes cloud. 'Go ahead,' he challenged against her mouth. 'Say it again.'

He didn't give her the chance. His lips were devouring hers, crushing then nibbling, then seducing apart so that he could take the kiss into the deep and the dark and the dangerous.

By Christ, he'd please himself. That's what he thought, even as he suffered. She was everything he'd remembered and sought to forget. Everything and more. Even as they sank beneath the surface, kicked back into air wrapped in each other, he knew it wasn't the sea that would drown him. But his desperate, endless need for her.

The taste of her, the smell and the feel. The sound of her breath catching on confused pleasure. The memories of the past and the reality of now tangled until he could almost forget there had been time between.

She hadn't known she could still feel like this. So hungry and out of control. She didn't want to think, not when her body was so intensely alive and every nerve in it on shivering edge.

It was just physical. She could cling to that as well as him. A man's hard, demanding mouth, that wet, slippery flesh, a tough, ready body molded to hers. No, she didn't want to think. But she had to.

'No.'

She managed one breathless syllable before his mouth came back and sent her mind reeling again. She felt her will slipping and struggled against both him and herself.

'I said no.'

'I heard you.' A dozen separate wars waged inside him. He wanted her, and knew by the way her mouth had fit on his that he could have her. He needed her, and read the mirror of that in her dazed eyes. If want and need had been all, the war would have been over quickly.

But he loved her. And that left him a victim bleeding on his own battlefield.

'I didn't do that alone, Tate. But you can pretend I did if it makes you feel better.'

'I don't have to pretend anything. Let go of me.'

He already had. And that helped curve his lips into something close to a smile. 'You're holding me, sweetheart.' He brought his hands out of the water, palms facing her.

On an oath, she released the grip her arms had somehow taken around him. 'I know the cliché, Lassiter, but this time history isn't going to repeat itself. We work together, we dive together. That's all we do together.'

'It's your choice, Red. It always was.'

'Then there shouldn't be a problem.'

'No problem.' He struck out in a lazy backstroke. 'Unless you're worried you won't be able to resist me.'

'I can manage,' she called after him.

He'd have been pleased to see the line was between her brows again. Muttering to herself, Tate went under to cool her head, then swam in the opposite direction.

'You're not going down again until you pass the written test.' Matthew shoved papers under LaRue's nose. 'That's the way it is.'

'I'm not a schoolboy.'

'You're a trainee. I'm your instructor, and you're going to take the written test. Pass it, you dive. Fail it, you're grounded. The first part's equipment identification.' Matthew leaned forward. 'You remember what a regulator is, don't you, LaRue?'

'It gives the air from the tank to the diver.' LaRue pushed the papers aside. 'So?'

Matthew pushed them back. 'And consists of?'

'Consists of, consists of.' Scowling, LaRue snatched his tobacco pouch. 'The, ah, mouthpiece, the hose, the what is it, stages?'

'What's a stage?'

'This is pressure-reducing unit. Why do you worry me with this?'

'You don't dive until you know the equipment inside-out, until I'm sure you understand the physics and physiology.' He offered LaRue a sharpened pencil. 'Take all the time you need, but remember, you don't dive until you're done. Buck, give me a hand on deck.'

'Sure, be right there.'

LaRue glanced over his test sheets, glanced at Matthew's retreating back. 'What is Boyle's Law?' he whispered to Buck.

'When the pressure–'

'No cheating,' Matthew called back. 'Jesus, Buck.'

'Sorry, LaRue, you're on your own.' Shamefaced, Buck followed Matthew out on deck. 'I was just giving him a little hint.'

'Who's going to give him a little hint if he forgets the basics when he's forty feet under?'

'You're right – but he's doing good, isn't he? You said he had a knack for diving.'

'He's a fucking fish down there,' Matthew said with a grin. 'But he's not skipping the details.'

He was already wearing his wetsuit and now zipped it. He gave his tanks and gauges a last check, then let Buck help him strap them on.

'We're just going down for a little recognizance,' Matthew commented as he adjusted his weight belt.

'Yeah.'

Buck knew they were over the site of the *Marguerite*. Both he and Matthew avoided discussing the wreck, or what had happened. Buck avoided Matthew's eyes as his nephew sat to put on his flippers.

'Tate wants some pictures,' Matthew said, for lack of anything better. Everyone knew they wanted a firsthand look at what VanDyke had left behind.

'Sure. She was always big on getting pictures. Kid grew up nice, didn't she?'

'Nice enough. Don't give LaRue any more hints.'

'Not even if he begs.' Buck's smile faded when Matthew slipped on his mask. Panic reared up and grabbed him by the throat. 'Matthew…'

Matthew paused, one hand on his mask as he prepared to roll into the water. 'What?' He saw the anxiety, struggled to overlook it.

'Nothing.' Buck wiped a hand over his mouth, swallowed hard while nightmare visions of sharks and blood swam in his head. 'Good diving.'

With a brief nod, Matthew slipped into the water. He ignored the impulse to dive deep, lose himself in the silence and solitude. He crossed the distance to the *New Adventure* in an easy crawl, gave up a hailing shout.

'Ready to roll up there?'

'Just about.' Ray, full-suited, came to the rail with a grin. 'Tate's checking her camera.' He lifted a hand in a wave to Buck. 'How's he doing?'

'He'll be all right,' Matthew said. The last thing he wanted to do was dwell on his uncle's fears. Now that they were here, he was impatient to begin. 'Let's go, Red!' he shouted. 'The morning's wasting.'

'I'm coming.'

He caught a glimpse of her before she sat to pull on her flippers. Moments later, he watched her graceful entry. With a quick pike dive, Matthew was following her down even as Ray dropped into the water.

The three of them descended, nearly side by side.

Matthew hadn't expected the memories to swarm up at him like the bright, quick fish. Everything about that summer came back, unbidden and unwelcomed. He remembered the way she had looked when he'd first seen her. The wary suspicious eyes, the quick flares of anger, resentment.

Oh, and he remembered his instant attraction, one he'd smothered, or tried to. The sense of competition when they'd teamed as diving partners, an edge that had never really dulled even after they'd melded into a unit.

There was the thrill he'd experienced when they'd found the wreck. Those times with her that had opened both his heart and his hopes as nothing and no one ever had before. Or had again. All the sensations of falling in love, of working together, of discovery and promise spun through him as they neared the shadow of the wreck.

As did the jarring aches of horror and loss.

VanDyke had left little but the shredded shell of the galleon. Matthew knew at one glance it would be a foolish waste of time to bring down the airlift and dig. Nothing of any value would have been left behind. The wreck itself had been destroyed, ripped apart in search of that last doubloon.

It surprised him to feel sorrow for that. With careful excavation, the *Marguerite* might have been saved. Instead she was in pieces, left for the worms.

When he glanced at Tate, Matthew could see clearly that whatever vague regret he felt for the ship was nothing to what she was experiencing.

It shattered her. Tate stared at the scattered planks, not bothering to attempt to block the wave of grief. She let it wash over her until she felt it deep inside.

He'd killed her, she thought. VanDyke hadn't been content with his rape, but had destroyed the *Marguerite*. No one would see what she had been, what she had meant. Because of one man's greed.

She might have wept if tears hadn't been so late and so useless. Instead, she shook off the comforting hand Matthew put on her shoulder, and lifted her camera. If nothing else, she'd record the devastation.

Catching Matthew's eye, Ray shook his head, gestured so that they swam a short distance away.

There was still beauty surrounding her. The coral, the fish, the waving plants. But it didn't touch her now as she recorded the scene that had once been the stage for such great joy.

It was fitting, she supposed, that it had been ruined, destroyed, neglected. Just like the love she'd once offered Matthew.

So, she thought, that summer was finally and completely over. It was past time to bury it, and start new.

When they surfaced, the first thing she saw was Buck's pale, anxious face leaning over the rail.

'Everything okay?'

'Everything's fine,' she assured him. Because it was closer, she pulled herself aboard the *Mermaid*. She stopped, turned and waved to her mother, who was recording the event on video aboard the *New Adventure*. 'Pretty much what we expected,' she told Buck after she had dropped her weight belt.

'Bastard tore her apart, didn't he?'

'Yes.' She glanced over as Matthew climbed on deck.

'Ray wants to head south right away.' He pulled off his mask, ran a hand through his hair. 'You might as well stay put,' he told Tate before she could rise. 'It won't take long. Buck?'

With a nod, Buck headed up to the bridge to take the wheel.

'Best plan is to do some swim-overs.' After tugging down the zipper of his wetsuit, Matthew sat beside her. 'We could get lucky.'

'Are you feeling lucky, Lassiter?'

'No.' He closed his eyes as the engine purred. 'She meant something to me, too.'

'Fame and fortune?'

The words cut, but not as keenly as the edge of her voice. His gaze, hot and hurt, swept up to hers before he stood and strode toward the companionway.

'Matthew.' Shame had her springing up after him. 'I'm sorry.'

'Forget it.'

'No.' Before he could take the stairs, she grabbed his arm. 'I am sorry. That was hard on all of us – going down, seeing what was left. Remembering. Taking it out on you is easy, but it doesn't help.'

In impotent fury, Matthew's hands whitened on the rail. 'Maybe I could have stopped him. Buck thought so.'

'Buck wasn't there.' She kept her hand firm on his arm until he turned to face her again. Odd, she thought, she hadn't realized he would blame himself. Or that he had room in the cold heart she'd assigned to him for guilt. 'There was nothing any of us could have done. Looking back doesn't help either, and certainly doesn't change anything.'

'The *Marguerite's* not all we're talking about, is it?'

She was tempted to back off, to shrug his words away. But evasions were foolish, and she hoped she was no longer a fool. 'No, it's not.'

'I wasn't what you wanted me to be, and I hurt you. I can't change that either.'

'I was young. Infatuations pass.' Somehow her hand had found its way to his, and linked. Realizing it, she flexed her fingers free and stepped back. 'I understood something when I was down there, looking at what was left. There is nothing left, Matthew. The ship, that summer, that girl. All that's gone. We have to start with what's now.'

'Clean slate.'

'I don't know if we can go that far. Let's just say we've turned a page.'

'Okay.' He offered a hand. When she took it, he brought hers unexpectedly to his lips. 'I'm going to work on you, Red,' he murmured.

'Excuse me?'

'You said we've got a new page. I figure I've got some say in what gets written on it. So I'm going to work on you. Last time around, you threw yourself at me.'

'I did no such thing.'

'Sure you did. But I can see I've got my work cut out for me this time. That's okay.' He skimmed his thumb over her knuckles before she jerked her hand free. 'In fact, I think I'm going to enjoy it.'

'I don't know why I waste my time trying to mend fences with you. You're as arrogant as you ever were.'

'Just the way you like me, sweetheart.'

She caught the lightning flash of his grin before she whirled away. Try as she might, she couldn't quite suppress the answering upward tug of her lips.

It was hell knowing he was right. That was exactly the way she liked him.

Chapter Eighteen

SWIM-OVERS TURNED UP nothing impressive. Tate spent most of the afternoon closeted with her father and his research while Matthew took LaRue, fresh from passing his written certification, on a practice dive.

She had already organized the heaps of notes, the snippets from the National Archives, wreck charts, the material Ray had culled from the *Archivo General de Indias* in Seville.

She'd separated his maps, charts, storm records, manifests, diaries. Now she concentrated on his calculations.

Already she'd figured and refigured a dozen times. If their information was correct, they were certainly in the right area. The problem was, of course, that even with a location, finding a wreck was like separating that one special grain of sand from a fat fistful.

The sea was so huge, so vast, and even with the leaps in technology, a man's abilities were limited. It was highly possible to be within twenty feet of a wreck, and miss it entirely.

They had been almost foolishly lucky with the *Marguerite*. Tate didn't want to calculate the odds of lightning striking twice, not with the hope and excitement she could see whenever she looked into her father's eyes.

They needed the *Isabella*, she thought. All of them did, for all manner of differing reasons.

She knew the magnetometer aboard the *Mermaid* was in use. It was a fine and efficient way of locating a wreck. So far the sensor being towed behind the *Mermaid* had picked up no readings of iron such as would be found in cannon, riggings, anchor.

They had depth finders on both bridges so that any telltale change in water depth caused by a wreck would be distinguished. They had set out buoys to mark the search pattern.

If she was down there, Tate thought, they would find her.

She stayed in the deckhouse after her father had gone out to starboard.

'You're not going to put roses in your cheeks in here, Red.'

She looked up, surprised when Matthew held out a glass of her mother's lemonade. 'You're back. How did LaRue check out?'

'He's a good diving partner. How many times are you going to go over all this?'

She tidied papers. 'Until I'm finished.'

'How about taking a break?' Reaching out, he toyed with the sleeve of her T-shirt. He'd been working on this approach all day, and still wasn't sure he had it right. 'Why don't we take a run into Nevis, have dinner?'

'Dinner?'

'That's right. You.' He tugged the sleeve. 'And me.'

'I don't think so.'

'I thought we'd turned the page.'

'That doesn't–'

'And I'm not keen on the big pinochle game that's being planned for tonight. As I remember, you weren't big on cards either. The resort has a reggae band out on the terrace. Some dinner, a little music. There won't be time for much of that once we find the *Isabella*.'

'It's been a long day.'

'You're going to make me think you're afraid to spend a couple of hours with me.' His eyes flashed on hers, blue as the sea and just as arrogant. 'Of course, if you're afraid you'll throw yourself at me again.'

'That's pathetic.'

'Well, then.' Satisfied he nailed the approach after all, he headed back for the companionway. 'Wear your hair down, Red. I like it.'

She wore it up. Not to spite him, she assured herself. But because she wanted to. She'd changed into a sundress the color of crushed blueberries borrowed from her mother's closet, at Marla's insistence. The full skirt made it easy to climb in and out of the tender.

Once she was settled in and the little tender was speeding toward the island, she admitted that she looked forward to an elegant restaurant meal, with a little music tossed in.

The air was balmy, the sun still bright as it traveled west. Behind the protection of her shaded glasses, she studied Matthew. His hair was whipping around his face. On the tiller, his hand was broad and competent. If there had been no history between them, she would have been pleased to have such an attractive companion for an evening's relaxation.

But there was history. Rather than diluting the pleasure, it added an edge to it. Competition again, she supposed. If he thought she would fall for that rough-and-ready charm a second time, she was only too happy to prove him wrong.

'The weather's supposed to hold all week,' she said conversationally.

'I know. You still don't wear lipstick.' When she instinctively flicked her tongue over her lips, he dealt with the resulting hitch in his pulse. 'It's a pity most women don't realize how tempting a naked mouth is. Especially when it pouts.'

Deliberately, she relaxed her mouth again. 'I'll enjoy knowing it's driving you crazy for the next couple of hours.'

She turned her attention to Nevis. The mountain's cone was swirled in clouds, a striking and dramatic contrast to the brilliant blue of the sky. Far below, the shore spread white against a calm sea. The sand was dotted with people, pretty umbrellas and lounging chairs. A novice sail-boarder struggled fruitlessly to stay upright. As she watched him fall into the water again, Tate laughed.

'Too bad.' She cocked a brow at Matthew. 'Have you ever tried that?'

'Nope.'

'I have. It's a hell of a lot of work, frustrating when you think you've got it then lose your balance and capsize. But if you catch the breeze and go, it's wonderful.'

'Better than diving?'

'No.' She continued to smile, watching the young man struggle onto his board again. 'Nothing's better than diving.'

'Things have changed around here.'

'Hmmm.' She waited as he maneuvered to the pier, tossed a line to a member of the resort's staff. 'I didn't even know they were planning to build when we were here last.' She took Matthew's offered hand and climbed to the dock. 'Now it looks as though it almost grew here.'

'Nevis isn't quite the secret it used to be.' He kept a hand on her arm as they walked down the pier to the beach.

Stone walkways offered a route through lush gardens and sloping green lawns where pretty two-story cabanas sat. They passed the pool-side restaurant, moving toward the marble stairs that led to the main building.

Tate glanced over her shoulder. 'We're not eating out here?'

'We can do a little better than light fare by the pool. The restaurant inside has terrace dining.' He led Tate inside toward the reservation pedestal, where a woman in the bright-patterned shirt of the staff beamed at him. 'Lassiter.'

'Yes, sir. You requested the terrace.'

'That's right. I called ahead,' he told Tate when she frowned at him. Her frown only deepened when he held out her chair. If memory served, his manners had smoothed out considerably. 'Can you handle champagne?' he murmured, leaning down so that his breath tickled her ear.

'Of course, but–'

He was ordering a bottle even as he took the seat across from her. 'Nice view.'

'Yes.' She took her gaze from his face and looked out over the gardens to the sea.

'Tell me about the last eight years, Tate.'

'Why?'

'I want to know.' Needed to know. 'Let's say it'll fill in some of the blanks.'

'I studied a lot,' she began. 'More than I bargained for. I guess I had the idea that I knew so much going in. But

I knew so little really. The first couple of months I ...' Was lost, unhappy, missing you so terribly. 'I needed to adjust,' she said carefully.

'But you caught on pretty quick.'

'I suppose.' Relax, she ordered herself and made herself turn back and smile at him. 'I liked the routine, the structure. And I really wanted to learn.'

She looked over as the waitress brought the champagne to the table to show off its label.

'Let her taste it,' Matthew ordered.

Obliging, the waitress uncorked the bottle and poured a swallow into Tate's flute. 'It's lovely,' Tate murmured, much too aware that Matthew's eyes never left her face.

When their glasses were filled, she started to drink again, but he laid a finger on her wrist. Gently, he tapped the glasses together. 'To the next page,' he said and smiled.

'All right.' She was a grown woman, Tate reminded herself. Experienced now. She had all the defenses necessary to resist a man. Even one like Matthew.

'So you learned,' Matthew prompted.

'Yes. And whenever I had an opportunity to use what I'd learned on an expedition, I took it.'

'And the *Isabella*, isn't she an opportunity?'

'That remains to be seen.' She opened her menu, skimmed it, looked up at him with wide eyes. 'Matthew.'

'I managed to hold on to a few bucks over the years,' he assured her. 'Besides, you've always been my lucky charm.' He picked up her hand. 'This time, Red, we go home rich.'

'So, that's still the bottom line? All right.' She shrugged. 'It's your party, Lassiter. If you want to live for today, we'll do it.'

While they ate, and the wine fizzed in their glasses, the sun lowered. It sank red into the sea, giving the air that brief and painfully lovely twilight of the tropics. On cue, the music from the patio beyond began.

'You haven't told me about your eight years, Matthew.'

'Nothing very interesting.'

'You built the *Mermaid*. That's interesting.'

'She's a beauty.' He looked out to the sea where, beyond his sight, she rocked. 'Just like I imagined her.'

'Whatever happens here, you'd have a career in boat design and building.'

'I'm never working to make ends meet again,' he said quietly. 'Never doing what needs to be done and forgetting what I want.'

It struck her, that fierceness in his eyes, so that she reached out to touch his hand. 'Is that what you did?'

Surprised, he looked back. With a careless shrug, he linked his fingers with hers. 'It's not what I'm doing. That's what counts. You know something, Red?'

'What?'

'You're beautiful. No.' He smiled slowly when she tried to slip her hand free. 'I've got you now. For now,' he corrected. 'Get used to it.'

'The fact that I chose you over pinochle has obviously gone to your head.'

'Then there's that voice,' he murmured, delighted by the way confusion flickered with the candlelight in her eyes. 'Soft, slow, smooth. Like honey spiked with just the right amount of good bourbon. A man could get drunk just listening to you.'

'I think you got a headstart with the champagne. I'll pilot us back.'

'Fine. But we'll have at least one dance.' He signaled for the bill.

A dance wouldn't hurt, Tate decided. If anything, she could use the close contact to convince him that she wasn't about to be seduced into the brief affair he was obviously after.

She could enjoy him without losing herself or her heart this time around. And if he suffered a little, she wasn't above enjoying that as well.

To show how little it mattered, she let her hand stay in his as they left the screened terrace for the open patio below.

The music was slow, sexy, with the vocalist adding a teasing interpretation to the words. A couple sat huddled together at a table in the shadows, but there were no other dancers when Matthew took her into his arms.

He took her close, so their bodies molded, so that her cheek had little choice but to rest on his. Without thinking, she closed her eyes.

She should have known that he would be smooth, that he would be clever. But she hadn't expected that her steps would match his so perfectly.

'I didn't know you could dance.'

He skimmed a hand up her back to where material gave way to flesh, flesh that shivered at the touch. 'There's a lot we didn't know about each other. But I know the way you smelled.' He nuzzled just under her ear. 'That hasn't changed.'

'I've changed,' she said, struggling not to react as fire licked along her vulnerable flesh.

'You still feel the same.' He reached up to pull pins out of her hair.

'Stop that.'

'I liked it short.' His voice was as quiet as the breeze, just as seductive. 'But this is better.' Softly, his mouth skimmed over her temple. 'Some changes are.'

She was trembling, those quick, involuntary shivers he remembered so well.

'We're different people now,' she murmured. She wanted it to be true, needed it to be. And yet, if it was, how could it be so easy to move into his arms as if not a moment had passed since the last time?

'Lots of other things are just the way they were. Like the way you fit against me.'

She jerked her head back, then shuddered when his lips brushed over hers.

'You still taste the same.'

'I'm not the same. Nothing's the same.' She broke away and darted down the steps toward the beach.

She couldn't seem to draw in enough air. The balmy night had suddenly turned traitor, making her skin shiver. It was anger – she wanted to believe it was anger that made her stomach clench and her eyes tear. But she knew it was need, and could only hate him for rekindling a long-dead spark.

When he caught her, she was sure she would round on him, clawing and spitting. Somehow her arms were around him, her mouth seeking his.

'I hate you for this. God, I hate you for this.'

'I don't give a damn.' He dragged her head back to plunder. It was all there, that energy, that verve, that passion. He had a wild, desperate thought to drag her off into the bushes, to plunge himself into the heat that vibrated from her.

'I know you don't.' And it was that which still hurt, a scar that throbbed under a fresh wound. 'But I do.'

She broke away, throwing her hands up to ward him off when he would have taken her into his arms again. She fought to even her breathing, fought to resist that reckless, compelling light in his eyes.

'You wanted to prove you could still strike a spark between us.' She pressed an unsteady hand to her stomach.

'Well, you did. But what we do or don't do about it is my choice, Matthew. And I'm not ready to make a choice.'

'I want you, Tate. Do you need to hear me say it?' He stepped forward, but didn't touch her. 'Do you need to hear me tell you I can't sleep at night for wanting you?'

The words, the rough, impatient delivery, spun in her head, swam in her blood. 'Maybe I do, but it doesn't change the fact that I'm taking whatever time I need to decide. I'd have gone anywhere, done anything for you once, Matthew. Once. What I do now, I do for myself.'

He hooked his tensed hands in his pockets. 'That's fair enough. Because this time around what I do, I do for myself.'

'This time around.' She gave a quick laugh and pulled her fingers through her tumbled hair. 'That part looks the same from where I'm standing.'

'Then you know what you're dealing with.'

'I'm not sure I do,' she said wearily. 'You keep shifting on me, Matthew. I'm not sure what's real and what's shadow.'

'This is real.' He cupped a hand behind her neck, lifting her to her toes until their mouths met.

'Yes, that's real.' As she eased away, she let out her breath. 'I want to go back now, Matthew. We start early tomorrow.'

She really didn't mind the way the teams split so that her father and LaRue worked together, leaving her and Matthew as the second team. She and Matthew had always worked well together underwater. After their first dive, she realized they still had the same natural and instinctive communication and rhythm.

The electronic equipment was the most efficient method of locating the *Isabella*, but Tate was grateful to have the chance to dive, to search by sight and by hand as she had learned to do.

Hours of fanning sand didn't bore her. Nor did hauling chunks of conglomerate to the surface for her mother and Buck to hammer apart. As far as she was concerned she was home again, with the fish as both audience and playmates. Every lovely sculpture of coral pleased her eye. Even disappointment was part of the whole. A rusted chain, a soda can might turn a quickly beating heart into a sigh. But it was all part of the hunt.

And there was Matthew, always close at hand to share some small delight with. A garden of sea plants, a grumpy grouper disturbed from his feeding, the bright silver flash of a fish in flight. If he tended to touch her just a bit too often, she told herself to enjoy it.

If she was strong enough to resist seduction, she was certainly strong enough to resist romance.

The days slipped by into weeks, but she wasn't discouraged. The time here was soothing a need she hadn't realized she'd held inside – to revisit the sea she loved, not as a scientist, an objective observer trained to record data. But as a woman enjoying her freedom, and the companionship of a man who intrigued her.

She examined a formation of coral, fanning sand away. Glancing over her shoulder, she saw Matthew tucking conglomerate into his lobster bag. She started to smile at him, the way she reserved for herself when she knew he wasn't looking. A sharp pain stabbed the back of her hand.

Jolted, she jerked back just as the head of a moray eel retreated into its slitted home in the coral. Almost before Tate could register the insult, and curse her own carelessness, Matthew was there, grabbing the fingers of her wounded hand as blood swirled into the water. The alarm in his eyes pierced through her own shock. She started to signal that she was fine, but he already had an arm around her waist and was kicking toward the surface.

'Just relax,' he ordered the minute he spat out his mouthpiece. 'I'm going to tow you in.'

'I'm all right.' But the throbbing pain made her eyes water. 'It's just a nick, really.'

'Relax,' he said again. His face was as pale as hers by the time he reached the ladder. Hailing Ray, he began unhooking Tate's tanks.

'Matthew, for goodness sake, it's a scratch.'

'Shut up. Ray, goddamn it.'

'What? What's wrong?'

'She got bit. Moray.' Matthew passed her tanks over. 'Help her in.'

'Lord, you'd think I'd been chewed in half by a shark,' she muttered, then winced as she realized what she'd said. 'I'm okay,' she hurried on as her mother came rushing over.

'Let me see. Oh, honey. Ray, get the first-aid kit so I can clean this up.'

'It only nicked me,' Tate insisted when Marla pushed her down on a bench. 'It was my own fault.' She blew out a breath and watched Matthew pull himself aboard. 'There's no need to get everyone in an uproar, Lassiter.'

'Let me see the damn thing.' In a move that had Marla blinking in surprise, he shouldered her aside and took Tate's hand himself. He smeared blood away from the shallow puncture with his thumb. 'Doesn't look like it'll need stitches.'

'Of course it doesn't. It's just–' Tate broke off as he snatched the first-aid kit from Ray. The next sound she made was a screech as he doused on antiseptic. 'You're not exactly Doctor Feelgood.'

His own blood pressure was gradually leveling as he was able to get a good look at the cleaned wound. 'Probably scar.' Annoyance was an easier emotion than fear, so he scowled up at her. 'Stupid.'

'Listen, it could have happened to anyone.'

'Not if they were paying attention.'

'I was.'

'You were daydreaming again.'

Ray and Marla exchanged glances as the argument and doctoring continued.

'I suppose you've never taken a bite. Your hands are riddled with scars.'

'We're talking about you.' It infuriated him that those lovely, narrow hands might be marred.

She sniffled, flexed her fingers. The bandage was small, neat and efficient. She'd have swallowed her tongue before saying so. 'Aren't you going to kiss it and make it better?'

'Sure.' In answer, he hauled her to her feet. While her astonished parents looked on, he fixed his mouth on hers in a long, hard, demanding kiss.

When Tate could speak again, she scrupulously cleared her throat. 'You missed,' she said, holding up her bandaged hand.

'No, I didn't. Your mouth's what needs the work, sweetheart.'

'Really?' Her eyes narrowed to slits. 'Now you're an expert on what I need?'

'I've always known what you need, Red. Anytime you want to–' Abruptly, he remembered they were a long way from alone. Getting a grip on his temper, he stepped back. 'You might want to take a couple of aspirin to take the edge off the pain.'

Her chin was angled like a sword. 'It doesn't hurt.' She turned and hefted her tanks.

'Where do you think you're going?'

'I'm going back down.'

'The hell you are.'

'Just try to stop me.'

As her husband opened his mouth, Marla patted his arm. 'Let them fight it out, honey,' she murmured. 'Looks like it's been simmering awhile.'

'You want me to try to stop you? Okay.' Letting temper lead, Matthew grabbed the tanks out of her hands and heaved them overboard. 'That ought to do it.'

For a moment, all Tate could manage was an open-mouthed gape. 'You idiot. You ignorant son of a bitch. You'd better get your butt in there and haul my tanks in.'

'Get them yourself, you're so anxious to dive.'

It was a small mistake, turning his back on her. And he paid for it. She launched herself at him. At the last instant, he realized her intent. In an effort to save himself, he shifted. But she dodged. The ensuing crash sent them both over the side.

'Shouldn't we do something, Marla?' Ray asked, as they stood at the rail.

'I think they're doing fine. Oh, look, she almost caught him with that punch. And with her bad hand, too.'

Matthew jerked back from the jab at the last moment. But he didn't quite avoid the fist to his midsection. Even slowed by the water, it earned a grunt.

'Cut it out,' he warned, snagging her injured hand by the wrist. 'You're going to hurt yourself.'

'We'll see who gets hurt. Go get my tanks.'

'You're not going down until we're sure you don't have a reaction to the bite.'

'I'll show you my reaction,' she promised and popped him on the chin.

‘Okay, that does it.’ He dunked her once, then hauled her up with an arm under her chin in a not-so-gentle rescue position. Every time she clawed or cursed at him, he shoved her under again. By the time they reached the ladder, she was wheezing. ‘Had enough?’

‘Bastard.’

‘I guess one more good dunk–’

‘Ahoy the *Adventure!*’

Matthew shifted his grip on her as Buck hailed from the *Mermaid*. She was coming in a good clip from her position to the southeast, where Buck and LaRue had been hunting with the sensor.

‘Ahoy,’ Buck shouted again from the bridge. LaRue leaned smugly on the rail at the bow. ‘We got something.’

‘Get aboard,’ Matthew muttered to Tate and all but carried her up the ladder.

Buck piloted the *Mermaid* neatly alongside, cut her engines. ‘Sensors picked up a pile of metal down there. Depth finder shows something, too. Marked it with a buoy – southeast, thirty degrees. Jesus, I think we might’ve found her.’

Tate took a deep breath. ‘I want my tanks, Matthew.’ Her eyes glittered as she turned to him. ‘Don’t even think about stopping me from going down now.’

Chapter Nineteen

THERE WERE SEVERAL ways to range a wreck for return to site. Standard methods included angular measurements taken from three fixed objects with a sextant, compass bearings with a nine-degree spread or simply ranging the wreck by using distant objects as gunsights. Matthew had used them all.

Though Buck had employed a simple buoy marker as a practical target, Matthew knew that had its drawbacks. A buoy could sink or drag. Or more important in this case, a buoy could be seen by other interested parties. For the sake of secrecy, he logged the compass bearings, targeted the distant Mount Nevis as a gunsight, then ordered Buck to move the buoy well away from the estimated position of the wreck.

'We'll keep the buoy on line with that group of trees on that point of the island,' he told Ray, passing over binoculars so that his partner could verify position by the point on Nevis.

They stood on the deck of the *New Adventure*, Matthew in his gear, Ray in cotton slacks and polarized glasses. Ray was already busy with his compass, marking the position for his ship's daily log.

'We're not going to moor here.' Matthew swept his gaze over the sea, noting the pretty catamaran carrying tourists on a snorkeling cruise from Nevis to St. Kitts. The cheerful sound of the ondeck band carried festively across the water. 'We'll use the buoy as a line and move inshore toward Mount Nevis.'

While Ray nodded and scribbled the marks, Matthew continued. 'Tate can make sketches of the bottom, and we can read them as we go.'

Ray slung the binoculars around his neck and studied Matthew's determined face. 'You're thinking of VanDyke.'

'Damn right. If he gets wind of us, he's not going to be able to drop right down on the wreck. He won't know the distances or the landmarks we select, or even if we're diving inshore or offshore of the buoy. That gives him plenty of possibilities to work through.'

'And buys us time,' Ray agreed. 'If this isn't the *Isabella*–'

'We'll soon find out,' Matthew interrupted. He didn't want to speculate. He wanted to know. 'One way or the other, we take precautions.' He pulled on his flippers as he spoke. 'Come on, Red, let's move.'

'I needed to reload my camera.'

'Forget the camera. We're not developing any film.'

'But–'

'Look, all it takes is one clerk passing the word along. Take all the pictures you want, but no film gets sent off until we're finished here. Got the board and graphite pencil?'

'Yes.' Assuming a nonchalantly professional pose, she patted her goody bag.

'Let's dive.'

Before she'd adjusted her mask, he was in the water. 'Impatient, isn't he?' She sent a quick smile toward her parents that revealed only a portion of the excitement humming through her. 'Keep your fingers crossed,' she told them, and splashed into the sea.

Following his trail of bubbles, she dived deep. Her inner sensor told her when she'd passed thirty feet, then forty. She began to make note of the landscape of the seafloor, knowing her assignment was to sketch it carefully. Every bed of sea grass, every twist of coral.

With her graphite pencil, she began to reproduce them, meticulously keeping to scale, marking distances in degrees, resisting the urge to add artistic flourishes. Science was exacting, she reminded herself even as she watched the dance of an angelfish duet.

She saw Matthew signal, and waved back querulously at the interruption. Efficient sketches took time and care, and since he was the one who'd insisted on them rather than photographs, he could damn well wait. When the clang of his knife on his tank intruded again, she cursed him mildly then stowed her board and pencil.

Just like a man, she thought. Always come here, and make it now. Once they surfaced, she'd tell him just what she thought of the arrangement. And then …

Her thoughts trailed off, went limp as her suddenly numb fingers as she saw what he was investigating.

The cannon was the lovely pale green of corrosion and alive with colonizing animals. She snatched her camera and recorded it, with Matthew at the mouth. But that didn't make it real. Not until she had touched it with her own hand, felt the solid iron beneath her exploring fingers, did it become real.

Her breath exploded in bubbles when he grabbed her, swung her around. Tate prepared herself for an exuberant embrace, but he was only pointing her toward the rest of the find.

More cannon. This was what the magnetometer had recorded. As Matthew towed her along, she counted four, then six, then eight, spread over the sandy floor in a rough semicircle. Her heart spun into her throat. She knew that cannon often literally pointed to a wreck.

They found her nearly fifty feet south, crushed, battered, and smothered by the drifting sand.

She'd been proud once, Tate thought as she plunged her hand into the sand and felt the soft give of worm-eaten wood. Even regal like the queen she'd been named for. For so long, she'd been lost, a victim of the sea that had come to be a part of its continuity.

Broken, what was left of the *Isabella* – for Tate never doubted it was the *Isabella* – was spread over more than a hundred feet of seabed, buried, encrusted. And waiting.

Her hand was steady enough as she began to sketch again. Matthew was already fanning, so she alternated her drawing with quick snapshots while he stuffed small finds into his lobster bag.

She ran out of boards, worked her pencils down to nubs and used every frame of film. And still, her heart thrummed and jittered.

Once in a lifetime, she thought with an ache in her throat, had become twice.

When he headed back toward her, she smiled, delighted that he would think to bring her a token. He gestured for her to hold out her hand, close her eyes. She rolled them first, but obeyed, only to have them spring open again when a heavy disk was dropped into her palm.

Heavy only because she'd been expecting a coin or a button, she realized. The round, biscuit-shaped object weighed no more than two pounds at her educated guess.

But her eyes went wider still at that unmistakable and stunning flash of pure and glorious gold.

He winked at her, signaled for her to put the ingot into her bag, then jerked a thumb toward the surface. She started to object. How could they leave when they had just begun?

But of course, there were others waiting. It jabbed her conscience a bit to realize she'd forgotten everything and everyone but what was here. Matthew's hand closed over hers as they kicked to the surface.

'You're supposed to throw yourself at me now,' he told her with a wicked laugh in his eyes that was more triumph than humor. 'That's what you did eight years ago.'

'I'm much more jaded now.' But she laughed and did exactly what he'd hoped by throwing her arms around him. 'It's her, Matthew. I know it.'

'Yeah, it's her.' He had felt it, known it, as if he had seen the *Isabella* whole, flags flying, as in his dream. 'She's ours now.' He had time to give Tate only a quick kiss before they were hailed. 'We'd better go give them the news. You haven't forgotten how to work an airlift, have you?'

Her lips were still tingling from his. 'I haven't forgotten anything.'

The routine was so familiar. Diving, digging, gathering. Onboard the *Mermaid*, Buck and Marla pounded away at conglomerate, separating pieces of treasure for Tate to examine and record. Each find, from a gold button set with a pink conch pearl to a gold bar a foot long, was meticulously tagged, sketched, photographed and then logged in her portable computer.

Tate put her education and experience to use preserving their finds. She knew that in the fairly shallow Caribbean, a wreck rotted, was further damaged by storm and wave action. The wood would be eaten by teredo worms.

She also knew that the history of the wreck could be read in the very damage it had sustained.

This time, she would see that every scrap brought up was protected. Her responsibility, she felt, toward the past, and the future.

Small, fragile items were stored in water-filled jars to keep them from drying out. Larger pieces would be photographed and sketched underwater, then stockpiled on the bottom. She had cushioned boxes for the fragile, such as onion-skinned bottles she hoped to find. Wooden specimens would be left in a bath to protect against warping in the small tank she'd rigged on the boat deck.

Tate delegated Marla to the position of apprentice chemist. They worked together, with daughter instructing mother. Even artifacts that resisted chemical change were soaked thoroughly in fresh water, then dried. Marla painstakingly sealed everything with a coat of wax. Only gold and silver required no special handling.

It was time-consuming work, but never, to Tate's mind, tedious. This was what she had missed and pined for aboard the *Nomad*. The intimacy, the propriety, and surprise of it all. Every spike and spar was a clue, and a gift from the past.

Ordinance marks on cannonballs corroborated their hopes that they'd found the *Isabella*. Tate added to her log all the information she had on the ship, its voyage, cargo and its fate. Painstakingly, she checked and rechecked the manifests, cross-referencing with each new discovery.

Meanwhile, the airlift was vacuuming off enough sediment to disclose the tattered hull. They dug. She drew. They hauled buckets filled with conglomerate to the surface. Matthew's sonar located the ballast stones before they found them by sight and hand. While Tate worked in the deckhouse and boat deck of the *New Adventure*, her father and LaRue were laboriously searching the ballast for artifacts.

'Honey?' Marla poked her head in. 'Don't you want to take a break? I've finished the waxing.'

'No, I'm fine.' Tate continued to add details to her sketch of a set of jet Rosary beads. 'I can't believe how fast it's going. It's been barely two weeks, and we just keep finding more. Look at this, Mom. Look at the detail on this crucifix.'

'You've cleaned it. I'd have done that.'

'I know, but I couldn't wait.'

Fascinated, Marla leaned over her daughter's shoulder to run a finger along the heavy, carved silver depiction of Christ on the cross. 'It's stunning. You can see the sinew in His arms and legs, count each wound.'

'It's too fine to have belonged to a servant. You see, each decade is perfectly matched, and the silver work is first rate. It's masculine,' she mused. 'A man's piece. One of the officers, perhaps, or maybe a rich priest on his way back to Cuba. I wonder if he held it, prayed with it as the ship went down.'

'Why aren't you happy, Tate?'

'Hmm?' She'd been dreaming again, Tate realized. Brooding. 'Oh, I was thinking of the *Santa Marguerite*. She was salvageable. I mean the wreck itself could have been preserved with enough time and effort. She was nearly intact. I'd hoped, if we did find the *Isabella*, she would be in a similar state, but she's ruined.'

'But we have so much of her.'

'I know. I'm greedy.' Tate shrugged off the gloom and set her sketch aside. 'I had this wild notion we could raise her, the way my team raised the Phoenician ship a few years ago. Now, I have to be content with the pieces the storm and time have left behind.' She toyed with her pencil and tried not to think about the amulet.

No one spoke of it now. Superstition, she supposed. Angelique's Curse was on everyone's mind, as VanDyke was. Sooner or later, she was afraid both would have to be dealt with.

'I'll let you get back to work, dear. I'm heading over to the *Mermaid* to work with Buck.' Marla smiled.

'I'll swim over later and see what you've come up with.'

Tate turned back to her keyboard to log in the Rosary. Within twenty minutes, she was lost in an examination of a gold necklace. Its bird in flight pendant had survived the centuries, the tossing waves, the abrasive sand. She estimated the relic to be worth easily fifty thousand dollars, and efficiently noted it down and began her sketch.

Matthew watched her for a moment, the competent and graceful way she moved pencil over paper. The way the sun was slanting he could make out her ghostly profile in the reflection of her monitor.

He wanted to press his lips to that spot just at the nape of her neck. He wanted to wrap his arms around her, to have her lean back into him, relaxed, easy and just a little eager for his touch.

But he'd been cautious for the last few weeks. Hoping to move her toward him without tugging. Patience was costing him dozens of restless nights. It seemed only when they were beneath the sea that they moved in concert.

Every part of him was aching for more.

'They sent up a couple of wine jugs. One's intact.'

'Oh.' Startled, she looked around. 'I didn't hear you come in. I thought you were on the *Mermaid*.'

'I was.' But all he'd been able to think about was that she was here, alone. 'Looks like you're keeping up with the haul.'

'I get antsy if I fall behind.' She brushed her braid off her shoulder, hardly aware she'd inched away when he sat beside her. But he was aware, and irritated. 'I can usually get in several hours in the evening, when everyone's turned in.'

He'd seen the light in the deckhouse every night when he'd restlessly paced his own deck. 'Is that why you never come over to the *Mermaid?*'

'It's easier for me to work in one spot.' Much easier not to risk sitting in the moonlight with him on his own turf. 'By my calculations, we're well ahead of where we were in the same amount of time in our excavation of the *Marguerite*. And we haven't hit the mother lode.'

He leaned over to pick up the gold bird, but was more interested in the way her shoulder stiffened when his brushed it. 'How much?'

Her brow creased. It was no more than expected, she supposed, that he could look at such a fabulous relic and think in dollars and cents. 'At least fifty thousand, conservatively.'

'Yeah.' With his eyes on hers, he jiggled the necklace in his hand. 'That ought to keep us afloat.'

'That's hardly the issue.' Possessively, she took the necklace back, laid it gently on the padded cloth she had covering her worktable.

'What is the issue, Red?'

'I'm not going to waste my time discussing that with you, but there is something we need to talk about.' She shifted, angling herself so that she could face him and still keep a fair distance.

'We could talk about it over dinner.' He trailed a fingertip down her shoulder. 'We haven't taken a break in more than two weeks. Why don't we take another run over to Nevis tonight?'

'Let's not cloud business with your libido, Lassiter.'

'I can manage both.' He picked up her hand, kissed her fingers, then the small scar the moray had given her. 'Can you?'

'I believe I have been.' But she drew her hand free, just to be safe. 'I've given this a lot of thought,' she began. 'We missed our chance to preserve the *Marguerite*. The *Isabella* is badly broken up, but we still have the opportunity to salvage some of her.'

'Isn't that what we're doing?'

'I don't mean just her cargo, I mean her. There are treatments to preserve ships' timbers, prevent their shrinking in open air. She can even be partially reconstructed. I need polyethylene glycol.'

'I don't happen to have any on hand.'

'Don't be cute, Matthew. Planks immersed in a bath of that solution are permeated with it. Even wood riddled with marine borers can be preserved. I want to call Hayden, ask him to get what's needed, and to come and help me salvage the ship.'

'Forget it.'

'What do you mean forget it? She's an important find, Matthew.'

'She's our find,' he tossed back. 'No way in hell I'm sharing her with some college professor.'

'He's not some college professor. Hayden Deel is a brilliant marine archeologist. One who's dedicated himself to study and preservation.'

'I don't give a damn what he's dedicated to, he's not coming in on this deal.'

'That's the bottom line, isn't it? The deal.' Disgusted, she shoved away so that she could scoot around the worktable and stand. 'I'm not asking for him to have a share of your all-important booty. He wouldn't expect it. Some of us don't measure everything in dollars.'

'Easy for you to say when you've never had to scrape one together. You always had Mom and Dad to fall back on, a nice cozy home with supper on the stove.'

Anger paled her cheeks. 'I made my way, Lassiter. On my own. If you'd ever bothered to think past the next wreck, you might have more than the loose change rattling around in your pocket. Now all you can think about is cashing in and living the good life. There's more to this expedition than auctioning artifacts.'

'Fine, when we've auctioned those artifacts, you can do whatever the hell you want, with whoever you want.' He'd damn well kill anyone who touched her. 'But until then, you don't contact anyone.'

'That's all it is to you, isn't it?' She slapped her palms on the table, leaning forward until her angry eyes were level with his. 'Just the money matters.'

'You don't know what matters to me. You never did.'

'I thought you'd changed, just a little. I thought finding the *Isabella* meant more to you than what you could take from her.' Straightening again, Tate shook her head. 'I can't believe I could be so wrong about you twice.'

'Looks like you can.' He pushed away from the table. 'You always accuse me of being self-involved, Tate, but what about you? You're so wrapped up in what you want, the way you want it, even if it blocks off what you feel.'

Driven, he grabbed her arms, dragged her against him. 'What do you feel? Damn it, what do you feel?' he repeated and closed his mouth over hers.

Too much, she thought as her heart went spinning. Too painfully much. 'That isn't the answer,' she managed.

'It's one of them. Forget the *Isabella*, the amulet, your goddamn Hayden.' His eyes were dark and fierce. 'Answer that one question. How do you feel?'

'Hurt!' she shouted over quick, useless tears. 'Confused. Needy. Yes, I have feelings, damn you, Matthew, and you stir them up every time you touch me. Is that what you want to hear?'

'It'll do. Pack a bag.'

He released her so suddenly, she stumbled. 'What?'

'Pack a bag. You're coming with me.'

'I – what? Where?'

'The hell with the bag.' She'd told him what he'd wanted to hear, and he wasn't going to let her rethink it. Not this time. He grabbed her hand again and pulled her on deck. Before she had a clue what he was planning, he'd scooped her into his arms and was lowering her over the rail into the tender.

'Have you lost your mind?'

'I should have lost it weeks ago. I'm taking her to Nevis,' he shouted to the *Mermaid*. 'We'll be back in the morning.'

'In the morning.' Shading her eyes, Marla stared at her daughter. 'Tate?'

'He's lost his mind,' Tate called out, but was forced to sit when Matthew leapt nimbly down. 'I'm not going with you,' she began, but was drowned out by the tender's engine. 'Stop the boat right now, or I'll just go overboard.'

'I'll pull you back,' he said grimly. 'You'll just get wet.'

'If you think I'm going to spend the night with you on Nevis–' She broke off when he whipped his head around. He looked too dangerous for arguments. 'Matthew,' she said more calmly. 'Get ahold of yourself. We had a disagreement, this is no way to settle it.' Her breath hitched when he cut the engine back. For one humming moment, she wondered if he would simply pitch her over the side.

'It's long past time we finish what we started eight years ago. I want you, and you've just said you want me right back. You've had plenty of time to think about it. Until we settle this, it's going to keep getting in the way.' His hand ached from his rough grip on the tiller. 'You look at me, Tate, and you tell me you didn't mean what you said, that it doesn't affect you, and everything we're doing here, and I'll turn around and go back. That'll be the end of it.'

Shaken, she dragged a hand through her tousled bangs. He'd shanghaied her, tossed her into a boat, and now he was putting the choice back in her hands. 'You expect me to sit here like this and discuss the effects of sexual attraction.'

'No, I expect you to say yes or no.'

She looked back toward the *Mermaid*, where her mother still stood at the rail. Then toward the smoky peak of Nevis. Oh, hell.

'Matthew, we don't have any clothes, luggage, we don't have a room.'

'Is that a yes?'

She opened her mouth, heard herself babble. 'This is crazy.'

'That's a yes,' he decided, and gunned the engine. He didn't speak to her again. They reached the pier, docked. As they crossed the beach at arm's length, he pointed to an empty lounge chair. 'Sit,' he told her. 'I'll be back.'

Too bemused to argue, she sat, staring at her bare feet, offering the wandering waitress who stopped by with a tray a vague shake of her head and a baffled smile at the offer of a drink.

Tate looked out to sea, but the *Mermaid* and the *New Adventure* were beyond sight. It seemed she'd cut her line.

If this was an answer, she could no longer think of the question. But when Matthew came back, held out his hand, she took it. They walked in silence through the gardens, across the slope of green lawn.

He unlocked a sliding glass door, pulled it closed behind them and flipped the latch.

The room was bright, airy, dreamy in pastels. The bed was neatly made, plumped with generous pillows. She stared at it, jerking only once when he pulled the blinds and tossed the room into shadows.

'Matthew–'

'We'll talk later.' He reached behind her to undo her braid. He wanted her hair loose, flowing through his fingers.

She closed her eyes and would have sworn the floor tilted beneath her feet. 'And if this is a mistake?'

'Haven't you ever made one?'

His grin flashed, and she found herself smiling in response. 'One or two. But–'

'Later.' He lowered his head and found her lips.

He'd been sure he needed to dive into her, the way he sometimes needed to dive into the sea, as if to save, or at least to find, his sanity. His hands had itched to tug at her clothes, to touch the skin beneath and possess what he'd once given up.

But the hot-edged hunger that had driven him to bring her here mellowed as her taste flowed through him. As sweet as yesterday, as fresh as the instant. Love, never quite conquered, swarmed through him in triumph.

'Let me see you,' he murmured. 'I've waited so long to see you.'

Lightly, gently, mindful of her trembling, he loosened her blouse, slipped it aside. She was pale ivory and soft satin beneath, a delicate feast for hands and eyes.

'All of you.' As his mouth skimmed over her bare shoulder, he tugged at her shorts, at the practical swatch of cotton under them.

His mermaid, he thought, almost dizzy with discovery. So slim and white and beautiful.

'Matthew.' She dragged his shirt over his head, desperate for flesh to find flesh. 'Touch me. I need you to touch me.'

With those words humming in his head, he lowered her to the bed and quietly, cleverly, pleasured them both.

Tenderness was so unexpected. So seductive. She had seen it once, hidden in the brash young man she had fallen in love with. But to find it now, after so long, was a treasure. His hands brushed and stroked and aroused while his mouth patiently swallowed her sighs.

Her own exploring fingers found muscle and scar, skin that heated under her curious caress. She tasted it, letting her lips and tongue skim over that flesh and savor the flavor of man and sea.

So she went dreaming, floating on a sea of shifting passions, thrilling to his murmurs of pleasure as he traveled over her. She arched to meet him, shuddering with delight when his mouth closed over her breast. So hot, so firm, so exquisitely controlled. All the while his hands moved steadily over her, sending tiny, eager pulses soaring.

When her sea began to toss, he soothed her back from the edge, teased her up again to the narrow verge until her breath came in gasps and she would have begged had she had the power. Storms brewed inside her so that the air was hot and heavy and throbbed with the threat.

He watched her, fascinated by the rapid flickers of pleasure, confusion and finally desperation on her face. His own mind was reeling when he sent her up and flying. His groan merged with hers as he felt her body tighten and shudder into wild release.

Fighting against a vicious slap of need, he closed his mouth over hers. When her breath began to settle, he nudged her gently, devastatingly over the edge again, into the tempest.

She couldn't stop the shudders. It seemed her body would break apart. So she clung to him as wave after wave of sensation battered her. She had ridden out a hurricane in the Indian Ocean, crawled through a blinding sand-storm thirty feet beneath the sea. She had felt the heat and need of a man's body meshed mindlessly with hers.

But nothing had touched her, stirred her blood or enticed her mind like this long, relentless loving. She had no secrets left to hide, no pride under which she might have buried them. Whatever she was, whatever he wanted from her, was there for him. Weak and wrecked and willing, she offered.

He slipped inside her slowly, savoring. Now he trembled as she did, resting his brow on hers as she took him deep, held him fast.

'Tate.' Emotions erupted inside him. 'Just this,' he whispered. 'Just you.'

His hands sought hers, fingers locking. He rocked inside her, struggling to keep the pace easy, to draw out the moment. He could feel his heart thudding in his chest, the blood that pounded, the deliriously soft, wet give of her.

Her nails dug into his shoulders, her body bucked and jerked. A sob tore from her throat and ended on his name.

Finally, when he was so steeped in her he'd lost himself, he dived.

While the sun lowered in the West Indian sky, VanDyke sipped Napoleon brandy thousands of miles away. He had the latest report on the activities of the Beaumont-Lassiter expedition on his desk.

It far from satisfied him.

From all appearances, they were still exploring the remains of the *Marguerite*. None of his contacts on St. Kitts or Nevis knew anything of importance. A busman's holiday, the report indicated, but VanDyke wasn't convinced.

His instincts were humming.

Perhaps it was time he followed them, he considered. A little trip to the West Indies might be in order. It would at least provide him with the opportunity to express his displeasure to Tate Beaumont.

And, if the Lassiters weren't going to lead him to Angelique's Curse after all these years, it was time he disposed of them.

Part Three

Future

The future is purchased by the present.
–Samuel Johnson

Chapter Twenty

TATE WONDERED IF it would be awkward. In her experience, mornings after routinely were. She'd been grateful to find herself alone when she'd awakened. It gave her the opportunity to shower and think.

They'd done very little talking the night before, she remembered. Then again, it was hard to hold a reasonable conversation while your brain was being fried with hot, demanding sex.

She let out a breath as she shrugged into the thick bathrobe the hotel provided. As far as the sex went, she thought, new precedents had been set in her body. Matthew Lassiter was going to be a very tough act to follow.

As she reached for the blow-dryer, she caught a glimpse of herself in the foggy mirror. Grinning.

Well, why not? she asked herself. She'd spent an incredible night having her system rocked. And, unless she was very mistaken, doing some rocking of her own.

But the sun was up, and it was time to deal with the reality of what happened next. They had a job to do, and though the tension had been wonderfully diffused, they were still bound to clash when it came to the bottom line.

It didn't seem fair that two people who could meld so gloriously together under one set of circumstances couldn't find solid mutual ground elsewhere.

Compromise, she supposed, sighing over the word, was the only solution.

Once her hair was nearly dry, she ran her tongue over her teeth and wished the pretty room included the amenity of a toothbrush. Worrying over it, she stepped back into the bedroom just as Matthew came through the glass doors.

'Oh, hi.'

'Hi back.' He tossed her a small bag. A glance inside had her shaking her head.

'You read my mind,' she said, taking out a toothbrush.

'Good. Now you can read mine.'

It wasn't difficult as he came to her, picked her up and dropped her back on the bed.

'Matthew, really.'

'Yeah.' Grinning, he stripped off his shirt. 'Really.'

It was an hour later before she could put the toothbrush to use.

'I was wondering,' she began as they crossed the beach toward the pier.

'What were you wondering?'

'How we're going to handle this.'

'This?' He took her hand as they crossed the planks to the tender. 'Being lovers? How much do you want to complicate it?'

'I don't want to complicate it, I just want to–'

'Establish the rules,' he finished, then turned to kiss her in front of several grinning crew of the resort's tour boat. 'Never change, Red.'

Once she was in the tender, he cast off, sent a cheery wave to the crew and kicked the engine to life. He felt incredible.

'Is there something wrong with rules?' she asked.

He grinned again, turned the boat skillfully. 'I'm crazy about you.'

That tugged a little too acutely at her heart. 'That's rule number one. Let's not confuse physical attraction and compatibility.'

'With?'

'Anything.'

'I've always been crazy about you.'

'I mean it, Matthew.'

'I can see you do.' And it stung. But he wasn't going to allow anything to dim his mood, or to wither the hope he'd begun to nourish while she'd slept beside him. 'Okay, how's this? I want to make love with you at every possible opportunity. Is that better?'

Her insides went liquid at the possibility, but she kept her voice brisk. 'It may be more honest, but it's hardly practical. There are six of us on two boats.'

'So, we'll be inventive. You up to diving this morning?'

'Of course I am.'

To entertain himself, he studied her. Windblown, tousled, barefoot. 'I wonder what it would be like to get you naked underwater.' He held up a hand. 'Just kidding. For now.'

If he thought the idea shocked her, he was wrong. But before she fantasized about it too deeply, she wanted to set the record straight. 'Matthew, there are still issues we have to resolve.'

He slowed the tender. Damned if she wasn't going to pick at it until she managed to spoil the mood. 'You want to get back to the idea of calling in your associate, or whatever he was to you.'

'Hayden would be invaluable on a project like this, if he's willing to take the time.'

'My answer stands, Tate. Listen to me before you start pissing me off again. We can't risk it.'

'Risk involving one of the top scientists in the field?'

'Risk VanDyke getting wind of it.'

'You're paranoid about this,' she said impatiently. 'Hayden understands the necessity for discretion.'

'Hayden worked for Trident.'

Her chin shot up. 'So did I. I'm sure Hayden was as unaware of the politics as I was. And even if he has been associated with VanDyke, he'd say nothing to anyone if I asked him.'

'You want to take the chance of losing it all again?'

She started to speak, hesitated because she was certain he was speaking about more than the hunt. 'No,' she said quietly. 'I don't. We'll table calling Hayden for now, but it's something I feel strongly about.'

'Once we've played her out, you can call every scientist you know. I'll even help you bring her up piece by piece if that's what you want.'

She stared, speechless. 'You would?'

He cut the engine with a jerk of the hand as they came alongside the *New Adventure*. 'You don't get it, do you, Red? Even now.'

Baffled, she lifted a hand toward his. 'Matthew.'

'Work on it,' he snapped out, and jerked a thumb toward the ladder. 'And be ready to dive in twenty minutes.'

Women, he thought as he steered the tender toward the *Mermaid*. They were supposed to be the sensitive, emotional ones. What a joke. There he'd been, all but dribbling with love like a sap and all she could talk about were rules and science.

LaRue, gold tooth gleaming, caught the line Matthew heaved to secure the tender. 'So, *mon ami*, you feel refreshed this morning, eh?'

'Cram it,' Matthew suggested. He landed lightly on deck, stripping off his shirt as he went. 'Save the comments. I want coffee.'

Not bothering to hide the grin, LaRue strolled toward the galley. 'Me, when I spend the night with a woman we both smile in the morning.'

'Keep it up,' Matthew muttered, checking his gear. 'You'll lose another tooth.' After grabbing swimming trunks, he moved to the port side.

She'd gone to bed with him, he thought, bitterly. She'd let him have her until they had both been delirious. And she still thought he was one small step up from slime. He tugged off his shorts, yanked on his trunks. What the hell kind of woman was she?

When he stalked back for his wetsuit, Buck was waiting.

'Just hold on a minute, boy.' After a night of soul-searching and worry, Buck was primed. He jabbed a finger in Matthew's chest. 'You've got some explaining to do.'

'What I've got is work to do. Get the airlift ready.'

'I never interfered with that – that hormone part of your life.' To keep Matthew in place, Buck jabbed again. 'Figured you knew what was what. But when you start taking advantage of that sweet little girl.'

'Sweet,' Matthew interrupted. 'Oh yeah, she's real sweet when she's tearing strips off you or kicking your guts out.' He grabbed his wetsuit and sat to begin the process of stretching it over his legs. 'What goes on between me and Tate isn't any of your business.'

'Hell it isn't. We're all part of a team, and her daddy's the best friend I ever had.' Buck rubbed a hand over his mouth and wished actively for a drink so that he could slide painlessly through the rest of the lecture. 'I ain't saying a man don't have needs, and maybe it ain't easy for you being out here all these weeks without any way to meet them.'

Eyes narrowed against the sun, Matthew stood to work the suit to his hips. 'I got a hand if that's all I need.'

Buck scowled. He didn't like talking about such matters. But he had a duty. 'Then why the hell didn't you use it instead of using Tate? I told you this eight years ago, and I'll tell you again. She ain't no throwaway, boy, and I'm not going to stand around–'

'I didn't use her, goddamn it.' He jammed an arm through the sleeve. 'I'm in love with her.'

'Don't you–' Buck stopped, blinked and decided he'd be better off sitting down. He waited, getting his bearings, while Matthew grabbed the coffee LaRue brought out. 'You mean that?'

'Just get off my back.'

Buck looked toward LaRue, who was busying himself studying the compressor. 'Look, Matthew, I don't know much about that kind of thing, but … Well, Jesus, when did that happen?'

'About eight years ago.' Most of his anger drained, but the tension remained fierce in his shoulders. 'Don't hassle me about this, Buck. Did you get the weather report?'

'Yeah, yeah. We got no problem.' Knowing he was out of his depth, Buck rose awkwardly to help Matthew with his tanks. 'Ray and the Canadian brought up some porcelain after you went ashore. Marla was going to clean it up.'

'Fine. Signal the *Adventure*, LaRue. I want to get started.'

'Better to finish,' LaRue commented, but walked to starboard to send up the hail.

⋆

'Of course I'm all right.' Tate strapped on her diving knife and tried to reassure her mother. 'I'm sorry if you were worried.'

'I wasn't worried, exactly. More concerned. I know Matthew would never hurt you.'

'Wouldn't he?' Tate mumbled.

'Oh, honey.' Marla gathered her close for a quick, hard hug. 'You're a grown woman. I know that. And I know that you're sensible and careful and responsible. All the things you should be. But are you happy?'

'I don't know.' Wishing she did, Tate hitched on her tanks, tugged the strap snug. 'I haven't figured that out.' She glanced up at LaRue's hail. 'Matthew isn't an easy man to understand.' Sighing, she hooked on her weight belt. 'But I can handle it. And I can handle him.' She pulled on her flippers and frowned. 'Dad's not going to do anything crazy about this, is he?'

With a light laugh, Marla offered Tate her face mask. '*I* can handle *him*.' She lifted her gaze, looked across the water to where Matthew stood on deck. 'Matthew Lassiter is an attractive and intriguing man, Tate. There are pockets in him the right woman could plumb.'

'I'm not interested in plumbing Lassiter's pockets.' Tate adjusted her mask, then grinned. 'But I wouldn't mind getting my hands on him again.'

He didn't give her much of an opportunity. The instant they were down at the wreck, he had the airlift sweeping. He worked fast and hard. At times the sand, shells and debris machine-gunned over her back and shoulders. She had to scramble to keep up with his progress, shifting through the fallout, filling buckets, tugging on the line that would signal Buck to haul them up. He gave her little time to delight in the finds.

A chunk of conglomerate struck her shoulder hard enough to bruise. Rather than wincing over the sting, she soothed herself by cursing him as she reached for the calcified form. The blackened silver coins fused together in an insane sculpture changed her mood. Swimming through the murk, she rapped sharply on Matthew's tank.

He turned, easing back when she stuck the conglomerate in his face in triumph. He barely glanced at it. With a watery shrug, he went back to work.

What the devil was the matter with him? she wondered, and dropped the monied find in a bucket. He should have grinned, tugged her hair, touched her face. Something. Instead, he was working like a maniac without any of the pleasure that always flowed through their partnership.

She thought he was only interested in money; meanwhile, Matthew fumed and played the airlift over the sand. Did she really believe a hunk of silver would make him rear up and dance? She could keep every fucking coin as far as he was concerned. Turn every last one of them over to her precious dream museum or her precious Hayden Deel.

He'd wanted her, damn it. But he hadn't known sex without her love, and goddamn it, her respect, would be hollow. Would leave him hollow.

Well, now he knew. That left him with only one goal. Angelique's Curse. He'd search every inch of sand, every crevice, every foot of coral. And when he had it, he'd take his revenge on his father's killer.

Revenge, Matthew decided, was a more satisfying goal than the love of a woman. God knew, it couldn't hurt as much to fail.

He worked until his arms sang with fatigue, and his mind went numb with the monotony of it. Then the pipe whisked away sand, and he saw that first stunning flash of gold.

He drew the pipe back, glanced toward Tate. He could see she was scrambling through the cloudy water, her eyes sharp behind her mask, even though Matthew could sense the dragging fatigue in her movements.

He'd worked her too hard, and he knew it. Yet not once had she asked him to stop, or slow down. Has pride always been our problem? he wondered, then looked back at the shining coins, tossed like a god's careless pocket change on the seafloor.

Smiling, he turned the pipe so that it would suck the coins. They flew back, clinking against Tate's tanks, bulleting against her back. He saw the moment the first glint caught her eye, watched her hand dart. She scooped up doubloons like a child scoops up candy from a shattered piñata.

And she turned to him. It soothed his edgy heart that she would seek his face with her hands full of old gold.

He grinned as she swam toward him, tugged the neck of his suit open just enough to slip coins down his suit. Her eyes brimmed with laughter as he turned the pipe aside. Curious fish watched them wrestle, spin, then clumsily embrace.

Matthew jerked a thumb toward the surface, but she shook her head, pointed toward the airlift. With a nod, he shouldered it again while she scooped handfuls of coins from the sand to the bucket.

She had filled two to overflowing, and was happily exhausted when she spotted the pouch. It had been velvet and was tattered and worn. Even as her fingers touched it, the corners crumbled in her hand. Through the thready hole, stars fell.

Her breath literally stopped. With a trembling hand, she reached down and lifted the necklace. Diamonds and sapphires exploded through the murk. It was three strands, ridiculously heavy and ornate. The gems had held their fire through the centuries and flashed now before her dazzled eyes.

Stunned, she held it out to Matthew.

For one numbing moment, he thought they'd found it. He would have sworn he saw the amulet dripping from her hands, felt the power humming from the bloody stone. But when he touched it himself, it changed. Priceless, sumptuous, it was. But it held no magic. In a careless gesture, he tossed it over her head so that gems sparkled against her snug, dark suit.

This time when he signaled to surface, she nodded. She gave a tug on the ropes. Together they followed the buckets.

'We found the mother lode.' Exhaustion forgotten, Tate reached out for him as they broke the surface.

'I don't think there's any doubt of that.'

'Matthew.' Reverently, she slipped her fingers under the necklace. 'It's real.'

'Looks good on you.' He closed a hand over hers. 'You still bring me luck, Tate.'

'Holy God Almighty!' came the shout from the *Mermaid*. 'We got gold here, Ray,' Buck yelled. 'We got ourselves buckets of gold.'

Tate grinned and squeezed Matthew's hand. 'Let's go let them pat us on the back.'

'Good idea. I was thinking' – he kicked lazily toward the *Mermaid* – 'if I were to swim over, say about midnight, go up to the bridge. There's a lock on that door.'

She reached for the ladder ahead of him. 'Now, that's a good idea.'

Within two days, they had hauled up over a million dollars in gold. There were jewels that Tate was struggling to appraise and catalogue. The more stunning their success, the more precautions they took.

They moored the boats more than a hundred feet from the site, and Buck made a show of fishing off the bow at least twice a day when the tour boats passed within hailing distance. Tate took countless rolls of film and stored them. She sketched, and filed the drawings away.

She knew her dream of a museum was almost within her grasp. There would be articles to be written, papers to be published, interviews. She and her father debated plans and ideas. To Matthew, she said nothing of her hopes. His dreams, she knew, were different from hers. They worked together, hunted together. In the quiet of midnight, they made restless love on a padded blanket.

And if he sometimes seemed moody, if she would catch him studying her with unreadable eyes, she told herself they'd reached their compromise.

The expedition, and the quiet flow of spring into summer, couldn't have been more perfect.

LaRue strolled, whistling, out of the deckhouse. He paused a moment, watching Buck and Marla hammer conglomerate. He admired the very attractive Mrs. Beaumont. Not only for her looks and slim, lovely body, but for her seamless class. The women who had flowed in and out of LaRue's life had been interesting, intriguing, but very rarely had they been classy.

Even sweaty and grimy-handed, the pedigreed Southern belle shone through.

It was a pity the woman was married, he thought. One of the few rules LaRue never broke was to seduce a married woman.

'I must take the tender,' he announced. 'We need supplies.'

'Oh.' Marla sat back on her heels, brushed beads of perspiration from her brow. 'Are you going to St. Kitts, LaRue? I was hoping to run in myself. I could really use some fresh eggs and fruit.'

'I would be happy to pick up whatever you would like.'

'Actually . . .' She offered him her most charming smile. 'I'd love to go ashore for a little while. If you wouldn't mind the company.'

His smile flashed as he quickly adjusted his plans. '*Ma chère* Marla, it would be my greatest pleasure.'

'Could you wait just a few minutes while I clean up?'

'My time is your time.'

All chivalry, he assisted her into the tender, watched her efficiently zip across the distance to the *New Adventure*. Nothing, he knew, would induce the lovely Mrs. Beaumont to swim even a few feet.

'You're wasting your charm on her, Frenchie,' Buck grumbled and whacked his hammer.

'But, *mon ami*, I have so much to spare.' Amused, LaRue glanced back. 'And what would you like me to bring you back from the island?'

A bottle of Black Jack, Buck thought, nearly tasting that first shock of whiskey in his throat. 'I don't need nothing.'

'As you wish.' He patted his pocket where his tobacco was stashed, then wandered back to the rail. 'Ah, here comes my lovely shopping companion. *A bientôt*.'

Gallantly, LaRue took the tiller, executed a sweeping turn so that Marla could wave to Ray before they cruised toward St. Kitts.

'I really appreciate this, LaRue. Ray's so wrapped up with his charts and inventory I didn't have the heart to ask him to run me in.' Delighted with the prospect of poking through markets, she lifted her face to the wind. 'And everyone's so busy.'

'You work very hard yourself, Marla.'

'It hardly seems like work. Now, the diving.' She rolled her eyes. 'That's work. You enjoy it, though.'

'Matthew is an excellent teacher. After so many years on the water, it's become a pleasure for me to explore beneath. Ray is the best of diving partners.'

'He's always loved it. Now and again, he still tries to convince me to try it. I actually tried snorkeling once. The reefs off Cozumel were very exciting, but I forgot myself and paddled out a bit. Before I knew it, I was looking down at open water. It's the oddest sensation.' She shuddered. 'A kind of vertigo.' Amused at herself, she patted the life jacket she'd strapped on. 'I'll stick with boats.'

'It's a shame you can't see for yourself the *Isabella*.'

'With all the sketches Tate's done, I feel as though I have. What will you do with your share, LaRue? Will you go back to Canada?'

'Spare me. Such cold.' He studied the shoreline in the distance. White sand, swaying palms. 'Me, I prefer a warmer clime. Perhaps I will build a home here, and look down on the water. Or sail the world.' He grinned at her. 'But whatever, I will enjoy being a rich man.'

It was, after all, a fine ambition.

Once he'd docked the boat, he escorted Marla into town, charmingly insisted on paying for their cab. Enjoying himself, he strolled through fruit and vegetable stands with her.

'Would you mind terribly if I took a turn through a couple shops, LaRue? I'm ashamed to admit such a female failing, but I'm feeling deprived. I'd just love to look at some trinkets. And I do need to buy some more tapes for my camcorder.'

'Then you must. I would like nothing more than to go with you, but I have an errand or two to take care of myself. Is it convenient to meet you here, in, oh, forty minutes?'

'That would be perfect.'

'Until then.' He took her hand, kissed it charmingly, then ambled off.

As soon as he was out of sight, he slipped into the lobby of a small hotel. He needed the privacy of a phone booth, and settled inside. The number he needed was inside his head. Such things were dangerous to write down for other eyes to see.

He waited patiently, humming to himself as the operator connected the call. Collect, of course. He sneered as the pompous voice announced, 'VanDyke residence.'

'I have a collect call for Silas VanDyke from a Mr. LaRue. Will you accept the charges?'

'One moment, please.'

'One moment, please,' the operator repeated in her lovely island voice for LaRue's benefit.

'I have nothing but time, mademoiselle.' To pass it, he rolled a cigarette.

'This is VanDyke, I'll accept the charges.'

'Thank you. Go ahead, Mr. LaRue.'

'*Bonjour*, Mr. VanDyke, you are, I hope, well?'

'Where are you calling from?'

'The lobby of a little hotel on St. Kitts. The weather is quite wonderful.'

'The rest of them?'

'The lovely Mrs. Beaumont is souvenir shopping. The others are at sea.'

'What are they looking for? The *Marguerite* is played out. I saw to it personally.'

'So she is. You left little even for the worms. Tate was very upset.'

'Was she?' A trace of malevolent pleasure crept into his voice. 'She should have stayed where I put her. But that's another problem to be dealt with. I want a full report, LaRue. I'm paying you very well to keep tabs on the Lassiters.'

'And I'm delighted to do so. You may be interested to know that Buck has gone on the wagon. He suffers, but he's yet to reach for a bottle.'

'He will.'

'Perhaps.' LaRue blew out smoke, watched it curl toward the top of the booth. 'He doesn't dive. When others do, he bites his nails and sweats. You might be interested that Matthew and Tate are lovers. They rendezvous nightly.'

'I'm disappointed in her taste.' The lovely, cultured voice tightened. 'Gossip is entertaining, LaRue, but I don't like to pay for it. How long do they intend to stay with the *Marguerite?*'

'We left the *Marguerite* weeks ago.'

The pause was brief. 'Weeks ago, and you didn't bother to inform me?'

'I have, as I always have, relied on my own instincts. I enjoy dramatic timing, *mon ami*. Now it seems more appropriate to tell you we have found the wreck of the *Isabella*. And, she is rich.' He drew in more fragrant smoke, blew it out. 'My diving companion, Ray Beaumont, believes quite strongly that she holds something most precious.'

'Which is?'

'Angelique's Curse.' LaRue smiled to himself. 'I think it would be wise for you to wire a bonus of one hundred thousand American dollars into my Swiss account. I will check in twenty minutes to see that the transaction has taken place.'

'A hundred thousand dollars, for a fantasy.' But there was a breathlessness in the words that came clearly over the wire.

'When I'm assured the money is in place, I will use the fax from this charming little hotel and send you copies of the documentation Ray has worked so hard and long to gather. I believe you will find it well worth the price. I will contact you again, soon, with our progress. *A bientôt.*'

Very pleased with himself, he hung up before VanDyke could finish the next sentence.

The money would come, LaRue thought. VanDyke was too much the businessman to ignore the investment.

LaRue rubbed his hands together and exited the booth, hoping the hotel ran a little coffee shop where he could pass a quiet twenty minutes.

It was so amusing, he decided, to stir the pot, and watch just how it simmered.

Chapter Twenty-one

She was late. Matthew paced the bridge, telling himself it was ridiculous to feel disappointed that she hadn't been waiting for him. He'd seen the light in the deckhouse when he'd started his swim over. Obviously, she was involved in something. Eventually, her concentration would break, she'd glance at the clock and realize it was after midnight.

Eventually.

He moved quietly to the pilot window again to stare out at the sea and stars.

Like any sailor, he could map the world with those stars. With them, he could find his way to any point of land or body of water. But he had no map, no guide to show him the route to what he coveted most. On that journey, he was blind and without direction.

All of his life it had been helplessness that had shamed him more than any emotion, any failing. He had been helpless to prevent his mother's desertion, his father's murder, Buck's mutilation. And he was helpless now to defend himself against his own heart, and the woman who didn't want it.

He wished he could blame this restlessness that chewed at him on something as simple as sex. But that basic thirst had been slaked. He still wanted her, he couldn't look at her and not want her. Yet it went so far beyond the physical.

He supposed it had always been beyond the physical.

How could he explain that he was a different man with her? Could be a different man if she felt even a shadow for him of what he felt for her. Living without her was possible. He'd done it before and knew he would do it again. But he would never be what he wanted to be, or have what he wanted to have, unless she was part of it.

There was nothing he could do but take what she gave him, and let her go when the time came.

He knew what it was like to exist for the moment. Most of his life had been like that. It was demeaning to realize that one woman could make him yearn for a future, for boundaries and responsibilities.

A woman, he knew, who didn't believe him capable of accepting any responsibility.

There was no way to prove her wrong. They both understood that if he found what he was looking for, he would take it. And he would use it. Once he possessed Angelique's Curse, he would lose Tate. There was no way he could hold both of them, and no way he could live with himself if he ignored his debt to his father.

Now, alone, watching the stars mirror themselves on the water, he could hope that the necklace and all it stood for remained buried under the grasping sea.

'I'm sorry.' She came in quickly, her hair flying as she turned to close and lock the door. 'I was sketching the ivory fan and lost track. It's fantastic to realize something so delicate could survive untouched and perfect for all these years.'

She stopped. He was staring at her in the way he sometimes did that made her feel awkward and terrifyingly transparent. What was in his mind? she wondered. How did he hide those emotions that drove him? It was like looking at a volcano and knowing that far beneath the surface, lava was boiling.

'Are you angry? It's only quarter past.'

'No, I'm not angry.' Those eyes, with all the secrets glinting, held hers relentlessly. 'Do you want some wine?'

'You brought wine?' Suddenly nervous, she shook back her hair. 'That's nice.'

'I filched it from LaRue. He picked up some fancy French kind when he went ashore with Marla the other day. It's already opened.' Matthew picked up the bottle and poured two glasses.

'Thanks.' She took the glass and wondered what to do next. Normally, they simply dived to the floor and tore off their clothes, as greedy as children unwrapping gifts. 'There's a storm brewing west of here. It could be trouble.'

'It's still early for hurricanes. Buck's keeping his eye on it, though. Tell me about the fan LaRue brought up this afternoon.'

'It's probably worth two or three thousand. More to a serious collector.'

He reached out to touch her hair. 'Tate, tell me about the fan.'

'Oh. Well.' Off balance, she wandered to the port window. 'It's ivory, sixteen spikes, carved in a swirl pattern that forms a rose in full bloom when it's opened. I'd gauge it at mid-seventeenth century. It was already an heirloom when the *Isabella* went down.'

He twined a lock of her hair around his finger, kept his eyes on hers. 'Who owned it?'

'I don't know.' Sighing, she turned her cheek toward his hand. 'I wondered if it might have belonged to a young bride. It would have been passed down to her. She might have held it on her wedding day, as something old. She'd never use it; it would be too precious to her. But now and again, she'd take it out of the box she kept in her dressing table. She'd open it, run her finger over the rose and think of how happy she'd been when she'd carried it down the aisle.'

'Do women still do that?' Touched by the vision, he took her untasted wine, set it aside. 'Something old, something new?'

'I suppose they do.' Her head fell back as he skimmed his lips along the line of her jaw. 'If they want a traditional wedding. The once-in-a-lifetime white dress and train. The music, the flowers.'

'Is that what you want?'

'I don't–' Her heart stuttered when his mouth cruised over hers. 'I haven't thought about it. Marriage isn't a priority for me.' Pulse quickening, she stroked her hands under his shirt to run them along his back. 'God, I love your body. Make love with me, Matthew.' Greedily, and a little rough, she nuzzled his throat, nibbling the skin. 'Now. Right now.'

If that was all there could be, he'd take it. He'd take her. But she wouldn't forget, by God, she'd never forget it had been he who had stripped away every layer of that logic.

In one fierce move, he wrapped her hair around his hand, used it to yank her head back. As she opened her mouth in surprise at the sudden ruthlessness, he plundered it.

She made a sound in her throat, part protest, part arousal. Her hands came to his shoulders to pry herself free, but his darted up the baggy leg of her shorts. His fingers drove into her and shot her into a shocking and violent orgasm.

Her legs buckled. He took no time for the niceties of a blanket this time, but dragged her to the floor. Even as she gasped for breath, he was on her. His hands and mouth were everywhere, tugging, tearing at her clothes to ravish the flesh beneath.

She writhed beneath him, clawed, but not in defense. Some part of her mind realized that the volcano had finally erupted. She churned in the dark, mindless pleasure as it poured its lethal heat over her. His mouth and tongue were on her, forcing her to accept a new and terrifying level of madness. As voracious as he, she arched against him, felt the hot spurt of her own jittery climax.

'Now.' She wanted to scream it. Desperate, she fumbled for him. 'Oh God, now.'

But he streaked up her body, pinned her hands over her head. When she opened her eyes, the light dazzled them.

'No, you look at me,' he demanded when her lashes fluttered down again. 'You look right at me.' His lungs were burning and the words ground in his throat like glass. But her eyes opened, an unfocused, swimming green. 'Can you think?'

'Matthew.' Her hand strained against his. 'Take me now. I can't stand it.'

'I can.' Linking her wrists in one hand, he cupped the other over her hot center so that she bucked wildly under him. She came again, violently. He bit back his own groan when her arms went to water under his grip. 'Can you think?' he repeated.

But she was beyond words, beyond sight. Her senses were scattered, a tangle of live wires that sparked and sizzled through her system. When he released her hands, she didn't move, but lay defenseless against the next onslaught.

He devoured her, inch by inch, pale flesh, delicate curves. When he could feel himself all but being absorbed into her, when her mouth was as hungrily avid as his again, he thrust into her.

She felt battered and bruised and blissful. His weight pinned her to the unforgiving floor, and she thought vaguely of the aches she would have in the morning. Somehow she found the strength to stroke a hand over his hair.

She felt sorry for every woman who didn't have Matthew Lassiter as a lover.

'I could use that wine,' she managed in a voice that came huskily through a dry throat. 'Any chance you can reach it? Or if not, if you can roll off, I might be able to crawl a few feet.'

He pushed himself up and wondered how he could feel drained, satisfied, pleased and ashamed all at once. He brought both glasses back, sat beside her on the floor.

With effort, she lifted rockily to her elbow and took the glass. A long, cooling sip did a great deal to steady her. 'What,' she asked slowly, 'was that?'

He jerked a shoulder. 'Sex.'

After a long, appreciative breath, she smiled. 'Not that I'm complaining, but it seemed a little more like war.'

'As long as we both won.' Since he'd already drained his glass, he rose to fetch the bottle.

The last thing she'd expected after such wild intimacy was the cool tone. Concerned, she laid a hand on his knee. 'Matthew, is something wrong?'

'No. Everything's dandy.' He tossed back more wine, stared into the glass. 'Sorry if I got too rough.'

'No.' Though she couldn't have said where it had sprung from, tenderness welled inside her. Very gently, she cupped his cheek. 'Matthew …' Words fumbled inside her head, inside her heart. She struggled to choose the ones best suited to what they had together. 'Making love with you is extraordinary, every time. No one's ever …' No, it seemed wise to back off from that. 'I've never,' she corrected, 'felt more free with anyone.' She tried a smile, a lightness. 'I guess it comes from both of us knowing where we stand.'

'Right, we know where we stand.' He cupped the back of her head, held firm as his gaze drilled into hers. 'Sometimes, you can stand in one place too long.'

'I don't know what you mean.'

He pulled her up, crushed his mouth against hers until he tasted his own mistakes. 'Maybe I don't, either. I'd better go.'

'Don't.' Compelled by emotions fighting to be free, she took his hand. 'Don't go, Matthew. I … it's a nice night for a swim. Will you come with me? I don't want to be without you yet.'

He turned her hand over, pressed his lips to the palm in a way that made her eyes film. 'I don't want to be without you, either.'

All this time, VanDyke thought. All these years, the Lassiters had played him for a fool. It was all clear now.

Unwilling to waste time with sleep, he pored over the papers LaRue had sent him, reading the words again and again until he all but knew them by rote. He had underestimated the Lassiters, he decided, and blamed himself for so careless a mistake.

Too many mistakes, he thought, carefully dabbing at the sweat that beaded above his lip. All because the amulet remained out of reach.

James Lassiter had known where to find Angelique's Curse, and had likely died laughing at his murderer. VanDyke was not a man to be laughed at.

Curling a fist around a jeweled letter opener, he viciously and mindlessly hacked through the creamy upholstery of a Queen Anne occasional chair. Brocade ripped like flesh, sounding like tiny screams as horsehair vomited out. The oval mirror on the wall reflected his face, wild and white, as he stabbed and tore.

His fingers were cramped and aching when the lovely little seat was no more than rags. His breath heaved in and out, sobbing on the air over the sounds of Mozart from the recessed speakers.

Shuddering once, he let the antique weapon drop onto the carpet, stumbled back from his latest work. It was only a chair, he thought as the sweat dried calmly on his skin. Only a thing, easily replaced. To help settle his uneasy stomach, he poured a soothing brandy.

That was better, he assured himself. It was natural for a man to let his temper out, especially a strong man. Holding it in only caused ulcers and headaches and self-doubt.

That's what his father had done, VanDyke recalled. Rather than making him strong, it had weakened him. It seemed he was thinking of his father, and his mother, more and more lately. Remembering how flawed they were, finding comfort in the fact that he had escaped all their weaknesses. No, no, had triumphed over the weaknesses of mind and body.

His mother's brain had betrayed her; his father's heart had killed him. But their son had learned to keep both strong.

Yes, it was better, much better to vent. Sipping, he took a calming turn around his office aboard the *Triumphant*.

Momentary physical release was sometimes necessary, he told himself, pursing his lips as he studied the rags of silken material that were scattered over the floor. It purged the blood.

But a cool head was imperative. And, of course, he rarely lost his.

Perhaps, just perhaps, he admitted, he had been a bit impulsive when he'd killed James Lassiter. But he'd been younger then, less mature. And he really had hated the bastard so.

Yet now to know that even in death James had tricked him … Fury clawed through him again, so ferociously that VanDyke had to close his eyes, struggle through his deep-breathing exercises to prevent himself from hurling the snifter and shattering the lovely Baccarat.

No, the Lassiters would cost him nothing more, he promised himself. Not even the price of a glass of brandy. Settled again, he walked out on deck to let the balm of the night air caress him.

The yacht moved swiftly through the Pacific, Costa Rica to the east.

He'd nearly taken his jet to the West Indies before he'd controlled the impatience. The time it would take to get there by sea would be put to very good use. His plans were already formulating, and with his own man part of Lassiter's team, it was almost like being there himself.

Of course, LaRue was a bit of a nuisance with his periodic demands for bonuses. VanDyke smiled to himself and swirled brandy. Then again, he, too, would be dealt with, after his usefulness had passed.

The ultimate termination of an employee, he thought with a low, long chuckle. And that would be a small but sweet pleasure.

The man had no ties, no family, just as VanDyke preferred his tools. No one would miss a middle-aged French Canadian ship's cook.

Ah, but that little diversion was for later. The real joy would come from disposing of the Lassiters, and their partners. He would use them first, let them dig and dive and work. The effort would give them a sense of satisfaction, the belief that they were deceiving him would delight them.

Oh, he could imagine their laughter, their excited meetings discussing their cleverness. They would be so smug and self-congratulatory that they had had the patience to wait so long when they had known just where to strike.

Matthew had worked eight years, VanDyke mused, in bone-chilling water, doing the kind of salvage work true treasure hunters scoffed at, certain his nemesis would lose interest. To be fair, VanDyke had to admire him for his efforts and long-range view of the prize.

But the prize would never belong to anyone but Silas VanDyke. It was his legacy, his property, his triumph. The owning of it would shove every possession he'd ever had into the shadows.

Once they had the amulet, held the prize in their trembling hands, were filled with the elation of success, it would be so much more satisfying to destroy them.

Chuckling to himself, VanDyke polished off his brandy. In one sharp strike, he shattered the delicate crystal on the rail and let the shards tumble glittering into the water. Not because he was angry, not because he was violent, he mused.

Simply because he could.

The storm came in hard, with sheeting rain and howling wind. Ten-foot seas buffeted both boats and made diving impossible. After a debate and vote, the Lassiter-Beaumont team opted to ride it out. Once she'd accustomed herself to the movement of the boat, Tate settled down with her computer and a jug of hot tea.

There would be no midnight rendezvous tonight, she mused. It surprised her how much the lack disappointed her. Perhaps the storm was a lucky break, she decided. Without realizing it, she'd let herself get entirely too used to having Matthew beside her.

It wasn't wise to become used to anything that included Matthew.

After a great deal of internal debate, she'd convinced herself it was all right, at least safe, to care about him. Affection and attraction didn't have to be a dangerous combination. However much they clashed, however much he tended to irritate her, she liked him. They had too much in common to remain truly at odds.

At least her heart was her own this time around. For that, she was grateful. To care and to want were a far cry from being in love. Logically, practically, sex was more satisfying when a woman felt affection, even friendship for her lover. Just as logically, practically, only a fool loved when the end had already been written.

Matthew would take his share of the *Isabella* and go. Just as she would take hers. It was a pity that what they wanted from that long doomed ship was so diverse. Still, it didn't matter as long as neither interfered with the other's goals.

Frowning, she switched documents so that the article she was drafting out on Angelique's Curse popped on screen.

> Legends such as the one surrounding the Maunoir amulet, also known as Angelique's Curse, often have

their roots in fact. Though it is illogical to ascribe mystical powers to an object, the legend itself has life. Angelique Maunoir lived in Brittany and was known as the village wise woman, or healer. She did indeed own a jeweled necklace such as described above, a gift from her husband, Etienne, the youngest son of the Count DuTashe. Documentation indicates that she was arrested, charged with witchcraft and executed in October of 1553.

Excerpts from her personal journal relate her story and her intimate thoughts on the eve of her execution. On October the tenth of that year, she was burned at the stake as a witch. Limited available data indicates she was sixteen. It is not indicated that, as was often done to show mercy, she was strangled first rather than burned alive.

On reading her words written the night before her execution, one can speculate on how the legend of Angelique's Curse grew and spread.

NOTE: transcribe last portion of diary.

A deathbed curse, from a woman distraught and desperate? An innocent woman grieving over the loss of her beloved husband, betrayed by her father-in-law and facing a horrible death. Not only her own, but her unborn child's. Such truths lead to myth.

Dissatisfied with her own take on the matter, Tate leaned back and reread. When she reached for her Thermos of tea, she saw Buck in the doorway.

'Well, hi. I thought you were battened down with Matthew and LaRue on the *Mermaid*.'

'Damn Canuk makes me nuts,' Buck grumbled. His yellow slicker ran with water, his thick lenses were fogged with it. 'Thought I'd come over and hang out with Ray.'

'He and Mom are up in the bridge, I think, listening to the weather reports.' Tate poured the tea, held up the half filled lid of the Thermos. She could see that it wasn't just LaRue that had Buck nervous. 'The last I heard, the storm was blowing herself out. We should be clear by midday tomorrow.'

'Maybe.' Buck took the tea, then set it down without tasting it.

Reading him well, Tate pushed back from the monitor. 'Take that wet thing off, Buck, and sit down, will you? I could really use the break and the company.'

'Don't want to mess up your work.'

'Please.' With a laugh, she rose to get another cup from the galley. 'Please mess up my work, just for a few minutes.'

Reassured, he stripped off his dripping slicker. 'I was thinking maybe Ray'd be up for some cards or something. Don't seem to have a lot to do with my time.' He slipped onto the settee, drummed his fingers on the table.

'Feeling restless?' she murmured.

'I know I'm letting the boy down,' he burst out, then flushed and picked up the tea he didn't want.

'That's just not true.' She hoped her basic psych course in college, and her understanding of the man beside her, would guide her instincts. No one spoke of the fact that he didn't dive. Perhaps it was time someone did. 'None of us could get along without you, Buck. Not diving doesn't mean you're not productive or an essential part of the team.'

'Checking equipment, filling tanks, hammering rocks.' He winced. 'Taking videos.'

'Yes.' She leaned forward to lay a hand over his restless one. 'That's as important as going down.'

'I can't go down, Tate. Just can't.' He stared miserably at the table. 'And when I watch the boy go, it dries up the spit in my mouth. I start thinking about taking a drink. Just one.'

'But you don't, do you?'

'Guess I figured out just one'd be the end of me. But it doesn't stop the wanting.' He glanced up. 'I was gonna talk to Ray about this. Didn't mean to hit you with it.'

'I'm glad you did. It gives me the chance to tell you how proud I am of the way you've pulled yourself together. And that I know you're doing it more for Matthew than for anyone else, even yourself.'

'At one time, all we had was each other. Some wouldn't think so, but there were good times. Then I cut him off, or tried to. But he stuck by me. He's like his dad was. He's got loyalty. He's stubborn, and he keeps too much inside. That's the pride working there. James always figured he could handle whatever came, that he could do it on his own. And it killed him.'

He lifted his eyes again. 'I'm afraid the boy's heading the same way.'

'What do you mean?'

'He's got his teeth in this, nothing's going to shake him loose. What he brings up day after day, oh, it's exciting for him. But he's waiting and wanting just one thing.'

'The amulet.'

'It's got hold of him, Tate, just like it got hold of James. It scares me. The closer we get, the more it scares me.'

'Because if he finds it, he'll use it against VanDyke.'

'Fuck VanDyke. Sorry.' He cleared his throat, sipped at the tea. 'I ain't worried about that son of a bitch. That the boy can handle just fine. It's the curse.'

'Oh, Buck.'

'I'm telling you,' he said stubbornly. 'I feel it. It's close.' He looked out the window at the lashing rain. 'We're close. Could be this storm's a warning.'

Struggling not to laugh, Tate folded her hands. 'Now listen to me. I understand the seafaring superstitions, but the reality here is that we're excavating a wreck. This amulet is very likely an artifact of that wreck. With luck and hard work, we'll find it. I'll sketch it and tag it and catalogue it just the way I do every other piece we bring up. It's metal and stone, Buck, with a fascinating and tragic story attached. But that's all it is.'

'Nobody who ever owned it lived to see a happy old age.'

'People often died young, violently and tragically during the sixteenth, seventeenth and eighteenth centuries.' She gave his hand a squeeze and tried another tack. 'Let's say, just for argument's sake, that the amulet does hold some sort of power. Why would it have to be evil? Buck, have you read Angelique's diary? The part your brother copied down?'

'Yeah. She was a witch, and she put a curse on the necklace.'

'She was a sad, grieving and angry woman. She was facing a terrible death, convicted of witchcraft and of murdering her husband, a man she loved. An innocent woman, Buck, helpless to change her fate.' Seeing he was far from convinced, she blew out a breath. 'Damn it, if she'd been a witch, why didn't she just disappear in a puff of smoke or turn her jailers into toads?'

'Don't work that way,' he said stubbornly.

'Fine, it doesn't work that way. So she put a spell or whatever on the necklace. If I read correctly, she cursed those who condemned her, those who would take her last link with her husband through greed. Well, Matthew didn't condemn her, Buck, and he didn't take her necklace. What he may do is find it again, that's all.'

'And when he does, what'll it do to him?' Desperate concern made his eyes glossy and dark. 'That's what eats at me, Tate. What'll it do to him?'

A shiver raced through her. 'I can't answer that.' Surprised at how uneasy she'd become, she picked up her cup and tried to warm her suddenly chilly hands. 'But whatever happens, it will be Matthew's doing, his choosing, not an ancient curse on a piece of jewelry.'

Chapter Twenty-two

LONG AFTER BUCK had gone off to find her father, his words and his worries haunted Tate. She couldn't dismiss them as absurd or mildly hysterical. She understood that the belief itself, the reality of it was what created legends.

And she'd believed once. When she'd been young and soft-hearted and ready to dream, she'd believed in the possibility of magic and myth and mystery. She'd believed in a great many things.

Annoyed with herself, she poured more tea, tepid now as she'd forgotten to close the Thermos. It was foolish to regret a loss of naïveté. Like childhood games, it was something that was set aside with time and knowledge and experience.

She'd learned the reasons behind such legends as Angelique's Curse. Indeed that was part of her fascination for her work. The whys and hows and whos were as important to her as the weight and date and fashion of any artifact she had ever held in her hands.

Innocence and wide eyes were lost perhaps, but her education hadn't diminished her curiosity or her imagination. It had only enhanced it, and given it a channel.

Over the years she, too, had gathered information on Angelique's Curse. Bits and pieces of research she had eventually filed away on disk. More, or so she had thought, out of a sense of organization than curiosity.

It didn't have the renown of the Hope Diamond, or the cachet of the philosopher's stone, yet its story and travels were interesting. Following the trail of any artifact gave a scientist facts, dates and a glimpse of the humanity of history.

From Angelique Maunoir to the count who had condemned her, from the count after his death to his eldest daughter, who had fallen from her horse and broken her neck on the way to a tryst with a lover.

Nearly a century had passed before it had turned up again in verified documentation. In Italy, Tate mused, where it survived a fire that had destroyed its owner's villa and left him a widower. Eventually it had been sold, and traveled to Britain. The merchant who purchased it committed suicide. It came into the hands of a young duchess who apparently wore it happily for thirty years. But when her son inherited the necklace, along with her estate, he drank and gambled away his fortune and died penniless and insane.

And so the necklace had been purchased by Minnefield, who had lost his life on the great Australia reef. The necklace had also been assumed to be lost there, buried in sand and coral.

Until Ray Beaumont had found an old, tattered book and had read of a sailor and an unknown Spanish lady who faced a hurricane aboard the galleon *Isabella*.

Those were the facts, Tate thought now. Death was always cruel, but rarely mysterious. Accidents, fires, illnesses, even poor luck were simply part of the cycle of living. Stones and metal could neither cause nor change it.

But despite all the facts, the scientific data, Buck's fears had translated to her, and had that well-groomed imagination working in overdrive.

Now the storm seemed eerie with its keening wind and lashing waves. Every distant flash of lightning was a warning that nature continued to thrive on possibilities.

The night seemed to warn that certain of those possibilities were best left untapped.

More than ever she wanted to contact Hayden, to call on a fellow scientist to help her put the *Isabella* and its treasures, all of its treasures, back into perspective. She wanted someone to remind her just what it was they had. An archeological find of significant importance. Not a witch's curse that seduced.

But the night was wild and full of voices.

'Tate.'

She had the unpleasant experience of discovering just what it felt like to jump out of her skin. After she'd knocked over her cup, spilled lukewarm tea into her lap, she had the presence of mind to swear as Matthew laughed at her.

'Little jumpy?'

'It's hardly a night for visitors, and you're number two.' She rose to grab a towel from a storage cabinet to mop up the spill. 'Buck's probably upstairs, trying to wrangle a card game. What are you–'

She looked at him for the first time, saw that he was soaking wet. His shirt and worn jeans clung to him and dripped water heedlessly on the floor.

'You swam over? Are you insane?' She was already grabbing more towels as she berated him. 'For Christ's sake, Lassiter, you might have drowned.'

'Didn't.' He stood cooperatively as she rubbed the towel over his hair and muttered at him. 'I had an uncontrollable urge to see you.'

'You're old enough to control your urges. Go to Dad's cabin and get some dry clothes before you catch a chill to go with your insanity.'

'I'm fine.' He took the towel, looped it around her neck and used it to pull her to him. 'You didn't really think a little squall would stop me from keeping our date?'

'I had the mistaken belief that common sense would outweigh lust.'

'Wrong.' His lips curved as they met hers. 'But I wouldn't turn down a drink. Got any whiskey?'

She sighed. 'There's brandy.'

'Good enough.'

'Put a towel on the bench before you sit,' she ordered as she turned into the adjoining galley to locate the bottle and a glass. 'You just left LaRue alone on the *Mermaid?*'

'He's a big boy. The wind's dropping some anyway.' Pumped up by the swim and the storm, he took the brandy, and her hand. 'Want to sit on my lap and neck?'

'No, thanks very much. You're wet.'

Grinning, he tugged her down and nuzzled. 'Now we're both wet.'

She laughed, and found it amazingly easy to give in. 'I guess I should consider the fact that you risked life and limb. Here.' She angled his face with her hand so that her lips could fit nicely over his. On a little murmur of approval, she sank into the kiss. 'Warming up?'

'You could say that. Mmm, come back,' he muttered when she lifted her head.

When he was satisfied, he cuddled her head on his shoulder, smiling as she toyed with the silver disk on the chain around his neck.

'I could see the light in here from the *Mermaid*. I kept thinking, she's in there, working away, and I'm never going to get any sleep.'

Finding it lovely to be snuggled in his lap, she sighed. 'I don't think anyone's going to get very much sleep tonight. I'm glad you're here.'

'Yeah?' His hand slipped nimbly up to cup her breast.

'No, not because of that. I wanted to … mmm.' Her mind slipped quietly out of gear as his thumb teased her nipple through her dampened shirt. 'How is it you always know just where to touch me?'

'I've done a study on it. Why don't you turn off that machine of yours, Red? We'll go lock ourselves in your cabin. I can show you a terrific way to ride out a storm at sea.'

'I'm sure you could.' And it was ridiculously easy for her to envision them tucked into her bunk, riding the waves, and each other. 'I need to talk to you, Matthew.' Greedily she angled her head to give his busy mouth freer access to her throat. 'I never realized I had such a hair trigger sex drive.'

'Looks like you needed my finger on your trigger, sweetheart.'

'Apparently.' Because that idea was more than a little unnerving, she shifted and rose. 'We do have to talk.' Determined to remember her priorities, she took a steadying breath and tugged her shirt back into place. 'I was going to try to find a way to get you alone tomorrow.'

'That sounds promising.'

'I think I'll have a brandy, too.' It would give her a minute to compose herself, she decided. At a safe distance, she poured a second glass, easily adjusting to the sway of the boat. 'Matthew, I'm worried about Buck.'

'He's getting his balance.'

'You mean he's not drinking. Okay that's good, that's important, even if he is facing his problem for you instead of for himself.'

'What are you talking about?'

'Take the blinders off.' She scooted onto the bench from the opposite side. 'He's here and he's dry because of you. He feels he owes you.'

'He doesn't owe me jack,' Matthew said flatly. 'But if it helps keep him from drinking himself to death, that's fine.'

'I agree, to a point. Eventually, he'll have to keep himself sober for himself. That's not going to happen as long as he's so worried about you.'

'About me?' With a half laugh, Matthew sampled the brandy. 'What's he got to be worried about?'

'About you finding Angelique's Curse, and paying for it.'

Annoyed to have the recklessly cheerful mood that had driven him into a stormy sea shattered, he dragged a hand through his wet hair. 'Look, as long as I've partnered with him, he's wanted that damn necklace. He worried about it, sure, but he wanted it. Because my father wanted it.'

'And now you do.'

'That's right.' He knocked back more brandy. 'Now I do.'

'And for what purpose, Matthew? Underlying it all, the nonsense about spells and witches, I really think that's what's eating at Buck.'

'So, now it's nonsense.' He smiled a little. 'You didn't always think so.'

'I used to believe in the Tooth Fairy, too. Listen to me.' With some urgency, she closed her hand over his. 'Buck's not going to feel easy in his mind or his heart as long as the amulet is an issue.'

'Don't ask me to forget it, Tate. Don't ask me to make a choice like that.'

'I'm not.' She sat back, sighed again. 'Even if I could convince you, I have to work on my father, probably LaRue. Even myself.' With a restless movement of her shoulders, she glanced over to the monitor. 'I'm not immune to the fascination, Matthew.'

'You've been writing about it.' Intrigued, he nudged at her to get a better look. 'Let me read it.'

'It's not finished. It's rough. I was just–'

'Let me read it,' he repeated, 'I'm not going to grade you on it.'

Huffing a bit because she felt exactly like a schoolgirl facing a quiz, she sat back out of his way.

'How does this thing work?' he asked after a moment. 'I never had much use for computers. How do you turn the page?' Absently, he glanced down as her fingers quickly tapped. 'Got it.'

Thoughtful, he read from beginning to end. 'Pretty cut and dried,' he murmured, and put her back up.

'It's a paper,' she said testily, 'not a romance novel.'

'Until you read between the lines,' he finished, and looked back at her. 'You've been giving it a lot of thought.'

'Of course I have. Everyone has, though nobody talks about it.' With a few expert taps, she saved her file and shut down. 'The fact is I want very much to find the amulet, see it myself, examine it. It would be the find of any professional lifetime. Truthfully, it's been playing on my mind so much that I've revised my entire thesis around it.'

She turned back with a weak smile. 'Myth versus science.'

'What are you asking me, Tate?'

'To reassure Buck, and I guess to reassure me, that finding it will be enough for you. Matthew, you have nothing to prove. If your father loved you even a fraction of the amount that Buck does, he wouldn't want you to ruin your life on some useless vendetta.'

Torn between comforting and convincing, she framed his face in her hands. 'It won't bring him back, give you the years you lost with him. VanDyke's out of your life. You can beat him if that's still important to you just by finding the necklace. Let that be enough.'

He didn't speak for a moment. The war inside was so familiar he barely registered the rip of battle. In the end it was he who broke contact.

'It isn't enough, Tate.'

'Do you really think you could kill him? Even if you managed to get close enough, do you really believe you're capable of taking a life?'

His eyes glinted as they sliced to hers. 'You know I am.'

She shivered as her blood chilled. There was no doubt in her mind that the man looking at her now was capable of anything. Even murder.

'You'd ruin your life? And for what?'

He shrugged. 'For what's right. I've ruined it before.'

'That's so incredibly ignorant.' Unable to sit, she shoved out and paced the room. 'If there's a curse on that damned thing, this is it. It blinds people to their better selves. I'm calling Hayden.'

'What the fuck does he have to do with it?'

'I want another scientist here, or at least I want to be able to consult with one. If you won't find a way to reassure Buck, I will. I can find a way to prove to him that the amulet is just an amulet, and that if and when it's found, it will be treated as a relic. With the scientific community backing me, that necklace will be put in a museum where it belongs.'

'You can toss it back into the sea when I'm done with it,' Matthew told her, and his voice was cold and final. 'You can call a dozen scientists. They're not going to stop me from dealing with VanDyke my way.'

'It always has to be your way, doesn't it?' If it would have done any good, she would have thrown something.

'This time it does. I've been waiting half my life for this.'

'So you'll waste the rest of your life. Not just waste,' she said furiously. 'But throw it away.'

'It's still my life, isn't it?'

'No one's life is theirs alone.' How could he be so blind? she wondered bitterly. How could he turn the beauty of these past weeks into something as ugly as vengeance. 'Can't you stop and think, for just a moment, what it would do to other people if you manage to succeed in this insane idea? What would happen to Buck if you get yourself killed or spend the rest of your miserable life in prison for murder? How do you think I would feel?'

'I don't know, Tate. How would you feel?' He pushed away from the table. 'Why don't you tell me? I'm interested. You're always so goddamn careful not to tell me anything you feel.'

'Don't turn this around on me, make it my responsibility. We're talking about you.'

'Sounds like we're talking about us. You put up the rules from the get-go,' he reminded her. 'No emotions or pretty words cluttering up nice, companionable sex. You didn't want me interfering with your life or your ambitions. Why should I let you interfere with mine?'

'Damn it, you know it's not as cold as that.'

'No?' He lifted a brow. 'It looks like that from where I'm standing. I don't remember you saying any different.'

She was very pale now, her eyes too dark against the white skin. He had to know how he was making everything they had together sound. Everything she'd given to him.

'You know I have feelings for you. I wouldn't sleep with you if I didn't.'

'News to me. Best I can figure, you're just scratching an itch.'

'Bastard.' Stunned by the sting, she'd swung out and slapped him hard before she could stop herself.

His eyes flashed, narrowed, but his voice was icily calm. 'Did that help? Or was that your answer to the question?'

'Don't attribute your own motivations and lack of sensitivity to me,' she shot back, both furious and ashamed. 'Do you think I'd pour out my heart and soul to you the way I did once? Not a chance. Nobody hurts me, especially you.'

'You think you're the only one who got hurt?'

'I know I was.' She jerked at her arm when his fingers wrapped around it. 'You'll never get a second chance to shrug me off again. I loved you, Matthew, with the kind of innocent, unrestricted love that only comes around once. You tossed it back in my face like it was nothing. Now your pride's ruffled because I won't put myself in the position where you can do it again when you're ready to move on. Well, the hell with you.'

'I'm not asking you for a second chance. I know better than that. But you've got no right to ask me to settle for sex then expect me to give up the one thing that's kept me going. I gave you up, now I'm taking what's left.'

'You didn't give me up,' she tossed back. 'You never wanted me.'

'I never wanted anything the way I wanted you. I loved you.' He dragged her painfully to her toes. 'I've always loved you. I cut my own heart out when I sent you away.'

She couldn't breathe, was afraid if she did everything inside her would shatter like glass. 'What do you mean, you sent me away?'

'I–' He caught himself. Shaken, appalled, he loosened his grip and stepped back. He needed a minute, he told himself, to get his balance. 'Nothing. It doesn't matter. Digging up old ground doesn't change where we stand now. I won't give you what you want. That's the bottom line.'

She stared at him, one part of her brain fascinated by the way he was able to close off. All those vivid emotions were dimming behind carefully shuttered eyes one by one. No, she thought. Oh no, not this time.

'You started digging this ground, Lassiter. Now we'll finish the excavation.' She balled her unsteady hands into fists. 'Eight years ago you laughed in my face, Matthew. You stood there on that beach and told me that it had all been for fun. Just a way to pass a summer. Was that a lie?'

His gaze never faltered, never changed, never sparked. 'I said it doesn't matter. The past is past.'

'If you really believed that, you wouldn't be so hell-bent on evening the score with VanDyke. Answer me,' she demanded. 'Was it a lie?'

'What the hell was I supposed to do?' he exploded. Outside the windows, the sky erupted in frenzied light. 'Let you throw everything away on some idiotic dream? I didn't have anything to give you. I ruined everything I touched. Christ, we both knew I wasn't good enough, but you were too stupid to admit it.'

Thunder grumbled, a nasty old woman's chuckling.

'But you would have,' he continued. 'And then you'd have hated me. I'd have hated myself.'

Unsteady, she braced a hand on the table. The storm outside was nothing compared to the one pitching inside her. Everything she'd believed, everything that had kept her from looking back in misery was shattered at her feet.

'You broke my heart.'

'I saved your life,' he snapped back. 'Get a picture, Red. I was twenty-four years old, I had no future. I had nothing but an uncle who was going to need every penny I could scrape together, maybe for the rest of my life. You had potential. You had brains, ambitions. All of a sudden, you're talking about ditching college and hooking up with me, like we'd just sail off into the sunset.'

'I never thought that. I wanted to help you. I wanted to be with you.'

'And you'd have ended up saving nickels and wondering what the hell you'd done to your life instead of making something out of it.'

'And you made that choice for me.' Oh, she could breathe now. She could breathe just fine. In fact, the air that filled her lungs was hot and pure. 'You arrogant son of a bitch. I cried myself empty over you.'

'You got over it.'

'Damn right I did.' She could lash back with that and be thankful. 'I got way over it. And if you think I'm going to weep gratefully on your shoulder because you see yourself as some self-sacrificing hero, you're mistaken, Lassiter.'

'I don't see myself as anything but what I am,' he said, wearily now. 'You were the one who saw something that wasn't there.'

'You had no right to make that choice for me. No right to expect me to be grateful for what you did.'

'I don't expect anything.'

'You expect me to believe you're in love with me.'

What the hell, he thought, he'd already ruined it. 'I am in love with you. Pathetic, isn't it? I never got over you.

Seeing you again, eight years later, carved a hole in me I've been trying to fill ever since with whatever you'd toss my way. No chance.'

'We had one once.'

'Hell, Tate.' He reached out to rub his thumb over a tear on her cheek. 'We never had a chance. The first time it was too soon. This time it's too late.'

'If you'd been honest with me–'

'You loved me,' he murmured. 'I knew you loved me. You'd never have left me.'

'No.' Her vision blurred with more tears, but she could see so clearly what had been lost. 'I'd never have left you. Now we'll never know what we might have had.' She turned away. 'So, what now?'

'That's up to you.'

'Ah, this time it's up to me.' She wished she could find even one small laugh inside her. 'That's only fair, I suppose. Only this time I don't have all that simple, innocent faith.'

And this time, she realized, she didn't know what to do, except protect herself from being so horribly hurt again.

'I guess the only answer here is to be practical. We can't go back, so we go forward.' She drew a deep breath. 'It would be unfair to the others, and shortsighted, to scuttle the expedition because of something that happened eight years ago. I'm willing to continue.'

He'd never expected otherwise. 'And?'

'And.' She blew out the breath. 'We can't afford to let personal problems undermine the excavation. Under the circumstances, I don't think it's in your best interest or in mine to continue the intimate aspect of our relationship.'

Again, it was no less, and no more than expected. 'All right.'

'This hurts,' she whispered.

He shut his eyes, knowing he couldn't hold her. 'Would you feel better if we switched teams? I can dive with Ray or LaRue.'

'No.' She pressed her lips together before turning back. 'I think the less upheaval, the better. We both have some sorting out to do, but I don't think we have to let it affect the others.' Impatiently, she brushed the heels of her hands over her face to dry it. 'But we can make some excuse to switch if you're uncomfortable ...'

He did laugh. It was such an absurd word for what he was feeling. 'You were always a piece of work, Red. We'll keep things status quo.'

'I'm only trying to make all of this as simple as I can.'

'Fuck.' Nearly undone, he scrubbed his hands over his face. 'Yeah, you go ahead and simplify. We keep the schedule as is, we cut out the sex. How's that for simple?'

'You won't make me fall apart,' she said, terrified she would do just that. 'I'm going to see this through. It'll be interesting to find out if you can do the same.'

'I'm game if you are, sweetheart. I guess that covers it.'

'Not quite. I want to contact Hayden.'

'No.' He lifted a hand before she could spit at him. 'Let's try this. We haven't found the amulet, and can't say that we will. If and when we do, we'll bring up the idea of calling in your backup scientist.'

It was a compromise that made sense, which was why she was instantly suspicious. 'I have your word? When we find it, I can contact another archeologist?'

'Red, when we find it, you can take out an ad in *Science Digest*. Until then, the lid's on.'

'All right. Will you promise to reconsider your plot for revenge?'

'That sounds pretty dramatic for something so straightforward. I'll give you a straightforward answer. No. I lost everything that mattered to me in my life, and VanDyke had a part in all of it. Leave it alone, Tate,' he said before she could speak again. 'The ball started rolling sixteen years ago. You're not going to stop it. Look, I'm tired. I'm going to bed.'

'Matthew.' She waited until he'd stopped at the companionway and turned back. 'You might consider the idea that rather than your ruining my life, I might have made a difference in yours.'

'You did,' he murmured, and walked out into the dying storm.

Chapter Twenty-three

THE ROUGH CHOP postponed the morning's dive. Tate was grateful to have some time alone, so she closed herself in her cabin with her work.

But work wasn't on her mind.

She indulged herself, lying on her bunk, watching the ceiling. A woman had a right to sulk when she discovered that eight years of her life had been determined by someone else's decision.

She'd already gone over all the standard lines in her head. He'd had no right. He'd broken her heart for what he'd deemed her own good. Every relationship in her life had been shadowed by what had happened on that beach in her twentieth year.

It did no good to go over it all again and again. But the arrogance of it, the unfairness of it stewed inside her.

Now he claimed he'd loved her. Loved her still.

What a crock, she thought and flopped over on her stomach. Obviously he'd seen her as a dim-witted child who hadn't been capable of making her own choices. She'd been young, yes, but she hadn't been stupid.

What games had fate been playing to have brought them full circle?

The hiatus had made her stronger, she acknowledged. She had used her opportunities and her brains to make her mark. There were degrees tucked away in the window seat in her room in Hatteras, an apartment in Charleston that was tastefully decorated and rarely used. She had a reputation, colleagues whose companionship she enjoyed, offers to teach, to lecture, to join expeditions.

Professionally, she had everything she'd ever wanted.

But she had no real home, no man to hold through the night. No children to love.

And she might have, she would have, if Matthew had only trusted her.

That was behind her now, she thought, and rolled over again. Who knew better than an archeologist that the past could be examined, analyzed and recorded, but it couldn't be changed. What had been, and might have been, was as calcified as old silver in seawater. It was the moment that had to be faced.

She hoped it was true, that he did love her. Now he could suffer, as she had, when a heart was offered and turned aside. He'd had his chance with her. This would be a case in point where history did not repeat itself.

But she wouldn't be cruel, she decided, rising to glance at herself in the oval mirror over her dresser. It wasn't necessary to pay him back in kind. After all, her own emotions weren't involved this time around. She could afford to be generously, certainly politely, forgiving.

Not loving him would help her be carefully detached. They would continue to dive together, work to salvage the *Isabella* as partners, colleagues. She was certainly able to turn aside her personal past in order to explore history.

Satisfied that she'd reached the only logical solution, she left her cabin. She found her father on the port deck, busily checking gauges.

'Wild night, huh, honey?'

In more ways than one, she thought. 'You'd hardly know it now.'

Above, the sky was blue and clear with no more than a few tattered powder-puff clouds. She glanced over atop the bridge to study the wind gauge. 'Wind's coming from the south now.'

'Bringing in drier air. The sea's calming, too.' He set a regulator aside. 'I've got a good feeling about today, Tate. Woke up full of energy, a kind of anticipation.' He rose, took a deep gulp of air. 'Your mother said it was leftover electricity from the storm.'

'You're thinking about the amulet,' she murmured and wanted to sigh. 'What is it about that one piece that pulls everyone so?'

'Possibilities.' Ray looked out to sea.

'Last night Buck was panicked at the thought of finding it. All Matthew can think about is using it to settle the score with VanDyke. VanDyke himself, a rich, powerful, successful man, is so obsessed by it he'll do anything to have it. And you.' She pushed impatiently at her hair. 'And you. You've realized a dream of a lifetime with the *Isabella*. There's a fortune down there, for you, for the museum we've always wanted. But it's the amulet that brought you back here.'

'And that makes no sense to you.' He slipped an arm around her shoulders. 'When I was a boy, I was fortunate to have a beautiful home, a yard with rich green grass and big shady trees to climb. I had a jungle gym, sliding board, pals. Everything a kid could want. But beyond the fence and just over the hill there was a swampy area. Dark, junglelike kudzu and ugly trees, a slow, almost stagnant river. There were snakes. I was forbidden to go there.'

'So, of course, that's where you most wanted to go.'

He laughed and kissed Tate on top of the head. 'Of course. Legend had it that it was haunted, which only added to the allure. Little boys went in, so I was told, and never came out again. I would stand at the back fence, smelling the honeysuckle that climbed there and think, what if.'

'Did you ever go in?'

'I got as far as the edge once, where you could smell the river and see the vines clogging the trees. But I lost my nerve.'

'Just as well. You'd likely have been snake bit.'

'But what if,' he murmured. 'I've never lost that curiosity.'

'You know it wasn't haunted. Your mother told you those stories so that you'd stay out of it. Otherwise you could have fallen in the river or lost your way. It wasn't ghosts she was worried about.'

'I'm not at all sure it wasn't.' He watched a gull soar overhead, then turn restlessly toward the horizon. 'I think it would be very sad if we lost our wonder, if we knew there was no possibility of magic-good or evil. I suppose you could say Angelique's Curse has become my haunted swamp. This time I want to go in and see for myself.'

'And if you find it?'

'I'll stop regretting I didn't take that next step through the kudzu.' Laughing at himself, Ray gave her a quick squeeze. 'Maybe Buck will stop believing he's not the man he was. Matthew might stop blaming himself for his father's death. And you …' He turned her to face him. 'You might let a little magic into your life again.'

'That's an awful lot to ask of one necklace.'

'But what if.' He drew her close for a hug. 'I want you happy, Tate.'

'I am happy.'

'All the way happy. I know you closed something off inside eight years ago. I've always worried that I handled things badly because I wanted the best for you.'

'You've never handled anything badly.' She drew her head back to study his face. 'Not where I was concerned.'

'I knew how Matthew felt about you. How you felt about him. It worried me.'

'You had nothing to worry about.'

'You were so young.' He sighed and touched her hair. 'I see the way he feels about you now.'

'Now I'm not so young,' she pointed out. 'You still have nothing to worry about.'

'I see the way he feels about you,' Ray repeated, his eyes sober and seeking. 'What worries me, what surprises me, is that I can't see the way you feel about him.'

'Maybe I haven't decided. Maybe I don't want to decide.' She shook herself, drummed up a smile for him. 'And maybe you shouldn't worry about something I have completely under control.'

'Maybe that's what worries me.'

'I can't win with you.' Rising on her toes, she gave Ray a quick kiss. 'So, I'm going to see if Matthew's up for diving.' She turned to walk away, but something stopped her, made her look back.

Ray was standing, one hand on the rail, a far-off look in his eyes as he gazed toward open sea.

'Dad. I'm glad you didn't walk through the kudzu. If you had then, you might not need to take the step now.'

'Life's all timing, Tate.'

'Maybe it is.' Mulling that over, she headed around to starboard. Timing, she supposed, could stop or start a war, save or end a marriage, take or give a life.

There was Matthew on the *Mermaid*, an elbow on the rail, a coffee mug in his hand. She didn't want that jolt of emotion, the stir and simmer. But they came nonetheless. Her heart went butter soft in her breast and melted out a sigh.

Did he have to look so lonely?

It wasn't her problem, she assured herself. She wouldn't let it be her worry.

But he turned his head. Across the choppy waves, his eyes met hers. There was nothing in them to read. Like the storm, whatever raged inside him had calmed, or was controlled. She saw nothing but that deep, enigmatic blue.

'We're down to a light chop,' she called out. 'I'd like to dive.'

'Could smooth out more if we wait an hour or two.'

Something was swelling in her throat. 'I'd like to go down now. If it's too rough once we do, we can scrub the dive.'

'All right. Get your gear.'

Turning, she walked blindly away. Damn him, damn the *Isabella*, damn Angelique and her cursed necklace. Her life had been manageable without them. She was afraid it would never be manageable again.

There was nothing to decide, nothing to control. She was still in love with him after all.

The storm had stirred and shifted the sand. Several of the excavation trenches needed to be cleared again. Matthew was grateful for the extra work. The skill and delicacy required to work the airlift left no room for deep personal thoughts.

He'd had enough of them during the night.

It gave him some small pleasure to suck away sand and see the hilt of a sword.

Déjà vu, he thought, almost amused. He turned the airlift aside. A glance around showed him that Tate was efficiently picking through the debris.

Matthew clanged on his tank, waited for her to look around. He signaled her over. Once she'd joined him, he gestured toward the hilt.

Take it, he indicated. This one's yours.

He watched her hesitate, knew she was remembering. Then her fingers closed around it, tugged it free.

Halfway down, the blade came to a jagged halt.

That, he supposed, studying the shattered sword, told the whole story. Struggling against keen disappointment, he lifted a shoulder. With the pipe, he widened the trench.

They saw the plate at the same moment. Even as she grabbed his arm to signal him to stop, Matthew was turning the pipe away. Hand fanning, Tate uncovered three quarters of the plate.

It was nearly transparent china, delicately painted with violets dancing around the rim. The rim itself was gold. With great care, she closed her fingers over the edge and tried to ease the plate free.

It was stuck fast. Frustrated, she looked at Matthew, shook her head. They both knew that dislodging it with the airlift was as chancy as cutting a diamond with an ax. If the plate was whole, which would be a miracle itself, the flow from the pipe could snap it.

They debated their options with hand signals until it was decided that they had to try. Ignoring the murk and discomfort, Tate kept her fingers lightly on the edge of the plate while Matthew removed the sand and debris, almost a grain at a time.

It was probably missing a fist-sized chunk, he thought, but ignored the strain in his back and shoulders. Degree by degree, he cleared the translucent china, exposing another sprig of violets, and the first swirl of a monogram.

Feeling a give, she stopped him. Working to keep her breathing steady, she eased the plate out another fraction before it jammed again. She could read the first ornate letter, painted in gold. *T*. Taking it as a sign, she nodded for Matthew to resume.

It would have a bite out of it, he was certain. The steel sword less than a foot away had been shattered. How could something as fragile as a china plate survive intact? Frowning in concentration he watched the next letter emerge. *L*.

If the *L* stood for Lassiter's luck, they were wasting their time. He wanted to stop, roll out the ache from his shoulders, but a glimpse at Tate's excited face had him keeping the flow steady.

The final letter came clear so that the monogram read *TLB*. She'd barely had time to consider the oddity of that when the plate, whole and miraculously undamaged, slipped effortlessly free.

Stunned, she nearly dropped it. With it held between her and Matthew, she could see the play of her own fingers under the base. The plate, so fine, so elegant, had once graced a gleaming table, she imagined. It had been part of a cherished set, carefully packed for the voyage to a new life.

And hers were the first hands to hold it in more than two hundred years.

In wonder, she looked up at Matthew. For an instant they shared the silent and intimate thrill of discovery. Then his face changed, became remote. They were only professionals again.

Sorry for it, Tate swam clear to set the plate beside the broken sword out of the range of fallout. She studied the two pieces lying side by side on the sand.

They had been on the same ship, through the same storm, had been tossed, then buried by the same sea. Two different kinds of pride, she mused. Force and beauty. Only one had survived.

What whim had chosen between them? she wondered. Snapping steel and leaving the fragile undamaged? Mulling through it, she went back to the chore of sifting debris.

Later, she would ask herself just what had made her look up and around at just that moment. There'd been no movement to catch her eye. Perhaps there had been a tickle at the back of her neck, or that visceral sensation of being watched.

But she looked up through the murk. The steely eyes and toothy grin of the barracuda gave her a jolt. Amused at herself for the reaction, she reached into the fallout again. And again found herself looking where the fish continued to hover – patient and watching. And familiar.

Surely it couldn't be the same fish that had joined them daily on their excavation of the *Marguerite?*

She knew it was foolish to think so, but the idea of it made her smile. Wanting to get Matthew's attention, she reached for her knife to rap on her tanks. Suddenly something flew out of the fallout and landed less than an inch from her hand.

It glittered and pulsed and gleamed. Fire and ice and the regal shine of gold. The water seemed to heat around her, move around her and grow clear as glass.

The ruby was a spreading of blood, surrounded by the iced tears of diamonds. The gold was as polished and bright as the day it had been fashioned into those heavy links and ornate setting.

There was such clarity to it that she could read the French inscribed around the stone perfectly.

Angelique. Etienne.

The roar in her head was her own blood singing. For there was no sound at all in the sea. No hum from the pipe, no clatter from the stone and shells that rained over her tanks. The silence was so perfect, she could hear her own words echo in her head as if she'd spoken aloud.

Angelique's Curse. We've found it, and freed it, at last.

With numbed fingers, she reached down for it. It was her imagination, of course, that made her think she could feel heat radiating toward her. An invitation, or a warning. When she held it in her hands, it was only fantasy that made it seem as though the necklace vibrated like something alive taking a long greedy breath.

She felt a terrible grief, and anger and fear. Almost, the wild flood of sensation made her drop it again. But there was love welling through all the rest, a fierce and desperate love that tore at her heart.

Tate closed a hand around the chain, another around the stone and absorbed the war of emotion.

She could see the cell, the thin light through the single barred window set high in the thick stone. She could smell the filth and the fear, and hear the screams and pleas of the damned.

And the woman in a dingy tattered dress, her red hair dull and chopped off rudely at her neck, sat at a tiny table. She wept, and she wrote while around her thin throat, the amulet hung like a bleeding heart.

For love. The words drifted through Tate's mind. Only and always for love.

Fire swept up greedily and consumed her.

Matthew. It was her first coherent thought. Tate had no idea how long she had clutched the necklace while debris fell like rain around her.

He was working steadily, his face angled away. Here it is, she thought. What you're searching for is right here. How did you miss it? Why, she thought with a shiver, didn't you see it?

She knew she should signal to him, show him what she held. The object that had drawn them together, twice, was right there in her hands.

And what would it do to him? she wondered. What would it cost him? Before she could question her own motives, she jammed the necklace in her goody bag, drew the drawstring tight.

Struggling for calm, she looked toward the barracuda. But the fish was gone, as if it had never been. There was only murk.

Five hundred miles away, VanDyke rolled off his surprised lover and got out of bed. Ignoring her complaints, he swung into a silk robe and hurried from the master suite. His mouth was dry, his heart throbbing like a wound. Stalking past a white-suited steward, he rushed up the companionway to the bridge.

'I want more speed.'

'Sir.' The captain looked up from his charts. 'There's weather due east. I was about to alter our course to swing below it.'

'Hold your course, goddamn you.' In one of his rare leaps of public temper, VanDyke swept a hand over the table and sent charts scattering. 'Hold your course and give me more speed. You'll have this ship to Nevis by morning or I'll see you captain nothing larger than a two-man paddle boat.'

He didn't wait for an answer, didn't need to. VanDyke's commands were always followed, his wishes always granted. But the flush of humiliation that had come across the captain's face didn't calm or appease VanDyke as it should have.

His hands were trembling, the bitter cloud of rage threatening to close over him. The signs of weakness infuriated him, frightened him. To prove his strength, he marched into the lounge, cursed at the bartender always on duty and grabbed a bottle of Chevis himself.

The amulet. He would have sworn he'd seen it flashing, felt its weight around his own neck as he'd ranged himself over the woman in his bed. And the woman in his bed had not been the increasingly tedious companion of the last two months, but Angelique herself.

Snarling at the bartender to leave, VanDyke poured the liquor, drank it down, poured again. His hands continued to tremble, to curl themselves of their own accord into fists looking for something to pummel.

It had been too real to have been a simple fantasy. It was, he was sure, a premonition.

Angelique was taunting him again, snickering at him from centuries past. But he would not be tricked, or outwitted, this time. His course was set. He accepted now that it had been set from the moment he'd been born. Destiny beckoned so that he could nearly taste it along with the liquor. And it was sweet and strong. He would soon possess the amulet, its power. With it he would have his legacy, and his revenge.

'Tate seems preoccupied,' LaRue commented, tugging up the zipper of his wetsuit.

'We put in a long shift.' Matthew hauled tanks over to the tender. Buck would be taking them to the island to be refilled. 'I guess she's tired.'

‘And you, *mon ami?*’

‘I’m fine. You and Ray want to work on that southeast trench.’

‘As you say.’ Taking his time, LaRue hooked on his tanks. ‘I noticed she did not linger on deck after you surfaced, as is her habit. She went inside quickly.’

‘So what? You writing a book?’

‘I am a student of human nature, young Matthew. It is my opinion that the lovely mademoiselle has something to hide, something that worries her mind.’

‘Worry about your own mind,’ Matthew suggested.

‘Ah, but the study of others is so much more interesting.’ He smiled at Matthew as he sat to put on his flippers. ‘What one does, or doesn’t do. What that one thinks or plans. You understand?’

‘I understand you’re wasting your air.’ He nodded toward the *New Adventure*. ‘Ray’s waiting on you.’

‘My diving partner. This is a relationship that must have full trust, eh? And you know, young Matthew …’ LaRue pulled on his mask. ‘You can rely on me.’

‘Right.’

LaRue saluted, then went into the water. Something told him he would need to make another phone call very soon.

She didn’t know what to do. Tate sat on the edge of her bunk staring at the amulet in her hands. It was wrong for her to keep the discovery to herself. She knew it, and yet …

If Matthew knew she had it, nothing would stop him from taking it. He’d alert VanDyke that he had it in his possession. He’d demand a showdown.

She knew without doubt that only one of them would walk away from it.

All this time. Slowly, she ran her fingers over the carved names. She hadn't really believed they would find it. What she hadn't realized was that, against all logic, all scientific curiosity, she had hoped they wouldn't find it.

Now it was real, in her hands. She had a foolish urge to open her window and heave it back into the sea.

She didn't have to be an expert on gems to know that the center ruby alone was priceless. It was certainly easy enough to judge the gram weight of the gold and figure that worth in current market value. Add the diamonds, the antiquity, the legend, and what did she have? Four million dollars in her hands? Five?

Enough, certainly, to satisfy any greed, any lust, any vengeance.

Such a stunning piece of work, she mused. Surprisingly simple despite the flash and fire. A woman would wear it and draw eyes and admiration. Displayed, it would be the centerpiece of any museum. Around it she could build the most impressive, the most spectacular collection of marine salvage in the world.

Her professional dreams would be realized beyond any of her wildest imaginings. Her reputation would soar. Any and all funding she desired for an expedition would flow to her like river to sea.

All of this and more would come. She had only to hide the amulet, to go to Nevis and make a single phone call. Within hours she and her prize could be on their way to New York or Washington to stun the world of ocean exploration.

She jerked back, letting the necklace spill onto the bed. Shocked, she stared at it.

What had she been thinking? How could she have even considered such actions? When had fame and fortune become more important to her than loyalty, than honesty? Than even love.

With a shiver, she pressed her hands to her face. Maybe the damn thing was cursed if having it for so short a time skewed her integrity.

She turned her back on it, walked to the window and, opening it, took deep gulps of sea air.

The truth was, she would give up the amulet, the museum, everything, if it would turn Matthew away from this course of self-destruction. She would hand it over to VanDyke personally if the betrayal would save the man she loved.

Perhaps it would. Turning, she studied the amulet again, spread like stars over the serviceable cover of her bunk. Driven by instinct, she scooped it up, pushed it under the neatly folded clothes in her middle drawer.

She needed to act quickly. Through the doorway leading to the bridge, she spied out at the *Mermaid*. She could see her mother hammering conglomerate to the rhythm of some top-forty station on the portable radio. Buck was on his way to St. Kitts, she knew, and her father and LaRue were at the wreck.

That left only Matthew, and of him she saw no sign. There was no better time, she decided, and no better way.

Heart pounding, she slipped up the stairs to the bridge. She hoped the operator on Nevis could help her contact Trident Industries. Failing that, she would work to track down Hayden. Surely between them, they could find a way to get through to VanDyke.

She made the ship-to-shore call, wishing she'd thought quickly enough to hitch a ride with Buck to the island. It would certainly have simplified the contact.

After twenty frustrating minutes, and countless transfers, she was able to reach Trident, Miami. For all the good it did, Tate thought when she disconnected. No one there would even acknowledge that Silas VanDyke was associated with them. All she could do was insist the silky voiced receptionist take her message and see that it was passed to the proper source.

Remembering the man she had faced years before, she had no doubt it would be. But there was little time.

That left Hayden, she decided, and hoped that he was off the *Nomad* and back in North Carolina. Again, she made the ship-to-shore, waited while the call was transferred north and over the Atlantic.

For all her trouble, her call was taken by Hayden's answering service.

'I need to get a message to Dr. Deel. It's urgent.'

'Dr. Deel is in the Pacific.'

'I'm aware of that. This is Tate Beaumont, his associate. It's imperative that I reach him as soon as possible.'

'Dr. Deel checks in for his messages periodically. I'll be glad to relay your message to him when he contacts me.'

'Tell him Tate Beaumont needs to speak with him urgently. Urgently,' she repeated. 'I'm at sea in the West Indies aboard the *New Adventure*. HTR-56390. He can contact the operator on Nevis for the transfer. Have you got that?'

Precisely, the service repeated the location and the call numbers.

'Yes. Tell Dr. Deel that I must speak to him, that I urgently need his help. Tell him I've found something of vital importance, and I need to contact Silas VanDyke. If I haven't heard from Dr. Deel in a week, no, three days,' she decided, 'I'll make arrangements to join the *Nomad*. Tell him I need his help badly.'

'I'll see that he gets your message the moment he calls in, Ms. Beaumont. I'm sorry I can't tell you how long that might be.'

'Thank you.' She could back up the message with a letter, Tate thought. God knew how long it would take to reach the *Nomad*, but it was worth a try.

She spun around, then stopped dead when she saw Matthew blocking the doorway.

'I thought we had a deal, Red.'

Chapter Twenty-four

DOZENS OF EVASIONS and excuses ran through her head. Plausible evasions, reasonable excuses.

She was sure the man who faced her now would swat them aside like pitiful gnats. Still, by the way he leaned negligently against the jamb, she thought there was a small chance.

'I want to check some data with Hayden.'

'Is that so? How many times have you felt the need to check some data with Hayden since we found the *Isabella?*'

'This is the first–' She yelped and instinctively stumbled back when he straightened. It wasn't the move, which had been slow and controlled. It had been the vicious temper that had leapt into his eyes. In all the time she'd known him, she'd never seen it fully unleashed.

'Goddamn you, Tate, don't lie to me.'

'I'm not.' She pressed back against the wall, for the first time in her life fully physically terrified. He could hurt her, she realized. Something in his eyes warned her that he'd like to. 'Matthew, don't.'

'Don't what? Don't tell you you're a lying, double-crossing bitch?' Because he did want to hurt her, was afraid he would if he let that last link of control snap, he slapped his hands on the wall at either side of her head to cage her in. 'When did he get to you?'

'I don't know what you mean.' She swallowed on a dry throat. 'I just needed to ask Hayden …' Her excuse ended on a whimper when he closed a hand over her jaw and squeezed.

'Don't lie to me,' he said, spacing each word deliberately. 'I heard you. If I hadn't heard you myself, no one could have convinced me you'd turn this way. What for, Tate? The money, the prestige, a promotion? A fucking museum with your name on it?'

'No, Matthew, please.' She closed her eyes and waited for the blow when his grip vised on her flesh.

'What were you so anxious to pass on to VanDyke? Where is he, Tate? Keeping a safe distance until we play out the *Isabella?* Then with your help he'll come along and take everything we've worked for.'

Her eyes swam with useless frightened tears. 'I don't know where he is. I swear it. I'm not helping him, Matthew. I'm not giving him the *Isabella*.'

'Then what? What the hell else would you have to give him?'

Staggered, she cringed back from the ripe violence in his face. 'Please, don't hurt me.' Cowardice had tears of shame spilling down her cheeks. Humiliated, she fought to keep her breath from sobbing.

'You can face down a shark, but you can't face yourself.' He let his hand drop, stepped back. 'You know, maybe you figure you've got a lot to pay me back for. I wouldn't argue with that. But I'd never have thought you'd betray the whole expedition just to get to me.'

'I didn't. I haven't.'

'What were you going to tell him?' She opened her mouth, shook her head. 'Fine. You tell him this for me, sweetheart. If he comes within a hundred feet of my boat, of my wreck, he's a dead man. You got that?'

'Matthew, please listen.'

'No, you listen. I've got a lot of respect for Ray and Marla. I know as far as they're concerned the sun rises and sets in you. For their sake, we'll keep this between the two of us. I'm not going to be responsible for them finding out what you really are. So you're going to come up with a real good reason why you've got to ditch this expedition. You make them believe you had to go back to the university, or back to the *Nomad*, or wherever, but you're out of here within twenty-four hours.'

'I'll go.' She dashed at tears. 'If you'll just listen to me first, I'll go as soon as Buck gets back with the tender.'

'You don't have anything to say I want to hear. You can consider it a job well done, Tate.' The heat had died from both his eyes and his voice. They were viciously cold again. 'You paid me all the way back.'

'I know what it's like to hate you. I can't bear knowing you'd hate me now.' She would have thrown herself at him when he turned for the door. It wasn't pride that stopped her, but fear that even begging wouldn't sway him. 'I love you, Matthew.'

It stopped him, sliced at him. 'That's a trick that would have worked even a couple of hours ago. Check your timing, Red.'

'I don't expect you to believe me. I just needed to say it. I don't know what's right.' She squeezed her eyes shut so that she didn't have to see his hard, unyielding face. 'I thought this was. I was scared.' Fighting for courage, she opened her eyes again. 'I was wrong. Before you walk away, before you send me away a second time, there's something I need to give you.'

'You don't have anything I want anymore.'

'Yes, I do.' She took a quick, shuddering breath. 'I have the amulet. If you come with me to my cabin, I'll give it to you.'

He turned slowly, completely around 'What kind of bullshit is this?'

'I have Angelique's Curse in my cabin.' She let out a thin, watery laugh. 'It seems to be working.'

He lunged forward, grabbed her arm. 'Show me.'

She didn't whimper this time, or complain though his fingers dug painfully into her flesh. Beyond tears now, she led the way into her cabin. Once inside, she opened the drawer and took out the amulet.

'I found it this afternoon, shortly after we dug out the monogrammed plate. It was just there, all of a sudden, lying on the sand. I didn't clean it,' she murmured, rubbing a thumb over the center stone. 'There was no calcification, no encrustation. It might have been lying on velvet in a display case. That's funny, isn't it? When I picked it up I thought I could feel … well, I don't suppose you're very interested just now in the tricks a mind can play.'

She lifted her head, held out her hands with the necklace dripping from them. 'You've got what you wanted.'

He took it. Glittering, gleaming, it was as stunning as he'd ever imagined. It was warm, almost hot, he thought. But perhaps his hands were chilled. Of course that didn't explain the sudden clenching in his gut, or the odd image of leaping flames that jumped into his head.

Nerves, he told himself. A man was entitled to be nervous when he'd found the treasure of his lifetime.

'My father died for this.' He didn't hear himself say it, wasn't even conscious that he'd thought it.

'I know. I'm afraid you will, too.'

Distracted, he glanced up. Had she said something? It had sounded more like weeping than words. 'You weren't going to tell me you'd found it.'

'No, I wasn't.' She would face his fury now, his hate, even his disgust. But in doing so, she would make him listen. 'I don't really know what made me keep it from you when we were down, I just felt compelled to.'

On unsteady legs, she crossed to her dresser, picked up a bottle of water to slake her burning throat. 'I started to signal you, then I didn't. Couldn't. I hid it in my pouch, and brought it in here. I needed to think.'

'To figure out how much VanDyke would pay you for it?'

The fresh barb dug deep. Tate set the bottle down again, turned back. Her eyes were eloquent with sorrow. 'However much I've disappointed you, Matthew, you have to know better than that.'

'I know you have ambitions. Ambitions VanDyke could turn into fact.'

'Yes, I'm sure that's true. And I admit, for a few minutes sitting in here alone with that, I indulged in speculating just what having that amulet could do for me.' She wheeled away to stand at the small window. 'Do I have to be flawless to be acceptable to you, Matthew? I'm not allowed to have any selfish needs.'

'You're sure as hell not allowed to double-cross your family, and your partners.'

'You really are a fool if you think I could. But you're right about one thing, I was trying desperately to contact VanDyke, to tell him I'd found it. I'd hoped I could arrange to meet him somewhere and give it to him.'

'Do you sleep with him?'

The question was so absurd, so unexpected, she nearly laughed. 'I haven't laid eyes on Silas VanDyke in eight years. I haven't spoken with him much less slept with him.'

Where was the sense in this? he wondered. Where was the logic that was so intricate a part of her makeup? 'But the first thing you did when you found this was to try to contact him?'

'No, the first thing I did was worry over what you would do to him if you had it.' She closed her eyes and let the light breeze that danced through the window play over her face. 'Or worse, what he might do to you. And I panicked. I even thought about throwing it back into the water, pretending I'd never found it, but that wouldn't really solve the problem. Giving it to VanDyke, I thought, asking him only to give his word that he'd leave you alone in exchange for it, would solve everything.

'I didn't know I still loved you,' she said, staring hard at the shifting water. 'I didn't know, and when I did, I guess I panicked there, too. I don't want to feel this way about you, and I know I'll never feel this way about anyone else.'

Grateful her eyes were dry again, she made herself turn. 'I guess you could say I thought I was saving your life, doing what was best for you. That should sound familiar. And it was as stupid for me to take the choice out of your hands as it was for you to take it out of mine.'

She lifted her hands, let them fall. 'Now you have it, and you can do what you need to do. But I don't have to watch.' Sliding open the door on the closet, she took out her suitcase.

'What are you doing?'

'I'm going to pack.'

He picked up the case, tossed it across the room. 'Do you think you can hit me with all of this then just walk away?'

'Yes, I do.' How odd it was, she realized, to be so utterly calm again. As if she'd punched her way through a hurricane to the thick, quiet air of the eye. 'Just as I think we both need to take time to sort through the mess we've made out of things.' She started to walk past him to retrieve her case, then lifted her chin when he blocked her path. 'You're not going to push me around again.'

'If I have to.' To settle the matter he turned and flicked the lock on her cabin door. 'The first thing we have to settle is this.' He held up the amulet so that it caught the light and exploded with color. 'We've all got a stake in it, but mine's the oldest. When I've done what I need to do, you can have it.'

'If you're still alive.'

'That's my problem.' He slipped the necklace into his pocket. 'You've got an apology coming for the things I said to you on the bridge.'

'I don't want your apology.'

'You've got it anyway. I should have trusted you. Trusting people isn't one of my strong suits, but it should have been where you're concerned. I frightened you.'

'Yes, you did. I suppose I deserved it. Let's just say we're even.'

'We're not finished,' he murmured and laid a hand, gently this time, on her arm.

'No, I guess we're not.'

'Sit down.' When she looked up, her eyes were guarded. 'I'm not going to hurt you. I'm sorry I did. Sit down,' he repeated. 'Please.'

'I don't know what else there is to say, Matthew.' But she sat, folded her tensed hands in her lap. 'I understand your reaction to what you heard and what you saw perfectly.'

'I heard you tell me you loved me.'

'Poor timing. Again. I don't want to,' she said with undertones of tired anger. 'I can't seem to help it.'

He sat beside her, but didn't touch her. 'Eight years ago, I did what I had to do. I did the right thing. I've screwed up enough to know when I manage to do the right thing. I wasn't going to drag you down with me. When I look at you now, what you are, what you've done with your life, I know it was right.'

'There's no point–'

'Let me finish. There're some things I didn't tell you last night. Maybe I didn't want to admit them to you. When I first started salvaging for Fricke, I thought about you all the time. I didn't do much but work, pay bills and think about you. I'd wake up in the middle of the night and miss you so much it hurt. After a while, things were so fucking bad, I didn't have the energy to hurt anymore.'

Remembering, he stared down at his hands. 'I told myself it wasn't such a big deal, a couple of months out of my life with a pretty girl. I didn't much think about you anymore. Now and again it would grab me by the throat, tear right down into the gut. But I'd shake it off. I had to. Things with Buck were as bad as they could get, and I hated every minute of what I was doing to make a lousy dollar.'

'Matthew.'

He shook his head to hold her off. 'Let me get it out. It's not easy stripping down this way. When I saw you again, it ripped my heart open. I wanted all those years back, and knew I couldn't have them. Even when I got you into bed there was this hole. Because all I really wanted was for you to love me back.

'I want a chance with you again. I want you to give it to me.' Now, at last, he looked at her, laid a hand on her cheek. 'I might even be able to convince you that you like being in love with me.'

She managed a shaky smile. 'You probably could. I'm already beginning to lean in that direction.'

'I'd start out by telling you that what I felt for you eight years ago was the biggest thing in my life. And it's not even close to what I feel for you now.'

She was near tears again, and more desperately in love than she'd thought possible. 'What took you so long to tell me all of this?'

'I was pretty sure you'd laugh in my face. Christ, Tate, I wasn't good enough for you then. I'm no better for you now.'

'Not good enough,' she said quietly. 'In what possible way?'

'In every possible way. You've got brains, an education, family.' Frustrated at trying to explain intangibles, he dragged his hand through his hair. 'You've got – it's … class.'

She remained silent a moment while it all simmered. 'You know, Matthew, I'm just too worn out to be angry with you, even for something that ignorant. I really had no idea you, of all people, had a problem with self-esteem.'

'It's not self-esteem.' The idea made him feel ridiculous. 'It's just fact. I'm a treasure hunter, broke most of the time. I've got nothing but a boat, and even that's part LaRue's. I'll make a fortune on this hunt and probably blow it in a year.'

She might have sighed if she hadn't begun to understand. 'And I'm a scientist with a carefully balanced portfolio. I don't have a boat, but I have an apartment that I rarely use. This hunt's going to make me famous, and I intend to use both that and my share of the fortune to make my mark a little deeper. Given those run-downs it appears we have very little in common and no logical reason to cultivate a long-term relationship. Want to give it a shot anyway?'

'I figure this,' he said after a moment. 'You're old enough and smart enough to live with your mistakes. So yeah, I want to give it a shot.'

'Me, too. I loved you once blindly. I see you much clearer now, and I love you more.' She framed his face with her hands. 'We must be crazy, Lassiter. But it feels good.'

He turned his head, pressing his lips to the center of her palm. 'It feels right.' Joy, he couldn't remember when he'd last felt the simple lift of it. Gathering her close, he nuzzled his face in her hair. 'I'd gotten over you, Red. Mostly.'

'Mostly?'

'I could never quite forget the way you smell.'

With a chuckle, she leaned back so that she could see his face. 'The way I smell?'

'Fresh. Cool. Like a mermaid.' He touched his lips to hers, lingered. 'I named her for you.'

His boat, she realized. The boat he'd built with his own hands. 'Matthew, you make my head spin.' Content, she laid her head on his shoulder. This time, she thought, they would sail off into the sunset. 'We'd better go out on deck before someone comes looking for us. We've got something to tell the rest of the team.'

'There's that practical streak.' He brushed a hand over her hair. 'And I was just thinking about getting you in bed.'

'I know.' A quick, satisfying shiver coursed through her at the pleasure of being desired. 'And that's definitely something I'm looking forward to. But for now … ' She took his hand and pulled him to the door. 'I like the way you locked this,' she said, flipping the latch. 'Very macho.'

'You like macho, huh?'

'In small, tasteful doses.' Outside, she hooked her arm through his and walked to the rail. She could hear the radio jingling from the deck of the *Mermaid*, and her mother's brisk, tireless hammering. The compressor kicked on, grinding. The air was filled with the sulfuric perfume of undersea excavation.

'They're all going to be shocked and excited when you show them the amulet.'

'We show them,' Matthew corrected.

'No, it's yours. I can't explain rationally how I feel about this, Matthew,' she continued over his protest. 'It seems I'm starting to accept that this whole business isn't meant to be rational. I felt the pull of that necklace, a kind of lust of ownership. When I was holding it earlier, I could actually see, vividly see,' she added, turning to look at him, 'just what it could bring me. The money, the outrageous fortune, the fame and respect. The power. It shakes me to realize that under all the fine lofty motives of education and knowledge, I want those things.'

'So, you're human.'

'No, it was very strong, that desire to keep it, to use it to gain my own ends.'

'What stopped you? What made you decide to turn it over to VanDyke?'

'I love you,' she said simply. 'I'd have done anything to protect you.' She smiled a little. 'Sound familiar?'

'Sounds to me like it's time we started trusting each other. The fact remains you found the amulet.'

'Maybe I was meant to, so that I could give it to you.'

'Meant to?' He took her chin in his hand. 'This from a scientist.'

'A scientist who knows her Shakespeare. "There are more things in heaven and earth." ' Keeping her eyes on his, she suppressed a shudder. 'It's in your hands now, Matthew. And for you to decide.'

'None of this – if you loved me you'd ...?'

'I know you love me. A woman can go her whole life and never hear the kind of things you've just said to me. That's why you're going to marry me.'

His hand dropped away from her face. A knee-jerk reaction that made her lips curve wryly. 'I am?'

'Damn right you are. It shouldn't be too difficult to arrange the necessary paperwork on Nevis. I'm sure we'd both prefer to keep it simple. We can have a small ceremony right here on the boat.'

His stomach jittered, then settled smooth. 'You've got it all worked out.'

'Working things out is my life, Lassiter.' Smug, she linked her arms around his neck. 'I've got you, from where I'm standing, exactly where I want you. You're not getting away again.'

'I'd probably be wasting my time arguing.'

'Totally,' she agreed, almost purring when he slipped his arms around her. 'Might as well give up now.'

'Sweetheart, I hoisted the white flag the minute you knocked me out of that hammock onto my butt.' The smile faded from his eyes. 'You're my luck, Tate,' he murmured. 'There's nothing I can't do if you're with me.'

She settled into his arms, closed her eyes. And tried not to think about the weight of the curse in his pocket.

The teams gathered on the deck of the *Mermaid* in the thinning light of dusk. The weeks of treasure-hunting had been prosperous. On the generous foredeck, bits and pieces of the latest haul were separated from debris. There were sextants, octants, tableware, a simple gold locket containing a lock of hair.

Tate did her best to keep her mind off the amulet Matthew still held and answered questions on the two porcelain statues her father was examining.

'They're Ching dynasty,' she said. 'They're called Immortals, depicting saintly human figures from Chinese theology. In all there are eight, and these two are wonderfully undamaged. We may find the other six, if indeed there was a complete set. They're not listed in the manifest.'

'Valuable?' LaRue tossed out.

'Very. In my opinion, it's time we started thinking about transferring the more valuable and the more fragile items to a safer place.' Deliberately, she kept her eyes averted from Matthew's. 'And that we call in at least one other archeologist. I need corroboration, and more extensive facilities in order to complete a proper study. And we have to begin work on preserving the *Isabella* herself.'

'The minute we make any move like that, VanDyke would be on us,' Buck objected.

'Not if we take the precaution of notifying the proper institutions. The Committee for Nautical Archeology in England, its counterpart in the States. If anything, keeping this to ourselves is more dangerous than going public. Once we're on record, it would be impossible for VanDyke or anyone like him to sabotage our operation.'

'You don't know pirates,' Buck said grimly. 'And government's the biggest pirate of all.'

'I'm leaning with Buck on this.' Frowning, Ray studied the Chinese figures. 'I won't dispute that we have an obligation to share what we've found, but we haven't finished yet. We have weeks more excavating, maybe months, before we've played her out. And we've yet to find the main thing we came for.'

'Angelique's Curse,' Buck said under his breath. 'Maybe she doesn't want to be found.'

'If she's there,' LaRue corrected, 'we'll find her.'

'I think you're all missing the point.' Marla spoke quietly. It was so rare she offered an opinion on excavation policy, everyone stopped and turned to her. 'I know I don't dive, don't work the airlift, but I understand the heart of all of this. Look what we've done, what we've found already. A small operation with only two diving teams, working frantically to keep it all so quiet and secret. Yet we've uncovered a kind of miracle. And we've made Tate responsible for caring for that miracle. Now that she's asking for help, we're all worried someone might come along and steal our thunder. Well, they can't,' she added. 'Because we've done it. And if we focus so narrowly on one piece, aren't we losing sight of the whole? Angelique's Curse might have drawn us here, but we don't have to find it to know we've done something incredible.'

With a sigh, Ray draped an arm over her shoulders. 'You're right. Of course you're right. It's foolish to think we haven't succeeded because we haven't found the amulet. Still, every time I go down and come up again without it, I feel as though I've failed. Even with all this.'

Tate's hot gaze skimmed over Matthew before settling on her father. 'You haven't failed. None of us have.'

Saying nothing, Matthew rose. He took the gold chain from his pocket, let it dangle. For an instant, Tate thought she saw light flash from the stone.

Ray got shakily to his feet. His vision seemed to blur and fracture as he reached out to touch the center ruby. 'You found it.'

'Tate found it. This morning.'

'It's a devil's tool,' Buck whispered, backing away. 'It'll bring you nothing but grief.'

'It may be a tool,' Matthew agreed, and his glance flicked over LaRue. 'And I'll use it. My vote goes with Tate. We make arrangements to transfer what we have. She can contact her committees.'

‘So that you can lure VanDyke,’ she murmured.

‘VanDyke’s my problem. This is what he wants.’ Matthew slipped the necklace from Ray’s hands. ‘He won’t find it easy going through me to get it. It might be best to suspend operations for a while. You and Marla and Tate could go on the island.’

‘And leave you here to face him down alone?’ Tate tossed back her head. ‘Not a chance, Lassiter. Just because I’m stupid enough to want to marry you doesn’t mean I’ll let you bundle me off.’

‘You’re getting married?’ Marla pressed a hand to her lips. ‘Oh, honey.’

‘I had intended to make the announcement a little more smoothly.’ Annoyance glittered in Tate’s eyes. ‘You jerk.’

‘I love you, too.’ Matthew hooked an arm around her waist while the amulet dripped from his free hand. ‘She asked me this afternoon,’ he explained to Marla. ‘I decided to give her a break and go along with it, since it means I get you in the bargain.’

‘Thank goodness the two of you have come to your senses.’ With a sob, Marla threw her arms around both of them. ‘Ray, our baby’s getting married.’

He patted his wife awkwardly on the shoulder. ‘I guess this is my cue to say something profound.’ Emotions warred through him, regret mixed with joy. His little girl, he thought, was another man’s woman. ‘I can’t think of a damn thing.’

‘If you will pardon me,’ LaRue said. ‘I suggest a celebration.’

‘Of course.’ Marla wiped at her eyes and stepped back. ‘I should have thought of it.’

‘Allow me.’ LaRue strolled off into the galley to unearth the bottle of Fume Blanc he’d hidden away.

After the glasses were poured, the toasts drunk and the tears dried, Tate walked to the starboard rail to join Buck.

'It's a pretty big night,' she murmured.

'Yeah.' He lifted his glass of ginger ale.

'I thought – I'd hoped that you'd be happy for us, Buck. I do love him so much.'

He shifted uncomfortably. 'Guess I know you do. I got used to thinking about him like my own the past fifteen years. I ain't been much of a substitute father–'

'You've been wonderful,' she interrupted hotly.

'Screwed up more than once, but mostly I done my best. I always knew Matthew had something special in him. More'n me, more'n James. I never knew how to make it come out. You do,' he added, turning to her at last.

'He's a better man with you than he would be without. He'll try harder with you there, and turn off that bad Lassiter luck. You gotta make him get rid of that damned necklace, Tate, before it curses your lives. Before VanDyke kills him for it.'

'I can't do that, Buck. If I tried, and he changed himself because I'd asked, what would I leave him?'

'I should never have told him about it. I made him think we could make James's death worth something if we found it. That was stupid. Dead's dead.'

'Matthew's his own man, Buck. What he does can't be because of me, or you, or anyone. If we love him, we have to accept that.'

Chapter Twenty-five

TATE STRUGGLED TO take her own advice to heart. As Matthew slept beside her in his cabin on the *Mermaid*, she tried to put her fears to rest.

He'd said it was time they trusted each other. She knew trust could be as strong a shield as love. She would make hers strong enough, she promised herself, to defend them both against anyone or anything.

Whatever happened, whatever he did, they would face it together.

'Stop worrying,' he murmured and nudged her closer.

The heat of his body, the hard length of it against hers, soothed. 'Who said I was?'

'I can feel it.' To distract them both, he ran his hand over her hip. 'You keep sending out all these nasty little worry darts. They're keeping me awake.' His hand inched back up, over her rib cage. 'And since I'm awake anyway …' He rolled on top of her to send kisses and shivers down her throat.

'Next time I build a boat, I'm going to make the master cabin bigger.'

She sighed as his lips nibbled their way to her ear. 'Next time?'

'Mmm-hmm. And I'm soundproofing it.'

She let out a chuckle. Buck's snoring from the next cabin battered the walls like thunder. 'I'll help you. How does LaRue stand it?'

'He says it's like the boat rocking in the current. It's just there.' Circling a finger around her breast, Matthew studied her face in the moonlight that drifted through the open window. 'When I designed the living quarters, I didn't have a wife in mind.'

'You'd better keep one in mind now,' she warned him. 'This one. And I think the living quarters are just fine.' Teasingly, she flicked her tongue over his jaw. 'Especially the captain's cabin.'

'You know, if I'd figured out that this engagement business would clear the way for this, I'd have tried it sooner.' To please himself, he spread her hair over the pillow. 'It beats the floor of the bridge.'

'All to hell.' She curved her lips under his. 'But I kind of liked those nights. Don't think this engagement business is going to last long,' she added. 'We're going to Nevis tomorrow to start the formalities.'

'Christ, you're bossy.'

'Yeah, and I've got you, Lassiter.' She vised her arms around him. 'I've really got you.'

Nothing, absolutely nothing, she vowed, was going to take him away from her.

'The minute you're finished, I want you to meet me in the boutique.' Under the bright morning sun, Marla shook the sand out of her sandals as she stepped from the beach onto the stone walkway of the resort. Small, informal wedding or not, she intended to take her duties as mother of the bride, and surrogate mother of the groom, seriously.

Tate sighed and flipped her braid over her shoulder. 'I don't suppose it's any use telling you again that I don't need a new dress.'

'No use at all.' Happily, Marla beamed. 'We're getting you a wedding dress, Tate Beaumont. If the boutique here at the resort doesn't have anything suitable, we're going to St. Kitts. And Matthew' – she patted him gently on the cheek – 'you could use a haircut – and a decent suit.'

'Yes, ma'am.'

'Suck up,' Tate muttered.

Ignoring that, Marla continued to smile. 'Now y'all go see the concierge. I'm sure he can help you find the way to push through the paperwork. Matthew, you and I will look into that suit later this afternoon. Oh, and Tate, ask him about shoes.'

'Shoes?'

'We'll want to get some to match your dress.' With a cheery wave, she headed up the steps toward the boutique.

'She's off and running,' Tate said under her breath. 'Thank God we're doing this here and now. Can you imagine what she'd be planning if we were getting married back on Hatteras? Showers and bridal shows. Flowers, caterers, cakes.' She shuddered delicately. 'Wedding consultants.'

'Sounds kind of nice.'

'Lassiter.' Bemused, Tate stared up at him. 'You're not telling me you'd like all that fuss and bother. If she had the chance, she'd stuff you into a tux, maybe tails.' She gave his butt a friendly pat. 'Not that you wouldn't look wonderfully dashing.'

'I thought women were supposed to want a big, splashy wedding.'

'Not sane women.' Amused, she paused halfway up the steps. 'Matthew, is that what you want, all the pomp and circumstance?'

'Look, Red, I'll take you any way I can get you. I just don't see what's so wrong with the fancywork. A new dress, a haircut.'

Tate narrowed her eyes wickedly. 'She's going to make you wear a tie, pal.'

He couldn't quite control the wince. 'Not such a big deal.'

'You're right.' With a little laugh, she pressed a hand to her stomach. 'I guess I'd better just come clean and admit it. I'm scared.'

'Good.' He clasped his hand over hers. 'That makes two of us.'

Together they went into the lobby to track down the concierge.

Fifteen minutes later, they walked out again, dazzled.

'It's going to be awfully easy,' Tate managed. 'Proof of citizenship, sign a few papers.' She blew the hair out of her eyes. 'We could pull this off in two or three days.'

'Cold feet?'

'They're blocks of ice, but I can handle it. You?'

'I never welch on a deal.' To prove it, he scooped her off her feet. 'Are you going to be Doctor Lassiter or Doctor Beaumont?'

'I'm going to be Doctor Beaumont and Mrs. Lassiter. Suit you?'

'Suits me. Ah, I guess we'd better head to the boutique.'

'I can save you from that.' Understanding, she gave him a hard, smacking kiss. 'If we manage to find a dress in there, you aren't allowed to see it. Mom will have a fit if we don't follow at least one tradition.'

Hope bloomed. 'I don't have to go shopping?'

'You don't have to go shopping until she snags you. Why don't you swing by in about a half hour? Wait, I forgot I was dealing with Marla the mad shopper Beaumont. Give us an hour. And since I'm feeling so generous where you're concerned, if Mom decides to drag me off to St. Kitts, we'll detour back to the boat and drop you off.'

'I owe you big, Red.'

'I'll collect. Put me down.'

He gave her one last kiss, then set her on her feet. 'I bet they carry lingerie up there.'

'I bet they do.' She laughed and gave him a shove. 'I'll surprise you. Get lost, Lassiter.'

Smiling, she watched him disappear back into the lobby. Suddenly the idea of a new dress, something flowing and romantic, didn't seem so frivolous. Something that would be flattered by a little gold heart with a single pearl dripping from its point.

Lassiter, she decided, I'm going to knock your socks off.

Flushed with pleasure, she started across the patio. The hand that clamped on her arm made her laugh. 'Matthew, really–'

The words, and her breath, clogged in her throat as she stared into the smoothly handsome face of Silas VanDyke.

Reality tilted on its edge for a moment. He looked exactly the same, she thought dumbly. The years had laid lightly on him. The thick, glossy pewter hair, the smooth, elegant face and pale eyes.

His hand was soft as a child's on her arm, and she could smell the subtle, expensive cologne he'd dabbed on his skin.

'Ms. Beaumont, what a pleasure to run into you like this. I must say, the years have been overwhelmingly generous with you.'

It was the sound of his voice, faintly European and coldly pleased, that snapped her back. 'Let go of me.'

'Surely you have a moment or two for an old friend?' Still smiling benignly, he steered her sharply around the garden of brilliant annuals as he spoke.

There were dozens of people around, she reminded herself as she fought back fear. Guests, staff, the early diners who lounged in the poolside restaurant. She only had to shout.

The realization that she was afraid, here, in the bright sunlight, had her digging in her heels. 'Oh, I've got a moment or two for you, VanDyke. In fact, I'd enjoy dealing with you very much.' Alone, she thought, without Matthew shouldering her aside. 'But if you don't let me go, right now, I'll start screaming.'

'Now that would be an unfortunate mistake,' he said mildly. 'And you're a sensible woman, I know.'

'Keep pawing at me and I'll show you just how sensible.' Furious, she jerked her arm free. 'I'm sensible enough to know there's nothing you can do to me in a public place.'

'Do to you?' He looked shocked, and vaguely offended. But his head was aching, pounding at the idea that she would defy him. 'Tate, my dear, what a foolish thing to say. I wouldn't dream of doing anything to you at all. I'm simply inviting you to come out and spend an hour or two on my yacht.'

'You must be insane.'

His fingers closed so quickly, so painfully over her arm, she was too surprised to shout. 'Be careful. I don't care for poor manners.' His face smoothed out again with a smile.

'We'll try again, shall we? I'd like you to accompany me for a short, friendly visit. If you refuse, or if you insist on making a scene here in, as you say, a public place, your fiancé will pay the price.'

'My fiancé will scrape your face over the pavement, VanDyke, unless I do it first.'

'What a pity that your mother's gentle breeding seems to have skipped a generation.' He sighed, leaned closer, keeping his teeth clenched to control his voice. 'I have two men watching your Matthew as we speak. They'll do nothing unless you force me to signal them otherwise. They're quite skilled and quite discreet.'

The blood drained from her face, leaving it cold and stiff. 'You can hardly have him killed in the lobby of the resort.' But he'd planted the seed of terror, and it was blossoming.

'You can always take that chance. Oh, and wasn't that your mother up in the boutique? She's chosen several lovely things for you.'

Numb with fear, Tate glanced up. She could see the glass doors and windows of the shop tossing back sun. And the man, broad shouldered, neatly dressed, loitering outside. He inclined his head slowly.

'Don't hurt her. You have no reason to hurt her.'

'If you do what I tell you, I'll have no reason to hurt anyone. Shall we go? I've instructed my chef to prepare a very special lunch, and now I have someone to share it with.' With a horrible gallantry, he tucked a hand under her elbow and led her toward the pier. 'The trip will only take a short time,' he assured her. 'I'm moored just west of you.'

'How did you know?'

'Oh, my dear.' Jaunty in his white suit and panama, pleased with his victory, he clucked her under the chin. 'How naive of you to think I wouldn't.'

Tate jerked her arm from his grip, gave one last look back at the resort before stepping down into the waiting tender. 'If you hurt them, if you so much as touch either of them, I'll kill you myself.'

She planned the ways she would do it as the tender cut through the water.

In the boutique, Marla sighed. After instructing the clerk to put aside her selections, she set out to track down her daughter. She searched the restaurants and lounges, scanned the beach and the pool. Mildly irked, she went through the gift shop, then back to the boutique.

When there was no sign of Tate, she marched back to the lobby intending to have the concierge do a page.

She spotted Matthew jumping out of a cab.

'Matthew, for goodness sake, where have you been?'

'Something I had to take care of.' He patted his pocket where the contract he'd just signed was neatly folded. 'Hey, I'm only a little late.'

'Late for what?'

'We said an hour.' Unconcerned, he glanced at his watch. 'It's just over that. So, did you talk her into a dress or is she still fighting it?'

'I haven't seen her,' Marla said grumpily. She was hot, frustrated. 'I thought she was with you.'

'No, we separated. She was going to meet you.' He shrugged. 'We were talking about different kinds of weddings, flowers and stuff. She probably got involved in something.'

'I know – the beauty salon,' Marla said, inspired. 'She probably wanted to check about getting her hair and nails done, getting a facial.'

'Tate?'

'It's her wedding.' Baffled by the casualness of youth, she shook her head. 'Every woman wants to look her best as a bride. She's down there right now going through pictures of hairstyles.'

'If you say so.' The idea of Tate getting herself polished and painted for him had him grinning. This he had to see. 'Let's go smoke her out.'

'I'm going to give her a piece of my mind, too,' Marla muttered. 'I was starting to worry.'

'Champagne?' VanDyke lifted a flute from the tray his steward had set beside a pair of peacock blue lounge chairs.

'No.'

'I think you'll agree that it sets the palate for the lobster dish we're having for lunch.'

'I'm not interested in champagne or lobster or your transparent politeness.'

Ignoring the little tremors of fear, Tate kept her shoulders braced. If she'd gauged it correctly they were about a mile west of the *Mermaid*. She could swim it if necessary.

'What I am interested in is why you kidnapped me.'

'Such a hard word.' VanDyke sampled the champagne, found it perfectly chilled. 'Please sit.' His eyes frosted when she stayed braced against the rail. 'Sit, now,' he repeated. 'We have business to discuss.'

Bravery was one thing. But when his eyes looked as flat and mindless as a shark's, she thought it wise to obey. She sat stiffly and forced herself to accept the second flute he held out.

She'd been wrong, she realized. He had changed. The man she had faced eight years ago had seemed sane. This one …

'To … destiny, perhaps?'

She'd have preferred to dash the contents of the glass into his face. Whatever small satisfaction that might bring her, she knew that it would cost dearly. 'Destiny?' It bolstered her to find her voice could be calm and even. 'Yes, I could drink to that.'

Relaxed, he sat back, holding the stem of the flute between his fingers. 'It's so charming to visit with you again. You know, Tate, you made quite a favorable impression on me during our last encounter. I've enjoyed watching your professional progress over the years.'

'If I had known you were associated with the *Nomad*'s last expedition in any way, I would never have been a part of it.'

'So foolish.' He crossed his ankles to better enjoy the wine and the company. 'Surely you know that I've financed a number of scientists, labs, expeditions. Without my backing, numerous projects would never have reached fruition. And the charities I support, worthwhile causes.' He paused to sip again. 'Would you deny those causes, Tate, charitable and scientific, because you disapprove of the source?'

She tipped her glass and sipped as delicately as he. 'When the source is a murderer, a thief, a man without conscience or morals, yes.'

'Fortunately few share your opinion of me, or your rather naive ethics. You disappointed me,' he said in a tone that had her pulse going thick. 'You betrayed me. And you've cost me.' Absently, he glanced up as a steward appeared. 'Lunch is served,' VanDyke told her, smoothly genial again. 'I thought you'd enjoy dining al fresco.'

He rose, offering a hand, which she ignored. 'Don't try my patience, Tate. Small rebellions only irritate me.' He demonstrated by clamping his hand over her wrist. 'You've already disappointed me deeply,' he continued as she struggled against his hold. 'But I'm hoping you'll take this last chance I'm giving you to redeem yourself.'

'Take your hands off me.' Temper spiked, propelling her around. Her fist was poised, ready to strike when he grabbed her braid and yanked sharply enough to have stars exploding in front of her eyes. When her body was dragged against him, she discovered the elegant clothes masked a tough, hard body.

'If you think I have any qualms about striking a woman, think again.' His eyes glittered as he shoved her roughly into a chair. He leaned over her, his breath hitching, his eyes blind. 'If I wasn't a reasonable, civilized man, if I let myself forget that, I'd break you, a bone at a time.'

Like a light switched, his eyes changed. The vicious temper turned into a smile that was edgy and thin. 'There are those who believe that corporal punishment is unwise, even uncivilized.' Daintily he fussed with his lapels, then sat. Brushing a hand back, he signaled for the stone-faced steward to retrieve the wine and glasses. 'However, I disagree. I'm a firm believer that pain and punishment are very effective for instilling a sense of discipline. And certainly respect. I demand respect. I've earned it. Do try one of these olives, dear.' The avuncular host once more, he offered her a crystal dish. 'They're from one of my groves in Greece.'

Because her hands were shaking badly she kept them locked under the table. What kind of man threatened to inflict pain one moment, and offered exotic tidbits the next? A mad one.

'What do you want?'

'First, to share a congenial meal in a lovely spot with an attractive woman.' His brow lifted when her cheeks went white. 'Don't fret, dear Tate. My feelings for you are much too paternal for me to entertain any sexual notions. Your honor, as you might think of it, is more than safe.'

'I'm supposed to be relieved that rape isn't on your itinerary?'

'Another ugly word.' Mildly annoyed with her choice of it, he helped himself to the dish of olives and the antipasto. 'A man who stoops to forcing himself on a woman sexually isn't a man at all in my opinion. One of my executives in New York browbeat and intimidated his assistant into having sex with him. She had to be hospitalized when he'd finished.'

VanDyke sliced through a piece of prosciutto. 'I arranged to have him fired – after I'd had him castrated.' He dabbed at his mouth with a pale blue linen napkin. 'I like to think she would have thanked me. Please, try the lobster. I guarantee it's superb.'

'I don't seem to have much of an appetite.' Tate shoved her plate aside in a gesture she knew was foolishly defiant. 'You got me here, VanDyke, and obviously you can keep me here. At least until Matthew and my family start looking for me.' Lifting her chin, she stared directly into his eyes. 'Why don't you tell me what you want?'

'We will have to discuss Matthew,' he mused, 'but that can wait. I want what I've always wanted. I want what belongs to me. Angelique's Curse.'

Worry gnawed at her stomach as Marla paced the hotel lobby. No matter how many times she told herself that Tate couldn't have simply disappeared, she was terrified. She watched people come and go, staff bustling along to perform duties, guests strolling from pool to lounge to garden.

She heard laughter, the splash of children swimming, the whirl of the blender that mixed frosty island drinks for those waiting at the bar.

She and Matthew had separated – she, to ask at the front desk, to question the doormen, the cab drivers, anyone who might have seen Tate leave the resort, he to check the beach and the dock.

When she spotted Matthew coming toward her, Marla's heart leapt. Only when she saw that he was alone, when she saw the grim look in his eyes, did it sink again.

'Tate.'

'Several people saw her. She met someone, left with him by tender.'

'Left? Who did she meet? Are you sure it was her?'

'It was her.' The panic that raced through him could be controlled. But not so easy was it to control the need to kill. 'The description I got fits VanDyke.'

'No.' Weak with fear, she reached out to take his arm. 'She wouldn't have gone with him.'

'She wouldn't unless he hadn't given her a choice.'

'The police,' she said faintly. 'We'll call the police.'

'And tell them that she left the island, without putting up any struggle, with the man who endowed her last project?' Eyes hard and hot, he shook his head. 'We don't know how many cops he owns either. We do this my way.'

'Matthew, if he hurts her …'

'He won't.' But they both knew he said it only to soothe. 'He has no reason to. Let's get back. My guess is that he won't be far from where we're moored.'

He doesn't know. Tate's mind whirled with possibilities. He'd known where to find them. Had somehow known what they were doing. But he didn't know what they'd found. Stalling, she reached for her glass again.

'Do you think, if I had it, I'd give it to you?'

'Oh, I think when you have it you'll give it to me to save Matthew and the others. It's time we worked together, Tate, as I've planned for some time.'

'You've planned?'

'Yes. Though not in quite the way I had hoped.' He brooded over that for a moment, then brushed it aside.

'I'm willing to overlook your mistakes, I'm even willing to let you and your team reap the rewards of the *Isabella*. All I want is the amulet.'

'You'd take it and walk away? What assurance do I have of that?'

'My word, of course.'

'Your word means less than nothing to me.' She gasped involuntarily when he crushed her fingers in his hand.

'I don't tolerate insults.' When he released her, her hand throbbed like a bad tooth. 'A man's word is sacred, Tate,' he said with eerie calm. 'My proposition stands. The amulet is all I want from you. In exchange for it, you'll have the fame and the fortune that goes with the *Isabella*. Your name will be made. I'm even willing to assist on that point wherever I have influence.'

'I don't want your influence.'

'You benefited from it many times in the past eight years. But I did that for my own pleasure. Still it wounds to have generosity met with ingratitude.' His face darkened. 'Lassiter's doing. I understand that. You realize that by aligning yourself with him you're lowering your expectations, your standards, your social and professional opportunities. A man like him will never be an asset to you on any level.'

'A man like Matthew Lassiter makes you look like a child. A spoiled, evil child.' Her head snapped back and her eyes watered when the back of his hand slashed across her cheek.

'I warned you.' Furious, he shoved his plate aside. The force of it sent it bulleting off the table to smash on the deck. 'I won't tolerate disrespect. I've made allowances as I admire your courage and intelligence, but you will mind your tongue.'

'I despise you.' She braced for another blow. 'If I found the amulet, I'd destroy it before turning it over to you.'

She watched him snap. The way his hands trembled as he surged to his feet. There was murder in his eyes. More than that, she understood. There was a kind of terrible delight. He would hurt her, she knew, and he would enjoy it.

The survival instinct kicked in over the numb fear. She sprang to her feet, leaping back when he grabbed for her. Without pausing, she sprinted for the rail. Water was safety. The sea would save her. But even as she poised to dive, she was dragged back.

She kicked, screamed, fought to find flesh that her teeth could sink into. The steward simply pinned her arms, yanking them viciously up behind her back until her vision grayed.

'Leave her to me.'

Dimly, she heard VanDyke's voice as she fell bonelessly to the deck.

'You're not as sensible as I'd hoped.' With the rage still in him, VanDyke snagged her abused arm and yanked her to her feet. Fresh agony had a sob catching in her throat. 'Your loyalty is displaced, Tate. I'll have to teach you–'

He broke off as the sound of a motor caught his attention. Hearing it, Tate swayed, turned her face toward the noise.

Matthew.

Terror and pain stripped aside all pride. She wept weakly when VanDyke let her drop to the deck a second time.

He'd come. She curled into a ball, nursing bruises. He'd take her away, and it wouldn't hurt anymore. She wouldn't be afraid anymore.

'Again,' VanDyke said, 'you're late.'

'It wasn't a simple matter to leave.' LaRue landed lightly on deck. He glanced briefly at Tate before reaching for his tobacco. 'You have a passenger, I see.'

'Fortune smiled on me.' Nearly steady again, VanDyke sat back down. He picked up a napkin to dab at his sweaty face. 'I was handling a few details on the island when who should cross my path but the delightful Ms. Beaumont.'

LaRue clucked his tongue and helped himself to Tate's champagne. 'There's a mark on her face. I disapprove of the rough treatment of women.'

VanDyke's teeth bared. 'I don't pay you for your approval.'

'Perhaps not.' LaRue decided to postpone his cigarette and enjoy the antipasto. 'When Matthew discovers you have her, he'll come looking.'

'Of course.' That would make up for everything. Nearly everything. 'Have you come only to tell me what I already know?'

'LaRue.' Trembling, Tate struggled to her knees. 'Matthew, where's Matthew?'

'I would guess he is speeding back from Nevis to search for you.'

'But–' She shook her head to clear it. 'What are you doing here?' Slowly it began to register that he was alone, that he was sitting comfortably at the table, nibbling.

He smiled when he saw the knowledge seep into her eyes, and with it disgust. 'So, the light dawns.'

'You work for him. Matthew trusted you. We all trusted you.'

'I would hardly have earned my keep if you hadn't.'

She wiped the weak tears from her cheek. 'For money? You've betrayed Matthew for money?'

'I have a great fondness for money.' Dismissing her, he turned back, popped an olive into his mouth. 'And speaking of my great fondness, I will require another bonus.'

'LaRue, I'm growing tired of your added demands.' VanDyke held up a finger. In answer, the steward stepped forward, flipped open his sharply creased white jacket and took out a highly polished .32. 'I might redeem myself in Tate's eyes by having you shot in several painful places and thrown overboard. I believe you'd draw sharks nicely.'

Lips pursed, LaRue contemplated his choice of peppers. 'If you kill me, your hopes for Angelique's Curse die with me.'

VanDyke clenched his fist until he calmed again. Another quick signal had the .32 disappearing under the tailored coat. 'I also grow tired of you dangling the amulet.'

'Two hundred and fifty thousand American dollars,' LaRue began, and shut his eyes briefly to savor the hot, sweet flavor of the pepper. 'And the amulet is yours.'

'Bastard,' Tate whispered. 'I hope he does kill you.'

'Business is business,' LaRue said with a shrug. 'I see that she has yet to tell you of our luck, *mon ami*. We have Angelique's Curse. For a quarter of a million, I'll see that it is safely in your hands by tomorrow, nightfall.'

Chapter Twenty-six

ANGELIQUE'S CURSE GLITTERED in Matthew's hands. He stood on the bridge of the *Mermaid*, his fingers wrapped tight around the chain. The hot white sun poured over the ruby, flashed the diamonds, sparkled the gold. Here was the treasure of a lifetime, fortune and fame in metal and stone.

Here was misery.

Everyone he'd loved had been hurt by it. Holding it, he could see the lifeless body of his father, crumpled on the deck of a boat. The face, so like his own, bleached white in death.

He could see Buck in the jaws of a shark, blood swirling in the water.

He could see Tate, tears in her eyes, offering him the amulet, offering him the choice of salvation or destruction.

But he couldn't see her now. He couldn't know where she'd been taken or what had been done to her. All he knew was that he would do anything, give anything to get her back.

The cursed necklace weighed like lead in his hands and mocked him with beauty.

Eyes blazing, he turned as Buck came onto the bridge.

'Still no sign of LaRue.' Spotting the amulet, Buck took a jerky step back.

Matthew swore and laid the necklace on the chart table. 'Then we move without him. We can't wait.'

'Move where? What the hell are we going to do? I'm with Ray and Marla on this, Matthew. We gotta call in the cops.'

'Did the cops do us any good last time?'

'This ain't piracy, boy, it's kidnapping.'

'It was murder once, too,' Matthew said coldly. 'He's got her, Buck.' He leaned against the chart table, warring against the old helplessness. 'In front of dozens of people he walked right off with her.'

'He'd trade her for that.' Wetting his lips, Buck forced himself to look at the necklace. 'Like a ransom.'

Hadn't he been waiting, praying by the radio, for VanDyke to make contact? Matthew thought. 'I can't afford to count on that. Can't afford to wait any longer.'

He grabbed binoculars, shoved them at Buck. 'Due west.'

Stepping up, Buck lifted the binoculars, skimmed the sea. He focused in on the yacht, hardly more than a glimmer of sleek white. 'A mile off,' he murmured. 'Could be him.'

'It's him.'

'He'd be waiting for you. Expecting you to come after her.'

'I wouldn't want to disappoint him, would I?'

'He'll kill you.' Resigned now, Buck set the glasses aside. 'You could give him that fucking thing wrapped in a bow and he'd still kill you. Just like he did James.'

'I'm not giving it to him,' Matthew returned. 'And he's not killing anyone.' Impatient, he seized the binoculars, searched the sea for a sign of LaRue. Time was up.

'I need you, Buck.' He set the glasses down again. 'I need you to dive.'

Terror and pain were no longer important. Tate watched LaRue eat heartily as he betrayed his partners. She no longer thought of escape as she lunged to her feet and flew at him.

The attack was so unexpected, her prey so complacent, that she was able to knock him out of his chair. Her nails scraped viciously down his cheek, drawing blood before he managed to flip and hold her down.

'You're even worse than he is,' she spat out, wriggling like an eel under him. 'He's just crazy. You're revolting. If VanDyke doesn't kill you, Matthew will. I hope I get to watch.'

Amused, excited by the display, VanDyke sipped champagne. He let the wrestling match play on, enjoying LaRue's grunts as he fought to restrain Tate. Then with a sigh, he signaled the steward. He couldn't afford to have LaRue overly damaged. Quite yet.

'Show Ms. Beaumont her stateroom,' he ordered. 'And see that she's not disturbed.' He smiled as his man hauled Tate to her feet. She kicked, cursed and struggled, but she was outweighed by a hundred pounds of solid muscle. 'I think you should have some rest, my dear, while LaRue and I complete our business. I'm sure you'll find your accommodations more than suitable.'

'Burn in hell,' she shouted, choking on tears of frustration as she was carried off. 'Both of you.'

VanDyke squirted a bit of lemon on his lobster. 'An admirable woman all in all. Not easily cowed. A pity her loyalties are so misplaced. I could have done great things with her. For her, as well. Now she's bait.' He nibbled delicately. 'Nothing more.'

LaRue wiped at the blood on his cheek with the back of his hand. The furrows she'd dug burned like fire. Though VanDyke frowned in annoyance, he used the linen napkin to staunch it.

'Next to money, love is the most powerful motivator.' More shaken than he cared to admit, LaRue poured the flute full and drank it down.

'You were telling me about Angelique's Curse before we were interrupted.'

'Yes.' Surreptitiously LaRue rubbed at his ribs where Tate's elbow had jabbed. Damned if he wasn't going to bruise. 'And about two hundred and fify thousand dollars. American.'

The money was nothing. He'd spent a hundred times that in his search already. But it bubbled in his blood to pay it. 'What proof is there that you have the amulet?'

Lips curled, LaRue lifted a hand to his shredded cheek. 'Come now, *mon ami*. Tate found it herself only yesterday, and with love guiding her, handed it selflessly to Matthew.' To soothe his frayed nerves, LaRue began to roll a cigarette. 'It is magnificent, more so than you had led me to believe. The center stone …' LaRue made a circle with his thumb and forefinger to indicate size. 'Red as blood, the diamonds around it iced tears. The chain is heavy but delicately wrought, as is the sentiment etched around the jewel.'

He struck a match, cupping it against the soft breeze, to light his cigarette. 'You can feel the power humming in it. Against your fingers it seems to throb.'

VanDyke's eyes glazed, his mouth went slack. 'You touched it?'

'*Bien sûr*. I am trusted, eh?' He blew out a lazy stream of smoke. 'Matthew guards it close, you see, but he doesn't guard against me. We are shipmates, partners, friends. I can get it for you, once I am assured the money is in place.'

'You'll have your money.' Need had VanDyke's hands trembling. His face was white and still as he leaned forward. 'And this promise, LaRue. If you cross me, if you try to bleed more money from me or if you fail, there is no place you can hide that I won't find you. When I do, you'll pray for death.'

LaRue dragged in more smoke and smiled. 'It's difficult to frighten a rich man. And rich is what I'll be. You'll have your curse, *mon ami*, and I my money.' Before he could rise, VanDyke held up a hand.

'We aren't finished. A quarter of a million is a great deal.'

'A fraction of the worth,' LaRue pointed out. 'Would you try to negotiate now when it is all but in your hands?'

'I'll double it.' Pleased to see LaRue's eyes widen, VanDyke leaned back. 'For the amulet, and for Matthew Lassiter.'

'You want me to bring him to you?' With a laugh, LaRue shook his head. 'Not even your precious amulet could protect you from him. He means to kill you.' He gestured in the direction where Tate had been taken. 'And you have the tool to bring him down already in your possession.'

'I don't want you to bring him to me.' That was a pleasure he would have to deny himself, VanDyke realized. The fact that he could make such a practical choice over an emotional one proved he was still in control of his fate. Business, he thought, was business. 'I want you to dispose of him. Tonight.'

'Murder,' LaRue mused. 'This is interesting.'

'An accident at sea would be appropriate.'

'You think he dives when Tate is missing? You underestimate his feelings for her.'

'Not at all. But feelings make a man careless. It would be a pity if something happened to his boat, when he and his drunken uncle were aboard. A fire perhaps. An explosion – tragic and lethal. For an extra quarter million, I'm sure you can be inventive.'

'I am known for a certain quickness of mind. I want the first two hundred and fifty deposited this afternoon. I will not move further until I am assured of it.'

'Very well. When I see the *Mermaid* destroyed, I'll make a second payment into your account. Make it tonight, LaRue, midnight. Then bring me the amulet.'

'Transfer the money.'

Hours passed. Tate resisted the fruitless urge to batter her fists on the door and shout for release. There was a beautiful wide window offering a spectacular view of the sea and sun sinking toward it. The chair she'd thrown had bounced off the glass without making a scratch.

She'd tugged and yanked until her already aching arms had wept with fatigue. But the window stayed firmly in place, and so did she.

She paced, she cursed, she planned revenge and she listened desperately to every creak and footfall.

But Matthew didn't come.

Fairy-tale heroes rescued damsels in distress, she reminded herself. And damned if she wanted to be some whiny damsel. She'd get herself out, somehow.

She spent nearly an hour searching every inch of the cabin. It was large and lovely, decorated in cool pastels under a ceiling of pale-gold wood. Her feet sank into ivory carpet, her fingers skimmed over smoothly lacquered mauve walls, around trim painted seafoam green.

In the closet she found a long silk robe in a brilliant pattern of cabbage roses, a matching nightdress. A linen jacket, a spangled wrap and a black evening coat had been provided for those cool night breezes. A simple black cocktail dress, an assortment of casual cruise wear completed the inventory.

Tate pushed clothes aside and examined every inch of the closet wall.

It was as solid as the rest of the cabin.

He hadn't skimped on the amenities, she observed grimly. The bed was king-sized, plumped with satin pillows. Glossy magazines fanned on the glass-topped coffee table in the sitting area. In the entertainment center under the TV and VCR were an assortment of the latest available movies on video. A small refrigerator held soft drinks, splits of wine and champagne, fancy chocolate and snacks.

The bathroom boasted an oversized whirlpool tub in mauve, a sink shaped like a scallop, brass lights around a generous mirror. On the pale green counters were a variety of expensive creams, lotions, bath oils.

Her search for a jerry-built weapon turned up nothing but a leather travel kit with all the necessities.

There were bath sheets, loofahs, a hotel-style terrycloth robe and dainty soaps shaped like starfish, conch shells and seahorses.

But the brass towel rack she envisioned wielding as a club was bolted firmly in place.

Desperate, she raced back into the main cabin. Her search through the elegant little writing desk unearthed thick creamy stationery, envelopes, even stamps. The perfect fucking host, she fumed, then closed her fingers over a slim gold pen.

How much damage, she wondered, could a designer ballpoint inflict? A good shot to the eye – the thought made her shudder, but she slipped the pen into the pocket of her slacks.

She slumped into a chair. The water was so close, so close, she wanted to weep.

And where was Matthew?

She had to find a way to warn him. LaRue, the bastard LaRue. Every precaution they'd taken over the last months had been for nothing. LaRue had passed every movement, every plan, every triumph, along to VanDyke.

He'd eaten with them, worked with them, laughed with them. He'd told stories of his days at sea with Matthew with the affection of a friend in his voice.

All the while he'd been a traitor.

Now he would steal the amulet. Matthew would be frantic, her parents wild with worry. He would pretend concern, even anger. He would be privy to their thoughts, their plans. Then he would take the amulet and bring it to VanDyke.

She wasn't a fool. It had already fixed in her mind that once VanDyke had what he wanted, her usefulness was over. He would have no reason to keep her, and couldn't afford to set her free.

He would certainly kill her.

Somewhere in the open sea, she imagined, coolly logical. A blow to the head most likely, then he would dump her, dead or unconscious, into the water. The fish would do the rest.

In all those miles, in all that space, no one would ever find a trace of her.

He assumed it would be simple, she thought, and closed her eyes. What could one unarmed woman do to defend herself? Well, he would be surprised what this woman could do. He might kill her, but it wouldn't be simple.

Her head jerked up as the lock on her door clicked. The steward opened it, his shoulders filling the doorway.

'He wants you.'

It was the first time he'd spoken in her hearing. Tate detected the Slavic song in the brusque tone.

'Are you Russian?' she asked. She rose but didn't come toward him.

'You will come now.'

'I worked with a biologist a few years ago. She was from Leningrad. Natalia Minonova. She always spoke fondly of Russia.'

Nothing flickered on his wide, stony face. 'He wants you,' the steward repeated.

She shrugged, slipping her hand in her pocket, closing her fingers over the pen. 'I've never understood people who take orders blindly. Not much of a self-starter, are you, Igor?'

Saying nothing, he crossed to her. When his beefy hand closed over her arm, she let herself go limp. 'Doesn't it matter to you that he's going to kill me?' It was easy to put the fear back into her voice as he dragged her across the room. 'Will you do it for him? Snap my neck or crush my skull? Please.' She stumbled, turned into him. 'Please, help me.'

As he shifted his grip, she pulled the pen out of her pocket. It was a blur of movement, the slim gold dart plunging, his hand shooting up.

She felt the sickening give as her weapon sank into flesh, and the warm wetness on her hand before she was hurled against the wall.

Her stomach roiled as she watched him stoically yank the pen from his cheek. The puncture was small but deep, and blood ran. Her only regret was that she'd missed the eye.

Without a word he clamped her arm and dragged her out on deck.

VanDyke was waiting. It was brandy this time. Glass-shielded candles glowed prettily on a table beside a bowl of dewy fruit and a fluted plate offering delicate pastries.

He had changed into formal evening attire to suit the celebration he planned. Beethoven's *Pathétique* flowed subtly from the outdoor speakers.

'I had hoped you might avail yourself of the wardrobe in your stateroom. My last guest left rather hurriedly this morning and neglected to pack all of her belongings.' His brow lifted when he saw his steward's bloody cheek.

'Go to the infirmary and have that dealt with,' he said impatiently. 'Then come back. You never cease to surprise me, Tate. What did you use?'

'A Mont Blanc. I wish it had been you.'

He chuckled. 'Let me give you a logical choice, my dear. You can be restrained or drugged, both of which are distasteful. Or you can cooperate.' He saw her glance involuntarily toward the rail and shook his head. 'Jumping overboard would hardly be productive. You have no gear. One of my men would be in the water in moments to bring you back. You wouldn't make it fifty yards. Why don't you sit?'

Until she could formulate a better plan, she saw no point in defying him. If he drugged her, she'd be lost.

'Where did you find LaRue?'

'Oh, it's amazingly easy to find tools when you can pay for them.' He paused a moment to choose the perfect glossy grape.

'A study of Matthew's shipmates showed LaRue to be a likely candidate. He's a man who enjoys money and the transient pleasures it buys. To date, he's been a good if occasionally expensive investment.'

He paused, eyes half closed in pleasant relaxation, and swirled his brandy.

'He kept close tabs on Matthew aboard ship, was able to develop a friendship with him. Through LaRue's reports I was able to determine that Matthew continued to keep contact with your parents, and that he never quite gave up the idea of finding Angelique's Curse. He knew where it was, of course, always, but he'd never tell LaRue where. Even friendship has its limits. He'd boast of it, but never drop his guard enough to tell the tale.'

VanDyke chose a second dark purple grape from the bowl. 'I do admire that. His tenacity and his caution. I wouldn't have thought it of him, holding onto the secret all these years, working like a dog when he could have lived like a prince. Still, he slipped when he resumed his partnership with your parents, and you. Women often cause a man to make foolish mistakes.'

'Firsthand experience, VanDyke?'

'Not at all. I adore women, much in the same way I adore a good wine or a well-played symphony. When the bottle is done, or the music over, one can always arrange for another.' He smiled as Tate tensed. The boat had begun to move.

'Where are we going?'

'Not far. A few degrees east. I'm expecting a show, and I want a closer seat, so to speak. Have a snifter of brandy, Tate. You may feel the need for it.'

'I don't need brandy.'

'Well, it's here if you change your mind.' He rose and crossed to a bench. 'I have an extra pair of binoculars. Perhaps you'd like them.'

She snatched them, rushed to the rail to scan east. Her heart leapt when she found the dim outline of the boats. There were lights glowing on the *New Adventure*, another holding steady on the bridge of the *Mermaid*.

'You must realize if we can see them, they'll be able to see us.'

'If they know where to look.' VanDyke stepped beside her. 'I imagine they'll scan this way eventually. But they're going to be very busy shortly.'

'You think you're clever.' Despite her best efforts, her voice broke. 'Using me to lure them here.'

'Yes. It was a stroke of luck well used. But now plans have changed.'

'Changed?' She couldn't stop staring at the lights. She thought she saw movement. A tender? she wondered. Cutting away toward shore. LaRue, she thought with a sinking heart, taking the amulet to some hiding place.

'Yes, and I believe the change is imminent.'

The excitement in his voice shivered over her skin. 'What are you–'

Even at nearly a mile's distance, she heard the blast. The lenses of the binoculars exploded with light, dazzling her shocked eyes. But she didn't look away. Couldn't look away.

The *Mermaid* was engulfed in flames.

'No. No, God. Matthew.' She'd nearly leapt over the rail before VanDyke yanked her back.

'LaRue is efficient as well as greedy.' VanDyke wrapped a wiry arm around her throat until her frantic struggles drained into wild weeping. 'The authorities will do their best to piece it together, what there is left to piece. Any evidence they find will indicate that Buck Lassiter, in a drunken haze, slopped gas too near the engine, then carelessly lit a match. As there's nothing left of him, or his nephew, there will be no one to dispute it.'

'You were going to get the amulet.' She stared at the fire licking at the dark sea. 'You were going to get it. Why did you have to kill him?'

'He would never have stopped,' VanDyke said simply. The flames dancing toward the sky mesmerized him. 'He stared at me over his father's body, with knowledge and hate in his eyes. I knew then that one day this would come.'

The pleasure of it shivered through him like wine, iced and delicious. Oh, he hoped there had been pain and understanding, even only an instant of it. How he wished he could be sure.

Tate sank to her knees when he released her. 'My parents.'

'Oh, safe enough, I imagine. Unless they were on board. I have no reason at all to wish them ill. You're terribly pale, Tate. Let me get you that brandy.'

She braced a hand on the rail, leveled herself up on her trembling legs. 'Angelique cursed her jailers,' she managed. 'She cursed those who had stolen from her, who persecuted her and cut off the life of her unborn child.'

Fighting to speak over her shuddering breaths, she watched his eyes in the glow of candlelight. 'She'd have cursed you, VanDyke. If there's any justice for her, and power left, the amulet will destroy you.'

There was a chill around his heart that was fear and deadly fascination. With the flickers of the distant fire behind her, grief and pain dark in her eyes, she looked powerful and potent.

Angelique would have looked so, he thought, and lifted the brandy to his suddenly icy lips. His eyes were almost dreamy on Tate's. 'I could kill you now.'

Tate gave a sobbing laugh. 'Do you think it matters to me now? You've killed the man I love, destroyed the life we would have had together, the children we would have made. There's nothing else you can do to me that matters.'

With the grief trapped inside her, Tate stepped forward. 'You see, I know how she felt now, sitting in that cell waiting for morning, waiting to die. It was anticlimactic really, because her life had ended with Etienne's. I don't care if you kill me. I'll die cursing you.'

'It's time you went back to your cabin.' VanDyke lifted tensed fingers. The steward, his cheek neatly bandaged, stepped out of the shadows. 'Take her back. Lock her in.'

'You'll die slowly,' Tate called as she was led away. 'Slowly enough to understand hell.'

She stumbled into her cabin and collapsed weeping onto the bed. When the tears were dry and her heart empty of them, she moved to a chair to watch the sea and waited to die.

Chapter Twenty-seven

SHE SLEPT FITFULLY and dreamed.

The cell stank of sickness and fear. Dawn sneaked stealthily through the barred window, signaling death. The amulet was cold under her stiff fingers.

When they came for her, she rose regally. She would not disgrace her husband's memory with cowardly tears and pleas for mercy that would never be granted.

He was there, of course. The count, the man who had condemned her for loving his own son. Hot greed, lust, an appetite for death gleamed in his eyes. He reached out, dragged the amulet over her head, slipped it over his own.

And she smiled, knowing she had killed him.

They bound her to the stake. Below, the crowds gathered to watch the witch burn. Eager eyes, vicious voices. Children were held up to afford them a better view of the event.

She was offered a chance to renounce, to pray for God's mercy. But she remained silent. Even as the flames crackled beneath, bringing heat and dazing smoke, she spoke no word. And thought only one.

Etienne.

From fire to water, so cool and blue and soothing. She was free again, swimming deep with golden fish. There was such joy her eyes teared in sleep and she had drops slipping down her cheeks. Safe and free, with her lover waiting.

She watched him swim effortlessly through the water toward her, and her heart almost burst with happiness. She laughed, reached out for him, but couldn't close the distance.

They broke the surface, feet apart, into air perfume sweet. The moon wheeled overhead, silver as an ingot. Stars were sparkling jewels displayed on velvet.

He climbed up the ladder of the *Mermaid*, turned and held out a hand for her.

The amulet was a spot of dark blood on his chest, as a wound drained from the heart.

Her fingers reached for his an instant before the world exploded.

Fire and water, blood and tears. Flames rained out of the sky and plunged into the sea until it boiled with heat.

Matthew.

His name circled her mind as she stirred in sleep. Lost in dreams and grief, she didn't see the figure creeping silently toward her, or the glint of the knife in his hand as the moonlight struck the blade. She didn't hear the whisper of his breath as he came close, leaning over the chair where she slept.

The hand clamped over her mouth shocked her awake. Tate struggled instinctively, her eyes going wide as she saw the silver gleam of the knife.

Even knowing it was futile, she fought, vising her fingers over the wrist before the blade could slash down.

‘Be quiet.’ The harsh whisper hissed next to her ear. ‘Goddamn it, Red, can’t you even let me rescue you without an argument?’

Her body jerked and froze. Matthew. It was a hope too painful to contemplate. But she could just make out the silhouette, smell the sea that clung to the wet-suit and dripped from the dark hair.

‘Quiet,’ he repeated when her breath sobbed against his muffling palm. ‘No questions, no talking. Trust me.’

She had no words. If this were another dream, she would live in it. She clung to him as he led her out of the cabin, up the companionway. Shudders racked her like earth tremors, but when he signaled her to climb over the side, she did so without question.

Clinging to the base of the ladder was Buck. Under that ingot moon, his face was white as bone. In silence, he hitched tanks over her shoulders. His hands trembled as hers did as he helped her with her mask. Beside them Matthew hooked on his own gear.

And they dived.

They stayed close to the surface to use the moon-light as a guide. A flashlight would mark a trail Matthew knew they couldn’t risk. He’d been afraid she’d be too frightened to handle the dive and the demanding swim, but she matched the pace he set stroke for stroke.

It was nearly four miles to where they had moved the *New Adventure*. There were squid and other night feeders, spots of color, blurs of movement in the shadowy sea. She never flagged.

He could have fallen in love with her for that alone, for the dogged way she swam, her hair and clothes floating around her, her eyes dark and determined behind her mask.

From time to time he checked his compass, corrected their course. It took more than thirty minutes of steady strokes to reach the boat.

Tate surfaced, fountaining water.

'Matthew, I thought you were dead. I saw the *Mermaid* explode and I knew you were on it.'

'Doesn't look like it,' he said lightly, but supported them both gratefully as she held onto him. 'Let's get you on deck, Red, you're shaking pretty bad, and your mom and dad are crazy with worry.'

'I thought you were dead,' she said again and sobbed as she crushed her mouth to his.

'I know, baby. I'm sorry. Buck, give me a hand with her.'

But Ray was already reaching over the side. His eyes, wet with relief, roamed over his daughter as he hauled up the tanks. 'Tate, are you hurt. Are you all right?'

'I'm fine. I'm fine,' she said again as Marla reached down to take her hand. 'Don't cry.'

But she was crying herself when her mother embraced her. 'We were so worried. That horrible man. That bastard. Oh, let me look at you.' Marla framed Tate's face, nearly smiled before she saw the bruising. 'He hurt you. I'm going to get you some ice, some hot tea. You sit down, honey, and let us take care of you.'

'I'm all right now.' But it felt wonderfully good to sink onto the bench. 'The *Mermaid*–'

'It's gone,' Ray said gently. 'Don't worry about that now. I want to take a good look at you, see if there's any shock.'

'I'm not in shock.' She sent Buck a grateful smile when he wrapped a blanket over her shoulders. 'I need to tell you. LaRue–'

'At your service, mademoiselle.' With a jaunty smile, he came out of the galley with a bottle of brandy.

'Son of a bitch.' Fatigue, fear and the fogginess of shock snapped clear. With a snarl she was on her feet and leaping. Matthew barely caught her before she could sink nails and teeth into LaRue's face.

'Did I tell you?' LaRue shivered and drank the brandy himself, straight from the bottle. 'She'd have clawed my eyes out if she'd had the chance.' He tapped his free hand on the medicated scratches scoring his cheek. 'Another inch north and I would be wearing a patch, eh?'

'He's working for VanDyke,' Tate spat out. 'He's been VanDyke's worm all along.'

'Now she insults me. You give her the brandy,' he said, shoving it into Ray's hand. 'LaRue, she'd hit over the head with it.'

'I'd tie you to the stern and use you for chum.'

'We'll talk about that later,' Matthew suggested. 'Sit down, take a drink. LaRue isn't working for VanDyke.'

'He only pays me,' LaRue said cheerfully.

'He's a traitor, a spy. He blew up your boat, Matthew.'

'I blew up my boat,' Matthew corrected. 'Drink.' He all but poured a shot of brandy down her throat.

She sputtered, and the heat hit her stomach like a fist. 'What are you talking about?'

'If you'd sit and calm down, I'll tell you.'

'You should have told her, and all of us, months ago,' Marla said testily as she bustled out with a steaming mug. 'Here's some soup, honey. Did you eat?'

'Did I–' In spite of everything, Tate began to laugh. It was only when she couldn't seem to stop that she realized it was borderline hysteria. 'I didn't care much for the menu.'

'Why the hell'd you waltz off with him?' Matthew exploded. 'A half a dozen people saw you get into his tender without a murmur.'

'Because he said he'd have one of his men kill you if I didn't,' she shot back. 'He had another right outside the boutique where Mom was.'

'Oh, Tate.' Shaken all over again, Marla sank to her knees beside her daughter.

'I didn't have any choice,' she said, and between sips of hot chicken soup, did her best to fill them all in on the events that had taken place since VanDyke had found her.

'He wanted me outside,' she finished. 'He even provided binoculars so I could watch the boat blow up. I thought you were dead,' she murmured, looking up at Matthew. 'And there was nothing I could do.'

'There was no way to tell you what was going on here.' Matthew sat beside her, took her hand. 'I'm sorry you were worried.'

'Worried. Yes, I suppose I was a bit concerned when I thought pieces of you were floating on the Caribbean. And why did you blow up your boat?'

'So VanDyke would think pieces of me were floating on the Caribbean. He's paying LaRue an extra quarter mill for it.'

'I will enjoy collecting.' LaRue's cocky smile faded. 'I apologize for not killing him for you when I found you on his boat. It was an unexpected turn of events. I didn't yet know you were missing. When I returned to tell Matthew, he was already making plans to get you back.'

'You'll excuse me if I'm confused,' Tate said coolly. 'Have you or have you not been passing information about Matthew to VanDyke during this expedition?'

'Filtering information is more accurate. He knew only what Matthew and I chose for him to know.' Squatting on the deck, LaRue took the brandy bottle again. 'I'll tell you the beginning. VanDyke offered me money to keep watch on Matthew, to become his companion and to pass along any salient information. I am fond of money. I am fond of Matthew. It seemed to me there was a way to take the first and assist the second.'

'LaRue told me months ago about the deal.' Matthew picked up the story, and the bottle. 'Of course LaRue had already been collecting for what, about a year, before he decided to let me in on the arrangement.'

With a flash of gold, LaRue grinned. 'Who is counting, *mon ami?* When the time was necessary, I shared with you.'

'Yeah.' To settle the stomach that had just begun to jitter in reaction, Matthew drank from the bottle. 'We figured we'd play along, split the profit.'

'Seventy-five, twenty-five, of course.'

'Yeah.' Matthew shot him a sour look. 'Anyway, the extra cash came in handy, and it did me a lot of good knowing we were bleeding it out of VanDyke. When we decided to come back after the *Isabella*, we knew we'd have to up the ante. And if we played it right, we'd harpoon VanDyke at the same time.'

'You knew he was watching us?' Tate said dully.

'LaRue was doing the watching,' Matthew corrected. 'All VanDyke knew was what we wanted him to know. When you found the amulet, LaRue and I agreed that it was time to reel him in with it. Only it got a little complicated when he reeled you in first.'

'You kept this from me, from all of us?'

'I didn't know how you'd react, or even if you'd be interested in my personal agenda. Then things moved pretty fast. It seemed logical,' he decided with a lift of brow, 'that the fewer people who were in on it, the better.'

'You know what, Lassiter?' She rose stiffly to her feet. 'That hurts. I need dry clothes,' she murmured and stalked off to her cabin.

She'd no more than slammed the door when he was shoving it open again. One look at her face decided him. He flipped the lock.

'You put me through hell.' She slapped open her closet, yanked out a robe. 'All because you didn't trust me.'

'I was playing it by ear, Red. I couldn't even trust myself. Look, it's not the first mistake I've made where you're concerned.'

'Hardly.' She fumbled to unbutton her wet shirt.

'And it won't be the last. So why don't we …' His words trailed off as she dragged off the shirt. There were purpling bruises on her arms and shoulders. When he spoke again, his voice was icily detached. 'Did he put those marks on you?'

'Him and his ham-fisted henchman from hell.' Still simmering, she peeled off her slacks, shrugged into the robe. 'I stabbed that Slavic robot with a hundred-dollar pen.'

He was staring at her face now, at the bruise along her cheekbone. 'What?'

'I aimed for his eyes, but I guess I froze up. Put a damn good hole in his cheek. Scraped a few layers off LaRue, too. I suppose I should be sorry for that now. But I'm not. If you had told me–' She squeaked in painful surprise when Matthew lurched forward and wrapped her tight in his arms.

'Yell at me later. He put his hands on you.' Eyes fierce, he framed her face. 'I swear to God he'll never touch you again.' He laid his lips gently on her cheekbone. 'Never again.'

Strapping on control, he stepped back again. 'Okay, you can yell now.'

'You know damn well you've ruined that for me. Matthew.' She reached out, let herself be folded in his arms. 'I was so scared. I kept telling myself I'd get away, then I thought you were dead. It just didn't matter anymore.'

'It's okay. It's over now.' Lifting her, he carried her to the bed to cradle her. 'When LaRue got back he told me how rough it was going on you. I never knew what it meant to be sick from fear until then.'

To comfort them both, he brushed kisses over her hair. 'We were already working on springing you when LaRue came onboard. Buck and I would swim over, he'd handle the tanks and gear while I looked for you. I figure it might have worked, but LaRue made it easier.'

'How?'

'For one, he found out which cabin you were in before he left, and snagged one of the duplicate keys. In his defense,' Matthew added, 'he was crazy at the thought that he had to leave you alone with that bastard.'

'I'll try to keep that in mind.' She heaved a long sigh. 'You had a key. And here I was imagining you swinging onboard like a privateer. Kicking in doors with a knife between your teeth.'

'Maybe next time.'

'Nope, I've had enough excitement for the next fifty or sixty years.'

'That's fine with me.' He took a breath. 'So, I laid everything out to Buck, then to Ray and Marla. The best I could think of was to use VanDyke's plan to burn the boat to our advantage. If we hadn't given him a show, he might have taken off, or done something to you.' Eyes closed, he pressed his lips to her hair. 'I couldn't risk it.'

'Your beautiful boat.'

'Hell of a distraction, and a foolproof way of making him believe everything was going his way. He'd see it go up, figure everything was going according to plan. I had to hope he'd relax enough thinking I was dead so that I could get on the yacht and get you off without risking a fight.'

He'd have loved a fight, he thought. He'd craved one. But not with her in the middle.

'Now we–' She stopped, jerked her head up. 'Buck. It just hit me. He went in.'

'It was tough on him. I wasn't sure he was going to make it. When LaRue got back, I thought about him going with me, but I wasn't sure I could keep you quiet if you spotted him. And Ray, well, he and Marla needed to stick together. That left Buck. He did it for you.'

'Looks like I've got a whole basket of heroes.' She touched her lips to his. 'Thanks for scaling the castle wall, Lassiter.' With a sigh, she settled her head on his shoulder again. 'He's not sane, Matthew. It's not just obsession or greed. He slips in and out of sanity like a shadow. He's only partially the man I met eight years ago, and it's terrifying to watch.'

'You won't have to watch again.'

'He won't stop. When he finds out you weren't blown up with the boat, he'll keep coming after you.'

'I'm counting on it. It'll be over this time tomorrow.'

'You still mean to kill him.' Chilled, she shifted away, moved out of his arms. 'I understand something of what you feel now. I would have killed him myself if I'd had the means when I thought you were dead. When I knew he was responsible for taking you from me. I could have done it then, in the heat of all that grief.'

Taking a steadying breath, she turned back to him. 'I don't think I could do it now, when the blood's cooled. But I know why you feel you have to.'

He looked at her for a long time. Her eyes were swollen from weeping, even in her sleep. Her skin was still pale so that the mark on her cheek stood out like a brand. She had, he knew, forgiven him any mistake he'd made.

'I'm not going to kill him, Tate. I could,' he continued almost thoughtfully as she stared at him. 'For my father, for the helpless kid who stood there doing nothing. For taking you, for touching you, for every bruise, every second you were afraid, I could cut out his heart without a flinch. Do you understand that?'

'I–'

'No.' His smile was thin as he rose to face her. 'You don't understand that I could kill him coldly, the way I've planned it for years. All those years I stared at the ceiling over my bunk on that fucking boat, with nothing to hold me together but the idea that one day I'd have his blood on my hands. I even used his money, setting what I could aside so I'd have enough to finish the boat, to buy equipment, to tide me over. Because I was going to find that amulet if it took a lifetime.'

'Then my father speeded things up.'

'Yeah. I could practically see "X" marking the spot. I knew I'd have it, and him. Then you …' He reached out to touch her face. 'Then you tipped the scales. You can't imagine how shocked I was to realize I was still in love with you. To know that the only thing inside me that had changed where you were concerned was that there was more.'

'Yes, I can,' she said quietly. 'I can imagine that perfectly.'

'Maybe you can.' He took her hand, brought it to his lips. 'I wasn't going to let that stop me though. I couldn't let it stop what had started sixteen years ago. Even when you put the amulet in my hand, I wasn't going to let it stop me. I told myself you loved me, you'd understand and come to accept what I had to do. You'd try to understand, but you'd have to live with it.'

Watching her face, he linked his fingers with hers. 'If I killed him, he'd always be between us. I realized that more than anything else, I want a life with you. The rest just doesn't come close.'

'I love you so much.'

'I know. I want to keep it that way. You can call the Smithsonian, or one of your committees.'

'You're sure?' she began.

'I'm sure it's what's best for us. What's right for us. The amulet's going into a vault for safekeeping until we get that museum off the ground. Make sure whoever you call hits the media hard. I want it to be worldwide news.'

'A publicity safety net.'

'It'll be tough for him to get around it. Meanwhile, I'm going to arrange to meet him.'

Panic grabbed her by the throat. 'You can't. God, Matthew, he's already tried to have you killed.'

'It has to be done. This time it'll be VanDyke who'll have to back down and sail away. A dozen news agencies will be sending reporters out here. The scientific world will be buzzing with the discovery. He'll know the amulet is out of his reach. There'll be nothing he can do.'

'It sounds reasonable, Matthew. But he's not a reasonable man. I wasn't exaggerating before. He's not completely sane.'

'He's sane enough not to risk his reputation, his position.'

She wished she could be so sure of that. 'He kidnapped me. We can have him arrested.'

'How are you going to prove it? Too many people saw you go with him, without a struggle. The only way to end it is to face him, to make him see he's lost.'

'And if he doesn't see, doesn't accept?'

'I'll make him.' He smiled again. 'When are you going to trust me, Red?'

'I do. Promise me you won't meet him alone.'

'Do I look stupid? I said I wanted a life with you. He's going to be meeting me, along with a couple of my pals, in the hotel lobby. We'll have drinks, a nice quiet chat.'

She gave a quick shudder. 'That sounds too much like him.'

'Whatever it takes.' He kissed her brow. 'After tomorrow, we're finished with him.'

'And then?'

'And then I guess we're going to be pretty busy for a while, putting this museum together. There's a piece of land at Cades Bay that ought to do.'

'Land? How do you know?'

'I checked it out the other day.' His eyes heated again as he stroked her bruised cheek. 'If I hadn't gone off to hunt up a realtor, VanDyke would never have gotten near you.'

'Hold on. You found a realtor and went out to look at land without telling me?'

Sensing trouble, he shifted back. 'It's not like you're committed to it. I just put a deposit on it to hold it for thirty days. I thought it would be like a wedding present.'

'You thought you would buy the land for the museum as a wedding present?'

Irritated, he jammed his hands in his pockets. 'You don't have to take it. It was just an impulse so– ' She moved so fast he didn't have time to yank his hands free and brace himself before she tumbled him onto the bed. 'Hey.'

'I love you.' Straddling him, she rained kisses over his face. 'No, I adore you.'

'That's good.' Pleased, if baffled, he pried his hands loose and cupped them comfortably over her hips. 'I thought you were mad.'

'I'm mad about you, Lassiter.' Bracing his hands on either side of his head she lowered to cover his mouth with hers in a deep, dreamy kiss that turned his brain to mush. 'You did this for me,' she murmured. 'You don't even care about a museum.'

'I don't have anything against it.' His hands slipped under her robe to flesh as her mouth jolted his system. 'In fact, I'm starting to like the idea. More and more.'

She skimmed her lips over his jaw and down his throat. 'I'm going to make you so happy.'

He let out a shaky breath as she peeled his T-shirt over his head. 'You're doing a good job so far.'

'I can do better.' She leaned back, her eyes on his, and slowly unbelted the robe. 'Just watch me.'

She was his oldest and most vivid fantasy, rising over him, slim and agile. Flame-colored hair, milky skin, eyes that echoed the sea. She was his to touch wherever he desired. His to hold when his heart thundered. His to watch as passion shimmered over her.

It was so quiet, so peaceful, so easy to join body and heart with hers. They might have been in that long-ago underwater dream, weightless, anchored only to each other. Every sense, every cell, every thought was tied to her, and only her.

He belonged, finally and completely.

Chapter Twenty-eight

TATE ROSE EARLY, and leaving Matthew sleeping, slipped from the cabin. She needed to think. The idea of a solitary cup of coffee in the galley seemed the best way to start.

Trusting Matthew was one thing, but letting him handle VanDyke on his own was another.

When she walked into the galley she found her mother already at the stove with the radio playing Bob Marley at low volume.

'I didn't think anyone was up.' Following the scent, Tate walked to the coffeepot and poured.

'I had an urge to bake bread. Kneading helps me think.' Marla vigorously massaged the dough on her floured board. 'And I thought I'd cook everyone a full breakfast. Eggs, bacon, sausage, biscuits. Cholesterol be damned.'

'You cook like that during emotional upheavals.' Concerned, Tate studied her mother over the rim of her mug. However carefully Marla had made up her face, Tate spotted the signs of a disturbed night. 'I'm okay, Mom.'

'I know.' Marla bit her lip, surprised tears were threatening again. Like most mothers facing a crisis, she hadn't broken down until Tate had been safe. Then she'd crumbled. 'I know everything's all right. But when I think of those hours that vile, unprincipled–' Rather than give in to tears, she punctuated each word with a sharp punch to the dough. 'Evil, conniving, murdering jackal had you I want to peel his skin away from his bones with a paring knife.'

'Whoa.' Impressed, Tate rubbed her mother's shoulder. 'Great image. You're a scary woman, Marla Beaumont. That's why I love you.'

'Nobody messes with my baby.' She let out a long breath, grateful there was no betraying hitch in it. The kneading and the venting had worked wonders. 'Your father talked about drawing and quartering and keelhauling.'

'Dad?' Tate set her mug down and chuckled. 'Good old mild-mannered Ray?'

'I wasn't sure Matthew was going to be able to convince him to stay aboard when they went after you. They fought about it.'

That brought her up short. 'Fought? Dad and Matthew?' Tate decided she needed more coffee after all.

'Well, they didn't come to blows, though it was close there for a minute or two.'

It took a conscious effort to close her mouth at the image of her father and her lover squaring off on the foredeck. 'You're joking.'

'Buck got between them until they'd both cooled off,' Marla remembered. 'I was afraid Ray would pop him instead.'

'Come on, Dad's never hit anyone in his life.' She lowered her mug again. 'Has he?'

'Not in the last few decades. Tempers were a bit heightened.' Marla's eyes softened as she brushed at her daughter's tumbled hair. 'You've got two men who love you sick with worry. And Matthew busy blaming himself.'

'He always does that,' Tate muttered.

'It's his nature to believe he has to protect his woman. Don't knock it,' Marla added with a chuckle at Tate's derisive snort. 'No matter how strong and self-reliant, a woman who has a man who loves her enough that he would literally give his life for hers is very lucky.'

'Yes.' Equality and common sense aside, she couldn't help but smile over it. Damned if she didn't have a white knight after all.

'If I could choose someone for you to spend your life with, it would be Matthew. Even eight years ago when you were both so young, too young, I knew you'd be safe with him.'

Intrigued now, Tate leaned a hip on the counter. 'I'd have thought the reckless, go-to-hell, adventurous type would have been every mother's nightmare.'

'Not when there's solid ground beneath.' Marla put the dough in a bowl to rise, covered it with a cloth. Finding her hands empty again, she looked around the already spotless galley. 'I guess I'll start breakfast.'

'I'll give you a hand.' Tate pulled a pack of sausage from the fridge. 'That way the guys'll have to clean up.'

'Good thinking.'

'Well, I wouldn't have time anyway. After we eat, I've got a lot of calls to make. The university, the Cousteau Society, *National Geographic* – maybe a dozen others.' Glad for the busywork, Tate chose a skillet. 'Matthew told you of his plan to make the discovery public before he confronts VanDyke?'

'Yes, we talked about it after you'd fallen asleep last night.'

'I wish I thought it was enough,' Tate murmured. 'I wish I thought it would ensure that VanDyke would just go away and stay away.'

'The man should be in prison.'

'I agree, completely. But knowing the things he's done and proving them are different matters.' As dissatisfied as her mother, Tate set the skillet on a burner to heat. 'We have to accept that and move on. He'll never pay for what he did to Matthew, to all of us. But we'll have the pleasure of seeing to it that he'll never have the necklace either.'

'Still, what might he do to pay you back for that?'

Tate lifted a shoulder as she set sausage to grilling. 'The necklace will be out of his reach, and I'll have to make sure I am, too. Along with my white knight.'

Absently, Marla reached into a bin and selected potatoes for home fries. 'Tate, I've been thinking. I had an idea – I know it's probably full of flaws, but …'

'An idea about what?'

'About VanDyke,' Marla said, gritting her teeth over the name as she scrubbed potatoes.

'Does it involve a paring knife?'

'No.' There was a giggle at that, followed by a self-deprecating shrug. 'Oh, it's probably stupid.'

'Why don't you tell me about it?' Tate flipped the browning meat with a spatula. 'You never know.'

'Well, I was just thinking …'

Ten minutes later, with sausage sizzling in the pan, Tate shook her head.

'It's so simple.'

Marla sighed and poked at her frying potatoes. 'It's a silly idea. I don't know what made me think of it, or that it could work.'

'Mom.' Tate took her mother's shoulders, turned her around. 'It's brilliant.'

Taken off guard, Marla blinked. 'It is?'

'Absolutely. Simple and brilliant. Keep cooking,' she said, adding a cheerful kiss. 'I'm going to wake everybody up so they can see I come by my genius naturally.'

With a sound of pleased surprise, Marla went back to her home fries. 'Brilliant,' she said to herself and gave her back a congratulatory pat.

'This may work.' LaRue took another scan of the spacious hotel lobby. 'But you're sure, Matthew, you wouldn't like to go back to your early idea of cutting VanDyke into small pieces and feeding him to the fish?'

'It's not about what I'd like.' Matthew stood out of view in the cozy library off the main lobby. 'Besides, it'd probably kill the fish.'

'True.' LaRue sighed deeply. 'It is the first sacrifice of the married man, *mon jeune ami*. The giving up of what he likes. A variety of women, the occasional drunken brawl, eating at the sink in underwear. Those days are over for you, young Matthew.'

'I'll live with it.'

Gingerly, LaRue touched his wounded cheek, and was able to smile. 'She is, I believe, worth even such wrenching sacrifices.'

'Maybe not eating in my underwear, but we'll work out a compromise. Everything set from your viewpoint?'

'All's well.' LaRue scanned the capacious lobby with its generous sitting areas, lush foliage and wide windows. 'The weather is so fine there is little traffic inside. And the timing, of course,' he added. 'We're late for lunch, early for the cocktail hour. Our man is prompt as a rule. He'll be here in ten minutes.'

'Sit down and order a drink. We don't want him choosing the table.'

LaRue straightened his shoulders, brushed at his hair. 'How do I look, eh?'

'Gorgeous.'

'*Bien sûr.*' Satisfied, LaRue moved off. He took a table by the patio window, across from a deeply cushioned sofa. He glanced toward a breakfront that held a variety of board games to amuse guests on rainy days, then took out his tobacco pouch.

He was enjoying the last of his cigarette with a frothy mai tai and a chapter of Hemingway when VanDyke walked in, tailed by his stoic steward.

'Ah, prompt, as expected.' He toasted VanDyke, sneered at the steward. 'I see you feel the need for protection, even from a loyal associate.'

'For precaution.' With a wave of the hand, VanDyke gestured his man toward the sofa. 'You feel the need for the protection of a public place for our business meeting?'

'For precaution,' LaRue countered, meticulously marking his page in his book before setting it aside. 'How fares your guest?' he asked casually. 'Her parents are terrified for her safety.'

VanDyke folded his hands, felt them relax. He had been fighting off a rage all morning after Tate's disappearance had been discovered. Obviously, he thought, she never made it back to the bosom of her family. Drowned, he supposed and glanced up at the waitress. A pity.

'A champagne cocktail. My guest is no concern of yours,' he added to LaRue. 'I'd prefer to get straight to our business.'

'I'm in no hurry.' Demonstrating, LaRue tilted back in his chair. 'Were you able to see the fireworks I displayed for you last night?'

'Yes.' Fussily, VanDyke flicked a speck of lint from his starched cuffs. 'I assume there were no survivors.'

LaRue's smile was thin and cool. 'You didn't pay me for survivors, eh?'

'No.' VanDyke let out a long, almost reverent breath. 'Matthew Lassiter is dead. You've earned your money, LaRue.' He broke off and gifted the waitress with his most charming smile as she served his drink.

'Your orders were to destroy his boat, along with him and his uncle, and your price, I believe, was two hundred and fifty thousand.'

'A bargain, to be sure,' LaRue murmured.

'Your payment will be transferred to your account before the close of the business day. Do you think he died instantly?' VanDyke said dreamily. 'Or do you think he felt the blast?'

LaRue contemplated his drink. 'If you had wanted him to suffer, you should have made it clear in the contract. For a slightly larger fee, it could have been arranged.'

'It hardly matters. I can assume he suffered. And the Beaumonts?'

'Eaten with grief, of course. Matthew was like a son to them, and Buck a dear friend. *Ils sont désolés*. For myself I pretend guilt and misery. If I had not chosen to take the launch to St. Kitts for a bit of nightlife …' He touched his heart, shook his head. 'They reassure me, tell me there was nothing I could have done.'

'Such generous spirits.' VanDyke pitied them for their open hearts. 'An attractive couple,' he mused. 'The woman in particular is quite lovely.'

'Ah.' LaRue kissed his fingers. 'A true blossom of the south.'

'Still …' Contemplating, VanDyke sipped his drink. 'I wonder if an accident on their voyage home might not be best.'

Surprised, LaRue sloshed his mai tai. 'You want the Beaumonts eliminated?'

'Clean slate,' VanDyke murmured. They had touched the necklace, he thought. His necklace. It was reason enough for them to die. 'Smaller prey, however. I'll pay you fifty thousand apiece to take care of them.'

'A hundred thousand for a double murder. Oh, *mon ami*, you are stingy.'

'I can handle it myself for nothing,' VanDyke pointed out. 'A hundred thousand to spare me the trouble of making other arrangements. I'd prefer that you wait a week, perhaps two.' To give me time, he mused, to plan your disposal as well. 'Now, with that settled, where is the amulet?'

'Oh, it's safe.'

The easy smile faded, hardened to stone. 'You were to bring it.'

'*Mais non*, money first.'

'I've transferred your asking price for the amulet, as agreed.'

'All of the money.'

VanDyke bit back on fury. It was the last time, he promised himself, that the little Canadian bastard would bleed him. In his mind murder flashed, the kind of murder that wasn't neat, wasn't practical. And wasn't handled by someone else.

'I told you you'd have the money by the end of the business day.'

'Then you'll have your treasure when the payment clears.'

'Damn you, LaRue.' With temper flushed on his cheeks, he pushed back from the table, nearly sent his chair toppling before he caught himself. Business, he repeated in his head like a chant. It's only business. 'I'll arrange it immediately.'

LaRue took the unexpected bonus philosophically. 'As you wish. Through that alcove you will find a phone.'

Chuckling to himself, he watched VanDyke stride off. 'Another quarter million,' he murmured into his drink, while his gaze roamed idly around the lobby, paused very briefly on the opening to the library. 'That's very sweet.'

Feeling generous, he decided to up Matthew's share to fifty percent, as a wedding present. It seemed, after all, only just.

'It's done,' VanDyke snapped when he returned a few minutes later. 'The money is being transferred immediately.'

'As always, it's a pleasure to do business with you. When I've finished my drink, I'll make my own call, see that the transfer is complete.'

VanDyke's knuckles were white against the table. 'I want the amulet. I want my property.'

'Only a few minutes longer,' LaRue assured him. 'I have something to amuse you until then.' From the pocket of his shirt, LaRue took a sheet of drawing paper. He unfolded it and laid it on the table.

The sketch was meticulously detailed, each link of the chain, each stone, even the tiny letters of the engraving.

The flush died from VanDyke's face until it was as white as his knuckles. 'It's magnificent.'

'Tate is quite skilled. She captured the elegance of it, eh?'

'The power,' VanDyke whispered as he skimmed his fingers over the sketch. He could all but feel the texture of the stones. 'Even in a drawing you can see it. Feel it. For almost twenty years I've searched for this.'

'And killed for it.'

'Lives are nothing compared to this.' Saliva pooled in his mouth and the champagne was forgotten. 'No one who's coveted it understood what it means. What it can do. It took me years to realize it myself.'

LaRue's eyes glinted at the opening. 'Not even James Lassiter knew?'

'He was a fool. He thought only of its monetary value, and of the glory he would reap if he could find it. He thought he could outwit me.'

'Instead, you killed him.'

'It was so simple. He trusted his son to check the gear. Oh, and the boy was careful, efficient, even suspicious of me. But just a boy for all that. It was ridiculously easy to sabotage the tanks, a matter of negating a contract.'

Resisting the urge to glance toward the library, LaRue kept his eyes on VanDyke's face. 'He must have known. Lassiter was an experienced diver, eh? When he began to feel the effects of the excess nitrogen, he would have surfaced.'

'I had only to restrain him for a short time. There was no violence in it, none at all. I'm not a violent man. He was confused, even happy. Once the raptures had overtaken him, it was only a matter of enjoyment. He smiled when I took the mouthpiece away. He drowned in ecstasy – my gift to him.'

VanDyke's breath quickened as he stared at the sketch of the necklace, as he steeped himself in it. 'But I didn't know then, couldn't be sure then, he died with knowledge.'

As he came out of his own spell, VanDyke reached for his drink. The memory had tripped his heartbeat pleasantly. And the realization that what he had done all those years before hadn't been a mistake after all. Only one of many steps to this point.

'All these years the Lassiters have kept what is mine from me. Now all of them are dead, and the amulet will come home to me.'

'I think you're mistaken,' LaRue murmured. 'Matthew, will you join us for a drink?'

As VanDyke gaped in shock, Matthew dropped into a chair. 'I could use a beer. Hell of a piece, isn't it?' he commented and lifted the sketch just as VanDyke lurched to his feet.

'I saw your boat go up in flames.'

'Planted the charge myself.' He glanced toward the steward, who had lunged to attention. 'You might want to call off your dog, VanDyke. A classy place like this frowns on brawls.'

'I'll kill you myself for this.' To keep from scrambling across the table, VanDyke gripped it until the bones in his fingers ached. 'You're a dead man, LaRue.'

'No, I'm a rich man, thanks to you. Mademoiselle.' LaRue smiled at the waitress, who'd hurried up and stared with anxious eyes. 'My companion is a bit overwrought. If you would be so kind as to bring us another round, and a Corona, with lime, for my friend.'

'Do you think you can walk away from this?' Shaking with fury, VanDyke snarled at his bodyguard until the man sat silently on the sofa again. 'Do you think you can cheat me, amuse yourselves at my expense, take what belongs to me by blood right? I can crush you.'

He couldn't quite get his breath, could see nothing but Matthew's cold and calm eyes. James Lassiter's eyes.

The dead came back.

'Everything you have can be mine within a week. I've only to whisper the right words in the right ears. And after I have, after you've lost everything you own, I'll have you hunted down, slaughtered like animals.'

'This is as close as you'll ever get to Angelique's Curse.' Matthew folded the sketch, slipped it into his pocket. 'And you'll never touch me or mine.'

'I should have killed you when I killed your father.'

'Your mistake.' Matthew could see the boy he had been, sick and trembling with grief, with rage, with helplessness.

Now, it seemed the boy was dead as well. 'I'm going to make you a proposition, VanDyke.'

'A proposition?' He all but spat it as his head threatened to explode. 'You think I would do business with you?'

'I think you will. Come on out, Buck.'

Red-faced from crouching in a jungle of decorative palms beside the breakfront, Buck puffed his way into the clear. 'I tell you, Matthew, them Japanese are geniuses.' He grinned at the palm-sized video recorder he held, then flipped out the tiny tape. 'I mean to tell you, the clarity's crystal, and the sound? I could almost hear the ice melting in that sissy drink of LaRue's.'

'I really prefer my brand.' Stripping a huge, floppy brimmed hat from her head, Marla strolled to the table. 'The zoom is superior. All the way across the lobby, and I could count the pores in his skin.' She too ejected the tape. 'I don't think we missed anything, Matthew.'

'Technology.' Matthew bounced the minicassette in his hand. 'It's amazing. On these little tapes we have video and sound recording, from two angles, of you confessing to racketeering. You know what racketeering is, don't you, VanDyke? That's when you pay somebody to do the crime.'

He smiled thinly as he palmed the tapes. 'I guess they'd get you for conspiracy to murder along with it.' He considered. 'That would be two counts. Then there's murder, that would be the first-degree murder of James Lassiter. Last I heard there was no statute of limitations on murder. Nobody forgets,' he added quietly.

He handed the cassettes to LaRue. 'Thanks, partner.'

'My pleasure, I assure you.' Gold flashed in his grin. 'My very *rich* pleasure.'

Matthew looked at his uncle. 'Buck, you and LaRue go take care of these.'

'On our way.' Buck paused, looked back at VanDyke. 'I thought the necklace was evil. I figured it had done in James, and that it hounded me and the boy here all our lives. But it was just you. Now we've done in you, VanDyke, and I gotta figure James is having a good laugh over it.'

'No one will take you or your tapes seriously.' VanDyke blotted his mouth with a handkerchief and sent a subtle signal to his steward.

'I think they will. Hold on a minute.' Wanting the entertainment, Matthew swiveled in his chair. He was in time to see LaRue bend down as if to tie his shoe. He came up like a bullet, directly between the legs of the bodyguard.

Two hundred and sixty-eight pounds of muscle bounced off the glossy floor, with barely a whimper, then curled up like a boiled shrimp.

'That was for Tate,' LaRue told him, then fluttered his hands helplessly as several staff members rushed over. 'He just fell over,' LaRue began. 'A heart attack perhaps. Someone should call a doctor.'

'You always underestimated the Canuk.' Matthew swiveled back. 'Thanks,' Matthew added as the now visibly nervous waitress brought the drinks. 'Marla, looks like you've got a mai tai.'

'Why, I'd love one, honey.' She settled at the table, smoothed the full skirt of her sundress, then aimed her frosty Southern gaze on VanDyke. 'I really want you to know this was my idea. The rough idea,' she temporized. 'It had to be refined a bit. You're very pale, Mr. VanDyke. You may want some cheese, a quick protein lift.'

'Isn't she terrific?' Madly in love, Matthew snatched Marla's hand and kissed it lavishly. 'Now, business. There are going to be copies of those tapes in various safe deposit boxes, vaults, law firms around the world. With the classic instructions – you know the drill – if anything should happen to me, et cetera. Me includes myself, my gorgeous future mother-in-law.'

'Oh, Matthew.'

'Ray,' Matthew continued after winking at her. 'Buck, LaRue, and of course, Tate. Oh, and speaking of Tate.'

Matthew's hand flashed out like a snake, snagged the meticulous Windsor knot of VanDyke's silk tie. With his eyes bullet hot, he twisted it like a noose.

'If you ever go near her again, if you ever have one of your walking dead put a finger on her, I will kill you – after I've broken every bone in your body, and peeled your skin with one of Marla's paring knives.'

'Tate wasn't supposed to tell you about that.' Flushing, Marla sucked mai tai through her straw.

'I think we understand each other.' Finished, if far from satisfied, Matthew loosened his grip.

'How nice. You're still here.' Tate strolled into the lobby. Despite the bruise, her face was glowing. 'Hello, lover.' Almost singing it, she bent to kiss Matthew's cheek. 'We're a bit late,' she went on. 'The plane was delayed. I'd like you to meet my friends and colleagues, Dr. Hayden Deel and Dr. Lorraine Ross.' She beamed at both of them. 'Also known as the new Mr. and Mrs. Deel. Dad.' Tate put a restraining hand on her father's arm when she saw him bare his teeth at VanDyke. 'Behave.'

'Nice to meet you.' Matthew rose and effectively blocked VanDyke in. 'Did you have a good trip?'

'Enjoyed every minute of it,' Lorraine told him. 'Jet lag included.'

Tate slipped off her sunglasses. 'It's very exciting. The captain of the *Nomad* married them just a few days ago.'

'We're going to combine a honeymoon here with business.' Hayden kept an arm around Lorraine's shoulder as if she might disappear without the contact. 'When we got Tate's message we were concerned enough to make the trip immediately.'

'It was great to be able to surprise them at the airport. When I called the university this morning to start the ball rolling on announcing the discovery of the wreck, they told me Hayden and Lorraine were already on their way.'

'Gives us a chance to beat out the others.' Lorraine leaned against Hayden's arm and struggled not to yawn. 'Nevis will be lousy with scientists and reporters in a couple of days. We're anxious to examine the relics from the *Isabella* before it gets crowded.'

'That's the plan.' Tate smiled sourly at VanDyke. 'I don't believe you've met my associates face-to-face, VanDyke, but you certainly know them by reputation. Oh, and wasn't that your servant I saw being loaded into an ambulance outside? He looked terribly pale.'

White with a choking, smothering fury, VanDyke rose. 'This doesn't end here.'

'I agree.' In restraint and unity, Tate laid a hand on Matthew's shoulder. 'It's just a beginning. Several very important institutes are sending representatives to observe the rest of our operation, and to examine the artifacts. Of particular interest is a certain amulet known as Angelique's Curse. The *Smithsonian Magazine* is going to do an extensive article on its history, its discovery and its lore. The *National Geographic* is considering a documentary.'

As all the pieces fell neatly into place, she smiled. 'It's very much on record now where the amulet was found, by whom, and to whom it belongs. Checkmate, VanDyke.'

'Want a beer, Red?'

'Yeah.' She squeezed Matthew's shoulder. 'Love one.'

'Take the rest of mine. I don't think the waitress will be coming back. I think that pretty much concludes our business, VanDyke. Anything else comes to mind, get in touch. Through our lawyer. What was that name again, Red?'

'Winston, Terrance and Blythe, Washington, D.C. You might have heard of them. I believe they're one of the top firms on the East Coast. Oh, and darling, the American consul was very enthusiastic when I spoke with him a couple of hours ago. He'd like to visit the site himself.'

God, Matthew thought, she was something. 'We'll have to accommodate him. Now if you'll excuse us, VanDyke, we have a lot of plans to make.'

VanDyke scanned the faces surrounding him. He saw triumph, confusion, challenge. He could meet none of them here, alone. With the sour taste of failure burning his throat, he turned stiffly and left.

He still had control.

'Kiss me,' Tate demanded and dragged Matthew hard against her. 'And make it good.'

'Ah ...' Hayden fiddled with his glasses. 'Would some-one tell me what's going on?'

'It feels like we walked in on the last act,' Lorraine agreed. 'Was that Silas VanDyke, entrepreneur, benefactor and friend to marine scientists?'

'That was Silas VanDyke.' Tate gave Matthew a violent squeeze. 'Loser. I'm crazy about you, Lassiter. Let's find that waitress and bring the newlyweds up to date.'

Chapter Twenty-nine

'IT'S A STORY with everything,' Lorraine mused.

On the deck of the gently rocking boat she studied the stars and the lovely silver moon. It was past midnight, the explanations, exclamations, victory dinner and celebratory toasts were over.

She'd left her new husband poring over treasures with the others and had slipped away for a quiet moment with her former shipmate.

'The ending's the best part.' Content to play truant, Tate lingered over the last glass of the last bottle of champagne.

'I don't know. You've got murder, greed, lust, sacrifice, passion, sex–'

'Okay, maybe the sex is the best part.'

With a chuckle, Lorraine tried to squeeze a few more drops from the bottle standing between their chairs. 'I left out witchcraft. Do you think Angelique Maunoir was really a witch?'

'This from a scientist.' But Tate sighed. 'I think she was

strong and powerful, and that love can work magic of all sorts.'

'Maybe you should worry about owning that amulet, gorgeous as it is.'

'I like to think she would have approved of who found it, and what we intend to do with it. We'll be able to tell her story. And speaking of stories …' Generously, Tate poured half her glass of wine into Lorraine's. 'What about yours and Hayden's?'

'It's not as legendary, but I like it.' Pursing her lips, Lorraine held up her hand to study her wedding ring. There was just enough starlight to make it glint. 'I hooked him on the rebound.'

'Don't be ridiculous.'

'Well, maybe it's not quite like that. You know, when you and I were working together, I never really understood you. There was Hayden, watching your every move with those wonderful cow eyes, and you never blinked. Of course now, meeting Matthew, it all comes clear.' She gave a dreamy little sigh.

'I hope you won't take this the wrong way, but I was thrilled when you were called away from the *Nomad*. Lorraine, I told myself, the coast just cleared.' Gesturing with her glass, she nearly sloshed out champagne. 'Get to work.'

'You worked fast.'

'I just love him. I swear, Tate, he made me feel like a clumsy puppy begging for scraps the whole time we were working together. I'd always been in control with men, you know? With Hayden, all bets were off. I finally had to swallow any semblance of pride. I cornered him in the lab one night when he was working late, and seduced him.'

'In the lab?'

'You bet. Actually, I'd made a few moves before, just to get his attention. I told him I loved him, that I was going to dog his heels wherever he went.

'He studied me very seriously before he said that it seemed best if we got married.'

'He said that?'

'Exactly that.' Lorraine sighed over the romance of it. 'And then he smiled. And then I cried like a baby.' Lorraine sniffled and tossed back the rest of her champagne. 'If I'm not careful, I'll cry again.'

'Don't, you'll set me off. I guess we both got lucky.'

'It's taken me practically my whole life to get lucky. Shit.' With a shrug she slurped more champagne. 'I'm just drunk enough to admit it. Forty-three years. I'm a goddamn middle-aged marine chemist who's really in love for the first time. Damn it, I am going to cry.'

'Okay.' Tate sniffled. 'Are you up to playing matron of honor in a couple of days?'

'Yeah.' Lorraine blubbered sentimentally into her empty glass. She looked up with a watery smile and misty eyes as Hayden and Matthew came on deck.

'What's going on out here?' Hayden asked.

'We're drunk and happy,' Lorraine told him. 'And in love.'

'That's nice.' Hayden patted her on the head. 'You be sure to mix yourself up something to fix the hangover you're going to have in the morning. We've got a busy day ahead.'

'He's so …' Lorraine rose, rocked and draped herself over him. 'Organized. Turns me to mush.'

'Lorraine, there are important people flying in from all over the world in the next day or two. We have to prepare.' When she only continued to beam at him, Hayden glanced at Matthew. 'Can I impose on you for a lift back to Nevis? I think Lorraine needs to lie down.'

'Buck and LaRue'll help you pour her into the tender, run you back.' He held out a hand. 'It's good to have you on our team.'

When the tender skimmed back toward the island, Tate leaned against Matthew. 'They look wonderful together.'

'I guess I can see why you kept tossing his name in my face. He catches on fast and he focuses in on what's most important.'

Resting her head on Matthew's shoulder, she watched the tender's light grow smaller. 'He's the best in the field, and his name carries a lot of weight. Lorraine's not small potatoes either. Having the two of them onboard cloaks the whole operation with efficiency and respect, and scientific purpose.' She let out a satisfied breath. 'And the more influential people who know about the *Isabella* and the amulet, the more impossible it is for VanDyke to interfere in any way.'

'Let's not lower our guard just yet. We're a lot better moored here, off island, miles from the site.'

'VanDyke's skulking off with his tail between his legs. He can call out every politician, every institute and official in his pocket. It won't change things now.' Turning, she wrapped her arms around him. 'I know you'd rather have handled things differently, but this is the best way for us.'

'Doing it this way was more satisfying than I thought. We win, he loses. All the way around.' He reached in his pocket, took out the amulet. 'It's really yours now.'

'Ours.'

'Rules of salvage,' he murmured and slipped it around her neck. 'I think when he had it made for her, he chose a ruby as the heart, for passion. The diamonds around it for endurance. The gold for strength.' Gently, he kissed her brows, her cheek, her lips. 'Love needs all those things.'

'Matthew.' She closed her hand around the stone. 'That's lovely.'

'I thought you might want to wear it for the wedding.'

'I would, yes, if I didn't have something else I treasure even more. It's a little gold locket with a pearl.'

Absurdly touched, he ran a finger down her cheek. He had to clear his throat before he could trust his voice. 'You kept that?'

'I tried to throw it away a dozen times, and never could. Nothing I've ever brought up from the sea was more precious to me. Not even this.'

'We're going to make it work.' He kissed her lightly. 'You're my luck, Red. Why don't we go in? Hayden's right about that long day coming up.'

'I'll be right along. I want to go over my records, make sure everything's perfect. Shouldn't take more than a half hour.'

'You're going to be practical when I was planning on driving you crazy?'

'Make that twenty minutes.' She laughed and gave him a nudge. 'I really need to be sure all my documents are in order. No way I'm going to look half-baked when the rep from the Cousteau Society shows up.'

'Ambitious and sexy.' He nipped her bottom lip. 'I'll wait for you.'

'Fifteen minutes,' she called after him, then hugged herself.

Everything she'd ever wanted was only a step away. The man she loved and a life with him, a career suddenly on fast forward, the museum that would showcase their work.

She closed her hand around the amulet, shut her eyes. And after four hundred years, perhaps Angelique would finally be at rest.

Nothing, she realized, was impossible.

She walked over to pick up the bottles and glasses she and Lorraine had left behind. The quiet footsteps behind her had her chuckling.

'Fifteen minutes, Lassiter. Maybe ten if you don't distract me.'

The hand that clamped around her mouth was damp and smooth. Her own had jerked up to claw at it even before true alarm registered.

'There's a gun at your back, Tate.' The sharp jab just above her kidneys had her going still. 'Silenced. No one will hear if I shoot you right here. If you scream or call out I'll kill you, and anyone who runs to your aid. Do you understand?'

The voice, the threat were sickeningly familiar. She could only nod.

'Be very careful.' VanDyke shifted his rough grip from her mouth to her throat. 'You can be dead in an instant.' Perhaps he could just snap her neck. He considered it, toyed with it, discarded it. Murder could wait. 'An instant later I'm in the water and away.'

'What do you hope to prove by this?' The words were weak and gasping as he squeezed her throat. 'The *Isabella* and everything she held is out of your reach. You can kill me, kill all of us, it won't change that. You'll be hunted down, thrown in prison for the rest of your life.'

'Don't you know that no one will be able to touch me once I have the amulet? You know the power it holds, you've felt it.'

'You're insane–' Her scream was involuntary and carried no more than a foot when his fingers crushed brutally over her windpipe.

'It's mine. Has always been mine.'

'You'll never get away. They'll know it was you. All your money and all your influence won't be able to protect you this time.' She wheezed out a breath as he loosened his grip.

'The amulet will be enough.'

'You'll have to go into hiding for the rest of your life.'

As she spoke, she shifted her eyes wildly in search of a weapon. The champagne bottle with its thick heavy glass was out of reach.

'We have the tapes, we've announced the find.' She hurried on. 'Hayden and Lorraine know, as do dozens of others. You can't kill them all.'

'I can do anything. I can do anything, and there's nothing and no one to touch me. Give me the amulet, Tate, and I'll spare your parents.'

Her head whirled as she remembered. She closed her hand protectively around the stone. It seemed to pulse quietly against her palm.

'I don't believe you. You'll kill me, you'll kill all of us, and for what, some wild notion that a necklace will bring you power and impunity?'

'And perhaps immortality.' Yes, he'd begun to believe that, begun to see the truth of that. 'Others have believed it, but they were weak, unable to control what they held in their hands. I'm different, you see. I'm used to command, to harnessing power. That's why it belongs to me. What would it be like to live with every wish, every thought possible? To win everything. To live forever if you wanted it.'

His breath quickened, coming hard against her ear. 'Yes, I'll kill you for that. I'll kill all of you for that. Do you want me to make you suffer first?'

'No.' She closed her eyes, straining her ears for the sound of the returning tender. If she could somehow signal them, or Matthew, there might be a way to stop VanDyke from killing all of them. 'I'll give it to you, and pray to God it gives you the life you deserve.'

'Where is the amulet?'

'Here.' She lifted the stone she still held in her hand. 'Right here.'

Stunned, he loosened his hold enough for her to jerk away. But she didn't run. There was nowhere to run. Instead she faced him, eyes cold and defiant, her fingers still circling the brilliant center gem. She could see his face go lax, soften like glass heated. But the gun never wavered.

'It's beautiful, isn't it?' she said quietly. She couldn't appeal to his reason. So she would appeal to his madness. Perhaps, just perhaps, she had a weapon after all.

'For centuries it's waited to be held again, worn again, admired again. Do you know there wasn't a mark on it when I took it from the sand?'

She turned the stone so that it caught the white beam of the moon. Light and shadows danced. It was quiet, suddenly so quiet, she could hear each separate whisper of the waves kissing the hull.

'Time, water hadn't touched it. It would have looked just like this, bright and gleaming, the last time she wore it around her neck.'

When he continued to stare, his eyes locked, hypnotized, on the amulet, she inched back, still holding the stone out. 'I think she wore it that morning. The morning they came to execute her. And he, the man responsible for condemning her, waited outside the cell, and took it.'

Her voice was quiet, almost soothing. 'He couldn't have her, but he could have that last physical link she had to the man she loved. Or so he thought. But he just couldn't break that very intimate connection between them. Neither could death. She spoke his name in her mind as the smoke filled her lungs and the flames licked at her feet. Etienne's name. I can hear her, VanDyke, can't you?'

Caught like a rat by the gaze of a snake, he stared. His tongue darted out to lick his lips. 'It's mine.'

'Oh no, it's still hers. It always will be. That's the secret, VanDyke, that's the magic and the power. The ones who didn't understand that, and coveted it for their own ends are the ones who brought the curse on their own heads. If you take it,' she said softly and with sudden certainty, 'you're damned.'

'It's mine,' he repeated. 'I'm the only one it was meant for. I've spent a fortune to find it.'

'But I found it. You're only stealing it.' She was nearly at the rail now. Was that a motor? she wondered. Or just her wishing? If she shouted now, would she save the people she loved, or kill them?

VanDyke's eyes snapped back to hers, and her heart sank like a stone in the sea. Those eyes were clear again, calm again, without that thin glaze of madness.

'You think I don't know what you're doing? Stalling for time until your broad-shouldered hero charges to your aid. A pity he hasn't so you could die together, romantically. Now I've indulged you long enough, Tate. Take off the amulet and give it to me or I'll put the first bullet in your gut instead of your heart.'

'All right.' Her fingers were oddly light and steady as she drew the chain from around her neck. It was almost as if they weren't her own, as if she were floating somewhere beyond her own flesh. 'If you want it so desperately. Get it, and pay the price.'

Braced for the bullet, she tossed it high and far over the sea.

He howled. The sound was inhuman, like a beast tasting blood. And like a beast he shambled to the rail and plunged into the dark water. Before he'd disappeared beneath, she was after him.

As she cut through the water, part of her brain registered the dangerous folly of the act. Yet she was compelled, driven to fill her lungs with air and dive blind.

Reason told her he would never find the amulet in the night sea without mask or tanks or time. Nor would she find him or the treasure she'd flung away.

Even as logic began to balance impulse, she saw the shadow of movement. Rage she hadn't even known had rooted inside her burst free. She was on him like a shark.

Here, in the airless world, his superior strength was countered by her youth and skill. His blind greed by her fury. There was no gun now, only hands and teeth. She used hers viciously.

He clawed at her, desperate to reach the surface and breathe again. With her own lungs aching, she dragged him back, until a kick sent her spinning away.

Up again through the dark water she rose, nearly despairing that she would reach the surface.

He waited for her there, lashing out wildly, and she fought to fill her empty lungs. His face was distorted by the water and salt in her eyes, obscenely feral as he struck out. They fought in a terrible silence broken only by gasping breaths and swirling water.

His eyes rolled white as he pulled her under. The sea embraced them greedily.

She swallowed water, choked. The salt stung her eyes as he held her down and gulped air for himself. Fumbling, her hands lost purchase on his slick wetsuit. The buzzing in her ears became a roar. There were lights glowing, bursting in her head, in front of her eyes.

No, she thought, fighting free. A light. A single light shining against the sand. He was racing toward it, diving, diving through the glassy black water to white sand where the amulet lay like a bloody star.

She watched him lift it, saw his hand close around it greedily. The soft red glow shone luminescently through his fingers, and deepened, darkened. Bled.

He turned his head, looked at her in triumph. Their eyes met, held.

Then surely he screamed.

'She's coming around. That's it, Red, cough it up.'

Through the harsh sounds of her own racking heaves, she heard Matthew's voice, the tremor in it. She could feel the solid wood of the deck beneath her, his big hands cradling her head, the damp rain of water leaking onto her skin.

'Matthew.'

'Don't try to talk. Christ, where's the damn blanket?'

'Here, right here.' With calm efficiency, Marla covered her daughter. 'You're all right, honey, just lie still now.'

'VanDyke–'

'It's all right.' Matthew glanced around to where the man sat hudled under LaRue's ready bangstick. He was half drowned and quietly chuckling to himself.

'The amulet.'

'Jesus, it's still around her neck.' Matthew slipped it off with an unsteady hand. 'I didn't even notice.'

'You were a little busy saving her life.' Ray squeezed his eyes tight and absorbed the relief. When Matthew had dragged Tate from the water, he'd been sure his only child was dead.

'What happened?' Tate finally found the strength to open her eyes. Overhead was a circle of pale, concerned faces. 'God, I hurt all over.'

'Just be quiet for a minute. Her pupils look normal. She's not shaking.'

'There could be delayed shock. I think we should get her out of those wet clothes and into bed.' Marla bit her lip, and though she knew it was foolish, checked Tate's brow for fever. 'I'll make you some nice chamomile tea.'

'Okay.' A little woozy, Tate smiled. 'Can I get up now?'

Muttering an oath, Matthew picked her up, blanket and all. 'I'll put her in bed.' He paused briefly for a last glance at VanDyke. 'LaRue, you and Buck better get what's left of him over to Nevis, give him to the cops.'

Vaguely curious, Tate stared. 'Why is he laughing?'

'That's all he's done since Ray hauled him in. He laughs and mutters about witches burning in water. Let's get you in a hot bath.'

'Oh, let's.'

He was patient. Matthew drew her bath, massaged her shoulders. He even washed her hair himself. Then he dried her, tucked her into a night-shirt and robe and put her to bed.

'I could get used to this,' she murmured, letting her still light head rest against plumped pillows while she sipped the tea her mother had brought in.

'You stay put,' Marla ordered, fussing with the blanket. She glanced up at Matthew. 'Ray went along to Nevis. He didn't want to let VanDyke out of his sight until he was in a cell. Do you want me to let you know when they get back?'

'I'll come up shortly.'

Marla only lifted a brow. She had a feeling Tate had one more crisis to deal with. 'I think I'll go brew a big pot of coffee. You rest, honey.' She kissed Tate's forehead and closed the door quietly behind her.

'Isn't she the best?' Tate began. 'Nothing ever shakes that wonderful Southern panache.'

'You're about to find out what shakes a Yankee temperament. What the hell did you think you were doing?'

She winced at the volume. 'I don't know, exactly. It all happened so fast.'

'You weren't breathing.' He caught her chin in fingers tensed and trembling like plucked wires. 'You weren't breathing when I pulled you out.'

'I don't remember. Everything after I dived in after him is jumbled and kind of surreal.'

'You dived in after him,' Matthew repeated, spacing each word.

'I didn't mean to,' she said quickly. 'I threw the amulet into the water. I had to take the chance that he'd go after it instead of shooting me.'

His heart, which had already suffered violently, stopped again. 'He had a gun?'

'Yes.' She could feel her mind begin to float again and struggled to concentrate. 'He must have lost it in the water. I was coming inside.' Gently she took his hand in hers. 'He was just there. Just there behind me, Matthew, with the gun jammed into my back. He must have come over from starboard. His gear's probably still there on the ladder. I couldn't call for you, Matthew. He'd have killed all of us.'

As calmly as she could, she told him what had happened on deck.

'I took the necklace off,' she murmured and closed her eyes to try to see it all again.

The play of light, the shifting shadows. The way the stone seemed to throb like a heart in her hand.

'I didn't even have to think about it. I just threw it. He ran past me; he never even looked at me. Just went in.'

'Why the hell did you go after him? I was right here, Red.'

'I know. I can't explain it. One minute I was thinking I'll get Matthew, and the next I was in the water. Even as I was diving I was thinking it didn't make sense. But I couldn't stop myself. I caught him, and we struggled.'

To bring the picture clearer, she closed her eyes again. 'I remember thrashing around with him on the surface, under it. I remember losing air, knowing he would drown me. Then there was this light.'

'Christ.' He dragged a hand through his hair. 'You're telling me you had a near-death experience? The white light, the tunnel, the works?'

As puzzled as he, she opened her eyes again. 'No, but it was just as odd. I must have been hallucinating. I saw this glow, and the glow was the necklace. The sand was perfectly white, and I could see it as clearly as I see you. I know it's not possible, but I did. So did he.'

'I believe you,' Matthew said quietly. 'Go on.'

'I watched him dive for it. I was just hovering there in the water.' Her brows drew together, forming a faint line between them. 'It was as if I had to be there, had to watch. I'm not explaining this very well.'

'You're doing fine.'

'I watched, waited,' she continued. 'He picked it up and held it, and I could see it bleed through his fingers, as if the stone had gone to liquid. He looked up. He looked right at me. I saw his eyes. Then …'

Because she trembled, he stroked her hair. He wanted to gather her close, tell her to forget all of it. But he knew she had to finish. 'Then what?'

'He screamed. I heard it. It wasn't muffled by the water. It was piercing, terrified. He kept looking at me and screaming. There was fire, everywhere. The light and color from it, but no heat. I wasn't afraid, not at all. So I took the amulet from him and let him go.'

She stopped on a nervous laugh. 'I don't know – I guess I blacked out. I must have. I must have been unconscious all along because it couldn't have happened that way.'

'You were wearing the amulet, Tate. When I pulled you out, you were wearing it.'

'I must have … found it.'

He brushed her hair back from her face. 'And that makes sense to you?'

'Yes, of course. No,' she admitted and reached for Matthew's hand. 'It doesn't.'

'Let me tell you what I saw. When I heard you calling for me, I ran out on deck. VanDyke was in the water. He was flailing around, and yeah, he was screaming. I knew you must be in the water, so I went in.'

There was no point in telling her that he dived until his lungs had all but burst, had never given a thought to surfacing unless she was with him.

'When I found you you were on the bottom, lying on your back the way you do when you sleep. And you were smiling. I almost expected you to open your eyes and look at me. I realized when I was pulling you up that you weren't breathing. It couldn't have been more than three, four minutes tops from the time you yelled for me to come, but you weren't breathing.'

'So you brought me back to life.' She leaned forward, set the cup aside so that her hands were free to frame his face. 'My personal white knight.'

'It wasn't like Prince Charming. Nothing romantic about mouth-to-mouth and CPR.'

'Under the circumstances, it beats a bouquet of lilies.' She kissed him gently. 'Matthew, one thing. I never called out.' She shook her head before he could protest. 'I didn't call out. But I did say your name in my head when I thought I was drowning.' She laid her cheek on his and sighed. 'I guess you heard me.'

Chapter Thirty

THROUGH THE BARS of the small cell, Matthew studied Silas VanDyke. Here, he thought, was the man who had plagued his life, taken his father, plotted to murder him and who had nearly killed the woman he loved.

He'd been a man of power, of far-reaching financial, social and political strength.

Now he was caged like an animal.

They'd given him a cotton shirt and pants, both faded and baggy. He wore no belt, no shoelaces, certainly no monogrammed silk tie.

Still he sat on the narrow bunk as if he sat in a custom-made chair, as if the dingy cell were his lushly decorated office. As if he were still in charge.

But it seemed to Matthew that he had shrunken somehow, that his body looked frail in the oversized prison clothes. The bones of his face had sharpened and pressed skeletally against the skin as if flesh had melted away overnight.

He was unshaven, his hair matted from seawater and

sweat. Livid scratches scarred his face and hands, reminding Matthew of Tate's desperate fight for her life.

For that alone he wanted to break through the bars himself, to hear VanDyke's bones snap in his hands.

But he made himself stand, and study.

And he saw that the dignity and appearance of power VanDyke struggled to maintain were stretched over him like thin, fragile glass. The hate was still there, Matthew realized, ripe, alive and burning in his eyes. He wondered if it was enough to keep the man alive, if he could feed on it through all the years he'd be locked away.

He hoped it would be.

'How does it feel,' Matthew wondered aloud, 'to lose everything?'

'Do you think this will stop me?' VanDyke's voice was barely a whisper that slithered through the bars like a snake. 'Do you think I'll let you keep it?'

'I came here to tell you that you don't matter anymore.'

'Don't I?' His eyes flickered. 'I should have killed her. I should have put a hole in her gut and let you watch her die.'

Matthew leapt toward the bars, nearly ripped at them, until the gleam of satisfaction in VanDyke's eyes stopped him. No, not this way, Matthew told himself. Not *his* way. 'She beat you. She's the one who finally brought you down. You saw it, didn't you? The fire in the water. You saw her watching you,' he continued, drawing on the scene Tate had described to him. 'She was so beautiful, so terrifying caught in that wild light. And you screamed like a child in a nightmare.'

Color that rage had washed into his cheeks had now drained, leaving them white as paper. 'I saw nothing. Nothing!' His voice rose as he jerked off the cot. In his mind a blur of terrifying images swam, took shape and threatened to tear at his sanity like eager claws.

The screams wanted to pump, wild and hot, out of his throat.

'You saw it.' Calm settled over Matthew once more. 'And you'll see it over and over again. Every time you close your eyes. How long can you live with the fear of that?'

'I'm afraid of nothing.' Terror was an icy ball in his belly. 'They won't keep me in prison. I have position. I have money.'

'You have nothing,' Matthew murmured, 'but years to think about what you did, and what in the end you couldn't do.'

'I'll get out, and I'll find you.'

'No.' This time, Matthew smiled, sharp and fast. 'You won't.'

'I've already won.' He came close, wrapped his fingers around the bars until they were as white as his face. His breath came fast, and the eyes that burned into Matthew's held the bright edge of madness. 'Your father's dead, your uncle's a cripple. And you're nothing but a second-rate scavenger.'

'You're the one in the cage, VanDyke. And I'm the one with the amulet.'

'I'll deal with you. I'll finish the Lassiters and take what's mine.'

'She beat you,' Matthew repeated. 'A woman started it, and a woman ended it. You had it in your hands, didn't you? But you couldn't keep it.'

'I'll get it back, James.' His lips peeled back. 'And I'll deal with you. You think you can outwit me?'

'I'll protect what's mine.'

'Always so sure of yourself. But I've already won, James. The amulet's mine. It was always mine.'

Matthew backed away from the bars. 'Stay healthy, VanDyke. I want you to live a long, long time.'

'I won.' The shrill, furious voice followed Matthew as he walked away. 'I won.'

Because he needed the sun, Matthew walked outside the station-house. He scrubbed his hands over his face and hoped Tate wouldn't be much longer giving her statement.

The air was hot and still, and he had a deep craving for the sea – for something fresh and scented. For Tate.

It was nearly twenty minutes later before she came out. He thought she looked exhausted, all pale skin and haunted eyes. Saying nothing, he held out a bouquet of vivid pink and blue flowers.

'What's this?'

'They're called flowers. They sell them at the florist down the street.'

That made her smile, and when she buried her face in them, her spirits lifted. 'Thanks.'

'I thought we could both use them.' He ran a hand down her braid. 'Rough morning?'

'Well, I've had better. Still, the police were very sympathetic and patient. With my statement, yours, LaRue's, the tapes, they have so many charges I'm not sure what they'll do first.' She lifted a shoulder. It hardly mattered now. 'I suppose he'll be extradited eventually.'

With his hand linked with hers, Matthew walked her to the rental car. 'I think he's going to spend what's left of his life in a padded cell. I just saw him.'

'Oh.' She waited until he'd climbed into the driver's seat. 'I wondered if you would.'

'I wanted to see him in a cage.' Thoughtfully, Matthew put the car in gear and pulled away from the curb. 'I guess since I couldn't pound his face in, I wanted to have the chance to gloat at least.'

'And?'

'He's right on the edge, and I might have given him a little shove to take him closer to it.' He glanced toward her. 'He tried to convince me – or maybe himself, that he'd won.'

Tate lifted the flowers to rub the fragrant blooms over her cheek. 'He hasn't. We know that, and it's what matters.'

'Right before I left, he called me by my father's name.'

'Matthew.' Concerned, she laid a hand over his on the gear shift. 'I'm sorry.'

'No. It's all right. It seemed just somehow. Like a closure. Almost half my life, I've wanted to turn the clock back to that day, do something to change what happened. I couldn't save my father, and I couldn't be him. But today, for a few minutes, it was like standing in for him.'

'Justice instead of revenge,' she murmured. 'It's easier to live with.'

As he turned the car toward the sea, she let her head fall back against the cushion. 'Matthew, I remembered something when I was talking to the police. Last night, when I was on deck with VanDyke, I had my hand on the amulet and I told him I hoped it gave him the life he'd earned.'

'Twenty or thirty years locked away from everything he wants most. Good call, Red.'

'But who called it?' She let out a long breath. 'He doesn't have the amulet, Matthew, but he certainly has Angelique's Curse.'

It felt good to be back at sea again, back at work. Warding off all suggestions that she take the remainder of the day to rest, Tate closeted herself with Hayden and her cataloguing.

'You've done a top-notch job here, Tate.'

'I had a good teacher. There's still so much to do. I have miles of film to be developed. We already have the videos, of course, and my sketches.'

Briskly, she ran a finger down one of her lists. 'We desperately need storage space,' she continued. 'More holding tanks and preserving solutions. And now that we've made the announcement, we can start bringing up the cannon. We couldn't risk using inflatables and cranes before.'

She blew out a breath and sat back. 'We need the equipment for handling the rest, and of course, for preserving and reconstructing what we can of the *Isabella*.'

'You've got your work cut out for you.'

'I've got a great team.' She reached for coffee, smiled at the vase of cheery flowers beside her monitor. 'Even better now that you and Lorraine are signing up.'

'Neither one of us would miss it.'

'I think we're going to need a bigger boat, certainly until Matthew can build one.'

But it wasn't that which preyed on her mind while Hayden muttered over her notes. Tate braced her shoulders and screwed up her courage.

'Tell me honestly, Hayden, when the reps and other scientists get here, am I prepared for them? Are my notes and papers organized and detailed enough? Without being able to use outside resources, I've had to guess on so many of the artifacts that I–'

'Are you looking for a grade?' he interrupted.

The amusement in his eyes had her squirming. 'No. Well, maybe. I'm nervous.'

He took off his glasses, rubbed the bridge of his nose, then replaced them. 'You spent last night fighting a madman, all morning talking to police, and giving a presentation to colleagues makes you nervous?'

'I've had more time to think about the colleagues,' she said dryly. 'I'm greedy, Hayden. I want to make a huge splash with this. It will be the foundation for the Beaumont-Lassiter Museum of Marine Archeology.'

She picked up the necklace that lay on the table. She'd needed, for reasons she no longer felt required analysis, to keep it close.

It was cool in her hands now. Beautiful, priceless and, she thought, quiet at last.

'And I … well, I want Angelique's Curse to have the home it deserves after four hundred years of waiting.'

'Then I can honestly tell you in my professional opinion, you have a very strong foundation.'

Very gently, she laid the necklace back in its padded box. 'But do you think that –' She broke off, glancing toward the window at the sound of clanging and motorized hiccoughing. 'What the hell is that?'

'Whatever it is, it sounds bad.'

They went on deck together where Matthew and Lorraine were already at the rail. Ray and Marla bolted out of the galley.

'What an awful noise,' Marla began, then her eyes widened. 'Oh my God, what is that thing?'

'I think it's supposed to be a boat,' Tate murmured. 'But don't take my word for it.'

It was painted a virulent pink which clashed interestingly with the heavy rust. The flying bridge shuddered each time the engine belched. As it drew alongside, Tate estimated that it was forty feet of warped wood, cracked glass and corroding metal.

Buck stood at the wheel, waving wildly. 'Ain't she something?' he shouted. He cut the engines, which showed their appreciation by vomiting a spew of smoke. 'Weigh anchor.'

There was a horrible grinding sound, a shudder and screech. Buck shoved up his shaded glasses and grinned.

'Going to christen her *Diana*. LaRue says she was a hell of a hunter.'

'Buck.' Matthew coughed and waved at the smoke carried cheerfully by the breeze. 'Are you telling me you bought that thing?'

'*We* bought this thing,' LaRue announced and strolled out on the slanted deck. 'We are partners, me and Buck.'

'You're going to die,' Matthew decided.

'Just needs some paint, little sanding, some mechanical work.' Buck started down the steps to the deck. Fortunately, it was the second riser from the bottom that snapped under his weight. 'Some carpentry,' he added, still grinning.

'You gave someone money for that?' Tate wondered.

'She was a bargain.' LaRue tapped the rail cautiously. 'When she's shipshape and our work is done here, we are off to Bimini.'

'Bimini?' Matthew repeated.

'There's always another wreck, boy.' He beamed at Matthew. 'Been too many years since I had a boat of my own under me.'

'How's it going to stay under him?' Tate murmured beneath her breath. 'Buck, wouldn't it be better to–'

But Matthew put a hand over hers and squeezed. 'You'll make her shine, Buck.'

'Coming aboard for inspection,' Ray called out. He stripped off his shoes and shirt and plunged into the water.

'They do love their toys,' Marla decided. 'I'm making lemon tarts if anyone wants a snack.'

'Right behind you.' Lorraine grabbed Hayden's hand.

'Matthew, that boat is a mess. They'll have to replace every board and spur.'

'So?'

Tate blew her bangs out of her eyes. 'Wouldn't it be more practical to put their money into something in better condition? Into something in any kind of condition?'

'Sure. But it wouldn't be as much fun.' He kissed her, and when she started to speak, kissed her again, thoroughly. 'I love you.'

'I love you, too, but Buck–'

'Knows just what he's doing.' Matthew grinned over the rail where the three men were busy laughing and examining the broken step. 'Charting a new course.'

Bemused, she shook her head. 'I think you'd like to go with them, bailing all the way to Bimini.'

'Nope.' He scooped her into his arms, spun a circle. 'I've got my own course. Straight ahead full. Want to get married?'

'Yeah. How about tomorrow?'

'Deal.' The reckless light came into his eyes. 'Let's dive.'

'All right, I–' She squealed when he carried her to the rail. 'Don't you dare throw me in. I'm still dressed. Matthew, I mean it. Don't–'

She gave a scream of helpless laughter as he leapt out into the water.